HEROES OF THE MISTY ISLE

King of the Stars

Saint Columba's
Journey to Scotland

SANDY DENGLER

MOODY PRESS
CHICAGO

ISBN: 0-8024-2296-9

1 3 5 7 9 10 8 6 4 2

Printed in the United States of America

Contents

THREE NOTES BEFORE COMMENCING:

As one of the oddities of history, Scotland was named for the Irish. The confusion began when the Romans called the inhabitants of Ireland the Scotii. Four or five hundred years later, a generation before Columcille, a branch of the Irish ruling family emigrated to the Hebrides and set up a political entity called Dal Riada. The Scotii of the Dal Riada became so dominant that the Angles, Saxons, and Jutes to the south began calling everyone up north "Scotii." As Roman influence died (it never really reached Ireland in the first place), calling the Erse "Scotii" died as well, leaving those invading, colonizing Irish to give Scotland its name.

To avoid confusion among the folks who never read historical notes and prefaces, thereby missing this first page, I will omit the use of "Scot" entirely. It will be either the Erse or all those other people.

Another point: several battles, including Cuil Fedha and Cuil Rathan, were fought somewhere around 587. In the text, I intimate that they occurred earlier, in the autumn of 579. I played loosy-goosey with history to keep the story moving—literary license, if you will.

Third, there is much talk here of angels and miracles. The very oldest biographies of Columcille and others, their lives as recorded before A.D. 1000, are rife with such, but, then, that was the purpose of these earliest works—to set apart the saints. Because they appear in the record and because they certainly enliven the story, I have employed them for dramatic purposes. Take them as fact or fancy as you wish.

Now to commence our tale . . .

PICTLAND

• Inverness

Aberdeen •

DAL RIADA

Isle
of
Skye

Rhum
Hinba •
Eigg

Glenelg •

Ardnamurchan

Coll

Tiree

Mull

Iona

Colonsay
Cronsay

Jura

Islay

Arran

Culrathan •

Derry
(Drumceatt)

Lough
Neagh

Armagh

Bangor
Moville
Down

Monaghan

Cionard

Bangor •

Isle
of
Man

CONNACHT

Kells

Telltown •

Tara

Lambay

Kildare •

Clonmacnois

LEINSTER

Kilkenny •

Cashel •

ERIN

1

Finnian's Bane

The Year of our Lord 537

Sing His praises!
  Sing with the heavens.
  Sing with the babes and infants. . . .

Finnian of Moville, a wise man in all respects, did not trust boys any farther than he could throw the bull in the south paddock. There reclined the bull in splendid repose under the rowan by the creek, his jaw placidly rotating. But where were the boys?

Nearly a score of promising lads resided at Moville at the moment, from tiny kings' sons to burly farm lads aspiring to monkhood. Usually the mix of pupils more or less canceled each other out, the big boys, having obtained a modicum of sobriety, acting as a damper to the younger ones' antics.

But now there was Mac Phelim.

Mac Phelim. The blond, hulking son of Phelim and Eithne. *Nothing* seemed to dampen him. Would that something could. Anything.

"Mac Phelim!" Finnian bellowed the name. Again. The bull's ear twitched. The abbot tried the name of Mac Phelim's cousin, frequent accomplice, and provocateur. "Mac Niall!"

The plowmen must be coming in from the east side, for a flock of fieldfares lifted out of the alders beyond the creek. In a fluttery mass they flew by and settled beyond the bier. Finnian waited. No plowmen appeared. *Aha!* He hurried down to the creek. *What would the boys be doing out by the alders? With Mac Phelim at their head, anything.*

A brilliant opportunity presented itself here. The boys had no way of knowing that Finnian had just deduced their precise whereabouts. He could sneak up on them and catch the culprits in the act—whatever the act was. Heaven only knew, but it couldn't be harmless.

Slipping and sliding, Finnian fumbled his way down the creek-bank. He really should lose a little weight. He would probably command better respect if he didn't waddle so. To his right the water glistened as it riffled across gravel beneath the surface. Loathe to soak his feet in the chilly creek, he instead hurried along the shore to the dry crossing, a series of stepping stones. They seemed a good fifty feet farther upstream than they ought to be.

He stepped out from flat rock to flat rock across the surging creek. The third stone from shore tipped when he put his weight on it. As it slid into the water beneath his foot, he gave a lunging leap for the next. No sturdier than its mate, the fourth stone went under. He dropped like—well, like a stone. Frigid water stabbed through his cowled dalmatic and numbed his bare toes. He hardly had time to cry out before his head went under.

His coarse wool dalmatic blotted up the freezing water. Intensely heavy, it sucked him down to the rocky creek bottom. He flailed. He twisted. He inadvertently filled his nose and throat and lungs with the racing, chilling water. *Those boys! Those hideous, irreverent boys!* He struggled to his feet, fighting for balance on the slick boulders of the creekbed. Water cascaded off him as he managed to pull himself erect.

Waves of childish laughter assailed his aching ears. They were gathered on the shore watching him, those infernal boys. None of them was wet.

None of them was Mac Phelim or Mac Niall either.

"Father! We will save you!" Comgall—good, stable Comgall, ripe with nascent manhood—Comgall would help him. The sturdy lad tossed him the end of a coarse tow line.

Finnian grabbed the proffered rope and let it steady him as he sloshed through waist-deep water. The lads pulled in concert on the other end. "Not so fast!" He staggered. The boulder-studded bottom and the rushing current tipped him again, but the water was not so deep now. He fell in to his armpits and managed to keep his head up. The rope broke—ropes of tow are never very strong, especially when wet. He floundered ashore and dragged himself up onto the stony bank.

He ought to intone a psalm of thanksgiving to God, for he was safe. He was essentially uninjured.

He was also on the wrong side of the creek.

Fury engulfed him. If he weren't careful, fury would drive him to do something unbecoming of an abbot, like killing a flock of rowdy boys. Or perhaps killing only one—Mac Phelim.

He reached out suddenly and seized the youngest, Kenneth, by the arm. "The rest of you fly home! Go! Get to your studies!"

With a chorus of "Yes, Father!" the boys romped away. Fifty or sixty feet down the creek, they hiked the hems of their tunics and waded across, splashing merrily, through water less than two feet deep.

"Well, Kenneth?" Finnian scowled his darkest.

Kenneth, looking near tears, stared at the stones. Small for his age to start with, and of tender years, the lad appeared so fragile, so vulnerable. His shaggy red hair gleamed like copper in the late-afternoon sun.

Finnian prodded. "This was planned, was it not?"

A hesitant nod.

"The stepping stones were moved from their usual place in the shallows."

Nod.

"Stacked precariously one upon another in deep water, to appear stable."

Nod.

"Who was the intended victim? Garth? Rinnon?"

Barely audible: "You, Father."

"How did they know I would come this way and cross the creek?"

"You'd come seeking us and see the fieldfares rise up, Father, and assume we were near."

"The timing. They would have had to wait until I approached, at least beyond the bull paddock, before letting the fieldfares fly. How did they entice the wild birds to fly up on command?"

Finnian waited . . . and waited. "Speak!"

The faltering voice: "We occupied the birds with bread crumbs, Father, and shooed them up when you drew near."

Finnian seethed. "Mac Phelim."

The miserable child shrugged mightily. Tears welled in those luminescent eyes and overflowed. He slurped his nose.

Finnian lurched to his feet and dragged the lad by an arm to the ford downstream. Fifteen inches of water. Thirty-six inches of lad. With a sigh, Finnian hoisted the little boy onto his shoulders, hiked his own sopping-wet dalmatic, and slogged across the frigid stream.

"Go." He set the lad down. Instantly the child's feet churned wildly. The lad stumbled in the rank grass, dropped to his knees, lurched erect, and took wing toward the safety of the monastery.

Still breathing murder—and dripping quite a bit—Finnian entered the monastery compound by the bier gate. The fewer who saw him thus, the better. When Finnian and his followers built this monastery, many argued that this second gate in the ringwall was a breach of safety. Nobody built two gates in a ringwall. Just wasn't done, you know. Raiders could penetrate twice as easily with two gates. Finnian had countered that on the contrary it improved safety, for herdsmen could quickly drive their cattle into the protection of the ringwall from either meadow, front or back. How glad he was now that he had stayed with this plan.

"Well, Finnian!" In the cookhouse doorway, arms akimbo, stood one of the people Finnian least hoped would see him wet. Aileen the Cook from Inishowen Head, as wide as she was tall, watched him with dancing eyes and a knowing smirk. "Mac Phelim again, aye?"

Finnian glared at her and continued toward his clochan. He was mere inches from his doorway—inches, mind you—his hand on the rawhide door cover when a familiar voice boomed his name.

If the irreverent, independent Aileen were one of the last people he wanted to see him thus, this man calling his name, Cruithnechan the wizard, was the very, very last. Finnian turned away from the comfort and safety of his humble little hut, dismal beyond description, and forced the corners of his mouth upward. Sort of. "Cruithnechan, and God's blessings upon you."

"Blessings on you." Cruithnechan was not a wizard actually. He was as much a man of God as any other priest. People dubbed him that because he was one of the few old Irish churchmen still reputed capable of calling up miracles. For some reason, the godly gift to perform miracles was abating rapidly among the faithful of Erin. No one felt the lack more keenly than Finnian, who at one time had pulled off a few minor miracles of his own. So he might be forgiven just a wee bit of jealousy regarding Cruithnechan's undiminished powers.

Cruithnechan allowed Finnian's present state the barest of notice, the barest of sneers. "Fell in, aye? You'd best lose some weight, Finnian, if you plan to tarry around water much. Hard to stay balanced when you waddle, you know."

"Indeed. Welcome, Father, to Moville. A safe journey, I trust."

"Good trip, thank you. My protégé, how's he doing?"

"Fine. Fine." *Altogether too fine, the rapscallion.* "Mac Phelim is brilliant as regards formal study. Has Greek and Latin both down pat, and now he's working on Hebrew."

"He was a quick lad when I had him at Temple Douglas. Glad he's coming on. Where is he? I want him. Have something special for him. I want you in on it too."

"The scriptorium, I would guess." *Something special. A whip? Chains? Banishment to Britain as a slave? Gladden my heart, Priest.* Finnian headed off at an angle across the compound, past the stone oratory toward the scriptorium. "What is the fine occasion, may I ask?"

Cruithnechan, when you thought about it, looked like a wizard too. Not that Finnian knew what wizards ought to look like, but Cruithnechan had that gaunt look, with a crook nose and tight, beetling eyebrows. He hunched a bit also as he walked. "His baptism. High time he was baptized into the work of God."

Finnian stopped, which drew Cruithnechan to a halt. "Oh? I assumed that had been done. He's approaching full adulthood, well within the age of accountability." *And much to be held accountable for.*

"It was done indeed. But in a private ceremony at Temple Douglas. This will be his public naming, for all the world to hear and see."

Finnian ought not question a point of faith with a man so esteemed, but he himself was, after all, an abbot and thereby entitled to. "My good father, does not the Scripture teach clearly,

15

one baptism for the remission of sins'? One is one, and done is done."

"Then call it a public naming. A christening. Whatever." Cruithnechan took off walking again. Always in a hurry to be elsewhere, this old man. "There's reason for the public ceremony, with plenty of witnesses. His father wants him called Phelan— 'The Wolf.' It's his totem. He's royal on both sides, you know."

"So I hear." *Royals. Not worth dirt, the lot of them.*

"His father's a great grandson of Niall of the Nine Hostages, direct line. Mac Phelim could take a high kingship if he wanted, you know. The highest. Ard ri. And his mother's connected to the kings up north across the passage. The Dal Riada. Has ties with the southern Ui Niell as well, I believe. But I'm convinced that he's destined for far greater things than a mere high kingship. Far greater!"

Cruithnechan stepped inside the scriptorium, from hazy sunlight into gloom. "You need more light in here. There he is! Mac Phelim! And Mac Niall as well! Excellent! Excellent!"

There they were indeed. The loathsome lads, the both of them, came running from a dark corner to embrace the priest. "My father!" Mac Phelim burbled, with some justification; not only was Cruithnechan Mac Phelim's first priest and tutor, he was the lad's foster father. The wizard's pet. What the wizard saw in him thoroughly escaped Finnian.

Taller than Finnian and growing more robust by the day, Mac Phelim already possessed a rich, clear baritone strong enough to call down migrating geese. And he didn't have his full growth yet. Imagine this lad in another five years, powerfully wrestling to a stand-still that bull out in the paddock. His white-blond hair glowed even in this gloom. Add to that his eyes—clear blue, they bored right through you. It was his eyes, most of all, that made Finnian so uncomfortable.

His cousin stood quite as bulky and tall. If Finnian had to decide between the two as to which frightened him most, he would have to give the edge to Mac Niall. The lad possessed a dark quality, perhaps because of his nearly-black hair and snapping jet eyes, perhaps because of the way he kept his own silent counsel.

16

Finnian studied the upstarts a moment. "You seem warm, Lads, even say sweaty. As if you've been running."

"Running?" Mac Phelim looked blankly at the abbot. He turned that vapid expression to Mac Niall.

Mac Niall shrugged casually. "I've been running—an errand for Garth. But so far as I know, my cousin here has been in the scriptorium most of the day."

Mac Phelim grinned suddenly, disarmingly. "I am overjoyed! My father is here."

"Show me your work." Cruithnechan strode off toward that dark corner from which Mac Phelim had emerged.

Good! Good! That boy was out watching the spectacle of my disgrace, not working at all. He raced back here ahead of me, and now he is to be caught in his deception! Finnian had to lace his hands together behind his back to keep from clapping them.

"See, Father!" Mac Phelim waved a hand across several pages of vellum. Why was Finnian's scriptmaster allowing this stripling to practice on vellum? Boys his age copied on cheap scraps, not book-quality pages. "The scriptarian has put me to copying the Pentateuch. He claims my work is masterful. It takes me quite a bit of time. I can't work quickly yet."

Not when you're traipsing all over the countryside fomenting mischief.

"Beautiful. Beautiful." Cruithnechan bent low to peer at the work. He straightened and glared at Finnian. "Why are these lads stuffed into this dark corner?"

"Their eyes are young, Father. They can see here, away from the door and windows, whereas some of the older copyists cannot."

"Build a decent scriptorium with plenty of light and use this miserable hovel for storage. It's a disgrace. Come along, both of you. We've work to do."

Who does this wizard think he is? Finnian was abbot of Moville, and Finnian would build as he saw fit! In a delicious snit, he followed Cruithnechan and the boys out into the glaring daylight. He was starting to feel intensely cold, chilled to the bone. He wanted to shed this wet dalmatic. He wanted to wrap up in a warm, dry wool blanket awhile. He wanted Mac Phelim to trip himself up.

The burly dastardly duo ran off on some errand, and Cruithne-chan slowed a few strides to fall in beside Finnian. "I'm thinking we'll perform the service at Vespers. You'll have the full assembly then."

"Father, must we entertain the whole world with this?"

"Absolutely!" Cruithnechan looked at Finnian as if he were sprouting green warts. "Mac Niall shows great promise. Since he's a full cousin to Mac Phelim, he also stands at the front of the line to ascend the high throne at Tara. But then you know that."

"Yes. Of course." Finian tried to picture the dark and brooding youngster as a high king. As a high anything.

Cruithnechan rolled on. "But Mac Phelim! This lad is going to move mountains for God! I know it. He belongs to the church, and the church belongs to him. The purpose of the church is to serve, you know. The whole church will send him forth. Send them both forth."

"Mm. Of course. Phelancille. The Wolf of the Church." *A clever and ravening beast without redeeming grace. How apt.*

"No, no, no. I was telling you his father wants him baptized Phelan, but then we got off onto something else. He's named Columba. Columcille. The Dove of the Church."

Finnian stopped cold. "Columba! The Dove! My Father, stop and think! Doves are peace. Doves are mercy. Doves are our Lord's Holy Spirit. When you think of doves, you think of affection and nurturing and gentleness. Nothing could be further from a description of that young man! Wolf, yes. Badger perhaps. Hawk. Vulture. But not Dove!"

"His mother expressed some concern that you were not the best of instructors for her son. Perhaps I should not have discounted her opinion. Is there a breach of faith between you? A conflict?"

"Well, er . . ." How to phrase this? "Not as such. I am fully in charge here, if that's what you're driving at. But he tends to lead the other boys astray."

The two miserable Macs came running. They had changed from their roughspun pupil's tunics into white wool dalmatics. Baptismal garb. And right there it struck Finnian how different were these two boys who were so much alike. The white garments vividly set off Mac Niall's dark complexion and black hair even as they made Mac Phelim's golden complexion glow. A son of light and a son of darkness—both with a sense of humor as black as the Styx.

Finnian eyed Mac Niall. "So you, lad, will be publicly named as well." No one had mentioned anything of the sort to Finnian.

"Aye, Master. I'm to be Gavin."

Gavin! What was this? Gavin meant White Hawk. The fellow might possibly grow into a decent sort of hawk, fierce and quick, but white? It didn't fit. But Finnian didn't feel like arguing. Obviously, Cruithnechan's mind was made up.

Cruithnechan twisted in midstride to address Mac Phelim. "So. I hear you lead the other lads astray."

Mac Phelim, all too soon to become Columba, of all things, looked confused. He brightened. "I lead, I hope, in acts of piety, Father, and also once in a while in a bit of harmless fun. *Astray* would hardly be the word. Never has anyone suffered injury or loss, nor entered into sin as such."

The wizard bobbed his head. "Not youth without a bit of frivolity." He angled off across the compound to the oratory.

Frivolity, he says. Columba. Dove. Gentleness and peace. Bah! How much more wrong could this terrible day go?

As one, the two boys stopped instantly. Mac Phelim cried out with a strangled, "Nooo!"

Mac Niall the Dark One bolted forward, calling over his shoulder, "Protect the Father!"

Mac Phelim the Light One grabbed not Finnian's arm but Cruithnechan's and began dragging the withered old man into the oratory. "Raiders, Father! We'll try to keep you safe."

Raiders? Where? What raiders? Finnian glanced toward the east gate, the only gate he could see. The truth dawned—this was a trick! This was another outrageous prank to discredit him before Cruithnechan, of all people. Misery of miseries, they would succeed too, for in the old man's eyes these two scalawags could do no wrong!

Then Finnian heard his bull bellow in pain. And he saw the black smoke of burning sheds boil up beyond the wall.

19

2

Anice's Tale

Blessed be the innocents of God,
  Children of beauty and praise....

Anice of the Oak Ridge wanted her mama, but her mama was dead. She wanted her papa, but her papa was long gone. She wanted to go home, but home lay beyond mountains and sea. She wanted safety, but peril surrounded her. And that seemed pretty much to sum up Anice's life.

Not that she'd lived all that much of it so far. At age twelve, though, she had already traveled farther and done more than most women manage in a lifetime, and none of it by choice. Who but a slave would go running down this grassy hillside wielding a battle-ax against strangers in a strange country to further the ambitions of a woman she hated?

She had tied her auburn hair up in the usual turban, but she was not good at winding turbans. It had slipped askew, partly covering one eye. Anice slowed to shove it back up.

Her handler behind her, a portly woman with a long pike pole, snarled, "Faster! Both hands on the ax haft!"

She shouted back, "But I can't see!" even though she knew it was no use to argue.

Directly ahead of them, the pasturage sloped downward to meet a sparkling little river, then beyond the stream it sloped upward into a low, domed hill. Crowning that hill stood a ringwalled rath larger than any other Anice had seen in this Irish coastland.

A dozen of Anice's fellow raiders, three of them slaves like herself, reached the little river. Several tried to cross on stepping stones, but the stones gave way and dumped them into deep water. Honestly! The Irish, stupid beasts, could do nothing right, for here just a few yards downstream were riffling shallows. Shallows were the place to set stepping stones. Any dunce knows that.

20

Goaded by her handler, Anice waded the riffles, jumped the narrow channel, and slogged up the slope through the thick grass. Running with this unwieldy battle-ax was wearing her out. Panting heavily, she passed a brush fence. In it, a massive bull struggled, trying to stand despite the javelins waggling loosely in its side at odd angles.

Rangers had already fired the corn skeps. Black smoke drifted up and over the rath. Now the main force—fifty-some spearmen and handlers—washed like a great ocean wave against the ring-wall. The gate held.

Anice ran forward as part of the second wave. She brandished her battle-ax, ululating the war cry, attacking the gate, knowing her handler would as soon thrust that pike pole into Anice's back as the enemy's. The prime warriors of this party fought naked, with nothing but the gold torques around their necks. Women and slaves fought clothed. It was an inconvenience, for Anice's coarseweave tunic, wet from the hasty river crossing, slapped against her legs and clung.

She swung her ax at the planked gate; as the blade thunked into the wood, her turban slid completely over her eyes. She swung again, blindly—literally—caring not whether she struck friend or foe. This was not her fight.

Someone—the unit commander, if she heard correctly—shouted about a second gate on the far side. Immediately, most of the fighting men ran off around the wall.

"Keep at it! Again!" Her handler's pike stabbed the back of her leg. Hot blood ran down her calf.

She so wanted to swing around and apply her ax to the handler, but that would mean instant death. On the other hand, that might be preferable to this long, frightening agony of battle. She shoved her turban up with one hand and chopped again. She hit either a knot or something metal, for a chunk chipped out of her ax's cutting edge.

With a mighty whack, the slave beside her split a plank, then wedged his blade in and pried. His ax handle broke. *What a great idea!* He was done with the war until they found him another ax. She shoved her slipping turban up, chopped a blow against the gate, and put all her strength into twisting her ax.

21

Nothing. The ax held. The gate held. She shoved her slipping turban up.

These Irish louts possessed no scruples whatever. Defenders at the top of the palisade were tossing boiling water down now. That's the kind of churlish behavior the Roman legions used to indulge in hundreds of years ago. Win at any cost, no matter how unprincipled the means. Barbaric!

A burly warrior stepped in beside her swinging a great stone ax. A *stone* ax, of all things! She shoved her slipping turban up. That massive sledge split a plank. Another. She shoved her slipping turban up.

They were breaching the gate! Much as Anice despised her mistress, much as she disliked and distrusted her mistress's current Irish consort, she found herself getting caught up in the thrill of pending victory. Yes! They would win! This ugly, bloody skirmish would end, and Anice could go back to serving as her lady's handmaiden. No more battle-axes, no more murder and mayhem. She shoved her slipping turban up.

Half a dozen warriors shouldered each other for the honor of being first inside. One of them fell back against Anice and collapsed. A second dropped at her feet.

Behind her, her handler shouted a war cry triumphant and pushed Anice through the breach ahead of herself. Anice stumbled and fell over the twitching bodies in the gate, struggled to her feet, shoved her slipping turban up—and gazed face to face upon the most splendid, handsome, frightening young man she had ever seen!

Strong he was, immensely tall and sturdy for someone with such a youthful face. And look at that shock of hair, nearly black. Dark complexions ran in some of the Irish kingly lines, they said, and he looked regal indeed, particularly clothed in white as he was. Proud! Defiant! Dangerous he was too, for his crackling black eyes burned with bloodlust. The short lance he wielded was bloodied tip to grip. The leathern shield on his left arm was generously blood-spattered as well.

And then Anice did a most foolish, foolish thing. To this enemy, he an Irishman and she a Pict, to this young man who was about to lose the fight and surely his life as well, she cried out, "Help me!"

He hesitated only the barest bit of a moment. His left hand darted toward her; the shield tipped aside, rendering him vulnerable. As with his right hand he thrust at her handler with his lance, with his left he grabbed her and yanked her toward himself. She went flying and skidding across the beaten dirt.

Someone stepped on her, stomping her arm as he passed over her. Someone else snatched her ax out of her hand. She used both hands to push her turban up and pull it off her head completely. Her hair cascaded down around her face, blinding her almost as badly as the loose turban had.

That great, hulking young man stood hard beside her now, wielding his lance expertly. She struggled to her knees.

He was bellowing "Kenneth!" over and over.

From nowhere a copper-haired child came racing, accompanied by a giant of a woman. Anice's rescuer cried out, "Hide her in the oratory!" Instantly, the giant grabbed Anice's wrist to drag her away. The small boy seized her other hand.

Such a small child on this churning battleground! Anice stumbled, tried to run, almost could not, for her stabbed leg was slow to function and threatened to give up completely. The large blonde woman scooped her bodily off her feet. Staggering, these two hauled her between mudhuts as the battle raged behind her with shouting and screaming and clouds of dust.

This was absolutely insane! As soon as her mistress's warriors secured the rath, they would dig Anice out and behead her for rebelling. She was doomed.

With a butcher knife in one hand and a roasting skewer in the other, a very fat woman came running out of what had to be the kitchen, a mudhut surrounded by fire rings and cauldrons. Cackling joyously, she lumbered off to join the fray.

This compound was overflowing with stunning young men! A fellow as big and burly and handsome as the other stood guard, sword in hand, at the door of a strange stone building. As dark as the other was, this one was just the opposite—bright blond, with intense blue eyes. He too wore a pure white woolen garment.

He had the door of the stone building open and waiting as

they approached. The hefty blonde woman dragged Anice inside; the door clumped shut, closing out the light along with some of the din of battle. Two small windows, much too narrow to admit weapons, let alone people, kept the interior from going completely dark. Anice could see daylight between some of the stones, and yet she noticed no miry puddles, suggesting rain leaks, on the dirt floor.

What a curious building this was, shaped rather like a huge, upside down boat hull, widest at the base and narrowing to a sharply angled pitch high overhead. All of stacked river stones, it looked like it ought to collapse of its own weight. Despite the appearance, Anice suspected that if this whole compound were reduced to ash and rubble, this building would still stand.

Several dozen boys and girls crowded in here, all children younger than Anice. Three aged women, withered and bent, knelt in a corner muttering.

A gaunt, gray old man with thick brows barked at her elbow, "Sit down! Sit down."

She did so.

He settled down to sitting beside her, casually, comfortably, as if there were no such thing as war raging outside. With a knife he cut a seam and ripped a couple inches off the hem of the tunic of the copper-haired lad called Kenneth. "Your leg," he said, and with the torn fabric commenced to bind her gash.

Too much was happening too fast. She tried to pay attention to what was going on here, but she could not. She ought to be listening carefully to the noise outside, ready to bolt and attempt an escape when it sounded as though these people were giving up. She couldn't concentrate. The noise and darkness swirled in a confused cacophony around her.

The blonde woman settled beside them, and for the first time Anice could get a good look at her. She was not nearly as big as Anice first thought—just a little larger than average, a wee bit heftier than average, and none of it fat. She had pulled her dark blonde hair back, not in a turban but in a braid. Anice envied that braid—no slipping, no blinding, no fuss, no muss.

The young woman spoke for the first time, and her voice floated, softly feminine. "Are you actually a warrior?"

"Not because I want to be."

The hawkish old man growled at the woman. "Don't even think of citing Pictish ways to support your opinions."

What was all that? Anice's leg, now that it was being tended to, hurt terribly. "I'm a slave to Forba of Drumderry. 'Tis she out there causing mayhem."

The old man froze. His hands paused in midwrap, he peered into her face. "Your strong Pictish accent makes you very difficult to understand." He said this as though it were a fault of Anice's. "Forba. A queen of the Picts?"

"She is, Lord. Actually, a princess. She'll probably become queen if she doesn't marry a royal above her rank."

The old man sniggered. He laughed. He sat back and roared. "Forba! Here!" The idea set him to laughing all over again. "Oh, I do hope Finnian survives this raid. Delicious. Absolutely delicious."

"Finnian?" Anice's ears perked. "My mistress knew a Finnian. She was in love with him once. I daresay she might still be so. He was an Irish monk, though, and refused to court her. 'Twas a wondrously sad and romantic story."

"Tell me more." The old man tucked her bandage in a bit carelessly and sat back.

This was a new kettle of porridge. What should she tell this old man, and what was best left unspoken? Her die was cast; either her mistress would win and Anice would lose her head, or her mistress would lose and Anice was free at last. Either way, what she said or did not say didn't seem to matter much.

"I heard, Lord—understand this was years before I was taken, so I don't know it firsthand—that my mistress Forba was enamored of a monk called Finnian, a young fellow somewhat on the portly side. He did not requite her love, but he did agree to arrange for her to meet a youth he deemed worthy of her. A charming rogue of a lad. So you see, the monk Finnian set up a romantic match."

"I heard a similar tale. Go on." The old man nodded, looking absolutely gleeful.

"Well, the match 'took,' as it were, and a wedding was arranged, the payments and exchanges all made—everything. But the princess tired quickly of the young man, and so Finnian helped her meet secretly with another who took her fancy. Sure and you know, Lord, that once the payments are made, the wedding's as good as done. It raised a scandal the like you've never seen. Forba's people drove Finnian right out of the country—would've driven him into the bedrock like a fencepost had they laid hands on him. We heard he fled home to Ireland."

"He did indeed," the old man cackled. "And it is his monastery, this very place, in whose oratory you've taken shelter. What a coincidence! What an amazing coincidence!"

Anice frowned. "I'm not so certain, Lord, that it's all that coincidental. Forba spoke of deliberately seeking Finnian out. She came from her homeland to Erin here specifically to that end."

"Indeed!" The man sobered instantly. "You're sure?"

"I am her handmaiden, Lord. I'll be combing her hair or tending her garments as she confers with her advisors and clan chieftains. And Irish kings as well who call upon her, such as the one who accompanies her now. I hear pretty much all."

"So Finnian was her purpose in coming."

Should Anice tell everything? Why not? "There were two purposes, Lord. The Irishman she is in league with is a prince of a kingly line. I forget who. He wants his cousins removed from consideration of a kingship, for they rank higher than he. Two birds with one stone, you might say. Apparently the cousins are in this general area. Close. So my mistress and the Irish taoisech joined forces to help each other."

"Kingly line. Name?" The man's gray eyes pierced.

A cold trill of fear ran down her spine. This man seemed to exude power far beyond the physical. He appeared the sort who could call down lightning and frizzle you on the spot. "Forgive me, Lord. I can't remember."

"Ui Neill?"

She bobbed her head. "Aye, Lord, the very same!"

His voice rose. "And the names of the cousins to be removed?"

She felt herself breaking into a sweat. "I'm sorry, Lord. Wait! I think I can remember one of them. Clum. Cumm. No. Wolf. No. Phelim. A son of a man named Phelim."

The old man's face hardened. "Mac Phelim. Columcille."

3

Gavin's Foray

A blond man, embattled,
girt in much blood . . .

Mac Niall, soon to be named Gavin the White Hawk, killed a man when he was twelve. The fellow, a foolish oaf, had thought to steal a calf from Finnian's herd, believing that the half-grown lad tending the cattle could do him no harm. That was three years ago. Today Gavin became a killer again. Four Pictish bodies pretty much blocked the bier gateway. These raiders may have breached the wooden gate, but they did not breach the Hawk.

Panting, dour Comgall, four years older than Gavin, came running and planted himself at Gavin's right elbow. "They're holding the main gate, so they sent me here."

A great bull of a fighting man came roaring over the top of the pile, ferocious in his ardor. He scrambled across the bodies, slipping on their blood, but managed to keep his balance. As he came at Comgall and Gavin, his ax flew forward and sank itself into Gavin's leathern shield. The blade protruded inside, gripping tightly; the force shoved Gavin's arm back against his chest. He slashed out with his sword before the bull could bring another weapon into play. He sliced air.

Comgall's sword connected; Gavin could hear it hit. The fellow went down at the brothers' feet, dragging the ax and shield—and Gavin's arm—along with it. Gavin fell forward on his knees, his neck and back exposed—totally vulnerable, except for the stalwart Comgall at his side. He struggled mightily to pull his arm free before the next man through the gate literally chopped his head off.

He managed to shed the weighted shield and regain his feet. But somehow the battle had departed from them. As he and Comgall valiantly defended this gate, everyone—enemy and friend together—

27

apparently decided to fight elsewhere. Gavin was sorely tempted to go find the fight and join it, but his assignment was to guard the bier gate. He would guard the bier gate.

Here came the two brothers from the monastery smithy. Crory they called the one. Of the other, Gavin remembered the face but not the name. Between them they carried split planks to repair the bier gate. They worked feverishly, clumsily, fearfully, spiking boards down haphazardly to shore up the shattered wood.

Gavin took the moment to free his poor gashed shield of that ax, then stood close guard as Crory and Whoever dragged the enemy corpses out of the way and rehung the gate.

What a botch job! Instead of artfully lashing the new wood in with sinew, the monks had simply hammered spikes here and there. The heavy nails did some plank-splitting of their own. But the sorry mess didn't look all that bad from the outside, where the hasty repairs did not show. Gavin fervently prayed that their foes would have more confidence in the gate's strength than he did.

"Gavin! The Wizard wants you!" Little Kenneth's pipsqueak soprano called to the Hawk.

"I can't! I have to guard the gate!"

"He says the battle's over, and we won. He says the enemy retired and sent their champion to negotiate. He says to come to the oratory."

Gavin looked at Comgall. Comgall's long, lanky, gloomy face looked blank. The warrior-brother shrugged. Was this a trick? If the enemy had broken through, it could be a ruse to disarm and defeat the Hawk.

Gavin asked little Kenneth, "Where's Colm?"

"In the oratory pouting."

Gavin frowned. That sounded right. Pouting was fairly common for Colm. "You said we won. *Now* why is he unhappy?"

The child shrugged. "He thinks you've been doing all his fighting for him, and he was able only to stand around looking fierce. And now Cruithnechan is put out because Colm is one part of the body of Christ and covets being another."

That sounded right also. Cruithnechan was inordinately ardent about what he called that cardinal spiritual truth.

Gavin asked Comgall, "Can you handle it?" The man nodded.

Gavin thrust the dead Pict's ax into Crory's hand. "You help guard the gate."

Crory turned white beneath his summer tan. "Brother, I am a simple blacksmith! I can't possibly . . ."

"He'll help you." Gavin grabbed Whoever's wrist and wrapped the terrified monk's fingers around the sword.

"I am a simple carpenter! I cannot possibly . . ."

Gavin trotted off toward the oratory at Kenneth's heels, leaving the two fearful brothers to whine their plaints to Comgall.

The compound within the ringwall, one of Erin's largest, churned with activity, but it seemed to be innocuous, almost-normal activity. Monks and sisters bustled among the cluster of little mud clochans to the east. With a smug, self-satisfied grin, the cook was heading back toward her kitchen complex, her cooking utensils in hand. The herdsmen had gathered the cattle in behind the scriptorium and now were penning them by brushing up the narrow passage between the scriptorium and the oratory.

Women and children came streaming out of the oratory as Gavin approached. Either the danger was past or this was an elaborate ruse indeed. Where was Colm? Gavin swam against the tide as it were, stepping into the dank darkness.

Finnian—hulking, overweight Finnian—hovered in the gloom near Cruithnechan. Finnian's face suggested that the end of the world, so richly promised in Revelation, was about to come to pass. At his side stood Colm, sword sheathed. And at their feet, huddled like a hare in its nest, sat that strange and compelling little auburn-haired girl.

"Listen to this." Cruithnechan scowled at the girl. "Tell these men your story."

"You won." She looked at Gavin, her original benefactor. Her voice trembled like a bird's song. "I didn't think you'd win."

"The story," the Wizard prodded impatiently. "About the princess and the heirs to the Ui Neill. That's these lads right here, you know. 'Tis them the enemy be seeking."

Her green eyes flicked from Gavin's face to Colm's, startled. She began her tale then, unfolding it in a flat, emotionless voice. She could not remember the Irish prince's name. Cruithnechan and Colm both tried her half a dozen ways on that.

Gavin listened. He laughed at Finnian's fecklessness as a matchmaker, though not aloud. And he wasn't the least surprised to hear that the swarmy Ui Neill bunch from the east would commit murder to put their man on the throne of Tara. It happened all the time. Well, a lot of the time.

The girl fascinated him. She was a child, a child who came at him with a battle-ax. She looked charming in a waif-like way, with overly large eyes and wispies of flyaway hair too short to stay with the bulk of her rich tresses. Her thin arms didn't look strong enough to wield a spoon, let alone a battle-ax.

Colm was asking her now about herself. Enslaved at nine, handmaid to a princess—she talked about it all with a cool detachment, almost a disdain for her own life. And this fascinated him most of all: Even though she had assumed that the monastery would fall to the enemy, she had switched sides. She had placed her life in Gavin's hands with no assurance that she was improving her situation. He had never before been trusted in quite that way.

They had beaten off the enemy. This time. Would it not be politic to avoid a next-time? Gavin caught his cousin's eye. "Do you mind a little risk-taking, Gentle Dove?"

"Is not all life a risk, Fierce Hawk?" Colm grinned.

Cruithnechan scowled, making the most of his thick brows and angular face. "What do you two think you're going to do?"

Finnian would have scowled as deeply, but his chubby face prevented him from achieving anything like the same effect. "No good, I'll vow."

Gavin stepped back to the door and paused. "I for one would love to see this headstrong princess who would have a crush upon our abbot. And as far as I know, you have no plans to take the throne, do you, Colm?"

The blond cousin shrugged. "I've pretty well decided to stay in the church and leave the ruling to others. Why?"

"Then you're not a threat to this Irish prince's ambitions, and I think he ought to know so."

"Confront him?" Cruithnechan shook his vulturine head. "Don't you dare!"

Colm's calm voice rumbled, "My father, you know I have two heritages, royalty and the church. Sacred and civil. You are the master of my faith, but not of civil matters. This is a civil matter." He joined Gavin at the door.

Gavin glanced back not at Finnian or Cruithnechan, for he knew what they looked like, but at that girl-child on the floor at their feet. Wide-eyed, she watched them leave.

As soon as they were outside, Gavin drew a deep breath. "You have more courage to oppose the Wizard than I ever could."

"And that surprises me too. He's been right up there next to God my whole life. Should we invite Comgall along?"

Gavin didn't have to think about that for very long. "He's too negative. Always comes up with the reasons why an idea won't work. Besides, we need minimum numbers if we would breach the Pictish defenses."

"Suit yourself." Colm looked down at himself. "We might want to shed these white baptismal garments—change to brown tunics, especially if you intend to go slinking around after dark."

"I intend to find out which of our sneaky relatives wants to do us in." Gavin led the way to their clochan.

"Don't try to fool me. You just want to look that princess over." Colm cackled.

So do you, cousin. So do you. Gavin didn't say it out loud because Colm tended to lose his temper if you second-guessed him too closely. Instead, Gavin put his thoughts to work on a plan. By the time they changed their clothes, he had formulated not one plan but two, a main course of action and a backup. He explained them to Colm as they headed for the bier gate.

The enemy's slain had been removed. Only the blackening pools of blood remained. Gavin and Colm didn't bother trying to get that makeshift gate open. They continued back behind the kitchen, climbed the grassy slope of the earthen ringwall, and scaled the palisade that topped it by climbing up the handholds they had chiseled into the logs years ago. An earthen wall with a palisade may stop the enemy, but it never stops boys who want to slip out of the compound undetected.

They settled down behind the smoldering ruins of the grain store. Colm dipped into the hot ashes for soot to smudge his glis-

31

tening blond hair. They talked about the girl's tale and about the girl and about Finnian's romantic misadventure. The day took forever to end.

Far out beyond the trees ahead of them, the waters of Strangford Lough glowed orange from the setting sun behind them. The water darkened, went flat, took on the gray of the night sky.

Colm stood up. "Time to go."

Gavin kept his sword sheathed, lest a fleck of moonlight glint off it, and hunched low as they jogged the track down into the oak grove beside the creek.

The enemy sat encamped not a hundred yards beyond the grove, in a rocky, deforested defile on the far side of the stream. From the number of tents pitched, Gavin would estimate their fighting strength at eighty or less. A great fire crackled in the center of the camp. Beside it, a giant beef hindquarter on a spit sizzled over a bed of glowing coals in a second firepit. From time to time, smoky yellow flames flashed up where fat dripped.

Gavin settled himself upon a rock and gazed across the creek to the encampment. "I do believe, Dove, they're roasting our bull."

"Certainly the size of him, isn't it? If God smiles upon us, the meat will be tougher than rawhide."

"And lay even more heavily upon their hearts than on their stomachs." Gavin raised a hand the way Cruithnechan sometimes did. "May remorse strike them to the very root."

Cruithnechan, however, performed miracles by so doing. Gavin did not expect God to honor him quite that richly.

Colm switched to hand signals as they moved down closer. He pointed out a logical ford and Gavin nodded. With a finger, Gavin traced their route up the other bank and Colm nodded. As one, they stepped quietly down to streamside.

It was almost impossible to cross the creek silently. They varied the rhythm of their strides, so that they would sound like cattle crossing and not men. Once they reached the other side, it wasn't hard to pick out the north and west watches. Gavin waited to draw his own sword until Colm had crept up on the north watch. They struck virtually as one, cutting the men's throats before they could cry out. They dragged the bodies downslope into the streamside brush and took over the watches' positions.

So far, so good.

Haze hid the moon, leaving a silvery blur of light to mark its position. The enemy would be measuring the night by that moon, but Gavin had no idea what the measures were. It seemed half the night, though it was less than two hours, before a very smelly Pict came climbing the hill out of the camp. The Pict took over Gavin's position with a muffled, "Good night."

Gavin mimicked the silly, boorish accent. "Good night." Casually he made his way down the rocky slope to the encampment.

The north watch, similarly relieved, joined him as he reached the outermost of the tents. Colm grinned so brightly that Gavin was afraid he was going to give them away.

The cousins stood about nonchalantly in the periphery of the group, watching, weighing, trying to look like something they were not. The cooks started hacking off slabs of the roasted outer part. Dripping juices hissed and smoked, raising a yellow cloud around the quarter. The burning juices smelled so good; too bad the meat would taste terrible. You just don't get a tasty portion from a quarter of beef that's been aged eight hours.

But food is food, and Gavin's stomach was screaming at him by now.

It wasn't hard to identify the Pictish princess. She sat in full battle garb of tunic, skirt, and mantle as others served her. Her blonde hair glinted reddish in the firelight. Actually, she could be quite a pretty woman if she would just get rid of the perpetual look of displeasure on her face. You would think that a princess being served so attentively would be a little happier with life, at least some of the time. She looked like one of those demanding, impatient people whom slaves hate to serve, and Gavin thought again about the auburn-haired girl-child who so lately had combed those blonde tresses.

At her side hovered what had to be the Irish prince the girl-child had talked about. Maybe seventeen or eighteen, he shared some of the same features—the eyebrow line, the shape of the nose, a relatively dark complexion—that a lot of Gavin's kin possessed. He was overweight and flabby looking—definitely not a

Niall characteristic—and he seemed completely enamored of the princess. Gavin tried to picture his abbot Finnian hovering around her, or she hovering around the abbot, and very nearly laughed aloud.

"Recognize him?" Colm muttered.

Gavin shook his head and whispered, "Got to be southern Ui Neill. We'd know him if he was from up here."

The druids accompanying the princess invoked nothing that even resembled a Christian deity. The princess was not a woman of Christ. The young Irish prince seemed not the least alarmed or put off by her Pictish ways. Gavin doubted his faith enough to assume he was nowhere near converted either.

The well-done meat was all distributed before any reached Colm and Gavin. They ended up with extremely rare, dripping, practically quivering slabs, barely edible, hardly palatable. Gavin ate part of it because he was ravenous and thought about how splendidly that bull's meat could have turned out, drawn properly and aged carefully for a moon and a half. What a waste. God, however, did grant a small bit of his request—the stuff certainly lay heavy on the stomach.

Finally—*finally!*—the princess rose and strode off to her tent, that puppy-dog prince at her heels. With a disdainful flick of the hand she sent him off to his own quarters, so apparently her favors, if bestowed at all, were bestowed infrequently.

Gavin gauged by eye the tent the prince seemed headed for, but Colm had already picked the probable tent and was circling around behind it. They guessed right. The prince entered with two retainers. Gavin moved in close to the curtained opening. They were far enough from the fire that Gavin could see no detail whatever, which meant that neither could anyone else.

One of the retainers, just inside the curtain, glanced out at him. Fear told his feet to fly. He stood firm. The retainer handed out the prince's leathern Roman-style breastplate. "Here."

Gavin took it and held it. Out came the tunic. Gavin folded his arms across it. It smelled funny. The retainer pushed out through the curtain without handing Gavin anything further. The second retainer came out, scooped Gavin's burden into his own arms, and followed his cohort off into the darkness. So the prince slept with his sword.

Colm moved in beside him, and they slipped inside, drawing their swords only after they'd entered the blackness of the tent.

"Now what? Get out!" The prince's voice told them where his head lay.

Gavin took two quick steps to where the right arm would be and stomped down. Colm dropped forward. Gavin felt the prince's arm squirm beneath his bare foot. The prince's voice, muffled by a hand across his face, went silent. Quite probably, a blade at his throat was giving him second thoughts about crying out. Colm whispered harshly in the prince's ear.

With almost no problem at all they escorted the terrified lad out the curtained doorway and down a rocky slope, past other tents, past other men upon whose stomachs that bull lay heavy. Between the west and south watches, they dragged the prince through a hazel thicket to the stream. Less than an hour later, soaking wet, they approached the main gate of Moville and identified themselves.

They had to roust Cruithnechan out of bed. Gavin had secretly hoped the old wizard, knowing the peril in which his charges were placing themselves, had spent the night in prayer in the oratory. Hardly. Besides, the old man snored.

Sullen and sleepy, Cruithnechan stuck an oil lamp in the prince's face. "So. The young man with big ambitions." No praise to the cousins for their daring coup. No surprise that they succeeded.

At the terrified lad's side, Colm announced, "I am Columcille, the Dove of the Church. Mac Phelim, in a direct line of the Ui Neill, eligible for the throne of Tara."

The prince shuddered.

"I am Gavin, the White Hawk. Mac Niall, in direct line of the Ui Neill and thinking about taking the throne at Tara."

"And I am a dead man," rasped the prince.

"A dead man with a name," snarled Cruithnechan. "What name?"

"D-D-Diarmaid. Mac Cerbaill."

"Ah. Diarmaid."

Gavin could not recite genealogy the way a fileh could. He tried to piece Diarmaid into the fabric of the clans and couldn't place him exactly.

Colm stuck his face closer still. "Listen closely, Diarmaid Mac Cerbaill. I have decided to devote my life to the church. Do you understand what that means? It means that I pose no threat to your dreams of a kingship. I'm eligible, but I'm not in the running. It also means that as I develop my skills as a church scholar—and that is my ambition—we will be called upon to work together from time to time for the sake of our people and for God."

"How did . . . Why are you . . . Huh?"

Ah, intelligence. It's what kings need most. Diarmaid, Gavin noticed, breathed through his mouth.

Colm raised his voice. "And when we are called to work together, you will ever and always remember that, from this moment forward, you owe your life to me."

"To us," Gavin corrected.

Diarmaid stammered and lapsed into silence. His eyes darted from face to face.

Cruithnechan raised an arm in that way of his. "God bless you, Diarmaid. May you never oppose His servants." If this feckless pretender was the pagan he appeared, Cruithnechan's blessing was pretty much lost on him.

Colm and Gavin escorted the lad out into the cold, black night, leaving Cruithnechan to his repose. They led him among the mudhuts to the gate and out onto the pasture slope.

They left the stark-naked prince then to let the intelligent Diarmaid figure out on his own how to make his way safely back home.

4

Colm's Gift

I wander among the stars;
I seek their counsel,
and they sing to me.

Gavin couldn't stand Comgall, and he didn't understand why Colm tolerated the old curmudgeon. Well, all right, so Comgall wasn't so old—a couple years older than Colm and Gavin. And he wasn't so much a curmudgeon as simply a sour apple. Now Cruithnechan, he was a curmudgeon. Curmudgeons have a strong, even if grumpy, personality and a viewpoint of at least some value. They serve a purpose. Comgall was simply negative and gloomy. It's not the same thing at all.

They sat in the shade of the rowan out in the bull pasture, for the lea was now safe, devoid of its bull. Gavin sprawled at perfect leisure, his back against the tree trunk, his legs splayed. By his left elbow, Colm also leaned against the tree, splayed out toward the creek and their encamped nemesis in the distance beyond. Little Kenneth sat at their feet, and Comgall perched cross-legged before them, his legs flaccid, his brow tight.

In a tight knot, her knees pulled up and her arms wrapped around them, Treasa gazed rapt at Gavin and Colm. Treasa with the long dark-blonde braid tended to make Gavin feel a bit unsettled. She was larger than usual for a woman and much stronger. Most of all, she aspired to full status as a warrior. That was the unsettling part. And yet she lacked no touch of femininity, so to speak. He admired her resolve and the constant determination in her battle with Finnian and Cruithnechan. They opposed her dreams; she persisted with them. Who would wear down whom was anybody's guess.

Comgall fumed, not for the first time. "You needed me. You shouldn't have gone off without me, and that's the end of it. If any

37

little thing had gone wrong, you'd be dead now. Besides, the whole plan was ill-conceived. I could have helped you devise a better means of obtaining the prince, with a better outcome."

Treasa giggled. Actually, she cackled, a derisive sort of chuckle that told Gavin her heart lay with the cousins. "Did it work?"

"By luck and providence. Certainly not by design."

"Don't speak ill of success, Comgall." Treasa's melodious voice was capable of quite a sharp edge. Gavin liked her opinion of Comgall too.

Kenneth's soprano floated in awe. "I wish I could've gone along. I know I probably would have messed it up, but I wish I could have been there."

"Build your strength for a couple more years." Gavin grinned at him. "You have a warrior's heart. Time will give you a warrior's body."

"Terrible plan, start to finish! Don't you see what you did?" Comgall was still off on his rampage. "You embarrassed him. Shamed him. I wouldn't be surprised if Diarmaid's own sentinels speared him. The idea was to gain his friendship, but you didn't forge an ally; you made an enemy. He'll get you for this, sooner or later."

Maybe Colm was patient enough to put up with these fulminations, but Gavin was not. "The only bad thing about our little coup—the *only* bad thing—was to get Finnian and Cruithnechan down on us."

Colm snorted. "Finnian's never been up on us. But I regret displeasing Cruithnechan."

"Cruithnechan." Gavin nodded in agreement. His hair scraped against the bark behind him. "I want to know how he knew my geis. Out of all the things in this world, he picked my taboo. That's uncanny."

Treasa asked, "What is your geis?"

"The hawk. I'm never to injure or misuse a hawk."

"Or eat its flesh, of course."

"Of course. What's yours?"

Treasa shrugged. "Girls aren't usually bound to a powerful taboo like yours. Sea gull. Mine's the sea gull. It was the first thing that spoke to my father when I was born."

38

Kenneth wrinkled his freckled nose. "Who'd want to eat a sea gull?"

"Exactly." Treasa grinned. "Sea gulls are safe as far as I'm concerned."

Everyone just sat there a few minutes pondering either the mysterious power of a geis or maybe nothing at all, which was what Gavin was thinking about mostly.

Colm stirred beside Gavin's elbow. "I've been thinking about moving on. South into Leinster and study there a while. My mother has relatives there."

Leave Finnian of Moville? That didn't sound like too bad an idea to Gavin. "Study what?"

"Poetry. Ever hear of a bard named Gemman?"

Comgall glared. "How can you think of it? He's not a proper Christian monk."

"But he's the world's greatest poet. There's a lot to learn from him."

Kenneth piped up. "My father was a bard. That didn't keep *him* from being a Christian. He sang wonderful hymns to Christ—until he died."

Gavin smiled. "Then he's still singing them." He jabbed Colm. "I'll go along. Let old stick-in-the-mud stay here. Comgall's one of Finnian's pets anyway."

"I am not! He respects my maturity and learning."

Gavin cackled. He hoped it sounded as derisive as Treasa's. "He respected Mobhi's too, and Mobhi left the first chance he got."

"Mobhi"—Comgall sniffed—"never did fit in here."

Gavin was about to give that nasty bit of falsehood the retort for which it cried out, but Colm dug an elbow into Gavin's ribs, sharply. Colm was Mobhi's friend as much as was Gavin. Why would he allow that unfair cut to pass? Gavin let it by for Colm's sake, not the grump's.

Treasa was looking from face to face. "This Gemman." She glanced at Comgall. "This improper monk. What's his position as regards women?"

The tree bark whispered as Colm shrugged. "He has a reputation for inviting the whole world, unrestricted."

39

"Then I want to go with you."

"Immoral!" Comgall snorted.

"If I want to be immoral, I don't have to travel clear to Leinster to do it." Treasa huffed.

But Colm took Comgall's part, at least mildly, by adding, "Appearances, Treasa. He's talking about appearances."

Gemman. Leinster. The idea appealed. Colm had established himself as being disinterested in a high kingship, assuming that Diarmaid halfway believed him. Gavin had not. Whether or not Diarmaid eased his homicidal designs on Colm, Gavin still posed a threat. It would be nice to leave the area a few years, then rejoin the clan when he was old enough to lay a claim to the throne, if such he wanted. He was still undecided about that.

Besides, Gavin had never traveled south. He looked forward to it. He tended to get restless easily, to crave excitement, and this latest adventure that Comgall bad-mouthed so thoroughly only whetted his appetite the more.

With an extensive parting lecture to Finnian on how a productive scriptorium ought to be built, Cruithnechan left that afternoon. Where did the wizard go? Gavin had no idea, and he doubted anyone else did either. The old man appeared. He disappeared. He showed up outside your gate. Sometimes he showed up inside it. Gavin feared no one who slung a sword, but he feared the mystical Cruithnechan.

Colm must have been thinking about Leinster for quite a while already, for to Gavin's surprise, he told Finnian his plans that very night. Finnian did not weep to see them go. Rather, he hastily built a very heavy bundle of books and partials to be delivered to the monastery at Armagh. Gavin had pictured himself footloose and unburdened in his peregrinations. Thirty pounds of books? Gavin's gentle disdain for the portly Finnian instantly turned into genuine dislike. Leave it to Finnian to spoil an otherwise delightful leavetaking.

After Compline that night, Gavin sat quietly in Colm's clochan as the Mac Phelim packed up his pens and inkpot. Gavin had no inkpot to pack. He did not do well with reading and copying. Even little Kenneth did better with letters than he. He did, however, remember an awl and sinew with which to repair his poor, lacerated shield. On second thought, he would leave the shield to others. Monks are generally expected to travel unarmed anyway, and the sword he used belonged to the monastery. He kept the awl and sinew though.

Matins the next morning dragged forever. Finnian prayed long and verbosely for the hand of God upon Columcille and Gavin, children of the King. He sent them forth, invoking safety, health, and anything else God might see fit to bestow. He did not mention Treasa. She must have changed her mind.

She was not waiting at the gate as they departed directly after Matins. That would be the other place she would be. Finnian quite too liberally slathered on his praise for their growth and progress under his aegis. His unction irritated.

Finnian's final "Godspeed," however, seemed to be working. By sunrise they had crossed the ragged ridge and descended into open farmland, great splashes of green across the undulating valley floor. Stumpfields extended halfway up the mountains to either side, and brown cattle grazed there.

As they walked down the dark valleys south of Strangford Lough, Gavin thought about the little twelve-year-old girl. *What was her name? Anice. That was it. Imagine sticking a battle-ax in such a child's hand and sending her out to die!*

They abandoned the bundle of books at Armagh, a bustling monastery perched on one hill among many in a tangle of slopes and woodlots. Most of these hills were denuded of trees, as were the hills around Strangford Lough. Curious, Gavin thought, how the church and wildwood seemed incompatible with each other.

Just as Gavin was about to put one foot before the other unburdened, the abbot of Armagh (a grandnephew of Patrick himself, the fellow claimed) handed Colm and him a bundle each, and each as heavy as the first had been. For Tara, the abbot directed.

To himself, Gavin fumed, *I am not a pack-beast!* Aloud, he mouthed the words all abbots love to hear: "With pleasure I serve the needs of Christ." *Pleasure up a pig's snout. This is not Christ's need; it's the abbot's convenience.*

He anticipated that as long as it took them to reach Armagh, that distance again would bring them to Tara. Hardly. No matter how long a day they spent toting those burdens, Tara still lay in the mists of forever to the south. Colm took to the track with an eager anticipation. He had relatives at Tara, and he looked forward to seeing them, he said, but then so did Gavin. Colm lived in the safety of his monk's robe. Gavin had made no such declaration.

Perhaps Gavin ought to. No. On second thought, Gavin dare not do that. Once Colm declared himself a noncandidate for high king, he was out of the running. Should Gavin do so and then change his mind, no ri ruirech would vote for him. No abbot would lend his weight to Gavin as a choice, for his word could not be trusted.

On the other hand, he could not envision the mousy little Diarmaid as being a better choice than he himself. Consorting with that Pictish princess was the least of it. His pagan tendencies didn't earn Gavin's dislike. Rather, the callow lad couldn't even defend himself worth spit. With Colm disallowing himself from consideration, Gavin stood a very good chance of gaining the regional kings' choice, should the seat of the high king open up.

Still and all, Tara was a long way away from Gavin's clan and kin. He felt nervous coming here. And always, popping in and out of his thoughts like dunnocks flitting among the hedges, the face and smile of Anice passed. Folly that the child should so frequently come to mind. His mind did that every now and then, but usually it was some lovely lass striking his fancy. He'd be glad when the foolishness passed.

Tara. Seat of the ard ri, the high king of the northern Ui Neill. In all truth, the hill of hills was more a meeting place for pomp and gesturing than a site of actual rule. This region of Erin, despite its proximity to the high throne, governed like any other. Cattlemen clients—boaires—in the neat little ringwalled raths scattered round about leased as many cattle as possible from their lords, the ris. Ri tuathe took care of the raths, providing judges for legal disputes and warriors for protection.

Ri ruirechs, regional warlords, threw their weight around as much as their fellow ri ruirechs would let them get away with. They provided titular homage to the ard ri, the high king, but, except in raids and war, they pretty much tended their own affairs, unaffected by distant claimants to thrones.

Simple in execution, orderly in its frequent chaos, the system worked well. Gavin liked it. He understood it. It was the way government had always been and the way it would remain forever. He wanted to become part of it and taste the power and honor it provided the strong of arm and heart. He could not begin to guess why Colm would deliberately turn his back on the opportunities his royal blood presented.

All the same, Gavin would probably have stilled his curiosity about the place and by-passed Tara completely were he leading this journey. He felt awed a bit too much by the mystique of the hall of kings. Colm, with no such reservations, walked right up to Tara's gate, his way as straight as a spearshaft.

Gavin felt a little better about coming when the people here unerringly addressed Colm and him as "prince." When the two were announced at court, the old fellow doing the announcing recited off Colm's royal lineage on both sides—without having asked Colm what it was! Would he get Gavin's connections to the Ui Niell right? He did. It wasn't so amazing, really. There were many men in the land, filidh and sages, who knew the genealogies of every clan in Erin. Some were committing their memories to the written word. But Gavin trusted memory better. The written word was subject too much to misspelling, let alone fire and plunder.

They spent three days at Tara. Colm seemed most interested in the abbot of the king's church and of the liturgy they used. Gavin found himself more impressed by the armory. The ard ri knew how to keep a ready blade sharp and employed splendid armorers and smiths. Finally, they got on their way again, this time unburdened by the weights of others.

Leinster was another one of those places you'd think you could get to fairly easily—one heard about it all the time. It comprised a full fourth of Erin, and hardly anyone in it knew where one might find Gemman. Besides, since Colm and Gavin were princes, tradition and tact required them to present themselves at Cashel.

As Tara was home to the ard ri of the northern Ui Neill, Cashel was seat to the southern branch. Colm had kin here as well, on his mother's side. Gavin did not. You think the pomp was bad at

Tara? It suffocated you at Cashel. Gavin performed the minimum of greeting and obeisance he could get away with and went exploring.

Tara up north sat on a green and rounded hill; Cashel was boulder studded, perched on the brink of near-vertical cliffs on one side and a steep slope on the other. Gavin rather liked its defensibility. Its armory, however, could learn a thing or two from Tara. The hostler cheerfully lent Gavin a horse whenever he wished, and the cooks were easily cajoled into providing tasty tidbits at odd times of day. All in all it was a hospitable place.

Three days later, detailed instructions to Gemman's firmly in mind, they sallied forth again. And sallied. And sallied. Many days later, they were at last approaching Gemman's monastic settlement. At least that's what the boaire at the gate of a little rath beside a quiet stream told them. "You'll know it when you get there." The old cattleman smirked.

Gavin didn't particularly look forward to settling in with this Gemman, truth be known. He rather liked wandering through countryside he had never seen before, stopping at this rath or that along the way, depending for food and rest upon the largess of the farmers and their wives. That largess almost always provided ample comfort.

He and Colm had both trimmed their heads in the monastic tonsure, the front shaved ear to ear. That opened doors to them. Everyone likes offering hospitality to monks. Their plainweave dalmatics told the world they did not come to threaten and plunder. Life was good, uncomplicated by Latin, Greek, the particular scan of a poetic line, the drudgery of daily chores in a monastery.

Twenty days out, midafternoon, and the track angled up a low hill, then lost itself in a jumble of rocks tumbling down the other side. Below the rockslide, the track continued on into an oak grove, presumably headed toward a distant river.

About halfway down the boulder pile on a round rock sat a grizzled old man, staring out across the trees. No staff, a worn, dirty tunic, tangled hair, no tonsure. His back was to them, but tips and fringes of a great gray beard fluttered at either side of his neck. He had wrapped himself loosely in a huge, threadbare wool cloak. Sure and a beggar he was. Gavin didn't mind encountering beggars, for he had nothing to give up, and they were generally quite equable fellows.

Colm led the way, picking a route from rock to shaky rock down the slide. The fellow gave no indication that he heard them approaching. And yet, when they drew abreast of him, he did not jump or act startled.

Colm worked downslope enough to speak comfortably face-to-face with the man and turned to greet him. "Good fellow, we are seeking a bard named Gemman. A boaire up the way claims he lives near here."

"Gemman." The man had quite a melodious voice. It purred and lilted. "Yes. I know the man. You're not far from there." Within that bushel of beard and moustache, he wrinkled his nose. "Why would you care to associate with Gemman?"

Colm was still smiling. "I've been told I have a gift for song and poetry. I wish to study under him."

The old man spat. "Bah! An irascible old fool. Believes his own reputation, which is greatly overblown."

Gavin grinned. "Were I Gemman, that's exactly what my brothers would say of me. You wouldn't be his brother, would you?"

The fellow cackled, a hoarse laugh not the least like his smooth speaking voice. And look at his bleary eyes twinkle! He stood up. "Gemman you seek. Gemman you shall find, to your own sorrow. 'Tis your misfortune, and none of mine. Come. I'll take you."

He lurched forward down the boulder pile, appearing every moment as though he would lose his footing and tumble to the bottom. The tails of that oversized cloak floated. Fifty feet ahead of Colm, the spry old buzzard emerged onto the grassy sward below the rocks.

Colm fell in beside the fellow, so Gavin tagged along behind. They followed the track through the oak grove and out the other side. The way opened up into river bottom.

What lush country this was! Grazing cattle ambled about, up to their bellies in daisies, and sheep lolled under the hazel hedges. The whole rivershore had been planted in barley and oats. Strips and patches of leeks and onions waved gracefully along the field margins. Someday soon, by various means, the pleasant scene before Gavin would be converted into barley gruel flavored with honey and onion, his favorite dish. And mutton stew with leeks. Not to mention a joint of boiled beef. He dearly hoped that Gemman set a well-laid table.

The old man and the blond cousin were deep into a discussion of some obscure book called Job when Colm paused, peering into the distance ahead. Gavin stepped in beside him. Just to this side of a distant bend in the track, a small person came running. Lad or lass? It was hard to tell from here. He or she was obviously being hotly pursued. The person would glance back, then run harder.

Around the same bend came a farmer, unmistakable in dress. Two colors in his flying cloak told Gavin he was a man of means and position. As he approached, Gavin could make out a javelin in his hand.

What's going on here? He glanced beyond Colm to the old man. The fellow stood straight. His watery eyes narrowed.

The farmer paused and flung the javelin at the fleeing girl, but the blade sailed past her. Gavin could hear her anguished cry from here. Why didn't she snatch up the javelin and turn upon her pursuer? The only answer that Gavin could think of was that she was a slave. A slave dare not, not even to protect her own life. Colm muttered something and crossed himself.

The lass was staggering now, her gait more a walk than a run. But the farmer appeared every bit as winded. The chase at half speed would look comical were the farmer's intent not so deadly. Here she came with brown hair flying. As she approached, she reminded Gavin more and more of Anice.

Gasping, sweat-slathered, she dropped to her knees in front of the old man. "Lord," she rasped. Her voice would sound like Anice's, too, if she weren't so exhausted.

As the enraged farmer came galloping up to them, the old man spread his oversized cloak. The girl rose up and flung herself against him. With sweeping arms he drew that cloak around her so that only the top of her head protruded outside its safety.

The farmer extended an accusatory pointing finger and arm at the old man. "I warned you before."

"And I warned you. I will sing you to disgrace."

"Meddler! She defies me!"

"You have the power of life and death over her. We all know that. You are in a position, therefore, to offer her grace and mercy."

With a blasphemy that ran a chill down Gavin's spine, the farmer cried out, "Here is mercy!" He thrust the javelin at the old man's belly.

Inside that encompassing cloak, the girl moaned, her voice not quite as loud as the ripping sound the cloak made. She collapsed in a hideous little heap at the old man's feet, the javelin still in her, a torn-away end of that protective cloak floating down upon her.

From the grove behind them a woman screamed. *Who . . . ?* There had been no one behind them a moment ago.

Treasa! She came running wildly toward them, that long braid flying. She carried a light ax in one hand and a short Roman-style sword in the other.

The farmer gaped at her a moment just as did everyone else. Suddenly he yanked out his javelin and waved its bloodied tip toward the old man. Gavin should do something. He should leap forward; he should snatch that hideous weapon away from that hideous man. *How could the farmer . . . ? That poor girl . . .*

"You'll not sing me to disgrace!" The farmer poised his blade to run the old man through.

Treasa was nearly here. *If only she would throw her sword or ax . . .*

Then Colm raised an arm, and the world stood still. Treasa's bare feet skidded to a stop in the track. The farmer froze, staring at that arm.

As Gavin gawked in disbelief, his cousin thundered, "You dare spill innocent blood and then threaten another? You risk the wrath of God. Beg His forgiveness, and seek penance."

Wide-eyed, the farmer swung his blade toward Colm. The iron tip wavered. It drifted downward until it dug into the wet dirt of the track. The warm, sweet smell of the girl's blood nauseated Gavin. The farmer stared unblinking at Colm's outstretched hand. He wagged his head. He mumbled something. His surly scowl deepened, and he spat in their direction.

Suddenly he looked pained and worried. The farmer turned white beneath his tan as he dropped his javelin. Gavin was looking at a man in pain. Excruciating pain. Pain so intense the fellow could barely breathe. Clutching at his breast, he seemed almost relieved when his knees buckled and he fell in a rumpled pile beside the girl-child he had murdered. His labored breathing ceased.

Gavin had just witnessed a miracle—a miracle not by the bony, withered hand of Cruithnechan but prompted by his own cousin Colm. Colm who loved pranks. Colm who loved books. Colm who obviously loved God, but had never mentioned so. Columcille, the Dove of the Church. A dove you dare not cross!

Colm lowered his arm. Treasa moved forward and stopped beside the bleary-eyed old man. She stared at the murdered girl. Her dumbstruck expression reflected what Gavin felt as well.

Colm turned to the distraught old man beside him and said quietly, "I perceive, lord, that you are Gemman."

5

Warriors' Escape

Majestic snorting from the war horse!
  He paws a furrow.
  He exults in his strength.
  He goes out to meet the weapons!

Watch moss grow on a rock. Watch a chicken set on eggs. Watch a mudpuddle shrink. Watch the hillside across the way. All equally boring. Gavin yawned elaborately.

He sat outside the gate to Gemman's monastery, such as it was, on watch. One would think that "on watch" would mean "on watch constantly." Not here. Gemman assigned watch duty to people only when there was nothing else going on. Half-a-watch is a fine mess of fish if your enemies decide to sneak up on you, say, at dinnertime. Gavin felt utterly useless.

The gray and lowering sky had been promising rain since noon. Now, at the close of day, a gentle shower commenced.

The only saving grace of his life just now was the season, the wonderful season. Erin surged in the warmth of her summer, and Gavin reveled in it. The girls all shed their wool cloaks and heavy woolen overskirts, flouncing about in their floating, clinging, light linen tunics. Calves and lambs frolicked, not yet locked into the stolid placidity of adulthood. Sharpening their grain sickles, farmers prepared to harvest the first of the summer's yield as their wives began picking early peas and beans. Wildflowers washed waves of nodding color across the leas. Bringing in the first cutting of hay, small children bossed lumbering oxen about, using nothing more than switches. Warm days and soft, damp, aromatic nights. *Ah, summer!*

The sun slipped out from beneath the cloud cover as it reached the horizon. It turned yellow-orange and flattened out as it touched the distant hills to the northwest. The rainshower fell harder.

On cue, the dinner bell rang from inside the ringwall. Gavin needed no second invitation. There ought to be a rainbow to the east, but he wasn't interested in looking for it. With alacrity, he abandoned his post and jogged up the muddy track to Gemman's semi-monastery.

What a motley assortment of would-be poets haunt this place! Some sported the standard Irish monk's tonsure, shaved across the front and long in back—the right way a monk should look. But then there were those who fancied the Roman style, with a round thatch of hair like a boaire's cottage roof and a bald spot shaved on top. *Ridiculous.* Some shaved their heads and others let their hair grow long and tangled, "The way God intended," they declared.

They differed in faith as much as in appearance. Some were druids, some Christians. Some aspired to the station of bard or fileh, others merely wanted to learn about poetry.

Women lived and studied here also, ranking as equals with the men. *Didn't Treasa revel in that!* She had found a home. Somewhat. She was not by nature a poet. What others came seeking she put up with as the price to pay for equality.

She and Gemman saw eye to eye that in Patrick's day a hundred years ago, women and men shared nearly equal responsibilities—in the home, in the fields, on the battleground. Back then, married men and women took up the brotherhood as comfortably as did the unmarried, and so it should be now. Marriage was ordained of God, was it not? And did not Scripture say there is neither male nor female but all are one in Christ? Who, then, should argue? It certainly sounded good to Gavin also.

Still, a confusion and lack of uniformity pervaded. Gavin would expect Gemman to impose some sort of order on this chaotic mishmash, but the old man simply crowed, "Celebrate diversity, my young friend!" and let pandemonium prevail.

Gavin grabbed his wooden bowl from his clochan and trotted across the compound to squeeze into the food line just ahead of a sullen young man from Kevin's new monastery at Armagh and right behind Colm.

Colm stared off into space, his lips moving slightly.

Gavin grimaced. "Can't you quit composing for a minute?"

Colm grinned wickedly. "I'll compose until I die, and then I'll decompose."

"Haw haw haw." Away up there at the head of the line, the cooks were still stirring the cauldron. For a while yet, at least, this line was not going to move. Gavin pressed in closer to his cousin and lowered his voice. "Colm? When you held your hand out and that farmer dropped dead, what did it feel like? A tingle or something? Anything?"

Colm pressed his lips together a moment. He shook his head. "I can't explain it. I didn't intend to put my hand up. It did that by itself, in a way. I felt more like an observer than a participant. I don't know how to describe it. I was enraged at the man, and that's what happened."

"That's scary."

Colm muttered, "I'm terrified."

The line began to move. Monks and laity and women and children filed past the cauldron, scooping gruel into their bowls. Each picked up a chunk of barleycake.

Colm and Gavin pushed their way into the crowded refectory and plopped onto the cut, dry grass beside a bench in the corner. Gavin would have to whittle a new wooden spoon one of these days. His was getting pretty ragged and splintery along the front edge.

"Colm? Do you think that would qualify as a miracle like the kind old Cruithnechan pulls off sometimes?"

"What else would it be? The man was healthy a moment before. You saw him. Ruddy face. Winded from running, but healthy."

Gavin grunted. That had been his observation too. "Did you notice about that slave girl, how like Anice she was?"

"Who's Anice?"

"The little girl with the big battle-ax, Forba's maid."

"Oh, her." Colm eyed Gavin suspiciously. "You're not in love again, are you?"

"What do you mean, 'again'? Grainne was a passing fancy, that's all. So was Shanna. And no, I'm not in love. I just happened

51

to notice they were a lot alike. And Anice is in the same situation that poor slave girl was—her mistress could kill her any moment, legally. Swish-swish, a flick of the blade, you're dead."

Colm shrugged. "That's true of any slave. Fortunately, most owners don't go to those lengths."

From the front door, a woman called. "Gemman, Father! The ri ruirech and his entourage."

Colm and Gavin looked at each other. Gavin grimaced. "You'd better hide. The only reason for a king to come is that farmer."

"Gemman's armory consists of two pothooks and a shepherd's crook." Colm leaped up and headed for the door, only ten feet behind Gemman.

"I get the crook. Or maybe we can take weapons off the retainers." Gavin abandoned his bowl of gruel and followed eagerly.

Actually, Gavin had not in the least expected Mac Phelim to hide. Colm's father's bravery was renowned—in fact, his mother Eithne's bravery and skill with javelin and ax were just as renowned—and there was no reason to think Colm would lurk in shadows.

A trill ran down Gavin's backbone. He heard the hooves of a dozen nervous horses outside the door. Twelve, more or less, against two, for Gemman was no fighter. It made his blood run hot just thinking about it.

Twelve against three. From nowhere Treasa appeared. She had her sword, poising with it two-handed, but not the ax.

In the drizzling rain, the biggest man Gavin had ever seen sat upon the biggest horse Gavin had ever seen. The fellow's great red beard tumbled nearly to his belt, completely hiding his torque and brooch. His thick eyebrows nearly matched it. Were they orange? In this faded light of dusk it was hard to tell. The beast beneath him, bay with black knees and white feet, held its head high, nostrils flaring. What a magnificent animal!

Surrounding this king, ten retainers waited for the next move. You could tell they were seasoned fighters by the loose way they sat upon their ponies, their swords and axes hung at ready on their saddles. No fidgeting, no nervous glances. Obviously, they were not only seasoned, they expected no resistance.

The party had hastened some distance, for the horses were partially winded. Their sweat and their steamy breath hung sweet on the damp air.

"We buried two bodies a while ago," claimed the king, without preamble. His deep bass voice matched his size.

"A slave girl and a boaire." Gemman nodded. "They were yours, I'm sure."

"They were. Who speared the girl?"

"The farmer."

The king might be addressing Gemman, but his eyes flitted from Gavin to Colm. Weighing their age and prowess? It was hard to tell what the hulking brute was thinking, hidden as he was behind that wall of hair. "And who killed the farmer?"

"God."

The king studied him a moment. "There was bad blood between the two of you, I know that. You had a run-in with him before."

"Regarding that very slave girl and his treatment of her. Yes." Gemman seemed not the least worried.

"I think God had help."

"On this occasion, apparently, God didn't need any. Your farmer dropped over untouched."

Colm was quietly moving out beyond Gemman's right arm. Gavin sidled around to Gemman's left as Treasa moved forward two paces. The three of them now stood between the old man and immediate danger.

That bass voice rose. "The man's clan insist upon revenge, and they're entitled to it. The boaire wasn't doing anything wrong when you attacked him."

"I did not attack. Their revenge, then, must be upon God, for I was nothing more than an onlooker." He did not mention Colm's part either. *Interesting.* "I must warn you"—Gemman raised his voice —"warn you all: Take revenge against God at your peril. He claims revenge as His own. 'Vengeance is mine, saith the Lord.'"

There is a way to seize a horse's bridle, give it a double twist while you lock your heel behind the horse's near the knee, and thereby throw the horse to the ground as it stands there. Gavin would never attempt the maneuver on that huge bay, but the nervous little dun pony directly in front of him would flip like a flat-bread. He gauged the position of the rider's battle-ax without actually looking at it. Rather, he watched intently the man on a gray horse between the king and the dun. Let them think that fellow was the first target.

Colm stepped up almost beside the retainer to the king's left. "Precious in God's sight is the blood of His innocents, Ri. The farmer may not have broken brehon law, but he violated God's law. That's infinitely worse. Gemman too is an innocent. God will avenge him just as surely as He avenged that little girl."

The bass voice boomed. "Who are you to address a king?"

"A prince by blood, Mac Phelim of the Northern Ui Neill, in direct line to Niall himself—great, great grandson—and your equal." Colm's voice carried just as powerfully as did the king's. Gavin would not have tweaked the big man's beard like that. Colm would do much better keeping his mouth shut. How could Gavin signal that bit of wisdom to his boastful cousin?

"I have no equal," the great man rumbled.

"Then, that be so, your superior."

Gavin's breastbone went thud. Colm wasn't even marrying age yet! *What does he think he's doing?*

The great man drew his sword. "Your words just sealed your doom, upstart."

Gavin grabbed the dun's bridle and hooked his heel behind its knee. He twisted sharply. With a squeal, the dun tried to regain its balance by sidestepping. Horses' front legs, though, possess little lateral motion. Gavin's heel cocked the horse's knee forward. As the startled retainer yelped, the pony dropped like a stone onto its left side.

The gray beside it lunged aside to avoid the falling horse and rider. It slammed into the king's huge bay. Instantly the bay shied away, dipping out from under the king. The ri and the gray's rider lurched into each other; the impact made the king drop his sword.

Even as Gavin was pulling the dun rider's battle-ax free of its loop, Treasa was taking out the rider with a sweeping stroke. When the dun struggled to its feet, Gavin was aboard it. He could fight mounted swordsmen much better if he himself were mounted.

The king, off balance, scrabbled for a grip on his saddle, but he slid artlessly into the dirt between the bay and gray. Two swordsmen were charging their horses toward Gavin but the nervous gray horse blocked their way.

Gavin's first impulse was simply to run. *Where's Colm? What next?*

There he was, weaponless, scrambling aboard that huge bay horse!

Treasa? Her dark blonde head bobbed right beside Gavin's free arm. He reached down to her. She used his arm to swing herself up behind him on the little dun horse.

Gavin reined the overladen dun pony aside and dug in his heels. With a whoop, he flailed his arms, spooking both his dun and the great bay. As Colm struggled to stay on top, his fingers laced into the mighty black mane, the bay bolted forward and lurched into a lumbering, ground-eating canter. Colm slammed his heels into that huge brown rib cage. The bay's gait evened out and extended into a gallop.

Gavin's little dun was not nearly so smooth and easy to ride. It galloped in rapid staccato—like riding on the teeth of an excited man who stutters. Behind Gavin, Treasa clung like teasel, throwing his balance awry. She had somehow lost her sword.

Where were they heading? North. Along what track? Who knew? The darkness closed down completely, and Gavin prayed that the bay up ahead enjoyed good night vision. Gavin couldn't see a thing. He could hear the thunder of pursuing horsemen behind them clearly enough, though. He was still hanging onto that bloodied ax. A single weapon between them, and their enemies riding in the hot, sweet fever of fury. Not good odds.

The drizzling rain became a downpour. None of them wore a cloak. It was going to be a long, cold night, assuming they survived it.

The track angled downhill. The dun horse slid in the loose mud and nearly went down. Gavin heard splashing ahead. Colm was fording a stream on that bay. The bay's legs were obviously long enough to negotiate the ford. Were the dun's?

"This way!" Colm rasped. He was not fording the little river but rather following it downstream. Gavin pushed the dun, keeping it close to the sound of the bay's wading. Up ahead, those platter-sized feet left the creek and scrambled up the streambank. Gavin did not have to guide his horse; it followed the bay willingly.

A hazel thicket grasped at Gavin's knees on both sides and tried to peel him off his mount.

"Here!" Colm whispered. He had dismounted, deep in the thicket. In the gloom, Gavin could just make out that Colm was holding the great horse's head by one ear and its nostrils, preventing it from whinnying, sneezing, or snorting. Treasa slid off and shuffled forward to grasp the dun's head. Gavin propped the ax against his leg and grabbed the horse also. Not that he didn't trust Treasa to keep the horse quiet, but she did drop her sword. The warm, velvety nose struggled against his grip.

They listened to the approaching hoofbeats. The stream gurgled. Less than a whisper, a white ghost swept by overhead. Barn owl. *Krerk-krerk!* A corncrake's crazy call, not forty feet away, made Gavin jump.

The odor of the horses' lather floated pungent in these close quarters. Would the pursuers be able to smell the horses? Not likely. Blessed by God were Colm and Treasa and Gavin that the ri ruirech had not brought dogs. The dun shook mightily, starting with its head, then relaxed. Its nose drooped so wearily that Gavin realized he was literally holding the little horse's head up.

They heard the hoofbeats rattle down into the stream. Rocks clattered. A crashing splash—a horse squealed. Men shouted. The corncrake squawked as wings fwooshed in rapid beat. The hoofbeats pounded up the bank and continued northward on the track. With much splashing and grunting, the fallen rider got mounted again; his horse followed the crew off into silence.

Peace.

"Now where?" Treasa whispered. "Back to Gemman?"

"No. North."

"Not the brightest of moves, Prince. Doesn't the ri ruirech live to the north? And they all just went that way!"

"I don't care where he lives. I'm going home." Colm sounded as weary as the dun acted.

Gavin listened to the so-familiar voice. Did he hear defeat and sadness there? He was certain he did.

Even whispering, Colm's voice carried well. "That girl dying —and the farmer. Watching the man drop. It's too much. I'm going back to my clan. I need my people near; I need their strength. Finish studies and get ordained. Then, I don't know. Something."

"Back to Finnian?" she whispered.

"Not Finnian of Moville. That grumpy lad from Armagh was talking about a Finian of Clonard. The way he was talking, I think the best scholarship in Erin is there right now. I'll go to Clonard."

"I'll go with you," Treasa announced. "Sure and I'm not going back to Moville. Maybe at Clonard I won't have to recite poetry. Think?"

Gavin kept his voice at a whisper too, even though the recalcitrant ri was surely half a mile off by now. "Scholarship. I realize you enjoy it, but it doesn't impress me."

Colm chuckled softly. "So I know, Cousin. Tell you what. Accompany me to Clonard, and since I won't need a horse while I complete my studies, you may have this one."

"Ah, sure and you do know how to bribe a fellow. To Clonard it is."

For a long moment, Colm remained silent in the silence. "Do either of you two happen to have any idea how to get to Clonard?"

6

Anice's Flight

The chariots are doomed to naught
beneath my Lord's fierce hand!

Anice had long since figured out that one thing worse than
being a slave to Forba the Pict was to be a kitchen maid to Aileen,
Moville's cook from Inishowen Head. Forba had been through two
husbands and was looking around for a third; mate-seeking made
her crankier than usual, and her usual crankiness was nasty enough.
But Aileen, despite advancing years, was still trying to snare her
first. That made her totally miserable to be around. At least Forba
didn't have the sense of desperation that you constantly felt in
Aileen.

Forba loved to lord it over everybody, but as a princess she
more or less could claim that right. Aileen's breeding was right
down there with the goats and cattle—hardly boss material. That
didn't keep her from ordering around everyone in sight, whether
they had anything to do with the kitchen or not. And poor Anice,
assigned specifically to the kitchen, bore the heaviest brunt of the
bossiness.

To top it all, Aileen, Finnian of Moville's monastery cook, hated
cooking. Every chore, from boiling pork to mixing stirabout, brought
forth a litany of complaint. She hated butchering, no matter that
the bulk of the butchering was handled by monks. She hated
maintaining the fires, no matter that novices to the brotherhood
were assigned that chore. She hated grinding grain, and yet it was
Anice who was invariably stuck with that chore. As Anice wrenched
the heavy quern stones round and round upon each other, Aileen
would stand idle and complain bitterly.

But what choice did Anice have? She dared not step outside
the ringwall, for Forba and her minions sat on the opposite hill in
a semi-permanent camp, much to the Father's chagrin. Anice dare

58

not even stick her head out of the kitchen when Forba's represen-
tatives (and often Forba herself!) were in the compound.

In theory, they were negotiating for local land upon which
Pictish immigrants might settle. Anice even in her tender years
knew better. Forba wanted some excuse, any excuse, to place herself in the presence of the fat, sweaty Finnian of Moville. Forba's
good taste was all in her mouth, if she had any at all.

It had been nearly a year, and Anice a prisoner within this
ringwall for just that long. Why didn't Forba give up?

Countless times Anice had thought about those two young
men, the cousins. Why did Forba not pant and lust after them?
Who could fail to? One with gleaming, golden spider-silk for hair
and one with raven's locks. Giants among men. Heroes, for all
their youth. She recalled again the vision of that black-haired one
defending the gate and the fair-haired one defending the oratory.
She could no longer remember their names. All she could remember was Hawk and Dove, and that couldn't be right.

Crory the smith brought the milk cows in. He seemed to do
just about anything in the settlement except smithing. He kicked
at the pile of brush between the kitchen and the grain bin, a half-
hearted attempt at penning the cattle in behind the kitchen. No
doubt they would break through the meager barrier by morning
and probably eat the thatch off the barley bin again.

Anice fetched the bucket and stool. Milking time. She would
milk the dark-faced brown cow first. That little cow was her favorite, and, besides, she let her milk down easily. Maybe, before Anice
had to tackle milking the obstreperous old black beast, a raid
would strike, or Jesus would come calling His own away, or
something—something to save her from the onerous chore.

Where the cows had chopped the ground up with their big
cloven feet, cold, loose mud pushed between her toes. The powerful sweet smell of cattle and their droppings wrapped around
her. Was there a world without cows? She would like to think that
cows would not accompany her and all other milkmaids into
heaven, but she could hardly imagine not needing them.

From out beyond the main yard came Finnian's angry wail,
"Why? They chose to go elsewhere. Let them stay elsewhere!"
Complaining lustily, Finnian sloshed through the mud toward the

gate. Behind him, tall, surly Comgall followed, like a stray dog in hope of a morsel from the dinner bowl. Comgall was leading the bay cart-pony. Either the two of them were bound for some distant visitation or had just returned from one.

Overriding his nasal whine, a deep, vaguely familiar voice answered, "Actually, I'm not here to visit you, Finnian Father."

That voice . . . ! Anice shoved a path back out through the brush barrier and ran out to the yard, stool and pail still in hand.

In the distance across the compound yard, the main gate stood open and the gatekeepers stood open as well—openmouthed. For *he* had entered. He of the raven hair and snapping black eyes, the dark-haired cousin, the heroic young man who had defended the bier gate, the burly fellow who accepted Anice's cry for help at face value and risked his life to help her.

He sat upon the most magnificent horse, a giant of a bay horse, that Anice had ever seen. She stood still, gaping as foolishly as the gatekeepers.

Wait! The other one—where? She looked all about, but the dark one seemed to be here alone. Finnian came waddling up to that great horse, glaring, and folded his arms across his ample chest. His shadow, Comgall, lost some of his natural scowl.

Casually, carelessly, the young fighter hopped off his huge mount and did obeisance to Finnian. "Father. God's peace." Then he and Comgall embraced enthusiastically, old friends long apart.

"God's peace." Finnian glanced about. "Mac Phelim did not accompany you? I thought you two were inseparable."

"Mac Phelim, Father, is studying with Finian of Clonard and having a wonderful time. As for me, I've decided that a scholar's life is not the life for me."

"Wise choice, since you never were worth mud as a copyist." Finnian paused, then scowled. "Finian of Clonard. He's but a youth! No older than yourself. What in heaven would he have to offer a scholar? He knows nothing."

The Dark One's voice took on a dangerous edge. Its ominous depth set Anice's breastbone to tingling. "My Father, Finian is drawing the finest scholars of Christendom to himself—nearly three thousand in his school now. All manner of people. Colm is an excellent judge of scholarship, and he rates Finian's school as the best in Erin."

"Nonsense! Foolishness. A callow youth. And you, what do you want back here? Surely not to complete your studies."

"Not at all, Father. I came to enquire regarding the slave girl, Anice."

Anice's whole world sort of collapsed together into a strange little jumble. *He's seeking me? Me? Some mistake, surely.* She was dreaming. She was mis-hearing.

This latest bit of conversation seemed to displease Finnian greatly. "To what end?"

"To enquire after her well-being. It was I who yanked her away from her Pictish princess, and I was wondering."

"Wonder no more. She is in the Lord's service here, preparing for a role as a nun, and in no need of young men chasing after her. If you've no desire to return to the studies you abandoned so precipitately—"

Finnian continued babbling in that fretful tone of voice, but Anice didn't hear the words exactly. Her mind was turning too rapidly. *Why would he be spouting that nonsense about preparation to be a nun? Since when did milking and grinding and serving in the kitchen prepare one for a life of service in a sisterhood? So far I've not been given a single moment of actual learning. And why, oh why, would this god-like young man bother to visit a slave girl? Sure and I could not have heard that correctly.*

Finnian was insisting that Anice was not available, and he didn't know where she was anyway. Helpfully, Anice called out, "I am here, Father!" She hurried out into the yard, only half mindful that she still carried the bucket and stool, badges of a lowly milkmaid.

The dark young man brightened visibly. He grinned as he stepped forward, that huge bay horse in tow. He came right toward her, as if he really did mean to visit her. Could it be? A dream come true!

From the open gate, a gatekeeper hastily called out, "Forba of the Picts and her brehons," his words stumbling upon each other.

61

Even his haste to announce her, though, was not haste enough, for here she came whistling past him in her war chariot, her usual mode of transport. Anice had ridden in it once and found it terribly uncomfortable, forever lurching and jerking. Its yawing movement had made her half sick. However, Forba did look royal riding in it, and she even managed to appear unperturbed by the lack of comfort.

Forba stepped off the back of her chariot with haughty disdain and strode directly to Finnian. Effusive in her false cheer, she crowed, "Why, Finnian dear! And Comgall." The bay cart-pony sidled nervously as one of the big chariot horses laid its ears back.

With a hard eye and an admiring expression, she paused suddenly to study Gavin's splendid bay horse. Behind her, two sage-looking old men in gaudy cloaks stepped through the gateway into the yard. Besides her charioteer, she had brought four retainers with her, and Anice recognized two of them.

"Lady!" One of them pointed toward Anice.

Forba turned her eyes toward the milkmaid standing out in the middle of the open yard. What could Anice do? Nothing. She was caught. Trapped.

Instant fury was Forba's specialty, as Anice knew all too well. Immediately and consummately enraged, Forba pointed finger and arm at Anice. "My slave! My handmaid!" She wheeled to Finnian, shrieking. "Liar! And here you told me . . . You had her after all! Lost in battle? Run away? Tucked away in your private harem just as I suspected all along, you hideous ogre!"

"Whoa!" The dark-haired youth exploded so suddenly that Forba was caught speechless for a moment. "Finnian has many shortcomings, but immorality is not one of them! And if he misled you, it was for the child's sake."

"Don't you try to defend that odious goat! He lied to steal my . . ." Forba's voice dribbled away to nothing. Her fury melted into what Anice could only read as fear. The princess took a delicate step backward from the raven-haired one.

The lad had darkened and taken on a frightening intensity, fire and ice and blackness like a Sammhain night. It was that same ferocious intensity Anice had seen when first she ever laid eyes on him.

He rumbled menacingly. "You put your slave girl behind an ax and sent her out to die. That's unconscionable. Finnian answered a higher call than your ownership rights—God's concern for His child. If you—"

"Don't you dare address a princess thusly, knave!" She regained a portion of her usual brazenness, in part perhaps because all four retainers had now grouped in close around her. She stood straight and stiff. "I am—"

"You are the daughter of a minor ri ruirech near Drumderry, and I am a prince of the Dal Riada. Sooner or later you will do obeisance to me as king. You'd best mend your fences now."

"A prince!" She made a highly derisive noise.

"Ask your feckless Diarmaid." With a smirk, the raven-haired one stepped back. He turned and motioned *come* to Anice.

Hesitant, Anice started toward him. These retainers would seize her. Forba would order her run through with a sword for deserting. Anice was marching directly toward certain punishment and probable death. She raised her chin and strode purposefully.

The dark youth waved a finger. "Give the princess your milk stool. You'll not need it, and she just might."

Confused, Anice moved toward her mistress. She heard whooshing movement behind her and hooves. And then a powerful hand grasped her arm and pulled her around. The stool and bucket fell to the ground.

The youth had swung aboard that gigantic horse. Without altering his grip in the least, he yanked her over against his horse and hauled upward mightily. Anice scrambled, kicking, and grabbed his tunic. As he reined his great horse aside, away from Forba and her minions, Anice managed to pull herself more or less astraddle up onto the horse's back behind him.

The horse lunged, very nearly unseating her. She wrapped tightly around the youth's waist, clinging desperately. The horse lurched upward and forward, upward and forward, in a powerful, flowing canter. Those hooves, huge as bee skeps, splacked through the churned mud of the gateway.

As Forba screamed "Stop them!" and Finnian roared at them to come back, they cantered out the gate.

Anice twisted to look behind. "The chariot! They'll bring the chariot after us!"

"Just hang on, whatever happens!"

Hang on? Sure and she would hang on! She had no choice. Death awaited her inside that ringwall, and death was pursuing her vigorously out here. They thundered down the track, angling south of the oak grove, heading away from the stream. Anice didn't know this country well enough to be able to guess where they were going, for she had never been allowed outside the ringwall, but Forba's Pictish encampment lay behind them on the other side of the creek.

The huge bay horse did not seem to be trying very hard. Like a child's toy swing-horse slung from a tree limb, the horse lumbered along at a casual, rocking gait.

"My lord! The chariot's coming! It's gaining on us!"

"I see it." The raven-haired youth didn't seem nearly as concerned as he ought to be. Didn't he know those Picts were brutes?

Behind the chariot came Comgall, drumming his heels in the ribs of the bay cart-pony. Was he here to help Gavin or to drag Anice back to Finnian and certain doom? He had picked up a pruning hook on the way out, apparently. He held it now like a lance.

"My lord—"

"Just hang on."

The bay left the muddy track and cantered out across a firm, grassy sward, the chariot hard behind. Now the chariot was pulling nearly abreast to the right of them. Snorting, winded, the chariot ponies looked ready to drop. And well they might, hauling five grown men in that clumsy vehicle across uneven ground. Two men is the normal load.

The dark-haired prince had pulled his sword, and Anice felt a slight glimmer of hope. But five against one?

The prince cocked his legs high against their mount's shoulders. As he swung his sword mightily, the massive bay horse plunged aside suddenly and slammed into the near chariot pony. The ponies screamed as the horse angled across in front of them, stumbled and lurched, regained its balance, and continued on.

Anice twisted to see Comgall thrust that iron pruning hook into the wheel spokes. The hook splintered and flew, but the wheel locked up. She watched then in horrified fascination as the chariot ponies tangled, tripping each other. The near pony's rump rose high in the air, twisting, as the off pony dropped to its knees. The forward butt of the heavy wooden shaft between them dug into the mud and the rearward end bucked upward, dragging the chariot up over the off pony's rump. The tangle defied sorting, as wheels and screaming men and swords and horses' legs tumbled and flew all over.

She shuddered and pressed the side of her head so firmly against the young man that her ear tight upon his back could hear his breathing. "I feel so sorry for those poor ponies."

His deep voice echoed oddly against her ear. "I would expect nothing less than a tender heart of you, lass!"

Just what do you expect of me, exactly? she wondered.

From time to time in his homilies, Finnian referred darkly to "the way of a man with a maid," though what that way might be, Anice had no idea. Finnian never gave any hint either. Whatever the way, it was obviously ugly and sinful, impossible for God to forgive unless you did an *awful lot* of penance. Anice could not imagine this perfect youth engaging in such sin, whatever it might be. He was far too magnificent for that.

He slowed his horse to a tooth-jarring jog, thence to a walk, as they wound down the way from lea to woodland. Comgall, still trying to draw more speed from his cart-pony than cart-ponies can deliver, came riding in behind them. Half a mile farther on, they picked up a little-used track.

Should they persist along this track, they would soon enter dark and moody mountains that Anice had seen only from afar. She did not particularly like that. She distrusted mountains. Robbers lurked there, and bitter wee folk. It was wise to leave the wee folk strictly alone.

On the other hand, Forba would be sending minions to avenge this blot on her honor, and any moment now. Anice kept glancing back, but the trail was too curvy to permit her to see far.

The young man spoke. "You're probably wondering why I snatched you away like this."

"Nay, Lord. I'm wondering why you bothered to remember me at all."

He chuckled. "You're a memorable lass, that's why." The mirth in his voice faded. "I was afraid your mistress would misuse you. It happens, you know."

"Aye." She waited for more, but nothing more came. All she could figure out from that strange exchange was that she had just learned nothing. She sallied out upon a fresh track. "To my shame, Lord, I cannot remember your name."

"No shame. Why should you? Gavin, son of the Nialls."

"White Hawk. I thought I remembered Hawk. And Dove. You have a cousin, true? A blond person?"

"Indeed. Columba. Columcille."

That was the name. She waited. Apparently, no more information was forthcoming. *Now what?* "Is he well?"

"Very. He's at a monastery called Clonard. We're going there. You'll see him then."

"Another monastery?" *Why not?* So long as her status remained *slave,* she could not be free to pursue a life most women pursued without thinking about it—marriage to some boaire, a family of lively youngsters, a little excitement, and a lot of routine work as one's life melded into the seasons, perhaps a few slaves or lesser workers of one's own, darkly fascinating stories told during the long winter nights around the fire.

"A lively monastery indeed! Finian of Clonard is only four years older than Colm and I—a brilliant man with an eager mind. He enjoys a great depth of wisdom, but he's constantly seeking to make it deeper still. So he's assembled round about him the best scholars and theorists in Erin. They feed each other, you might say. It's an exciting place to be if you've an interest in study."

I haven't. But Anice didn't say it aloud.

Comgall grumbled. "I'm willing to wager that you're sketching a far rosier picture than I'll find when we get there."

Gavin twisted around, grinning. "You're going with us? Good for you!"

"As if I had any choice now that I've cast my lot in your foolishness."

True.

66

Gavin was not done sketching. His crackling dark eyes met hers briefly before he twisted back straight. "Men and women alike study there. You'll meet girls your own age. I think you'll enjoy it."

Perhaps.

"And it's safer there for you."

Comgall growled, "This Finian of Clonard is a bishop, I trust."

"No, so some of the fathers there sent Colm and a few others down to the bishop of Clonfad, to be ordained as priests." Apparently for Anice's benefit he added, "Only bishops can do that, you know. Ordain people. Or ordain other bishops. Etchen is his name."

She at last felt safe enough to unwrap from around his waist. "Will your cousin become a bishop someday?"

"Undoubtedly."

"And you've no plans to become a bishop yourself?" She thought he certainly deserved it, as heroic as he was. And smart, to best a chariot full of seasoned fighters like that.

"No. I plan to become ard ri someday. My course lies other than with the church."

"Cruithnechan is a bishop. Does the title of bishop confer the ability to work miracles? Is that why your cousin is being ordained?"

And the man to whom she clung stiffened. He froze the way washing freezes on the line on a winter day.

She tried, but she could not twist far enough to see his face. "What did I say?"

He chuckled. "Nothing, lass. And no, being a bishop is not what gives a person the power to perform miracles. You'll recall, the dear saint Brigid herself performed miracles long before she was ordained a bishop."

"No. I never heard. Brigid. As in Imbolc?"

"Not that Brigid; not the Celtic goddess. The church Brigid."

"Finnian has spoken of such a one. I thought they were the same. He never made a point of difference between them."

"And that, lass, is why Colm loves Clonard so. They not only preach clearly there, so that you understand, they spend hours in lengthy discussions about things."

"What things?" She loved listening to him speak. She didn't want him to lapse into silence again.

"Things such as the two Brigids and the role of the church in society and Patrick's influence. When to hold Easter. Things like that."

"Ah." Things of scant interest to a slave girl just recently emancipated from milking that horrid old black cow. Her thoughts paused in midstride, as it were. She had wished to be relieved of that onerous duty, and it happened. Would that be a gift from God? Never once had Finnian intimated that God bestows gifts upon slave girls. According to Finnian's homilies, such gifts went to wise men in the church.

They rode through to dark and took shelter that night in the rath of a small ri tuatha. The next morning, Gavin and Comgall tarried for an hour helping the man gather the cattle he would drive to the feast of Lughnasa, so Anice helped the goodwife with the milking—compliant cows, placid cows, cows that were a joy to milk.

They took to the track then, pressing with due speed to stay ahead of any forces Forba might send after them. Anice was becoming exceedingly stiff and sore, riding behind like this. She would much rather be walking, but she said nothing, for she so much enjoyed being near this White Hawk.

Seven days they spent on the track, doing nothing but ride, accepting hospitality and alms from whatever raths they passed, talking in fits and spurts. Perhaps "talking" was not exactly it. Anice would get Gavin to talking about something and then would listen, loving it, having nothing wise or important of her own to add to the conversation.

A week. It seemed like a year, for she sported open sores on her bottom now, places that rubbed. But then again, it seemed like a day, for time spent with this young fighter sped by on hawks' wings.

Gavin began to assure her that they were nearing Clonard. And then they encountered travelers afoot, and Anice recognized the younger. It was the little blond boy who dragged her off to the oratory that first day she entered Moville. Kenneth. She remembered his name. She had never met his companion, a rather stand-offish young monk named Kieran. Kieran wasn't half the fellow Gavin was, or Colm either for that matter. He was tall like they were, but he stood with shoulders hunched, so that he looked smaller. His sallow, nondescript complexion could not compare with the strong, manly features of the Hawk and Dove.

Kenneth embraced his old acquaintance Comgall and introduced the sallow Kieran. Kieran explained that Finian had blessed a number of his charges and sent them forth to expand their theological horizons. Columba was among those sent forth. He was on his way to join a friend of theirs, Mobhi, who had just established a dandy little monastery to the south. Would Gavin and Comgall care to come?

Gavin would. Without conferring a bit with Anice, he committed them to more days on horseback. They weren't going to Clonard anymore. They would travel over to the coast to a place near a ford across the River Liffey. Near a Dublin Crossing it was.

Now they were going to Glasnevin.

7

Treasa's World

Dangers may assail me
  and foes torment me. . . .

"Like this, you mean?" Treasa gripped the little gray pony mare's bridle and shoved the shaggy head up and to the side.

"Right. Now like this." Beside Treasa, Gavin stood on one leg and curled the other in empty air.

Treasa's balance didn't seem as good as his. Propping on one foot, she hooked her other heel behind the mare's near knee. The mare jerked her nose high, reared, and rocked back on her hocks. The unexpected move yanked Treasa's leg and threw her into the mud. Dejected, she lay on her back a moment as wetness soaked through her tunic and the little mare jogged off across the paddock.

From over by the gate floated a girlish giggle. A spectator, and Treasa knew who.

Gavin, the pig, didn't even offer a hand up. "It'd probably help, I suppose, if you practiced on a horse that hadn't been thrown twice already this morning."

"Probably." *You slog of rotten fodder. You're the one threw her, demonstrating.* Treasa sighed. Why was she constantly so out of sorts? She had enjoyed remarkable freedom at Gemman's quasi-Christian monastery. Here at Mobhi's Glasnevin, her freedom extended even further, to the point that she was practicing sword-work almost daily with one of half a dozen fighting men, Gavin among them. It was a dream come true. She was polishing the very skills she had long dreamt of mastering.

She should be happy. Elated. Instead, she felt anger burning, and very close to the surface. Nothing seemed right.

She lurched to her feet. Over by the gate, that little Anice girl picked up her milk pail and continued on to the next paddock, still snickering. Treasa glared at the snippet's departing back.

Gavin raised his hands. "It's all right. It's something that comes with strength and practice. You'll get it, eventually."

She wheeled on him. "Don't you patronize me!" She stormed off across the muddy paddock, caught up the gray mare and took the bridle off. When she looked back, Gavin was disappearing out the gate. *Riddance. Let him go.*

Two other horses were penned here, a dun pony and Gavin's big, broad-backed bay gelding. On impulse she approached the gelding. He lifted his nose and trotted across the mud a-splacking. She walked toward him. He trotted wide around her, hugging the stone wall. It took her five minutes to walk him down until at last he admitted defeat and let her approach his backside. She laid a hand on his rump, slid it along his back to his withers. At the last moment he started to swing his head away from her. He even commenced the first step in his next jaunt across the paddock.

But she managed to slip an arm under his neck, up and around, and grab an ear. He swung around to face her in order to back out of her grasp. With her other hand she gripped his upper lip firmly, twisted his head, and hooked her leg behind his knee. A shove and a yank, and he went down like a hod of rocks, squealing.

"Take that, Gavin White Hawk Mac Niall." She turned her back on the squirming, panicky horse and headed for the gate. She stepped from paddock mud onto the sheep-cropped grass of the real world and drew the gate behind her.

The River Finglas, running narrow and crooked between these gentle hills, managed to sparkle despite the overcast day. Nearly all the trees had been cut in the area. Stumpfields were being replaced by clear, open pastures as the herds grew and people chopped up the dry stumps for firewood. A cluster of alder along the shore, a coppice of hazel here, an occasional spreading oak in the pasture there—trees still beautified the land, but they did it in remarkably subtle ways for things so large.

In the swale on either shore of the stream, scores of mud huts clustered like gaggles of cold, hunched geese, the living quarters of the brethren gathered here. After all, the closer you lived to one of the oratories, the less you had to walk through rain for the services. Treasa, one of the latest to arrive, lived on what could only be called the outskirts—back a muddy path through a

71

soft crease in the slope, practically out of sight of most of the Glasnevin monastery.

The alternate choir would begin Tierce soon. She'd wait until Noonsong to wash the mud out of her braid. Her thick hair wasn't going to dry anymore today anyway, so she might as well do it after the day warmed up better. *That lout Gavin.*

Here came the lout's partner in crime. Columcille Dove of the Church Mac Phelim, shining like an angel, came traipsing down the slippery path. He smiled at her, beaming, and stopped. Sunlight on the hoof, this prince. "You're going in the wrong direction if you expect to attend Tierce. They start shortly."

She reversed directions. She did not particularly care to attend Tierce, but it was expected. Members of Mobhi's monastery were supposed to attend every canonical, just as you were supposed to pray in between times and sing in adoration of the Father at least twice in the day. Colm, she knew, was good at it. She fell short in just about every department.

With a baritone voice that in full cry could call in cattle from Donegal, Colm commenced a hymn in undertone. "Thou king of moon and sun, thou king of stars . . ." He sang so softly now, barely a rumble, that she very nearly missed it: "Thou queen of mud . . ." With her knuckles, she jabbed him so wickedly in the ribs that he grunted and staggered.

"Churl!" She marched ahead down the wet track. She could feel her mud-caked braid swinging stiffly, like a too-short tail on a cow. It gave her a certain ugly delight to note that he took quite some time to regain enough breath to laugh at her.

He followed her into the crowded little oratory up here by the rowans. Thin, vertical shimmers of daylight showed through between the rough planking of its wooden walls. Hastily built and constantly occupied, the oratory was little more than a cattle shed, with no hope of improvement in the future. The dirt beneath her bare feet turned from clammy mud to cold, dry powder.

The overcast without multiplied the gloom within. A smokey torch at the lectern up front provided a miserably inadequate circlet of light in this miserably inadequate building. How Treasa preferred the naked sky and forests to this cramped substitute—

72

not to mention clean grass to this dirt floor. They didn't even spread rushes in here.

Flexible as wet linen, Colm folded into a kneeling posture of prayer. Treasa knelt beside him without worrying about whether her skirt hem were getting dirty. She was all mud in back; mud in front wouldn't make a bit of difference. At the far end, the lector began the chant for this midmorning salute to God.

"Diarmaid!" Colm snapped to upright.

The lector droned on. Colm hopped to his feet. Right out loud he said, "Comgall! Come with me!" He pushed through the few latecomers and out the door.

The lector droned on, faltering only a little at the disruption. Stumbling, Treasa scrambled to her feet and followed him. Behind lanky Comgall, the sallow Kieran and little copper-haired Kenneth tumbled out the doorway. Treasa had to run like a hare to keep up with the Dove.

How could Colm talk and run so hard simultaneously? The man had the lungs of a bull. "I saw Diarmaid here, attacking Gavin! Not the pagan prince himself. His minions."

"Where?" Comgall had his hem hiked above his knees. His long legs worked like churn blades.

"I don't know. I'm letting God lead me." Colm charged on.

Treasa's heart sank. Gavin wouldn't be more than ten minutes away or so, but it could be any direction—a fine time to run around on whim. Guilt welled up in her breast, and regret.

Every now and again Colm received the sight—a vision of something or other, a sure knowledge of some datum no human being could understandably know. She had never known the sight to be in error. Diarmaid here? But running around at random couldn't be a sensible response.

Little Kenneth was too tender of years yet to join a battle unarmed. Was he keeping up? She glanced back and roared, "No!" For here came that Anice snip, running free with her skirts held high, ahead of Kenneth and behind Kieran.

"There!" Colm cried and his speed picked up.

Ahead on the pasture hillside grew a solitary wych elm. More than once Treasa had sat beneath that very tree eating her lunch of bread and cheese as she tended cattle or sheep. Round its trunk today churned the hounds of hell in the guise of Pictish rangers. Six of them! The forces for good numbered six as well, but two of them were Kenneth and Anice.

The seventh, Gavin himself, was little use to anyone. He had wedged himself into a crotch of the elm ten feet off the ground. As the limb that held him bobbed, he jabbed at his attackers with a long stick. His tunic was bloodsoaked, his face cut in a couple places.

Two of the rangers were chopping at the tree trunk, the logical thing to do, but they carried only battle-axes. Battle-axes bend and buckle quickly when flung against hard elm wood. A third fellow had laid his ax on a smooth stone nearby and was stomping on it. A fourth was dressing the eye of a fifth, binding the fellow's head with a strip the color of his cloak. The sixth wheeled and howled a happy war cry as these simple, unarmed monastics swarmed toward him. He swung his sword up, readied. The two chopping didn't even bother to pause.

In fact, the fellow trying to flatten out his ax blade just kept stomping, and the other two, medical practitioner and medical practitionee, seemed in no rush to join a fray.

Grinning like the sun itself, Gavin whooped.

Treasa focused her every sense upon the fellow with the sword. At the last moment she lunged aside and bowled into the fellow flattening his blade. They tumbled together across the wet grass. She flipped around to her knees, fell forward and grabbed the ax. Then she whip-snapped her body, tucking, giving that ax lethal momentum as she swung it around at her foe.

An ax blade can be bent and still save the day. One out, five to go.

Treasa twisted around to her knees again just in time to see Colm bodily lifting the fellow with the bandaged eye. The bandage-tail fluttering, the man sailed through the air at the fellow with the sword. That ranger managed to stumble backward in time to avoid being squashed by his flying companion, but the move unbalanced him long enough for Comgall to barrel into him. They went down in a tangle, knocking the legs out from under one of the choppers.

Treasa's wide swipe with the bent ax just missed the bandager. He took off at a run northward into a grassy draw and around the rise. Gavin dropped from his perch, presumably on purpose, and fell on the other chopper, literally.

Colm had commandeered an ax of his own. Treasa stopped. She stood gaping in awe as she watched a true expert wield a battle-ax. The burly blond monk feinted, parried, attacked, and fended as two seasoned rangers came at him. He bested them both in less than a dozen heartbeats.

With no further ado, the two Picts still capable of fleeing did so.

Comgall had pulled the bronze sword from his downed chopper's scabbard before he fled; its tip had been broken off. In horror, Treasa realized where the tip had ended up—it stuck out of Gavin's hip, in front, near where the leg joined.

The fallen hero sprawled on his back beneath the wych elm, his face a pasty white. Kieran and Colm, Pictish weapons in hand, stood at defense, their backs to the elm, as Comgall ran up the draw to reconnoitre the whereabouts of those Picts—and quite probably the hordes of foreigners of which they were the vanguard.

Quick as a stoat, Kenneth squirmed down under Gavin and cradled the dark head in his lap. He was sniffling, his fragile facade of manhood rapidly crumbling like a pastry shell left too long on the shelf.

That ridiculous little Anice, look at her hover over the fallen hero, her hands flying! As if she knew what she were doing, she tipped his face aside, wagged her head at that bronze stub in his hip, and then pressed her linen neckerchief against his upper arm. Treasa could not figure out why.

She stomped on the angled ax herself a couple times, but she couldn't straighten it either. She resigned herself to a weapon of reduced effectiveness and took up a position between Colm and Kieran.

Comgall came down off the hill calling, "Flee!"

Barking "Treasa!" Colm tossed his purloined ax not to Kieran but to her. With a few terse words he helped Gavin to his feet. And then this golden bear of a man scooped up that dark bear of a man as if he were a child and began walking swiftly, powerfully toward the monastery. That Gavin weighed every bit as much as Colm did apparently made no difference.

Well armed at last, Treasa cast the bent ax aside and ranged out to Colm's left. Straight as a well-cast lance they marched, up the hill the way they had come, away from the wych elm with its blood and its fallen Picts, away from the first real kill-or-be-killed skirmish Treasa had ever entered.

Her heart and her head and her senses suddenly flamed super-bright, like a Beltane fire the druids ignite merely by pointing a finger at the wood. Effectively outnumbered and totally unarmed, these cohorts had just bested seasoned fighters, and she was a part of that. Indeed, she'd drawn first blood. They had singlehandedly rescued Gavin, and she took part in it. They were a unit, a true camaraderie, and she was one with them. She had held her own and acquitted herself well. She could not contain her joy.

Her senses had brightened also. She heard more, saw better, tasted the air, felt the undercurrents and whispers that might be the wee folk round about discussing this heady victory. The world glowed.

She did not elate, though. The group shared as one a grim fear for Gavin. Their faces broadcast that fear as a peasant broadcasts barley seed. Gavin's head flopped back, and Anice quickly moved in to support it as they hastened along. His free arm dropped and dangled.

Kieran had moved out to protect their other side, so Comgall took up the defense of their rear. Kenneth pressed close to Colm, his outsized blue eyes terror struck. An odd lot they were as they came sweeping up the hill toward the monastery gate.

Mobhi himself came hustling out to meet them. He skidded to a halt, called "The oratory!" and hustled back in, shouting orders. As Colm carried his cousin in through the gate, he seemed not the least bit winded or wearied, though he had broken into a sweat.

Treasa stopped at the gate, reversed, and stood guard, the good ax Colm had tossed her balanced in her hands. It hefted well. She had no idea what of a medical nature to do. She must

76

leave that to others, even if "others" included the brazen little Anice. Grim as a grave digger, Comgall took his place beside her.

Truth be told, Gavin's extremity dulled her exuberance. She thought about how angry she had been, lying on her back in the mud. Her braid was stiff as a pike now.

She watched and listened carefully all around for any change in the rhythms of life in the pasturage before her. A flock of lapwings working the meadow near the Finglas behaved normally. The two jays airing their litany of complaints in the hazel thicket near the bier continued to do so. The great tits nesting in the thicket complained about the jays. Horses and cattle grazed on the hillside, none raising a wary head, none turning suddenly toward some unheard sound. They would detect anyone who approached long before Treasa could.

"How many are coming after us?"

"I don't know."

She looked at him. "How many did you see?"

"None. But there's a Pictish settlement ten or fifteen miles away . . ." He let it drop, as if she ought to plainly see something.

Treasa felt her anger rising, about to explode. Her fury burned, but she said nothing. *Rangers. Outlaws. And he fears a phantom army!*

Comgall fidgeted and scowled, his youthful face forced into creases it shouldn't be seeing for years yet. He paced a while, glanced in the gateway maybe a thousand times, then charged inside. But for the usual watchmen, Treasa held the ground alone.

Suddenly very weary, she backed up against the ringwall and sat against it. So steeply did it slope, she could sit and still remain standing, a sort of half one and half the other, not one or the other.

Just like she herself. Not one thing, not the other. That delicious feeling of oneness that had so buoyed her drained away, leaving her the outsider again. The wet grass soaked her clothes.

Kieran and Colm appeared in the gateway. Silently the towering blond bear handed her an iron sword, then stationed himself on the other side of the gate where Comgall had vacated. Kieran settled in beside Treasa—crowding her, it rather seemed.

They didn't need her. She carefully slipped the sword into her leathern belt—she certainly wasn't going to give that up—and elected to carry the ax. This was her ax, a prize of war. On impulse, she took off down across the lea.

She knew of three places to find ash trees. The nearest was the hedgerow over the hill beyond the stone oratory, but the largest trees grew down by Patrick's well. Old trees were most likely to yield dead limbs. She went that way.

Patrick's well. Why was every second well in Erin called Patrick's well? And most of the others were Brigid's well. If Patrick really did bless all the wells tradition attributed to him, he died with a mildewed right hand. A fine drizzle had commenced. Slipping in the wet grass, she passed the sheep flock and negotiated the steep hillside toward the sea. The ash grove, a dozen trees at most, sat in wet and moody silence, staring at distance.

She had to climb the tallest of the ash trees to find dead branches, shinning up the unforgiving trunk. The bark and twigs did not take kindly to her efforts. They scratched her mercilessly. It took nearly an hour to gather an abundant armful of branches, to carry them back to the monastery, to find a high, flat place north of the cluster of huts on the far side of the Finglas.

She fetched fire not from within the ringwall or from the cookhouse but from the casual fire of several shepherds down by the hazel coppice. For some odd reason, she didn't want to have to pass by Colm.

Even with good, open flame with which to start, she found it terribly hard to get the fire going—wet wood and not enough dry tinder. It blazed up eventually despite the drizzle, a brave little fire on a bald, windswept hill.

Movement behind her—she sensed rather than heard it. With a gasp she wheeled, spiraling to her feet, her ax swung up at ready.

Colm stopped and raised his hands.

She plopped into the grass beside her fire and cast the ax aside. "Don't sneak up like that."

He hunkered down to sitting, not beside her but across the fire from her, facing south.

She tossed another branch onto the fire—she had only a few left—and glanced at him. "Will he be all right?"

"Prayer vigil's already set up. That will cure him if anything can. Anice is very good with war wounds—better than that monk from Kildare—what's his name? Came just before we did."

"Eamon?"

"Him. She's taken over—removed the sword tip, dressed wounds in his arm and ribs. Says the cuts in his face are nothing. Doing a great job."

"Praise God."

"Praise God indeed." That lilting baritone voice paused. "But you don't trust Him completely."

"Why would you say that?"

He gestured toward the little fire. "Burning ash wood drives away the devil. Every true child of the sod knows that."

"It also warms cold fingers and toes," she added defensively.

"A fire for warmth on an open hill with the wind blowing and rain falling? An exposed hill that just happens to be directly north of the monastery?"

Why deny it? He knew what she was doing. And he knew she knew he knew. She snapped, "And every true child of the sod knows the devil comes out of the north."

"So do the Picts. Which gives them much in common with the devil."

"Aye and aye again." She watched the flames dip and feint, then tossed on another broken branch.

He let the silence ride a while. "They say your father was a druid."

"He still is."

"And you have learned from him."

"Not enough."

"Too much, perhaps."

She knew where he was headed. Had not Mobhi himself preached just yesterday against the evil of diluting the true faith with pagan practice? Fine words, but yesterday no one from Mobhi's monastery lay at death's door. The devil had no opening to come in and rob a life, to snatch a weakened soul. The world was neat and orderly yesterday. Not today.

She unhorsed his topic and substituted her own. "Gavin will be safe so long as he remains here. There are so many of us to protect him. And of course, the power of corporate prayer."

"He'd be stronger among his own clan, but there's no society of this size in that area. Ever hear the book of Jeremiah?"

"No."

"About a third of the way through is written 'Accursed is the man who trusts in man and makes flesh his arm.' The essence of the passage is, you don't depend on the strength of man but on the strength of God. Clans are the strength of man. Prayer is the strength of God. God's power."

She was going to ask him if he had memorized all of Jeremiah, but she didn't bother. If he heard it or read it once through, he had it.

Why did she always feel so useless and secondary when Colm was near? Silly question.

Silence.

"Treasa? Remember when the boaire killed the slave girl under Gemman's aegis, and you appeared out of nowhere?"

She looked at him startled, not expecting that. Not now. "So?"

"So how did you get there?"

She laughed. She roared. "Has that been preying on you all this long time? When you announced your going, I told Finnian that I too would be leaving on the morrow. Finnian denied my release. As if I were a slave or prisoner. 'Very well,' I replied, went back to my clochan, and gathered some bread and my cloak. I chose a sword from the smithy—Finnian owed me at least that much for three years' service—and climbed over the back palisade."

"The same notches we boys used for climbing out and finding mischief." Colm was smiling.

"The very same. Sure and they fit a girl's hands and feet quite as well. I waited down by the poplars until I saw you two come out in the morning, then followed you."

"Living off the land for weeks." He wagged that gloriously shining head.

"I had the easy part," she said smugly. "I didn't have to carry parcels of books around. While you were flitting about Tara being

80

a prince, I took the armorer aside and got him to teach me how he puts an edge on a sword. At Cashel I showed the armorer how the fellow at Tara does it."

Colm laughed aloud. And then he was sitting up straighter, frowning as he watched the compound in the distance below.

She twisted around to look behind her. The ringwall, the biers, the paddocks, the cote. Nothing unusual. "What?"

"The woman sitting on the ground by the sty. She staggered and fell against the wall." He hopped to his feet.

She waited to put the rest of her ash wood on the fire until he turned his back and started down the hill. Then she snatched up the ax and followed.

She recognized the woman as one of the milkmaids, though she didn't know her name. Colm settled down beside the milkmaid, cupped her cheeks in his hands, and asked her what was wrong. She answered in glazed, hesitant phrases.

Treasa might not know much about war wounds, but from earliest childhood she had watched an endless parade of maladies appear at her father's door. Many the time she watched her father pronounce the names of those maladies and, oftener than not, banish them. This looked like one of those he never could banish.

She checked for fever. None. She asked regarding nausea or diarrhea. None. She pulled a gap into the neck of the woman's tunic and thrust a hand deep down in, pressing the woman's armpit. The apple-sized boil under the left arm told Treasa more than she wanted to know.

She sat back as Colm glanced toward her curiously. How she dreaded saying the word. "Plague."

8

Anice's Gloom

The year of our Lord 544

I am Heaven shaken and stars fall.
I am a tree shaken and apples fall.
I am a heart shaken and tears fall.

The best place to watch the mighty conflagration was from the bald hill north of the monastery. From there you could see both banks of the Finglas and almost all the huts and other buildings clustered along them. The stockade along the top of the ringwall had been pulled down, the logs stacked in haphazard piles inside. Some of those logs were ash. The devil was in trouble now.

The great wooden oratory within the ringwall on the south side burned wildest. For a few minutes, a tall spiral of fire swirled heavenward in the midst of its bubbling, boiling smoke column. The spiral died of hunger before long, but now the thatch on the mud huts nearest it had caught and were smoldering.

Here on the north bank the little wooden oratory burned eagerly. The biers and cotes with their roofs of jumbled sticks didn't last long. The wicker granaries melted in moments. The fire skipped from thatch to thatch among the huts. Some of them began charring along the lower edges. The charring eventually would erupt into open flame. Some commenced smoking because of the firebrands falling on them. Thatch hates to burn, though, preferring instead to put up dense clouds of gray-black smoke, smoke so thick that it seems you could climb up it to ask God questions.

And Anice of Drumderry had many questions. She pressed as close as she could manage to Gavin on her left without crawling in under his cloak. Monstrous in size now that he had his full growth, the burly Columcille stood near, protecting her right. Tears made his piercing blue eyes bluer.

Perhaps five hundred other monastics clustered on this hillside watching. They were all that remained of Mobhi's brotherhood after the hundreds of plague deaths in this last year or so, and hundreds more fled the place in search of safety.

Anice, despite her few years, knew for a fact: There is no safety, not in place, not in strength of arm, not in clan, not in numbers. Fools they were to fly.

The only person not enthralled by the stinking, smoking inferno, it would appear, was Mobhi himself. The young abbot came walking across the hillside among the remnants of his magnificent Glasnevin scholars with nary a glance toward the ravaging fire. In her mind's eye, Anice recounted the memory of him again as he and he alone hurried from building to building inside the ringwall, setting the fires in the oratory and scriptorium, lighting the biers outside the wall and the summer cookhouse. The black smoke of his mutton-fat torch seemed so thick and ominous then as he thrust it in this pile of kindling and that. Now, in retrospect, it was nothing.

As he approached, Anice was about to say, "This must be terribly hard for you," but she bit her tongue and kept silent. The haggard sorrow on his face made any words sound silly.

He embraced Gavin, Colm, Anice, and Treasa beyond Colm. He paused and looked at Colm. "You were in prayer this morning, so I didn't disturb you. Do you know yet where you're going?"

"North. When Gavin lay so sore, there was no good church to take him to among his clan or mine. I'll try to rectify that."

"Godspeed. When the plague abates I'll begin assembling another body of scholars, bigger and better than this one. Where will I be able to find you?"

"Word left at Tara and Armagh will reach me soon enough."

Mobhi nodded. "Good. Good. Spread the faith." He did not move nearly as quickly or as smartly now as he had at the beginning of this terrible day. He Godspeeded Gavin also and young Kenneth and Kieran, but not Anice and Treasa. He moved on to others.

Spread the faith. It had been the message of his final address in the great oratory this morning.

"Spread the plague is more like it," grumbled Gavin.

What is that oozing out from under the burning cattle bier? Rippling, sort of. Dark. Smoldering in spots. Curious, Anice left the cover of her friends and moved down closer.

Rats. The dark ooze consisted of hundreds of rats leaving the bier and haystacks. They did not scamper and scurry as you would expect. They did not bother to hasten at all. As stunned as anyone else by this turn of events, they ambled blindly, confused. The backs of some were burned; a few still smoked. Anice could not picture a rat casually remaining in a fire to burn. Rats are too canny.

A pair of jackdaws swooped down into the pasture grass. One of them seized a rat; the other immediately commenced fighting for it. They engaged in a silly tug of war as many, many rats waddled by to either side of them.

Anice climbed the hill again to rejoin her friends. Crows and jackdaws, all a-chatter, were gathering in the poplars below the settlement.

It seemed the display was ended. The fire still crackled and sang of its conquest, but the wind was shifting, drawing the smoke this way. No doubt the site would flare and sputter for days yet. Anice was of no mind to sit about watching it.

Apparently, neither were the others of Mobhi's erstwhile Glasnevin school. In clusters and pairs, the few remaining brethren picked up their bundles and wandered away. Colm started off across the hill northward.

"I don't understand." Anice fell in beside him. "If he's going to start another school, why did he burn this one?"

"What causes plague?"

"God. Punishment for wrongdoing."

Colm nodded. "Wrong question. *How* does God cause plague? Does He have an instrument of death, and, if so, what is it?"

Anice shrugged.

He waved a hand. "Healthy people walk about one day and the next day drop dead. But the telling clue: Healthy outsiders arrive at the school and within weeks fall victim. It could be something in the buildings. He didn't want anyone to move in after we left and possibly drop dead."

That made sense. Anice nodded. "Then he'd feel responsible for their death. He tends to do that anyway."

Gavin rumbled, "I don't accept it." His big bay horse, on lead behind him, sneezed noisily, spraying everyone within an arm's span. "People out in the raths are dying too. Farmers who were perfectly hale. Boaires, peasants, ris, everyone. It wasn't just the buildings. Ah well. One bright spot."

The horse shook, rattling the bridle tied to its saddle.

"What?" Anice knew the dark cousin better than to believe he valued anything bright.

"Think of all the fleas and flies and ticks that died today. Makes a heart feel good. Even a smoke cloud has its silver lining."

"You're grotesque." Treasa stopped and turned for one more look.

But Anice was watching Colm's face. He obviously considered Gavin's stab at humor not only grotesque but infuriating. Colm bothered her. He seemed remote, dark, though in a different way from his cousin. That wasn't like him.

"There." Treasa pointed aloft.

Three ravens circled high, spiraling downward beside the smoke. Now they were five and now six. A hen harrier skimmed in close across the hilltop and in a great, sweeping arc soared downslope.

"The rats." Anice took one last glance at the great, undulant column of smoke and resumed walking. "They've come for the rats."

Whether Colm doubted her or was merely curious she couldn't tell, but he turned back to watch. Then he jabbed his cousin's elbow, an attention-getter, and pulled the bay's lead line out of Gavin's hand. He didn't bother to bridle it. He threw a loop of the lead line over the horse's nose, a temporary war bridle, and swung aboard. His knees high on its shoulders, he wheeled it and trotted it off back toward the fire.

Gavin scowled at his departing horse and its thief, then with a sigh settled to the trail again. Colm caught up to them five minutes later.

Anice felt as safe as a person can reasonably feel, traveling with these two young giants. Treasa was as good with the ax, lance, and sword as anyone, but she despised Anice. She made that clear enough. Anice would not trust Treasa with old chicken bones, let alone her life. Kenneth and Kieran walked a bit behind. Half an hour later, huffing and panting, sweaty, sour Comgall caught up.

They by-passed Tara at Colm's insistence, and Anice had no idea why, for Colm seemed to like Tara so much. They followed one track or another northward for three days, in no hurry and yet not wanting to lag, putting the past behind but not too quickly. Several times, usually in mountains, they saw highwaymen eyeing them from afar, but no one challenged them. That impressed Anice, for the bay horse was a prize worth fighting for. Did the brigands defer out of respect for the faith of the monks among the party or the size of the young men? No matter.

They ran out of bread on the eighth day. On the ninth they ran out of patience.

The day started all right. How it ended was the trial. They learned much too close to dusk that what they thought was a traveler's route was actually a cow path. Merrily it led them up into a dense wood, then dissipated itself into a fan of cattle hoof prints that spread up and out across the mountain. Discouraged, they built ragged brush shelters roofed with birch boughs, set too few deadfalls and snares, and retired. There was no fire, for Kenneth had accidentally drowned their brands while crossing a rocky little mountain stream that afternoon, heralding the trial to come had they only known. The men sang Compline huddled under their cloaks, while Treasa and Anice under the other brushpile shivered individually, for Treasa would not share her cloak to make a double layer.

It began to rain, casually at first, then driving chilling fingers down through the birch leaves. As soon as everyone was quite wet enough, the storm broke off and the sky cleared. The temperature dropped ten degrees in an hour. Anice glimpsed the Pleiades overhead just before she finally fell asleep.

She slept through Matins and had no idea whether the others did as well. The men were singing Prime when she awoke. From the degree of light abroad already, it seemed they were at least half an hour behind. Three or four hours of sleep is not enough.

One of Gavin's deadfalls yielded a squirrel. A squirrel hardly feeds one, let alone seven. It feeds no one at all when there is no fire. Gavin cleaned it and stretched the skin over a thick birch branch, a gift for whomever provided them fire.

They backtracked down the cow path, out of the forest into open bush. New trees were coming in—hazel scrub, a few sloes, and raggedy little hawthorns. The hooves of sheep and cattle had chopped the ground nearly bare. The slope looked just as dismal as Anice's spirits felt.

And then the unthinkable happened. Still miles, apparently, from the nearest rath, they paused to sing Tierce beneath a dull-gray overcast. They sat in a sort of circle, as if they were gathered around a fire instead of a cold, wet patch of beaten grass. The final "Thanks be to God" had hardly faded when Gavin waved an arm and announced, "I'm striking out that way. Straight west across the River Derg to the sea."

Comgall sneered. "Wild land. You'll find nothing there."

And Gavin replied quietly, "My birthplace, eventually, and my parents if they still be living. I've been too long away from my clan. I'm tired of roaming the wide world."

Then Colm said the unthinkable. "North. Lough Neagh and beyond. The north coast. I'm too strongly called to go anywhere else."

Gavin wagged his head. "Sammhain in two weeks. Come home with me, and we'll go north after the new year."

"North now. Then you can follow the coast west and go upriver to home."

Treasa's head swung back and forth, partly a "no" and partly trying to watch both faces at once. Anice could tell her that these young men were equally brave, equally stubborn, and equally stupid. Neither would back off. The party was about to break up. Unthinkable!

But, then, why did Anice think it would last? Nothing good ever lasts. Despite the cold and rain, getting lost and going hungry, this was a good time.

Comgall was sputtering like porridge left cooking too long. "It's too dangerous! This is wild country. We stay together." He looked from face to face and apparently realized what Anice knew. You did not tell these cousins what to do. He shifted tactics. "Look at Kenneth here. You've terrified him just talking about breaking up. You're not—"

Colm raised a hand. "The loss of one member isn't going to damage your strength that much. Continue with Gavin. Many's the time I've traveled alone."

Gavin exploded. "None of the time you've traveled alone! I'm always with you."

"And I don't know why. Sure and you're not interested in glorifying God. Every time we're singing an office, you're traipsing off somewhere doing something else."

"Somebody's got to feed this flock of wandering sheep, and standing there counting off the hours isn't going to do it."

"Man does not live by bread alone."

"Or one lousy little squirrel, for all that." Gavin lurched to his feet. "Did I mention I'm also hungry? Enough of this. Comgall, Kieran, Kenneth, and the two women are big enough a party to stay safe. You go your way and I'll go mine, and they can go to Armagh." He brushed off his seat, which was all prickled with wet yew needles.

"Armagh!" Comgall's puckered face looked like he was drinking rotten beer. "If I wanted to go to Armagh I would have gone to Armagh. It's not two days east of here, and I'd be a far sight more comfortable than I am now. If I go anywhere, I'll go back to Clonard. We never should have left there in the first place."

Anice's ears listened to the storm and thunder, but her heart was still dwelling on Gavin's careless words. *The two women.* He called her a woman. Treasa certainly was by now, having attained her full growth. Anice, though, was a child, a straw doll, a plaything tossed about by the hand of fate or God or whoever that was.

Colm too was standing now, twisted hard around, trying to pick the tenacious needles out of the back of his coarse wool dalmatic.

"Clonard." Treasa nodded. "We walked right past the front gate. It's hard by Tara; that should appeal to you, Colm. Tarry there a while. Let the wound of Glasnevin heal."

Comgall was still fuming. "—don't know why we wander about like this to no good end." No one offered him any reasons why.

Kenneth, usually so quiet, said, "I was born in Glengiven. That's up north where Colm is going. I'd like to go there." No one save Anice gave any indication they heard him.

"Clonard." Gavin flapped both arms with an I-couldn't-care-less gesture. "If you go to Clonard, stop by Armagh. I'm sure the bishop will have lots of books he'll want you to carry to Finian for him."

Treasa burst out laughing. "Not if you work it right. Just hang around the armory."

Gavin glared at her. Colm chuckled. Anice was confused. What were they talking about? See? She was a simple child, unable to follow an ordinary conversation.

And suddenly, with hardly any leave-taking, Gavin had untied his big horse and was marching off to the west, straight out across the wooded hillside with his horse in tow. The trees swallowed him almost instantly.

Colm turned into a monk then, which was not so surprising, since he was ordained. He raised his hand not in the Latin position of blessing but in the Celtic, mumbled things, and signed the cross to Gavin's back. He turned and blessed the rest of them in the same way. He wished them Godspeed wherever they may go, asked their mercy, and walked away along a track that was either the way north or another cow path.

Anice's world, already wet and cold, turned frozen. The last time the cousins walked out of her life, they returned for her a year-and-some later. This time they would not know where to find her.

She probably should go with them to this Clonard. But what if it were like Moville? She aspired to far more than milking that obstreperous black cow. She didn't want to go back to a place like Moville, laboring endlessly for some unappreciative master or mistress like Aileen of Inishowen Head. Or Finnian either.

Complaining mightily, Comgall announced that he would take over the leadership and they should all get moving toward Armagh. His announcement was not received favorably. In fact, it appeared not to be received at all. Treasa remained sitting cross-legged, staring at the ground before her and wagging her head in disbelief. Kenneth sniffled. Kieran apparently prayed, since his lips moved a while and he subsequently crossed himself.

In a huff, Comgall urged them forward. Arguments and complaints and cranky retorts fluttered around Anice's head like a flock of confused butterflies. She listened to none of it. Her heroes had deserted her. *She* must determine her path now. She was nothing at all like these companions of the track. She was not a monastic but a milkmaid. She was not a person of means but a slave. She was not a woman but a child.

She wanted to follow Gavin, but he was traveling cross-country. She could never keep up, never find him, even if he didn't have that magnificent horse. She did not dare plunge off into the woodland alone. And so, while the other four berated each other and debated their destination, she walked away unnoticed, hungry, alone, hastening northward up the track after Colm.

9

Gavin's Past

The spirits linger on the night.
  The memories linger on the heart.
  Sammhain touches them together.

"It's dreadfully unlucky to use oak for roof rafters, Niall! Don't do it. Our Lord's cross was made of oak, you know."

Gavin remembered clearly his mum saying that, her feet apart, her arms akimbo, her brow puckered in a worried frown. He recalled her standing in the dooryard of their brand new rath, watching their clients and house-slaves shave rafters.

And his father had airily replied, "Nonsense, Glenna. That's ignorance speaking. We'll use what the Lord provided. These tall-oak beams will last a thousand years. You know how durable tall-oak is."

Gavin stood on the very spot where once his father's clients had spent days stripping oak bark with drawknives. They must have tanned two dozen hides with the oak bark from the new round house inside the freshly built ringwall of which his da was so proud.

Durable, yes. Tall-oak is known for that. It burns well too. Now nothing was left of Da's rafters save a few charred stubs anchored in the walls. Da's steep, conical roof had collapsed down into his round walls, walls partly fallen, partly burnt, partly still standing. Blackened and matted, spoilt thatch lay like a grotesque troll's nest inside. Looters had dug around in it here and there. Gavin thought about the jewelry his mum so loved, golden torques and brooches that had been in the family for ten generations.

Lost. Lost to looters. Lost to greedy political foes. Lost to the four winds. It was all lost.

Numb with cold and loss, he wandered out Da's ringwall gate and down to the springhouse. Still tied to the hitch post by the gate, the bay nickered to him. "You forgot me."

The wicker-and-thatch roof on the springhouse needed repair, but flame and pilferage had passed it by. His mum kept a small fired-clay mug down here that she might draw a cool draught at any time. Here it lay, just inside the little doorway. Gavin had to stoop almost double to reach in and retrieve it.

A vertical crack ran down one side of the mug. *Did time or the elements or mum herself crack it?* As he turned it over in his hands, the mug fell apart into halves.

If I had been here rather than out studying with my cousin, would all this have happened? Had my father possessed just one more strong sword, could disaster have been averted? As ri ruirech, his father could command a small army. But his army—boaires and ri tuatha under Da's aegis—would have to be here to fight. Da rarely assembled a force for a preemptory attack on someone, and never had attackers entered the area of his tutelage before. Gavin was looking at the results of a surprise raid, striking before Da could call his army out of their fields and pastures.

Da's strength was Gavin's. Da was gone. *What now?*

In his early childhood, Gavin had spent long hours dreaming, plotting, and simply vegetating in the oak grove over beyond the creek. He would go there now, where thoughts came freely and imagination soared. He turned his back on the ruins of his childhood home and crossed the pasture eastward toward the creek.

The birches that once lined the creek draw were gone. There used to be a score of birches here. And alder. *Where were the alders gone?* The creek still ran bravely, tumbling through the rocks to the sea, but now its face was in the sun.

Gavin's oaks? Gone.

He flopped to sitting in the rank grass and stared across the creek to the stumpfield on the far slope, utterly drained. *With my father gone, who now would be ri ruirech?* Chances were better than even that it was his father's murderer, whoever that might be. Politics worked that way.

Fury and Frustration joined hands with Sorrow to whirl round and round in his heart. Their wild dance swept away every sane thought, every gentle feeling. Not a little of that fury and frustration centered on Colm. Gavin needed his cousin here. Now. He needed Colm's strength and common sense. He needed another good sword arm. Colm and his infernal, "I am called." Well, Gavin was calling now, to no avail. And Gavin was blood, close blood. Serve the clan first, always.

He slogged up the hill through tangled, ungrazed grass to the bay. He untied the gelding and swung atop the broad back with no plan in mind, no destination.

He rode away from the useless home of his early years. No need to come here again. His head and heart were too muddled to be of any use, so he'd let his stomach lead. In his childhood, the best bread baker among all his father's tuathe was a crone named Swaya, down by the sea two miles to the north. Swaya was older than most rocks when Gavin was six. She must be in her grave by now, but perhaps she passed her art on to someone else in her family. He aimed the gelding toward the sea.

The track wound half a mile through pasturage and stump-fields before ever it passed beneath a tree. Then Gavin had to slide off and lead the bay through the second-growth alder along the creek shore lest he be wiped off the broad back by overhanging branches. Old Cruithnechan claimed that the law required all roads to be brushed at least once every three years so that the brehons could travel freely to the triennial assemblies. Gavin had not seen that done much anywhere that he had traveled, and he knew his father had paid no attention to it.

The track opened into the Mac Harra pasture and then carried Gavin to one of his favorite haunts. The ragged hill to the east of the track dropped off steeply here. A thick oak-and-hazel forest covered the sharp gray outcrops tumbling down the hillside, and a broad band of ferns hid completely the little rivulet that darted down through the rocks toward the sea. It was cool and dark in here, as always. Gavin stopped the horse a few moments, blotting up the sensations of childhood.

"Hazelnuts gathered from oak woods impart wisdom," his mum often claimed. "You should eat more of them, Son."

"Many more," Da would add.

Gavin slid off the bay. The first of the season's hazelnuts were ripening. Most of the clusters of burs still clung on the trees, half green. Some, though, had split. Gavin gathered a dozen with hardly any effort at all. He made a sling in his cloak tail to hold them and sought out more. His trove wrapped in his cloak tail, he led the bay out the familiar track to the Maas meadow, scooping up a hand-sized rock along the way.

As the bay grazed near the chair-shaped Seat Rock of Gavin's childhood, he settled himself beside it and methodically began hulling hazelnuts, cracking them open with stone upon stone. Some were wormy. A few were shriveled, ill formed in the shell. Some were too green yet, pasty and bitter. He ate them anyway. A few, though, were ripe enough to give him the sweet savor that delighted his mouth and his memories.

His stomach and his wisdom refreshed, he mounted the bay and took off again toward Swaya's. The track plunged down a steep hillside and rounded a smaller rise. The smell of the sea greeted him before ever he saw the water. Then, just past the final gentle rise, the sea spread out before him with its arms open wide, like a maiden aunt come to visit—a bit too eager to greet him, he a bit reticent to come too near. He knew people who had died in the rough waters and odd tides. Over across the arm, Crohy Head sulked beneath the overcast. *Nothing new there.*

Nothing new at Swaya's rath either. Her whole farm, ringwall and all, could have fit inside his father's house. The space between her ringwall and the house wall was barely wide enough to admit one cow. He didn't see how a cow could turn around within it. Swaya must drive them in one side at night and on around her house and out the gate next morning, a single-file parade. Her walls needed repair. The gate was a pile of brush, pushed aside at the moment. Smoke curled out the hole in the peak of the conical roof. Someone was home.

Gavin dismounted and walked carefully through ankle-deep mud at the gate into ankle-deep mud at her house door. Tentatively he called her name.

Silence inside. Then rustling.

"Swaya? Goodwife? It's Mac Niall, Glenna's boy. The dark-haired one."

More rustling inside. An ancient, withered, disembodied head loomed in the near darkness inside. It took on a body as it moved closer to the door—dark garments in the gloom. A cold, gnarled hand shot out suddenly and grasped Gavin's tunic down by his belt. He sucked in air and almost leaped backward. He caught himself in time, for she was clinging to his tunic and he would yank her right off her feet if he moved.

It was Swaya, looking older than the oldest rocks in Erin. Her eyes were closed and seemed content to remain so. Did light hurt her aging eyes so much? Gavin let himself be dragged in closer to her.

"Mac Niall, aye? The dark one." Her hand trembled; her voice croaked. A dozen or so hairs clothed her head.

And all Gavin could think about was the Morrigan. That dreaded Erse goddess could turn herself into a wizened old hag or an irresistible auburn-haired beauty. Here stood the hag. Did the Morrigan assume a known identity? Gavin couldn't remember aye or nay from the tales he heard in childhood, except that the hero Cu Chulainn had failed to recognize her to his woe. Was this old Swaya or a divine impostor? And the thought of auburn hair brought the girl-child Anice suddenly to mind.

Anice. What if . . .? Surely not!

The tiny house smelled musty inside. Gavin could tell even without entering the door. *What a stupid, foolish thing to do, coming here! This is the last time I'll listen to my stomach.*

"Mac Niall," she repeated. The claw hand let go his tunic and groped up to his face. It was cold and dry; its coldness and dryness startled him. She ran her smooth, chilly fingers over his face, his ear, his hair. "Could be. Could be. Enter, Mac Niall. You want to know about your parents and your cousin." She turned and led the way back to her fire.

Gavin followed two steps and stopped. "You need more wood, Old Woman. I'll fetch some for you." Swift as a stoat he hurried outside, away from the must and darkness. He took from the brush pile at the gate because he had no time to seek wood farther afield. But how he wished he could.

He brought an armload in, sat down on the floor beside the fire, and began breaking up sticks. "It's been many years, Old Woman. I was a small child when last I visited." Her dirt floor was damp, and no dry covering of rushes or strewn grass. Its moisture began instantly to seep into his clothes.

She had settled onto a small stool about as close to the fire as a person can get without igniting. "Seeking my wheat bread. I remember you well."

"I remember your bread well. It brought me back today."

She cackled. "A fair answer and a bold one. No pretense. You're Mac Niall, aye. Your father, the rascal, was as great a beggar for my bread as you, you know. Many the time he'd show up fresh from the hunt, his hounds yapping at my gate. He'd give me a hare or two, and I'd give him a loaf. Then we'd sit at this very fire and talk. Good times they were!"

"Talk about what?" Gavin smelled no bread—saw no food of any sort, in fact. The hazelnuts had not made much of a meal. He fed her fire from the pile of sticks.

"Politics. People." She paused. "You. Your father was not an aggressive sort. Honest and true. Under his kingship, the district prospered, for he was noble. He saw in you the qualities he lacked—eagerness to fight foremost among them—but he worried about your nobility."

"My integrity's intact. And I'm sure Da's was, to the end."

Her sunken eyes still had not opened, not even in this deep gloom. "Indeed, indeed. 'Twas decisiveness he lacked. It was his undoing."

Gavin's breastbone trilled. He measured his words carefully, keeping them casual. "By whose hand?"

She began rocking gently back and forth. "Many a loaf of bread I baked. There's secrets to it, you know—a secret in the kneading and in the rising of it. No one could match my bread, though well they tried."

"Sure and you're the master of it."

"I took a stab at baking a few loaves now and again after my eyes went, but without the eyes to see its progress, a loaf is aught more than a loaf. The touch is gone. Now I must sit here blind and content myself to eat what others bring me. Sorry bread it is, but am I to complain? Truth, and women don't bother to bake as once they did. The art is lost."

Gavin pondered her answer a few minutes, mulling it—what she said and what she would not say. "Old Woman, give me this, I pray thee. Who brings you food?"

She smiled slightly. "Your cousin Oran."

"And so shall I, as I am able, in gratitude that you suffered an impudent child with a yearning for good bread." He took his leave then, hauled aboard the bay, and headed back to the oak-and-hazel glen. He gathered all the hazelnuts and downed wood he could transport in his cloak and brought them to Swaya. He found her two flat stones to crack the nuts with and rode up to the eastbound track.

The track crawled through a crease in the hills and out across an unavoidable bog. The causeway of brush and oak limbs his father had built was now almost totally obscured by bog vegetation that had grown in from both sides and up through the sticks from underneath. Good thing too. His bay horse was nervous enough about walking on this bouncy, creaking togher it could not see. The animal would probably explode if it had to traverse a fresh new walkway.

The hills beyond seemed much the same as they had in Gavin's youth. But then, hills are hills.

He arrived at Oran's rath late in the afternoon. The ringwall crowning Oran's hill was so new the grass on its sides had not yet rooted well and the palisade along the top smelled of green wood. A dozen more than the usual complement of four outbuildings were scattered down the slope, with rockwalls and paddocks all across the hillside. A busy place for a boaire with humble credentials.

Gavin was not alone in coming here. Travelers were pouring in from all directions—along the westbound track from the River Foyle, the road from the Swilly up north, from the south, mayhap clear up from Lough Derg and the Ballyshannon. From the time Gavin laid eyes on the gate until the moment he actually reached it, eleven other people had entered it—not counting retainers.

Gavin might be dirty and unkempt from his journey (not to mention sitting on Swaya's crumbling dirt floor), he might be arriving without arms or retinue, but he was a prince, and he knew how to act like one.

He abandoned his bay's reins, swung his right leg up over its neck and slid to the ground with his back to his saddle. He announced casually, just a wee bit imperiously, "Mac Niall the Dark," and watched a gray-haired old man just inside the gate hasten toward the hall beyond.

A stable boy led his horse away. He hoped it was a stable boy, or he had just lost a horse. He stepped inside the gate and waited. A score of people were bustling from building to building in the enclosure, carrying pots and kettles and great wooden bowls from here to there.

By and by the gray-haired man returned. Smiling, he dipped his head. "You were unexpected. A place is being prepared for you, Prince. Would you care to refresh yourself from the journey?"

"I would, thank you." As the warder led him to a clochan hard by the kitchen, Gavin looked all about for familiar faces. He saw no one from his youth among these people.

The warder watched him step into the tiny beehive hut and drop the hide that served as a door behind him. But Gavin immediately tipped a corner of the hide back to watch the warder depart. As soon as the man had passed beyond easy earshot, Gavin slipped out of the clochan and into the next one. How fortunate he was that no one was in it at the moment.

The tub of wash water was too much used to consider, the linen towel just as sorry. No matter. Gavin quickly wiped the dirt off parts that showed, brushed the mud out of his clothes as best he could, and stepped outside into the waning daylight.

He continued around the back side of the compound, past the closely clustered clochans and granaries, the leatherworker's shed and what must be, from the piles of wood chips at the door, a woodcarver's hut. The smithy at last. The smith's fire was banked, his forge cooling. Gavin ought to call out, but that would draw attention. Attention he did not need.

From behind him a woman screamed, muffled. He jogged ten paces back the way he came. In the clochan next to the kitchen, the clochan to which he had first been ushered, two men with swords drawn were backing out hastily, nearly tripping over each other. An older woman appeared in the doorway wagging her finger, obviously scolding loudly, though Gavin couldn't make out words. The hide at the clochan door dropped closed. The two swordsmen beat a hasty retreat around the far side of the compound.

Gavin returned quickly to the smithy and opened a heavy wooden door to a closed shed at the back of the smith's shade frame. This had to be it, and it was. The armory. He passed up the spears and javelins and anything of bronze. The axes were more Colm's weapon than his. He ignored them. He chose a sword off the back rank, hefted it, replaced it, and chose another. He went through four before he found a perfect weight that was neither too long nor too short. He slid its haft up into his belt and let the cloak fall over it. Fully dressed at last, he continued around the compound wall to the door of the banqueting hall.

On second thought. . . . He walked out to the stables, ordered his horse resaddled and tied beside the gate, and went back inside.

Cousin Oran's vast rectangular hall was so new that smoke had not yet darkened the rafters overhead. This might even be its first use. It smelled strongly of freshly peeled wood and newly laid fire. Down its wide open center burned four fires. A great caldron hung on a tripod over one of them. Fresh rushes covered the floor thickly. A tiny fraction of these rushes, were they laid on Swaya's floor instead of this one, would dispel the mustiness and chill from her house.

Despite the ample center aisle, room enough remained to array two tiers of tables along each side. This place was very nearly as capacious as the new hall at Tara. In fact, as Gavin gave the steward his name and followed the fellow across the room, he more and more smelled the aroma of Tara, or perhaps, pretensions to Tara.

Oran and his wife had not yet arrived. Gavin recognized and greeted a dozen aunts and uncles, as many cousins, and Colm's father's old brehon. Phelim's aged lawkeeper spent at least five minutes commenting on how big and strong Gavin looked and enquired less than delicately why Gavin was not yet married.

Gavin finally got to ask, "Why are Phelim and Eithne not here?"

The old brehon hesitated the barest bit of a moment. "They no longer celebrate Sammhain in the way most do, as you know, and sent their regrets."

Gavin knew their religious proclivities well enough. But somehow that wasn't it. He let the matter by and took his place to the left of Colm's brother Eoghan, who sat to the left of Oran's wife, who sat to the left of Oran.

Oran arrived all smiles and wellwishes and greeted each of the nobles and Aes Dana personally, allowing most profusely how happy he was that the Mac Niall should appear. The lesser guests were greeted with a general speech.

Gavin sipped from the mead goblet as it passed by. He was famished, and the speeches far from over.

Oran's chief druid had a few words. Then Oran rose again. "The plague raging in the south is spreading northward rapidly, I hear. We will see it here any day. Whom will it lay low? God alone knows. Therefore, let us be merry tonight and drink good ale, knowing not when God calls." With an expansive gesture and a few more words, Oran launched his feast.

He called for heroes to describe their exploits, that the bravest present might carve the roasted boar. It was all ceremonial; the other eleven roasted hogs would be carved in the kitchen by slaves and unpedigreed cooks' assistants. Gavin, who so loved a good fight, found this part of a feast rather boring, frankly. Lots of bombast and flowery speech for no real honor to speak of.

Plague. The word kept springing back into his heart, no matter how often he kicked it out. With difficulty, Gavin turned his mind's eye away from the pillar of smoke and fire, from the black-blotched bodies he buried. Immediately the troll's nest popped into his thoughts, the devastated rath. Another goblet came by, so Gavin tried it. The raw brew must have been aged eight hours at most. Worst ale he ever tasted.

"*I said,*" Eoghan repeated loudly at Gavin's right, "what have you heard about the high kingship?"

Gavin made his flitting thoughts settle down and behave. They didn't do it willingly. "Nothing. Why?"

"I hear the ard ri is dying and half his court is gone, courtesy the plague. That he's already named his successor."

"A tanaiste? News to me."

Eoghan grunted. "You and my brother being at the top of the pile of candidates, I thought you would have heard. Of course, we're northern Ui Neill, and it's the southern folks' turn to field one."

"Sure and the crown usually alternates between north and south. But that's nowhere near a sure thing. When I was down in Cashel a year and some ago, I didn't see anything in the south worthy of ard ri. They have to offer a competent candidate."

"They did. Diarmaid Mac Cerbaill."

Gavin stared. He almost blurted *"That* Diarmaid?" but he didn't. Of course that Diarmaid. The little puppy dog who tagged after a disenfranchised Pictish princess. The jealous cur who learned Gavin was at Mobhi's and sent his rangers down to remove him—seasoned, well-armed rangers who were trounced by a couple of weaponless monks and a woman. "I said competent. Besides, he's as non-Christ as they come."

"He's not that bad. A little slow in some regards, but not bad. Learns fast. Dogged. Has a good fighting force behind him."

Gavin made a messy noise. "Slave children and Pictish expatriates. If you call that g—"

The tall double doors slammed open with enough clatter to alert old Swaya that something was up. A huge bay horse came thundering down the center of the hall—Gavin's horse! And aboard it Treasa, sword in hand!

Gavin gaped, unable to move, to speak, to breathe. Treasa, her long braid flying! *How . . .?* Others were laughing—no doubt most of the banqueters thought it was all part of the show, an early start to the deviltry and foolishness of Sammhain.

She dragged the horse to a halt in the middle of the hall and pivoted it a full turn, searching faces. "Gavin!" She waved her sword toward him. "Come quickly!"

His mind stood still; his feet did not. They hauled him upright and in one giant stride brought him up onto the table. Another giant stride carried him forward onto the table tiered in front. His mind was finally beginning to function as his feet, with a flying leap, sent him hurtling toward his horse.

Treasa was swinging the bay broadside toward him. The gelding's wide back sort of came up under Gavin as he slammed into it, and they connected well enough that he didn't slide ignominiously to the floor. As he struggled to find his balance and get

101

properly astride, Treasa dug her heels in and leaned forward, urging the horse toward the door. Gavin must have hooked his heel up under the bay's stifle, for the horse gave a little kick and a crowhop. Then its gait evened out and they flew through the opened doors, from Oran's orange-lighted, stuffy banqueting hall into the cold, dark night.

10

Gavin's Exile

How sweet, how desired . . . the marriage bed.

Treasa could feel the difference as they jogged along the track across a broad, open stumpfield: The bay horse was working up enough of a sweat now that Gavin, riding behind her, wasn't slipping and sliding so much. The resinous sweat helped him stay put, except for the deliberate squirming.

He twisted around again to look back from where they'd come. "Where are we going?"

She wished he'd quit doing that. The overcast night was so dark you couldn't see anything anyway. "How should I know? I've never been up here before."

He barked right in her ear. "Wait a minute! We're trotting along at eight miles an hour and you don't know where?"

"We're supposed to be headed for Derry, around where the River Foyle meets the Lough. Any of that sound familiar?"

"Somewhat. I've never been there, but I know about it. It's right near Grianan Fort."

"We don't want to go there, according to the bishop at Armagh. There's a ri ruirech around Derry somewhere. If a regional king can't get you out of the country secretly, I don't know who can."

"Get me out—" He wrapped an arm around her and grabbed the reins. The horse bobbed to a confused stop.

He roared, "This is the second time you popped into my life. Now explain. And I'm not going anywhere until I'm convinced it's the thing to do."

Treasa took a deep breath. How do you explain all this? "Can we talk while we ride?"

He released his hand on the reins and sat back. Treasa kept the bay at a walk, which was the bay's frame of mind as well, apparently. The big horse settled to the track.

"When we got to Armagh—Kenneth, Kieran, Comgall, and I —a fileh was just—"

"What about Anice?"

"She took off north after Colm. We figured if she was going to be that stupid, let her. Anyway, a fileh was just arriving from Tara with the news. Diarmaid is the new high king." She paused a moment. *"Your* Diarmaid. The one you and Colm spirited out of his own tent all those many years ago. You don't act surprised."

"No surprise. Rumor had it he was tanaiste."

"Oh. So the first thing he did when he took the seat was put a price on your head. There are people all over Erin just hoping to earn themselves twenty cows by giving you over to Diarmaid."

"Why me?"

"You're a criminal, Gavin, didn't you know that? Theft of a slave. Theft of a horse. Some friend of his lodged the horse charge down in Leinster. Am I right that we're riding on it?"

"Right. Is that all?"

"Dishonoring a prince. There are some other charges too. Everyone knows it's political, but the reward is real enough. You don't dare stay in Erin."

"And I suppose you have a solution all worked out." His voice dripped sarcasm.

"We're doing this to help you, so don't try so hard to avoid sounding grateful, all right? Kenneth and I worked it out. In his own quiet way he's a really smart lad, you know that? The word at Armagh was that a new ri ruirech out here was throwing a three-day feast to usher in Sammhain."

"The word got all the way over to Armagh?"

"All the way to Tara, as I understand it. It sounded like your clan territory, and the filidh said you had a cousin named Oran, so we figured that either you'd be at the feast or someone there would know where you were. So I came straight to Oran's rath to find you. Only had to ask directions four times."

She waited. Silence behind her. She continued, "Colm said he was going up past Lake Neagh to the sea. Kenneth was born somewhere up here. So the lad thought about it a while and said that Colm is most likely to go to Derry. We should look there first for him."

104

"Why do we need Colm?"

"He has connections through his father's side to the Dal Riada. We figure he can get you an introduction somewhere up there in the Hebrides or maybe even the Caledonian mainland, set you up as a prince where Diarmaid can't get at you. The Dal Riada is pretty much independent of Tara."

"I have connections too, you know."

"Yes, but do you know Conal personally?"

He grunted, a negative sort of noise. "I notice you didn't ask me whether I'd like to do all this."

"No time. There are buggers all over Ulster right now, headed for your clan territory, ready to drag you away. I'm less than half a day ahead of at least two bands that we know about. You're going to attract cutthroats like a cow pie attracts flies."

"Beautiful poesy. You're such a flatterer." That sarcastic tone again.

"You're such an ingrate!"

The least he could do was apologize for his attitude. She was struggling her best to save him, and he grumped like a dog whose bone was stolen. *Aha.*

She twisted around to look at him. "Did you eat today?"

"A couple hazelnuts around midmorning."

She returned frontward. "I should have known. You always get testy—no, make that impossible—when you're hungry."

"I was sitting at a feast with twelve roast pigs just waiting for me. You could have put off your wild ride for another hour without too much trouble."

"Did you forget I mentioned 'highwaymen less than half a day behind me?' And you're worried about roast pigs. When you get to the Hebrides, maybe they'll roast you a pig."

"I don't want to go to the Hebrides."

"You don't have much choice." She licked her lips. "Mobhi's school isn't the only one breaking up. Most of them are. The big monasteries are so decimated that there's no safe haven for you anymore. Even Clonmacnois is down to a couple hundred people. We heard that at Armagh too. Mobhi's is just the latest, is all. Homeless monks by the hundreds."

He sighed heavily behind her. "Yes, but monasteries are sanctuary. As long as I stay with a brotherhood, they can't come in after me."

"You? Trapped inside a monastery the rest of your life? Singing services every three hours?"

"Soon as we meet up with Colm and Kenneth we'll be doing that anyway."

"Not Kenneth. He was fostered out to Finnian when he was so young he doesn't remember much of the area here, so he's not coming up. We pretty much agreed he probably couldn't be much help. Besides, he has bigger plans."

"Bigger plans?" Gavin seemed to be loosening up a little, losing a bit of the testiness.

"A trip to Rome!"

"Rome! Little Kenneth?"

"Isn't it something? And to some teacher named Cadoc at Llancarfan."

"Colm mentioned the name before. I'd think Kenneth would want to come home to relatives if he hails from up here."

"He's an orphan, Gavin, remember?" She shifted in the saddle. Her backside was getting stiff. "You said you were going home. Did you have time to look up your parents?"

"No."

Silence. They rode from darkness through darkness into darkness. The horse descended a hillside and either lost the track or the track lost them, for now the gelding was picking its way through boulders and thorns. Treasa pulled her feet clear up onto his withers, trying to avoid being scratched to the bone.

"Follow this creek." Gavin's voice sounded tight and angry again. "It will join the Foyle and take us to Derry."

"Not the easy way, I'll wager." She wished they had some light, but they didn't dare stop and wait until morning. The night was too cold, too long, too dangerous. "How long?"

"If the horse doesn't drop dead, late tomorrow, probably. And there better be a roast pig waiting at Derry."

The horse did not drop dead. There was no roast pig waiting at Derry. And unfortunately, there was no Colm there either.

Derry was a pleasant vale, home to perhaps half a dozen raths scattered about its gentle dips and rises. The valley widened casually as the river widened. The complaints of sea gulls replaced the whispers of falling leaves. The river became an arm of the sea, a lough not potable and bound by land but saline and subject to tidal rise and fall. Were Treasa to ride north to land's end, she would stand on the shore of the ocean.

She did not. She accompanied Gavin to the rath of the regional king at Drumceatt, there to eat anything and everything set before them. She bathed in warmed water, a luxury beyond price, and gently pampered her sorry, sore backside. She was as good a horseman as anyone, but twenty hours in the saddle is ten too many. A few hours' conversation with such a thoughtful and convivial host was the least she could return. Finally, about the time Colm and Kenneth in their various somewheres were singing Compline, she was able to retire. She slept nearly to Tierce.

This Drumceatt, as befits the rath of a regional king, offered far more amenities than did the farm of your average boaire . . . or did a monastery, for all that. When Treasa arose and dressed, a house girl offered to wash her hair for her and comb it out. Treasa accepted. Luxury. Instead of the braid, she let her hair fall loose, the better to get it dry in this damp weather of waning autumn. The same girl directed her to the kitchen.

A breakfast of porridge set her day to rights. She stepped out into the compound, and her day went suddenly to wrongs.

Colm the Dove came striding in the gate, and tagging hard at his heels came the little snip Anice! So somewhere, somehow, the two of them had connected up. Colm she was glad to see.

And here too Treasa discovered a cardinal truth that in the egalitarian atmosphere of a monastery usually slipped past her: She was not a royal; Colm and Gavin were. She watched them formally present themselves to the king. Their prince-ness showed through in every word, every gesture. They walked in this world with a bearing befitting rulers, and they did it comfortably. Treasa couldn't help but wonder whether the feckless Diarmaid wore the seven colors as effortlessly and as well.

She spent ten minutes braiding her hair up after all. Loose to blow in the wind, it was nuisance, getting in her eyes, firmly tethering her head in one place when she sat down on it.

She realized, once that was done, that she had nothing to do. The royals were probably ensconced in the close presence of a pitcher of ale, discussing Gavin's fate and future. It was Treasa who rubbed sores in unmentionable places getting Gavin out of harm's way, and now she was excluded from the talks. And it had been her idea—hers and Kenneth's.

Very well. If the high and mighty princes were engaged, she would play the lowly servant and go check on Gavin's horse. The poor old beast was muckle tired when they dragged in yesterday. Then she would seek out the armorer and talk about sharpening edges. She walked out the gate toward the horse sheds—and froze.

Not all the princes were courting ale. Two very familiar voices came from the paddock containing Gavin's horse, and neither of them would be the horse's. Quickly, Treasa gathered up her cloak, lest it snag on a paddock pole and make noise, and worked her way forward.

Treasa ventured a cautious peek. To say that Gavin and Anice were engaged in conversation would be inaccurate. Anice was interrogating Gavin as the brehons would question a murderer, with queries and accusations pressing hard, one after the other. She had him backed up against the wattle-woven paddock fence. Half his size and half his weight, and she had him thoroughly cowed. Treasa loved it! She hunkered down to listen.

Anice was fuming. "Then if that's so, why did you come back on that big horse and rescue me? Because as soon as you did, you ignored me again!"

Gavin: "I told you about the slave girl the boaire killed, and then Colm put out his arm and the man dropped dead. Colm could work a miracle, but even he couldn't save that girl. I was terrified that something like that could happen to you. I didn't want you to die by the hand of an owner. Forba would be cold enough to do that."

"Yes, but—"

"So I had to get you away from there. But then I didn't know what to do with you. After you were away from the danger . . . I didn't have any plan for what to do then."

Anice: "And do you happen to have any plan for what to do now?"

Gavin: "It looks a lot like those plans are being made for me. Colm has a boat lined up, and he's writing a letter."

"I mean about us!"

"What about us?"

"I'm old enough to marry. Fourteen."

Treasa's heart went thump. *That brazen vixen!*

Gavin: "I can't get married, Anice. Not now. Not with Diarmaid out to get me. It wouldn't be fair to the woman. And besides, I don't have any way of supporting a family. Never have. I'm not attached to any king, and I don't have a farm. I'm like a leaf floating down a stream."

"You're going to be attached to King Conal himself, as soon as you get to the Hebrides."

"Maybe. We'll see."

"I want to come with you."

"No."

"Yes!"

"End of it. No."

"Why not?"

"Not proper, just two of us. Colm would tell Conal to throw me into the sea. No."

"Why? I traveled with Colm to here, just the two of us. Nothing happened."

"And he's furious about it. Livid. If he could have dumped you safely, he would have. The answer is no." The wattles creaked. He was moving. If he headed this way, Treasa was undone.

She stood erect quickly and came strolling out around the fences, casually watching the ground ahead of her. She looked up at them, smiled and nodded. "I was going to check the horse. He was knackered last night. I see you beat me to it."

Gavin grinned. "He's still knackered. Look."

Treasa had to stretch on tiptoe to see over the fence, and she was not a small woman. The bay stood listlessly in a corner with one hind foot cocked, dozing, his ears a-flop.

Treasa cleared her throat. "You're sailing soon, right? The plan isn't messed up, is it?"

"Still on."

"Sure and this old beast isn't going to swim the distance, and I can't picture him in a curragh. Trade you the horse for my sword." She turned and looked at him.

"I have a sword." He gestured toward his hip.

"Then may I borrow him until you get back?"

"As far as I'm concerned, he's a prize of war, but Diarmaid doesn't see it that way. You don't want to get caught with a stolen horse."

"Then give him back to Diarmaid. I'm sure the little king would be pleased. And I'll wager the original owner will never see it again. It might even become a gift for a Pictish princess." She shrugged with mock carelessness. "Could happen. Do you suppose she's still around?"

The way he smirked told her he knew what she was doing. "You can borrow him until I need him again."

"Thank you." And then Treasa turned away and started back toward the gate before they could see her own smirk. She had successfully wheedled that splendid horse from Gavin. More important, the prince would soon be safe from Diarmaid's machinations.

But best of all—the very best of all—Anice's bold attempts to snare a hero were all gang aglee. Gavin had refused her. Colm had refused her. Treasa's day, now bright, was set to rights again.

Much against his better judgment, or so he claimed, Gavin allowed a little sailing curragh—a twelve-foot boat with one sail and two oarsmen—to carry him away, down the River Foyle to the sea and beyond. Treasa and the ex-snippet stood side by side, watching the boat shrink into a murky little dot and disappear.

To Treasa's right, Colm hooked his thumbs in his belt and watched. There went his cousin, his lifelong companion. Did the loss hurt? Surely so; yet from the outside it appeared he felt the separation not at all.

Treasa sighed. "What now? Sit quietly and wait for the plague to come?"

"It won't." Anice was still staring off down Lough Foyle.

Treasa glanced at her. "You're so sure?"

Anice nodded. "At Lough Neagh, where I caught up to him, a little stream on this side—where was that called, Colm?"

His voice, tight as a drum with anger, rumbled, "The Bior. Moyola Waters."

"There. He prayed out loud that the stream there would be the northern limit of the plague. We must have passed a dozen raths with fresh graves south of there. But not one since we crossed the Bior."

Treasa looked at Colm. He too intently watched nothing in the distant haze of Lough Foyle, as if he hadn't heard. Maybe he didn't hear. He seemed lost in thought.

Anice then captured his attention thoroughly, and Treasa's. She asked simply, in a dull tone of voice, "Marry me."

He stared. Treasa stared. There she went again, the snippet, her second proposal in two days. You couldn't fault her taste, but her tact was execrable.

Colm wagged his head, stammering. "I can't . . . you know . . ."

Her voice didn't brighten the least. "You're ordained. You can perform marriages. There have to be eligible boaires in Derry. And you're a prince. You can find me a good one."

Treasa stood there stunned. Double stunned. Gavin, as much a part of her life as her long braid, was gone. And now, this childwoman seemed hell-bent upon marriage with any warm body who had a cow to spare for a bride-price. She probably wouldn't even demand a bride-price, since her clan, the recipients, were nowhere near.

With a sudden clap of the hands Colm announced, "There's work to do," and he hastened back toward the rath.

Work to do indeed. Matchmaking. The shining prince as a matchmaker. The very thought brought Treasa's smirk back unbidden.

It took him two months. The next Imbolc, Anice was married to a rather stodgy and pedestrian overly-mature ri tuatha with two wives already in the grave, three sons older than the bride, and three thousand cattle leased out. Not a bad choice by a monk who was so scared of women.

111

Over the next several years, Treasa stayed with Drumceatt because she had no place better to stay. Her clan was becoming ever more closely associated with Finnian of Moville over on Strangford Lough, and her own mother had her to know that she was going to have to change her ways if she wanted to come home.

Why Anice wanted to stay in Erin, Treasa could not guess, nor would Anice say. They were less than a week's sailing-and-walking to Anice's ancestral home over in Pictland. Why didn't she return to her clan and her roots to find a man?

Diarmaid took time out from being ard ri to go home and kill the successor to his Connaught regional kingship, Ailill Inbanna. Why he thought Ailill was a threat or disappointment remained unclear. How much help the Picts offered, if any, Treasa never heard. Diarmaid, though, was developing a reputation for ruthlessness.

At the age of twenty-five, Colm established his first monastery at Drumceatt in pleasant Derry. Mobhi, who burned his monastery lest any more lives end within it, died of the plague before he could establish his new one. Finian of Clonard, the highly successful teacher who gathered so many of Erin's saints to study, died three years later. He was thirty-two.

11

Colm's Trial

Year of our Lord 561

The Three in One—
The hope of all
The glory of all
The judge of all

"I never thought I'd be coming back to Moville." Treasa settled into a corner of the kitchen with her pig rib and began stripping the succulent meat off the bone.

With a practiced flick of her knife, Aileen of Inishowen Head sliced the roots off a leek and reached for another. "No more surprised than I. Come to meet Colm, eh?"

Treasa nodded. "He sent for me to join him here, but I haven't seen him yet. Have you talked to him since he came?"

The cook snorted. "That lad's talked to nobody since he came. Spends all his days and nights in the scriptorium, copying. I bring him meals. Claims he needs books."

"'Tis true. Do you realize how many monastic churches he's started? Some of them considerable. Up at Drumceatt—"

"Derry."

"Derry. That area. It's huge. Now he has one down south at Kells, near Navan and Tara—Durrow. He even started one out on Lambay, that little island off the mouth of the Liffey. And they all need books." Treasa abandoned pulling at the meat and just gnawed directly. So much easier.

"And I take it ye never married." Aileen's interest in books was about as great as Treasa's.

"Thought about it a couple times. You never did either."

"Times have changed." Moville's dumpy old cook paused from maiming vegetables. "Me mum tells of the old days, with the brotherhoods freely admitting the married and the women. Once,

113

she says, 'twas a fine place to seek out a decent man, a monastery. No more. They listen too much to Rome, with her misguided ways. Excluding women—Bah!—except for the menial work, of course. We're good enough for that part."

"So you've given up looking?"

"Too fat and old to expect luck to prevail over circumstance."

Treasa snickered. Already nearly thirty-five, she also would probably be able to say that, and in too few years.

Aileen de-rooted another leek and began beheading purplish roots of some sort. "You gave up babies for battles."

"Well put, Aileen. Mercenary for a ri tuatha at the moment. One of the Monaghan, over west of Armagh."

Aileen eyed her with a wicked twinkle. "And who, pray tell me, wins?"

"When I fight we do pretty well. When I lead the sortee we prevail mightily. I have five hundred cattle, prizes of war, leased out to the Monaghan clients, and I'm not even a member of the clan."

The cook chuckled. Her ample middle bobbed, jiggling her equally ample bosom. She glanced out the doorway and stilled. Puzzled, Treasa leaned way forward and twisted to see.

A horse was clattering away out the gate. But you couldn't see the gate for the man standing between it and the kitchen.

Out in the yard, a mountain that was Finnian of Moville stood arguing with a person or persons unknown. All Treasa could see was an acre or two of cloak. She might not be able to see his opposer, but sure and she recognized both voices! She bolted to her feet, wiped her greasy hands on the linen towel at Aileen's waist, and hurried outside.

She jogged out across the beaten dirt of the compound and slipped in beside Finnian and his opposer. "Hello, Colm."

The blond giant grinned. He was forty years old and look at him—still no crinkles in the corners of those intense blue eyes.

"Treasa! See, Finnian? To insure the safety of any books I send, I've employed a capable mercenary. With Treasa on guard, they'll pass safely."

So that was why he sent for her. But sure and he wouldn't depend on her alone. She wondered who else was coming.

114

Finnian of Moville, tubby in his youth, had become a blob in his old age. If the man still had a neck, it was completely buried; his jowls and chins (plural) rested directly on his collarbone. His voice, a gravelly tenor, was the only solid thing about him. "No. It's not yours. No."

Colm's face hardened with barely-contained fury. "I spent how-many-weeks copying it! You knew that I intended to send it to Kells. You knew that all along. If you had no intention of releasing it, why didn't you say something at the start of my labor?"

Treasa picked a string of pork out of her teeth with a thumbnail. "What's going on?"

"You!" Finnian turned on her, blazing. "You disobeyed me and left Moville against my express orders. You're not welcome here. Leave!"

Treasa gaped in disbelief. "And you're *still* angry? That was twenty years ago! Things were different then. I was a child!" She paused for effect. "You could still fit through a door then."

Colm turned red with laughter. Finnian just turned red. He roared, "Your parents sent you to me. You were under my aegis!"

"I was under your roof and no more. Anybody can thatch a roof." She turned to Colm. "You have a problem?"

"He seems to think that now I've copied his book of Psalms for him, that I should not have the copy."

Finnian flung his attention back at Colm just as viciously as he had attacked Treasa. "You did it covertly. Sneaking around. You knew it wasn't yours, and it never will be."

Treasa looked from face to face. "I can't believe you two good brothers in Christ are arguing over a book. A simple, lousy book."

Colm fumed. "Do you know how long it takes to copy the complete text of the psalms? I did it by lamplight outside my regular duties and—"

"Without my knowledge!"

"And now he wants to rob me of a piece of my life. A considerable piece."

Treasa scratched her head. "Well, let's see. There's how many armed brothers here at Moville now? Five hundred? Eight hundred? So if we take your book by force of arms, it should be quite a pretty war. Or we could simply do old Finnian in. He's well past his prime anyway." She watched with delight as his red fury blanched to white. "But I'm not sure how. My sword isn't long enough to reach a vital organ through the fat. Garrotting is out of the question—look where his neck should be. He'd never feel it. Poisoning?"

Colm picked up the spirit of it instantly and shook his head. "He's been eating Aileen's cooking constantly all these years. He's enured to poison."

Finnian's fury returned. He glared from face to face. "You would make sport of me, your master, the lord of your youth? You owe me honor, not jibes!" In an absolutely perfect snit, he stormed away.

Treasa watched the man depart. Even with his draped tunic, you could see the fat bob lugubriously. "His sense of humor got suffocated under one of those layers of pudge."

"He never had one. However"—Colm sighed heavily—"he has a point. We do ill toward God to make sport with God's servant. Penance and apology are due."

Neither appealed to Treasa. "You're certain that book is yours?"

"Positive. I formed every character on its pages."

"Then let's just take it."

"Two of us against eight hundred? You're good with a sword. I'm good. But not that good."

Treasa kept her voice low and even, knowing full well exactly what she was saying. "If you really think the book is worth it, I can have five hundred blades under your orders in a week."

Colm knew too. "Let's give him a few days to see the light."

Giving Finnian ample time to muster whatever resources he wanted did not seem like good strategy to Treasa, but it was Colm's affair. She advised him, and then she shut up.

She had intended to spend a considerable part of her time at Moville putting decent edges on Finnian's weaponry. In sorry shape indeed were Finnian's blades. Now, with the prospect of facing that weaponry looming large, she went fishing instead. She didn't like fish. She detested eels. Flounder tasted all right, but it didn't look edible. Oysters? Bleh.

She could go hunting, but that would carry her away from the monastery into the hills—quite some distance from the monastery, the way the land was being stripped of its forests here—and with hell about to yawn wide open any moment she wanted to remain near.

Most of all, she wanted to fight again beside Colm. She still remembered that skirmish beneath the wych elm and the elation of it. Watching him wield a blade the way an ax should be wielded. Watching him move, throwing that immense and powerful body wherever he wanted it to be. Watching the fury in him unleash itself, the way the old stories described the hero Cu Chulainn.

And she thought about an earlier time, when the church in Erin would have welcomed her role as a warrior, would have welcomed the union of a monk with a defender of the monastery.

One spends altogether too much time thinking when one is fishing.

A fortnight passed, and Treasa began to lose patience with Colm's patience. The morning after new moon, she fell in beside Colm as he came out of the oratory following Tierce. "I have an idea."

"That worries me immediately."

"Burn the scriptorium, and we'll rescue all the manuscripts and just keep going. I can have Finnian's own chariot ready and waiting in half an hour."

Colm laughed. In fact, he laughed more than the suggestion warranted.

"What's so funny?"

"An old saint they called the Wizard, Cruithnechan."

"Cruithnechan. That means 'Little Pict.'" She hoped this didn't have anything to do with Anice.

"He was the authority of God in these parts, one of the old-time fathers whom God honored by giving the power to perform miracles. And he was my foster father."

"I hear tales, from Aileen mostly, that Finnian too had that power once upon a time."

"So I hear, though I never saw it. Cruithnechan insisted that Finnian should tear down his scriptorium and build a decent one. He never did. You'd be doing the spirit of the old Wizard an immense favor by torching the place." He stopped. His face melted into a scowl. He was looking toward the gate. "Diarmaid!"

Diarmaid, high king at Tara. So this was Diarmaid. Colm and Gavin had described him as a slow-thinking, somewhat flabby and effete suckling. Treasa saw instead a man who kept himself in excellent condition, an imposing man who wore all the colors well. But time had not dealt kindly with him. His dark hair was graying, but not gracefully, and an intricate spiderweb of lines spread out around his eyes and mouth.

Fifty armed mighty-men accompanied his chariot. In a gilt-trimmed chariot behind his, two brehons rode in haughty splendor. Most of the cortege and all the pack animals remained outside the gate of necessity. Just the chariots and a few retainers filled Finnian's little dooryard, and the obese abbot wasn't even taking up his part of it yet.

Colm did the minimal obeisance due an ard ri. Diarmaid did none of the obeisance due an abbot and founder of monasteries.

The king stepped down. Instantly his charioteer drove out the gate, probably to make room for Finnian.

Colm's voice, normally resonant enough to make mountains vibrate, purred like a dog's cautious growl. "Many years ago, when we were both young and foolish, I recommended we work together in the Lord's will. I trust you remember."

"Ever so clearly." The king stood a head shorter than Colm. He didn't seem the least intimidated. "We were young indeed, weren't we? And some of us more foolish than others."

"Some of us have not outgrown foolishness. You took the throne according to druidic ritual, with no mention at all, as I hear it, of God's power in your life. No invocation to God, no acknowledgment of Jesus or His sacrifice, no bow toward His divine lordship."

"Had you been there you would have known firsthand."

"I was on the track to Derry according to divine call. I didn't immediately hear of your good fortune."

Diarmaid's head bobbed, a dismissal. "The matter is of no consequence. Matters immediately at hand are the issue. Because Moville is under the leadership of Tara, Finnian made appeal to me to settle the problem of a purloined book."

"Hardly purloined."

"The problem of a disputed book. So I have brought the court's brehons to settle it."

"This is an ecclesiastical problem. Why not a council of abbots?"

"Because the world operates under brehon law, it has always done so, and so it shall always be. You want the decision to be both binding and lasting, do you not?" He turned away without actually learning whether Colm wanted a permanent decision and strode off toward the oratory, his obedient flock falling in behind.

Treasa doubted he was going there to pray. "If you get a fair call out of that mob, I weave daisy chains for a living."

"We'll see. Brehons are notoriously difficult to buy." Colm trusted the whole stuffy outfit a whole lot further than Treasa ever would.

If the blond abbot would not prepare for an unseemly outcome, she would. With the vernal equinox coming up shortly, the brehons would want to get this over with quickly. She didn't have much time. Colm's power centers were Drumceatt on the north coast and Durrow clear down by Cashel. The Monaghan at the moment were Treasa's, and they were Ulstermen with scant regard for Diarmaid. She spent a very, *very* long day in the saddle reaching the closest rath of the clan, and another very long day hastening back toward Moville. It took her until nearly noon the following day to get there.

She arrived with the court in full swing and her first wave of warriors at least a day behind her. The porter, a pimply young man with a bronze sword (what was Diarmaid thinking of, arming his people with that junk?), was going to deny her entrance to the refectory, the largest building available. She reduced him to a little pile of quivering semi-consciousness by raking the hard leather sole of her Roman-style caliga down his shin, stomping his instep, then disabling him with a well-placed knee. She felt a little guilty—just a wee bit—as she strode past him into the assembly. He was young and hadn't been expecting any of that.

She pushed through the crowd of monks and retainers, keeping close to the wall. A puncheon platform had been raised at one end. On it sat Diarmaid with his kingly snoot in the air. To one side sat Colm, glowing like sunlight. To the other, in a heavy oak chair of artful joinery and tight rawhide binding, sat the rotund Finnian. His chair creaked whenever he moved despite the fancy carpentry.

Clearly, the brehon who heard the case had been sitting with his back to the room and his face toward Diarmaid. His chair stood empty now.

In the oratory across the yard, a child's soprano began the call to the office of Nones. Midafternoon. Treasa had not eaten since before daybreak. No wonder she felt famished.

Commotion at the door caught her attention. Finnian and Colm stood up. Diarmaid did not. A tight wedge of warriors plowed a furrow down the middle of the refectory crowd. Behind them strolled the brehon and half a dozen assistants. Apprentices, probably. Behind the judge and his lawyers, the furrow closed in almost instantly.

The brehon acknowledged the king, Finnian, and Colm, and, still standing, turned to face the room. "The question before us today is not addressed in the main body of law. I venture the opinion that this is because books are such a new thing, and of value almost exclusively to monastics. The general population has no need of them. Therefore, the law has not dealt with them in detail. Related law, however, applies here. In husbandry law—"

A low murmur interrupted him. Treasa got a sinking feeling. Colm's case was being tried by a brehon who either didn't care or wasn't informed. She trusted brehons a lot better when they were delivering judgments out under a rowan tree, the proper place to try a case, and not in a dark, close box.

The judge continued. "In husbandry law, ownership is determined not by the sire but by the dam. Not the bull but the cow. By loose but apt analogy, we compare Finnian's ownership of the original book as possession of the cow. The copy then would be the calf arising out of the original, regardless the male who made it happen, as it were. To every cow its calf, and to every book its calf-book." With the barest of movements, the brehon gave his nod to Finnian, did a perfunctory obeisance to Diarmaid, stepped down off the platform, and headed toward the door behind his plow.

"The law has spoken. The crown concurs." Diarmaid smirked at Colm. Treasa saw the expression only in profile; even so, were she Colm she would have sliced it right off the cow's face. The ard ri followed his brehon out the door even as the stunned silence collapsed into a roaring swell. Happy monks laughed and shouted and began a couple of hasty *laudatums* that didn't really get anywhere.

The crown concurs. His brehon inserted the knife and Diarmaid twisted it. By law it didn't matter a whit whether the warlord agreed with a judge's pronouncement. Brehons operated independently despite being under a ri's tutelage. Not even the ard ri determined legal matters. His concurrence was a slap in the face, and nothing else.

The crowd quieted and parted. Colm was leaving the room, and he didn't need a phalanx of warriors to part a way for him. People looked at his face and stepped aside, fell back, squirmed to get out of the way. He strode forward, staring at the door before him, or perhaps the hills beyond, or perhaps the face of a God from whom he would call vengeance.

Once Colm was out the door, Diarmaid's steward announced a feast at Tara to follow equinoctial observances and invited all to attend. One might think that Columba the Dove of the Church was not welcomed.

From experience of the past, Treasa was aware of Columcille's three degrees of anger: mumbling, loud, and silent. When he muttered, you knew the pique would pass shortly. When he raged, the ire took longer to subside. This, though—this was his silent fury. He said nothing. The black scowl said all. This fury would not subside, no matter how long the time.

He gathered up what materials he could—the calf-book of Psalms not among them—and left within an hour of the verdict. He did not bid Finnian farewell or ask the abbot's blessing. Treasa didn't bother either.

Through Aileen, rather than Finnian's steward, Treasa left instructions for her arriving Ulstermen. Without saying a word to Colm, she slung two roughweave panniers across her saddle to help carry the books he could take. He had brought along three scribes from Kells and Derry. They loaded their donkeys with supplies and followed him in muted respect, even fear.

They took some work to Down, a considerable loop out of the way, and difficult road at that. Treasa made no complaint. Colm needed the time for healing. The monastery at Down received them well, but they stayed only a few days and headed northwest up the track to Drumceatt.

Now and again in her childhood, when water puddles had frozen overnight, Treasa would break out the thin sheet of ice and look at the world through it, endlessly interested by the way it twisted lines and shapes and blurred the edges of things. The rain laid a coarse gray bleariness just like that across the land as they arrived at Drumceatt. Treasa had always enjoyed playing with ice. She was rapidly developing an intense distaste for rain.

Eager monks carried the oilskin-wrapped books and partials into the scriptorium. Through one of the large windows, Treasa watched them gently, reverently, unwrap this piece and that. The brehon may have rendered the wrong verdict, but he had it right about books—except to monastics, books weren't much use.

Two days after their return, Treasa for the first time felt it safe to head back down to the Monaghan. Colm still brooded, but he had lost most of the patina of murder. He and his rosy-cheeked cohorts here faced months of copying in order to provide books for all his churches. Copying occupied the mind as well as the body—just what the blond lad needed.

She saddled up after Primes, accepted a gift of bread and boiled pork for the journey, and let Colm accompany her to his gate.

"You sure you're going to be all right?" She watched his face for any sign of lying or suppressed emotion.

He smiled grimly. "You worry too much, Mother."

"Not without cause. Diarmaid is going to pay dearly for this. You know it, and I know it. You've accomplished a multitude of wonderful things. If you misstep now, those things could—"

She stopped because his attention had been wrenched away from her to the lea beyond his gate. He wheeled and yelled, "To arms!"

Treasa had drawn her sword before she realized what she was doing. An army was approaching the gate, an army wet and bedraggled from a long journey. She raised a hand. "Colm! Peace. It's the Monaghan." She slammed her sword back into its sheath. "I left word with Aileen that they could go home. What they're doing here I have no idea. Rest easy in the knowledge that they're Ulstermen and no more impressed with Diarmaid than you are."

She stepped out the gate to greet the leader. Declan, ri ruirech of the Monaghan, soaking wet in the rain, grinned at her. Behind him, seventy-five or eighty men drew to a halt. Treasa smiled. His second-in-command, Fergus Gray Beard, looked like a drowned rat.

Beside Declan, a young man Treasa had never seen leaped off his horse and came running. He seemed a nice enough lad, at least on the outside. If his face were not so twisted by anxiety, he'd be quite a handsome bit. He brushed past Treasa and fell at the feet of Columcille. He grabbed Colm around the knees and nearly yanked the prince's legs out from under him.

His voice quavered. "My Lord Columba, I pray thee. Sanctuary! The high king, Diarmaid Mac Cerbaill, is trying to kill me!"

12

Curnan's Tragedy

In springtime, when kings go forth to war...

One of the primary reasons for a monastery's existence—and as far as Treasa was concerned it was the only important one—was to brew good ale. Left in the hands of cow farmers and minor ri tuathe, the brewing of ale could sing like a lyric ode or, far more frequently, curl the sides of the tongue and bite its tip.

"What we have here is a serious lack of uniformity across the land," she mused to herself. But then, hardly anything across Erin was uniform, except perhaps a fierce independence and a dogged delight in picking a fight.

Columcille's Drumceatt brewed fine ale. Treasa pondered this verity as she stared at the earthen ale jug on the table before her. Fergus Gray Beard, ri tuatha of Ballykeady, scooped up the jug for a swill and passed it to his right. Declan, ri ruirech of the Monaghan, appreciated fine ale when he tasted it. Treasa knew this because she had tipped many a jug with the man and for a while had considered marrying him. He sipped and passed the jug to Colm. He passed it on to Treasa.

He seemed more relaxed tonight than he had in weeks. Treasa attributed it to the company of kings sitting round his table. Colm, a prince forever, drew nourishment from royalty the way others draw nourishment from porridge.

She took a drink and passed it on to Curnan.

Curnan Mac Colman was still as anxious as a hedgehog in a fox den. His eyes flitted about, and he started at every little sound outside the door. He frequently reached up and fingered the shining brooch that held his cloak, apparently a nervous tic. His behavior was not particularly stolid, as would befit a hero, but it was certainly understandable—having the hounds of Connaught on your tail tends to make a person jittery.

His thick shock of light brown hair would benefit from some cutting, washing, and combing. It was healthy hair, though, crowning a handsome head. His eyes would never be as penetrating as Colm's, but they were almost as blue. And his physique, firm and well shaped, left nothing to be desired. How old was he? Treasa would guess late twenties, but she wasn't particularly good at estimating ages.

Curnan wiped his mouth on his sleeve and passed the jug to Fergus. Fergus set it back on the table before them. "We'd received your message through that big cook—what's her name?"

"Aileen of Inishowen Head. Been there since God made His first crabapple." Treasa sat back and leaned against the wall.

"Her. Telling us to go on back home—that you'd left for Drumceatt with Columcille here. We were some disappointed, I'll have you to know. A chance at lopping some Connaught heads, and all for naught. So we hung around a while, thinking maybe you'd come back unannounced. That Aileen said Columcille here was furious beyond words."

Beside him, Declan the loon grinned wickedly. "Quite the gossip, Aileen, and a delight to talk to. She told us things about you the like I've never heard."

Fergus grinned just as wickedly, and Treasa would have loved to lop Aileen's blathering head, should heads be lopped. Fergus picked up the tale. "We'd more than worn out our welcome—old Finnian made that abundantly clear—so we took our time folding up to leave. Suddenly, along comes Curnan here, blazing up the track."

Curnan rubbed his face wearily. "I asked Finnian for sanctuary. He said—"

"Wait." Colm spoke for the first time in minutes. "Kells is very close to Tara. Why did you not seek refuge at Kells? Or south to Lambay or Clonmacnois? Or completely out of Diarmaid's way into Durrow or Cashel?"

Treasa scowled. "Think, Colm! Clonmacnois is the very middle of Diarmaid's patrimony."

Curnan shook his head. That shock of hair floated. "He was after me, driving me north. Pressing me. I couldn't go where I wanted. When my horse dropped dead under me I thought sure I was lost, but apparently their horses were in little better shape. So I pushed on to Moville. I knew it was a large monastery, and I thought it would offer safety." He wagged his head. "I never was very good at politics."

"I should think not. Showing up at the gate of one of Diarmaid's most ardent supporters." Treasa glanced at the jug, but she was too comfortable and too lazy to sit forward and start it on another round. "The ard ri was probably shoving you intentionally into Finnian's lap."

"So we took him in," Fergus concluded, "and decided to bring him up here."

"To murder a king on purpose . . ." Colm's voice carried the rumbling freight of heavy warning.

"He wasn't a king; he was a civil servant. Basodan Mac Nonneadh, and—"

"Nonneadh is a king of Erin."

"But Basodan wasn't in a direct line. And I swear, it wasn't on purpose!" The anxiety began to build again in the fugitive. "Anger. Heat of the moment. 'Twas a silly game, played at leisure. At hurley we were. Outside the wall at a game of hurley. He insulted me, and I responded without thinking. One thoughtless sword stroke, and my life is ruined forever."

"That depends," Colm purred. "Have you ever been a copyist?"

Treasa let fly an impolite word unfit for kings, princes, or abbots. "Colm, can't you think of anything else?"

The big man shrugged. "He's welcome to sanctuary here. He can sit in idleness and quietly go crazy or put himself to productive labor."

Apparently to mollify Treasa, for he looked right at her, Curnan offered, "I can learn. I'm considered a ready pupil."

"Aargh!" Declan, bless him, took a swill and started the jug around. "So the dust settles and again we have no action. Young Curnan holes up with the prince here—through him, therefore, under the protection of all the sons of Earc. Everyone sits around cheerfully writing books, and we get to ride home to Monaghan and stare at our fingernails some more."

Fergus gazed roofward. "Ah, the sweet charm of life! So

much adventure, so little responsibility." He turned his eager attention to the progress of the jug.

"The luck." Colm again passed the jug without sampling. "I fully expected Diarmaid at our gate by now. You think you've got a ride. I already sent for a couple detachments to back up my own force here. Now I'm going to have to tell them to turn around."

"Feed them first." Treasa sat forward to receive the jug. "Who?"

"Cheartach—"

"Earca's lad?"

"The same. Aidmire, Sedna's son; Nainidh. Their tuathe. Some others from up in the Dal Riada."

"It must be nice to be related to so many good military men." Treasa sent the jug on to Curnan, her thirst momentarily slaked. She sat back. No one in her clan was a fighting man to speak of, especially her father. A cobbler and harness maker, he constantly reeked of half-tanned leather. His ri more than once said that for the protection of his own fighting force, he kept her father well away from swords.

"None better than the Earc." Colm didn't say it in a proud or haughty way. He simply said it. And it was true.

They spent another three hours in relaxed and easy repartee. Colm told stories on Treasa that Declan had not heard from Aileen, and Treasa, with plenty of dirt on Colm, returned in kind.

Curnan began to loosen up a little. You could watch him change as he finally grasped that he was safe here. He actually became somewhat animated and told a couple of woolly tales of his own.

Treasa noticed that he fit comfortably among this royalty. Curnan Mac Colman. The only two Colmans Treasa knew were both abbots. If Curnan had been playing hurley with the son of Nonneadh at the ill-fated feast, though, he was either a royal or a relative of royalty. And if so, why did he not call upon his own clan for safety? She would ask him sometime. He was their responsibility, not Colm's.

She didn't get the chance. The next morning, Colm sent Declan and Fergus Gray Beard on their way. Treasa had no reason to stay here at Drumceatt, and she could not understand why she so much wanted to do so. She saddled up for the long ride home with her Monaghan.

With the effusive prayers for blessing you would expect of a church leader, Colm signed the cross in front of everyone's faces —even the horses'. The little army took to the track, and Drumceatt melted into the rain mist the way honey melts in water. You see it, and then you think you see it only because you know it's there.

They would follow the rivers, taking the easy way home. They had to string out into single or double file when the track entered the forest ten miles south of Derry. Treasa fell in behind Fergus.

Ahead of Fergus, Declan twisted in his saddle and leaned on his horse's rump. He called back, "Finnian and the abbot of Kildare —you really did braid their horses' tails together while they were in Vespers?"

"Not Vespers. Compline."

Fergus twisted around also. "Is it true that Columcille can perform miracles?"

"You went to bed relatively sober last night. That's a miracle."

Declan guffawed. Fergus, undaunted, pressed on. "I mean real ones. Did you ever see a miracle? See him do one?"

"Remember the dried apples they served last night?"

"Soaked soft and awash in fresh cream. Delicious!"

"They came from that crabapple tree on the south side of the monastery."

Fergus made a noise. "Kind of big for a crabapple tree, isn't it? Besides, I know crabapples when I eat them. These were the sweetest I ever tasted."

"That's because soon after Colm arrived in Derry, so I hear, he stood in front of that very tree, did his sign-of-the-cross motion, and said, 'In the name of the Almighty God, Bitter Tree, let all your bitterness depart and all your apples be now changed into the sweetest.'"

Fergus's eyes practically popped. "But you didn't see it yourself."

"Well, actually, no. But I heard about it. A story—you know?" The strangest feeling suddenly seized her. She heard Declan and Fergus asking her if something was wrong. They seemed distant.

She drew her horse to a halt. "No, nothing's wrong. At least, I wouldn't exactly describe it as wrong. I feel like Colm is calling us to come back."

Declan wrenched his horse around and pulled up beside her. "What do you mean?"

"Sure and I don't hear voices or anything. It's not a vision. It's just this strong feeling that Colm wants us to return."

Fergus squeezed his horse in at her other side. "I say do it. They've been good friends for a long time—close connection—and he has the gift. If the feeling's false, why, we've ridden a little farther is all and nothing lost."

That momentary dreamy feeling abandoned her. Now it was as if it had never happened. "There's an urgency about it. I'm going back, Declan. I hope you do too."

Declan nodded abruptly and barked orders back through the line. Long, long moments later, the track behind them began to clear as the men streamed north, toward Drumceatt.

This was foolishness. In another hour, Treasa was going to look absolutely stupid. Comfortably seated in his bright and airy scriptorium, Colm would glance up momentarily, say, "What are you doing here?" and return to his precious copying.

Declan pushed hard, keeping the pace up. Treasa's horse broke into a sweat. Lather foamed up on its neck and flanks. A couple of the small ponies fell well behind.

Two miles below Drumceatt, as the river plain widened out and the skies opened, the ranger named Harlaigh came clattering back to join them.

"Tracks of another army," he reported, "mostly afoot. Marched west and returned toward the east. Very fresh. Within hours."

Declan spurred his horse forward with renewed vigor.

Treasa's horse was spent to the point of dropping dead when they pressed up the slope of the lea before Drumceatt. The gate stood open and unattended. Keening inside rose above the ring-walls, above the peaked roofs. Keening and cries. Gray-white smoke curled up from somewhere around the refectory.

Treasa leaped off her horse before it had settled to a stop and yanked her sword on the way through the muddy gateway. "Colm? We're here! We're back! Colm?"

The slaughter had begun at the gate with the two porters and extended out into the courtyard. No Colm. Her sword at ready two-handed, Treasa jogged over to the open doorway of the oratory, the next logical place to look.

He was here. At the far end of the big room, Colm stood leaning against the lectern looking dazed, his hands empty. A book from the lectern had fallen at his feet, spoilt by blood. From the blood that spattered his tunic and soaked him from his armpit to his shoe, Treasa could gauge the battle—a mighty one.

Curnan Mac Colman, so lately a fugitive, so lately admitted into sanctuary, lay ten feet to this side of the lectern. Treasa recognized him from his body build, that gleaming brooch, and the clothing. The head was gone, severed and stolen.

She stepped forward. "Colm?" Her sword tip drooped, digging into the rushes on the floor.

She pivoted, swinging her sword up to meet a noise and a sudden darkening of the light behind her.

He filled the doorway, blocking the sun. Gavin Mac Niall, the White Hawk, burly and handsome as ever.

His sword wavered in front of his face a moment. He lowered it. "Treasa!"

Surprised as she was to see him, Treasa was even more startled by the darkness and fury in his face.

"Colm asked me to come down and help tend a baby." He looked at Colm, at the decapitated remains, at her. "I can see there's going to be a war."

13

Culdrevny's Glory

You do not go forth with our armies, God.
O grant us aid against our foe,
For vain is the help of man.

The song began, "O God, you have rejected us and broken our defenses." Colm's voice at full throat could call whales in from the sea. With Gavin at his side, he sat his horse by the gate of Drumceatt, his arms uplifted, and raised his voice, that magnificent voice, to heaven. It rolled forth out over the lea, down the hill, along the rivershore. It rolled forth above the heads of myriad fighting men and women, thousands upon thousands, spread across the lea and hill and shore.

A dot amid that myriad, Treasa stood in awe of the man, of his family, and of the army he had mustered out of his clans of the Ui Neill. Not directly of the Ui Neill, the Monaghan were there anyway. Sure and they wouldn't miss it for the world, claimed Declan, with Fergus Gray Beard nodding hearty assent. Declan stood at Treasa's elbow with his mouth open, as rapt as everyone else.

That voice swelled ever more powerfully as the song ended. "With God we will fight valiantly! Who will squash our enemy? Our God!"

Sudden, dashing silence rang across the sky, as if the world were holding its breath. Then the shout went up, a war cry of all war cries, exuberant, reverberating, deafening. Who could doubt victory? Treasa shouted as loudly as kings, as free clients and base, and no one heard her for the din. No one heard the kings either. Declan's shout beside her was buried just as deep.

With Gavin at his side, Colm came riding down off the hill. Cheartach Mac Earc, Aidmire Mac Sedna, and Nainidh fell in behind them, a roll call of Erin's finest warriors. Other kings joined the lead, men from up north whom Treasa had never met. The column drew nigh, and Declan left Treasa's side to take his place as a ri ruirech.

"The sons of Earc have been violated," Gavin had declared in his pep speech preceding Colm's prayer. Until this undertaking, Treasa had barely ever heard of the Earc, one of the ruling families of the northern Ui Neill. Now she rode with them. She fell in beside Fergus.

The Gray Beard rearranged himself on his saddle, settled in for the long haul. "One of Gavin Mac Niall's people tells me that Columcille there writes songs. Composes poems and sets them to music."

"He does. Poetry is a love of his. But he didn't write that one. That one is a Hebrew song he translated into Gaelic; he told me it comes out of the very book Finnian denied him."

"Indeed."

They rode in silence awhile, savoring the delicious irony of it. Would Colm have gone after Diarmaid over that book if Diarmaid had not violated sanctuary? Treasa would almost think so. Sooner or later, Colm would have picked a fight. Propitious it was, that the fight was picked for him.

Did Diarmaid do that on purpose? Probably. Diarmaid did not think much of monastics or the church. He held sanctuary in much lighter regard than did Colm. Still, he surely knew what he was doing when he blazed through the gate of Drumceatt, cutting down its defenders.

Another idle speculation: Did Curnan's head now hang from Diarmaid's saddle, a trophy? Undoubtedly.

Fergus grunted. "Did you see the slice in Columcille's side? The sword wound?"

Treasa nodded. "Took out a part of his rib. He went down fighting."

"Aye! Ribs are the worst for hurting, besides feet. If not the weakness, there's the pain. How does he manage to stay in the saddle?"

"Tough enough to rust, both of 'em."

Fergus grunted appreciatively. "Sure and Diarmaid knows we're coming."

"A mob this size is hard to miss, ri. He'll be waiting."

"Can you speculate where?"

"We were talking about that last night. Cheartach and Aidmire think he'll beat it back to Tara. Colm and Gavin say he'll head for Connaught. Declan thinks Cashel."

"I don't remember any conversation of the sort."

"You passed out before we got to that subject. Next time take smaller sips when the ale jug passes by. Either way, Diarmaid will surround himself with as big a force as he can muster."

"Quite the battle 'twill be, where e're we meet!"

Quite a battle.

They met at Culdrevny, near the ford. Colm's thousands arrayed out across the hills. On the slope opposite, nearly as many thousands gathered. The sheer enormity of the forces stunned Treasa. If Diarmaid was concealing half his chariots and nearly all his cavalry, as Gavin was doing, the power was pretty evenly divided.

Suddenly Treasa couldn't sit still. She abandoned her place as just another soldier and rode forward through the mob to join Declan and Gavin.

Gavin was studying the forces lined up across the way. He glanced at Treasa as if she belonged there. "Recognize anyone?"

She was looking not for familiar faces but for a familiar head. If Diarmaid still had Curnan on his saddle, it was on the far side by his other knee. Treasa saw no trophies hung from this side. "Diarmaid, of course, dun horse with the red plume there. The two on the matching bays are sons of Murray—Domhall and I forget who the other one is."

"Fearghus." Declan pointed to a regal-looking fellow at the fore of a chariot crew on the east edge. "Hard to tell, but isn't that the son of Eochaid?"

Treasa had never seen that particular prince of Connaught before. Sword fodder, like all the others.

Beyond Gavin, Colm the warrior of warriors carried no spear or javelin, no sword, no ax. Just how he planned to meet the enemy escaped Treasa.

"Shall we call for champions," Gavin asked, "or just wade into them?"

Declan snorted. "If you don't wade into them, you'll have a couple thousand angry, disappointed people cursing your back. We're spoiling for a fight. Give it to us."

Without pointing or moving in his saddle, Gavin nodded. "Treasa? You're in charge of cavalry. Split them. Send that Fergus of the Monaghan with half of them east around the oak copse and in from the side. You take the rest. Dismount and lead the horses along behind those hawthorns to the west of us. When you see the rest of our chariots rush forward, mount up and hit them from the rock outcrop there. Know what I mean?"

Treasa twisted left to study their east flank, turned to study the west. "Got it."

"Then here's where we have the fight."

Declan purred, "Have at it. They're watching us."

"The fight?" Treasa gaped as Gavin suddenly barked something angry and unintelligible. Declan shook his fist and shouted at him. He muttered. "Want to join in?"

"Love to! What are we doing?"

Gavin yelled at her. She yelled back. Gavin swung at her, pulling the punch by inches. She slid off her horse and plopped into the grass as Declan's mount danced nervously aside to give her room.

Gavin waved his arms, shouting. Colm made wild peacemaker gestures.

In the midst of all this, Gavin explained in normal tones, "Letting Diarmaid think we're at odds with each other. Disunited. We're going to engage the enemy in disarray, so to speak, and then suddenly firm up. Colm's idea, to put them off balance."

Declan purred, "Can't hurt," and waved his arms angrily at Gavin.

Treasa grabbed up her horse's reins and led it hastily away, limping, shouting threats. Beautiful! Beautiful!

Colm bellowed "Peace! Please!" in that penetrating voice. Sure and Diarmaid heard it plain as thunder.

With a final shout and a raised fist, Treasa buried herself within the mass of troops. She pushed on, headed to the back, and she could not restrain her grin.

She joined Fergus. "Come."

He slid off his horse and fell in beside her. "That part went well. Gavin cued us this morning. Columcille's cousin was telling me about himself. Exiled to Dal Riada. He's taking a chance, coming back to Erin, aye?"

"Aye." *If everyone else in the army knew about the diversion, why wasn't I told?* "We're pretty certain Diarmaid can recognize Gavin as an outcast, even after all these years. It should be interesting. There was a price on his head before. I'll bet ten cows it's just gone up."

A noisy argument broke out along Gavin's west flank. With a loud and impatient "We quit!" the whole two-hundred-man force of the Cathray lowered their spears and walked away in apparent disgust. Gavin called to them in vain to come back. They took the three hundred troops of the Mountain Behr with them. The Behr had stripped for battle. With disgruntled gestures, they put their tunics back on as they walked away.

The Gray Beard giggled. "Know where they are going to turn up? They're going to run the two miles back that creek and down behind the hill there and show up right near Diarmaid's horse's tail."

Treasa cackled delightedly. She sent Fergus and his four hundred horsemen on their way. Even as she led her four hundred and fifty in that clever sneak behind the hawthorns, she heard the war shouts ululate across the vale.

The struggle was on, and she couldn't see it all hunched over behind the hawthorns. She tried to imagine Diarmaid surging forward against the scattering northern Ui Neill, only to have them come swooping around as one against him.

Diarmaid was too good a leader to lay all his troops out in the open. Sure and he must have more than one nasty surprise in store, just as Gavin did.

She assembled her cavalry in the shelter of the outcrop and sent rangers up the hill to make sure equally sneaky men of Diarmaid would not stumble upon them. Now she must wait, a harder thing by far than attacking. The Tyrone stripped. In their glittering gold torques and leathern belts they waited. The Catheir stripped. The Doughals.

135

Treasa's skin prickled, for over to the east the second wave of chariots came rumbling forward, threading down across a rocky little stream bed at the rear. They picked up speed on the open upslope. Here they came hurtling, over the crest and down the slope. They rolled wildly, recklessly, thunder on wheels, out of sight beyond the outcrop.

"Now." Treasa swung aboard her horse and drew her sword.

She waited until they were bursting out into the open before shouting. Her riders picked up the shout behind her. Their cry became a howl of joy and fury, four hundred and fifty voices raised against the enemy, fresh to the attack. First among them, she drove her horse forward toward the exposed west flank of the prince of Connaught.

Many the time she lay alone in the dark at night, questioning the wisdom of choosing the life she led. No man. No babies. As always, in the heat of battle her doubts became the first casualties. *This moment! Yes! This moment right here, with chaos and blood and screams all around. This moment of horror and splendor. Yes!* Her blood roared; her senses sang. *Yes!*

The son of Eochaid, prince of Connaught, was falling back. As Treasa's horsemen pushed toward him, he fell away. Then one of Diarmaid's surprises burst forth upon them as a troop of cavalry came roaring out of an alder grove to the west.

Treasa kneed her pony aside to meet them. The Tyrone reached them first. And now Mac Eochaid came a-roaring, renewing a frontal attack swiftly upon them.

Hard pressed on two sides, Treasa veered east, getting out of the way of the cavalry behind her. She changed directions again, kneeing her pony south into Mac Eochaid's line. She missed by a yard skewering a warrior, and he missed by a hair skewering her. Her backswing took out the man behind him.

Two women were coming at her. She slammed her horse into one as she parried the lance thrust of the other. Her horse bobbed to a halt, penned by warriors. In the periphery of her vision to the right, a mounted warrior was raising something against her, and she was too entangled to respond in time. Then Clavis Mac Ewin pushed in beside her, protecting her off side, engaging the figure.

Here came the Mountain Behr and the Cathray! With screams to put banshees to shame, they ripped into Mac Eochaid's rear. They hamstrung the prince's chariot horses, for the team literally dropped out of sight. Men from the east came running to Mac Eochaid's aid, but they were too late.

Slashing, spinning her horse, driving it up over fallen bodies, Treasa and her cavalry cut a wedge through the Eochaid.

And then it was over. The fight had not abated, the screams had not lessened, but you knew it was over. More would die in the next few moments, but it was over.

Diarmaid's men broke and ran. Jubilant, the Derrymen pursued. *Yes! Yes!*

Squealing, Treasa's horse dropped out from under her. She hit the ground rolling, tucked, and came up on her knees facing backwards. Whoever hamstrung her horse would fall upon her immediately. Her arcing sword and the charging warrior met in the middle. He collapsed artlessly beside her horse.

She bolted to her feet and turned a half circle. No one alive and moving was close enough to engage. The battle roared south, departing from her. She stood amid the carnage a moment, slashed her crippled horse's throat, and headed for high ground.

Colm! She recognized the white-blond head a quarter mile away on the crest of the slope. It would appear he had not moved five feet from where he'd been at the start of battle. She ran to him, slipping repeatedly in the bloody grass, stumbling, falling. And she stopped.

His eyes closed, that fair face sweaty, he knelt in ardent prayer. She did not speak. Silently, she moved in enough to read the sign on the ground around him. So far as she could tell, his troops in their thousands had streamed past him on both sides into the battle. Chariot wheels cut marks not six feet from him. As far as she could tell, he had not moved a muscle the whole time. The grass immediately around him remained untrodden.

She backed away, leaving Colm to his prayer, and walked down the hill again. How many dead there were! Hundreds. Tens of hundreds. Already the buzz of flies was picking up where the shouts and screams had left. One crippled horse or another would nicker or neigh. Here and there the wounded moaned. A raven called in the distance.

In the eerie near-silence, her heart began to thump audibly. The fight was over. This time right now was always the hardest time of all for her. She wanted her vibrating body to settle, and it would not.

Her people, Colm's army, commenced streaming back to strip the dead, canty in their joy of victory. Treasa would celebrate as heartily as all the rest tonight. Just now, though, standing in the middle of this horror with so many graves to dig, her heavy, heavy heart could not sing.

It didn't have to, for from the hill came Colm's voice. She turned to look.

He stood radiant in the waning sun, his arms aloft. Already loud enough to be heard for half a mile, that voice began to swell with a most wonderful song of praise. The tune was Celtic, probably one of Colm's own, but the words sounded straight out of that psalm-book.

"Praise the Lord from the heavens! Praise Him, you sun and moon. Praise Him, you shining stars!" And then, a couple verses later, "Praise the Lord from the earth!"

The happy hubbub of the victors quieted. They stood in bunches and crowds among the slain, listening. The final words, "Praise the Lord," died away. And then Colm began a hymn Treasa knew well, one of Patrick's songs of praise.

"You, the king of moon and sun, you the king of stars, beloved . . ."

Without fully realizing what she was doing, Treasa picked up the melody and joined the song. Behind her, several monks from Drumceatt began singing also. The music built, voice upon voice upon voice, hundreds of voices raised in praise, until both sky and valley filled end to end with the exuberant Celtic hymn.

Even when the melody died, the praise lived on. Colm gave the victory to God. Was Treasa to say otherwise?

A month after his glorious triumph, and his rib not quite healed, Colm received word from Finnian of Moville to hasten south. A synod was being called in Telltown. For his part in the slaughter of three thousand, Colm was to be excommunicated.

14

Culdrevny's Woe

Sweet Beltane Lamb who goes before
  to lead us safe to golden shores
Sweet Mary's Lamb who died before
  to lead us into Evermore

Resplendent in white robes was he, their fluting held neatly in place with a jeweled belt. His heavy gold collar draped from shoulder to shoulder, covering half his chest. The chief druid stepped between the two fires, laid but as yet unlit.

Anice always loved this part. She and hundreds of others waited and watched in anticipation.

The first sunstreak of dawn shot out from behind the eastern hills. Imperiously, the druid pointed a long, bony finger toward the great, propped cone of birch logs beside him. To the oohs and aahs of the assembly, it *fwooshed* into open flame. He pointed to the other. It ignited just as dramatically. Beltane observances had begun.

Of the fire festivals, Anice liked Beltane best. Not the least of the reasons for her preference was that by the first of May you didn't freeze your toes off, the way you did with the winter festivals. Boaires by the score commenced to drive their livestock between the fires, to purify them and render them safe from most harms. Pimply boys and nubile girls leaped the fires to bring fertility or luck or both.

So far, Anice had precious little of either.

Anice of Drumderry, she was once. Then, Anice the wife of Colin of the High Wall, ri tuatha near Limavady. And now? Nothing, probably. Anice of Nothing. She could not fight them all.

Traveling down the tracks of Erin was highly dangerous for a woman alone. Anice, though, had learned a thing or two during her abortive year at Moville, besides how to milk that obstreperous black cow. She wore a plain wool tunic without dye or embroidery, and over it a dark brown cloak with a hood. Barefoot, she looked just like one of the devoted sisters of Moville's monastery. Highwaymen, rapists, and robbers usually left nuns alone.

Telltown in Meath. She could find Meath just fine. Hadn't Gavin traveled her all over Erin on the huge bay horse? She wondered whatever came of that horse. Treasa had it for a while, she knew —Treasa with that long blonde braid.

Ancient memories mixed with new. Anice rehearsed the memory of Treasa leading four hundred horsemen against eight hundred Connaughtmen. There was a daring there, a boldness, a foolhardiness that Anice hungered for. She had none of that. She thought of Treasa's matchless horsemanship; the woman gripped her sword in both hands, the reins looped loose on the horse's neck, and yet the horse veered and dipped and feinted wherever the rider wanted it to go. It was the first Anice had ever seen Treasa in battle.

She thought about Columcille, her hero of yore. The moment the battle began he dropped to his knees in prayer, and he stayed there unmoving until the last foe fled.

And that song, Patrick's song, joyously ringing out! Her voice, added to all the others, had been a part of that.

Her other hero, Gavin—she had never expected to see the Hawk again. The sight of him stirred in her feelings she had known nothing about in her earlier innocence. She understood them now.

She must press on. As the sun made a full appearance, she left behind the fires and feasting and the druids' magic. The track wound in leisurely esses down the hill to join the main road to, eventually, Kildare. Going down would have been easy were not so many cattle and sheep coming up. The numbers of lambs and calves suggested that last year's Beltane fertility rites certainly worked handily. The baaing and lowing blotted out much of the spring bird song.

She sat at the roadside and waited a while where the tracks joined. Should a ri or boaire with retainers happen by, she could improve her safety by attaching to them. Here came three monks. That was almost as good as swords and brawn. She greeted them, they greeted her, and in moments she had been invited along. From Kells they were. From Drumceatt she was. Delighted. Likewise.

The down side of traveling with monks was to listen to incessant discussions of topics of no interest to her. They talked about the preferred dating of Easter observance. This being Beltane, they talked at length about lambs and sacrifice. And then the subject shifted to Telltown.

"You three are going there, I presume," Anice said.

"Certainly, for we're Columcille's monks. He built a splendid, splendid monastery at Kells. Have you seen it?"

"No. I've not been there."

"Bright, airy scriptorium, windows in the oratory and rushes on the floor, and a refectory big enough to hold everyone at once."

Another monk ventured, "Curious. And sad. Consider: Some of us have traveled to Rome. Now there are buildings! Stonework that will last forever. Marble floors. And spacious! Vast! And yet— this is the sad and curious part—when we come home and build our own facilities, we make them dark and crude and much too small. Look at Finnian's scriptorium at Moville. Dark as a cave and twice too small to hold his copyists' benches. And yet the books he copies there came from Rome, by his own hand."

Another chimed in, "And Aghaboe! Have you been to Aghaboe? Hundreds of monks stuffing themselves into an oratory built for fifty. And yet Kenneth spent quite some time in Rome."

"Kenneth?" Anice interrupted. "I know a Kenneth; coppery hair, a pleasant young man. Hardly a warrior. And I believe he indeed went to Rome."

"That would be him." The monk nodded. "And he's a warrior indeed. A prayer warrior! Works miracles through prayer."

"As does Columcille."

The man nodded sadly. "As does Columcille. But miracles seem to count for naught when the synod meets. Bishops. Bah. Bunch of grumps inflated by their own importance."

"Be fair," said the first. "'Twas not the bishops who called this one."

They murmured as to how that was so.

141

"Then who did?" Anice asked.

"Why the man who's made Telltown one of the royal centers for his patrimony."

Another: "The man who was sorely trounced despite superior numbers and the cream of the south's fighters. That sort of thing irritates an ard ri." And they all laughed.

Diarmaid called the synod? That did not bode well at all. Anice traveled thenceforth under a heavy cloud of gloom.

By the time they found Telltown and arrived at the site—not a church or monastery but a royal banqueting hall—the session was apparently well under way. Dressed as monastics, they had no difficulty getting past the porters. Well, not much, anyway. Apparently, brehons and druids were more welcome than Christians. The place was jammed with listeners, standing elbow to elbow.

All manner of church men—and women—sat in a great semicircle at the far end of the room. Only one woman took her place as a bishop. That would be the abbess of Kildare, for since the time of Brigid, Colm once explained, that seat was a bishopric. The very, very broad shoulders seated amongst the abbots would have to be Finnian of Moville. There could not be two that size.

Colm? Where was the hero of her childhood? There! Proud and tall, he stood to the side with his hands folded before him, able to watch but nowhere near the center, flanked by brehons. Not monks.

Treasa of all people stood in the little open space in front of the semicircle. With animated gestures, she was telling about the crabapple tree. Surely everyone had heard the tale of the crabapple tree.

Anice worked her way down closer, quietly slipping between this standing spectator and that one.

The woman before them now, the widow of a ri, lamented about the deaths of her husband and sons, fallen at Culdrevny. She wept. She cursed the Ulstermen. Anice pressed in closer.

Another took the floor with virtually the same testimony, the needless deaths of loved ones. Anice could see the rhythm and method of what was happening here. She thought a moment about what she might do. When she entered this building she had assumed she was powerless to alter the outcome. All the monastics thought that. Perhaps that was not entirely true.

Silently she pushed in front of a woman near the semicircle and whispered, "I don't know why, but the fellow says I'm to be next. I'm frightened. Are you?"

The woman stepped back to give her room. "Terrified. Blessings, Lady." Her face was already tear-streaked.

"And the same to yourself."

The witness in the circle walked away, dabbing at her weepy eyes. The brehon behind the circle waved impatiently to Anice, frowning.

She stepped forward, her insides frozen absolutely stiff with terror. She had to stand silent a moment, her mind forcing her legs to remain still, for she so intensely wanted to run. She could not bear to look at Colm at the far side there.

"I am Anice, widow of Colin of the High Wall, uh, a ri tuatha of good name, uh, near Limavady."

From behind her, "Louder!"

She thought about Treasa plunging recklessly into the midst of the foe, that sword slashing, her very life on the line. Anice was plunging recklessly as well, but the worst they could do was eject her from the building. She had, in essence, nothing to lose here. A Pict, she possessed little interest in the hereditary animosities between the houses of Erin. A friend of Columcille, she possessed intense interest in presenting another side to these women's tales.

She squared her shoulders and raised her voice, in effect plunging forward with both hands on her sword. "My husband, the father of five, died with a lance through his neck at Culdrevny. I fought by his side in that battle. When we opened the fighting, my husband was leading fifty fighters from our tuath, including all four of his sons. Thirty-two still stood when the enemy fled. Two of the sons are gone, the other two covered in glory. They acquitted themselves well.

"But their glory comes not just from battle, or even mostly from battle. Their greatest glory is their good name and their high standards. The brehons will attest to this: Before ever there were monasteries or the name of Christ was known in the land, a just man could find sanctuary with a ri. Once the ri accepted that man, the man was as safe as a member of the ri's own family. Sanctuary is holy. It always has been."

She paused a moment. "The great beauty of brehon law is its justice. My husband fell in with the monks of Drumceatt because all law—both monastic and brehon—and all decency had been violated, and he would not allow that to go unanswered. He did not have to follow Columcille. No one in that army did. We followed willingly to protect and avenge our honor, and nothing less. Were any man other than Columcille leading the army, they would have marched anyway. My husband and his sons died for honor. Not Columcille. Honor. There is no better death than that. I am immensely proud of them, and I'd send them forth again. I beg you not to censure a man over an affair of honor."

She stepped out of the circle dry-eyed. She did not look at the brehon behind her. She did not look toward Colm. She couldn't. She pushed through spectators and lost herself among them to listen to the proceedings buried among backs and cloaks. Her breastbone still trilled. She could not calm down despite that, for better or worse, her part was ended.

Hours more testimony followed. Anice couldn't see that the many widows of Connaught had much of a case, but that apparently did nothing to stem the tide of them. Men with booming voices pontificated on details of church law. Anice had never noticed any particular influence of church law on daily life of the monastics among whom she had ever lived. In fact, they tended to take more than a little pride in ignoring Rome. Why did they make such an issue of it now?

By the close of deliberations that day, Anice perceived that the line was drawn not between good and evil, or between honor and falsity, or between sanctity within church law and the breaking of it, but between political factions in Ulster and Connaught, enemies eons before the like of Cu Chulainn and the gods beneath the earth.

Deliberations continued yet another day. Anice, bored beyond words, went berrying. She tried to pick enough for her companions from Kells as well as herself and left their berries at their campsite, wrapped in one monk's spare cloak.

On the way back to the gathering she passed a patch of with-erod. She cut enough for a basket. Inside the building, she found a place near the wall where she could strip the withes and listen at the same time. Occupying her hands seemed to help her ears to hear.

Someone called for a preliminary vote. Anice didn't want to hear it. She did anyway.

Overwhelmingly for excommunication.

A Brendan of Birr protested eloquently. He urged those present to put the ancestral animosity aside. *Ha, ha. Hardly.*

Another abbot protested about Brendan. Brendan responded that Birr being halfway between Columcille's church center at Durrow and Diarmaid's church center at Clonmacnois, he was uniquely qualified to present an objective view. All this was bandied about a while.

And then a familiar voice spoke in defense of Columcille. Startled by it, Anice wormed her way to a point where she could see the circle. *Finnian of Moville.*

In his magnificent tonnage he stood in the circle and pleaded on Colm's behalf. He mentioned nothing about that disputed copy of the Psalms or the brehon's decision regarding cow-books and calf-books. He spoke only of the promise in Colm, the will of the miracle-working saint Cruithnechan, and of the fact that he himself had produced an occasional miracle in the past. The Holy Spirit, he reminded all, moves miraculously. The Holy Spirit takes His own vengeance. "Destroy a worker of miracles at your peril."

Finnian waddled away. Suddenly, Colm lurched forward from his place at the wall. The brehon in charge of the circle moved to stop him, looked at his face a moment, and stepped back.

He took his place in the circle, and that splendid voice that had carried across lea and river and field of battle now filled the room.

"My brothers, forgive me, for I have sinned. It is sin to answer sin with the arm of man. Vengeance is God's, not man's.

"What is done cannot be undone, but it can be balanced. My father Phelim of Gartan is closely related to Conal, ard ri of the Dal Riada. I have already sent my emissary north to make arrangements to negotiate a parcel of land for a monastery up in Dal Riada, to be used as a base to evangelize the Picts."

The room buzzed; Anice's head buzzed even louder. *Emissary. That would have to be Gavin. Gavin is of the same blood, the same link to the king of Dal Riada. So Gavin is back in the Pictish isles.*

Anice knew for fact that the Picts to the northeast of Dal Riada cared nothing for the things of Christ. She knew vaguely that Ninian and others, a generation or more before Anice's, had worked among the southern Picts and the Britons and who knows who else—perhaps even the Erse in that region, the Scotii. So a pattern was already set, a precedent. *Colm would not be the first, but wouldn't he be magnificent?*

The bare bones of a plan formed immediately in Anice's mind, a plan that seized her heart and her imagination and instantly consumed her as nothing had before. She would become part of Colm's bold move into Pictland, her native country.

He continued. "Three thousand fell at Culdrevny. Let me, in answer, win three thousand new souls to Christ."

More deliberation followed, but the synod was as good as ended. Excommunication had failed, but Diarmaid could be quit of Colm anyway. Politically, it worked out all right. Religiously, it worked out all right.

Best of all, one way or another, Anice would be going north —going home—with her heroes.

15

Finnian's Guilt

The salmon leaps! Oh, the joy!
He whips forward through the riffles,
The rapids.
Oh, the joy!
Death close at hand cannot still the pleasure.

Would that summer persisted forever. *An endless summer. Ah, my, yes!* How Treasa loved the summer with its plenty, its warmth, its vigor. Summer bowed in with leeks and onions, eels and strawberries, honey, ample milk and butter and soft curd. Sunshine, gentle breezes, rich grass, cheer. Not content with that, as it aged it offered berries, vegetables, fish, and ale. With its dotage came meat, nuts, wheat, and barley, new mead, and tender venison. And long, long days.

She lounged at rest on shore with the setting sun on her face and watched Kenneth standing in the shallows of a small stream. Kenneth was now an abbot, a veteran of journeys to Rome and to Wales and a founder of monasteries, not to mention a delegate to the just-past synod at Telltown, and he looked even yet like the copper-haired lad of yore. His round face was never going to wizen, his burning hair never turn to gray ash. His neck was still the width of an ax handle when by this age it ought be the diameter of a house post.

Kenneth was fishing. The salmon were running thick enough to walk on, but still Kenneth seemed to have a little trouble grabbing one. He would stand rock still with his hands poised just on the water surface, ready to snatch when the crush of swimmers forced a salmon between them. Thanks to execrable timing, he always managed to grab the water just behind the fish's tail. Thanks to that same execrable timing, he had arrived at Telltown the very evening the synod dissolved.

Here came the auburn-haired Anice down to the shore. She was never going to age either, it appeared. Without a word she waded out across the gravelly riffles and took a stance wide-legged just behind Kenneth, her hands hovering on the water.

He grabbed; she grabbed—and came up with the fish.

She smiled, the first smile Treasa had ever seen on her. "We make a good team. I just grab blindly when I see you move." She handed Kenneth his fish.

Treasa lurched to her feet and walked upshore toward the main track. Sit in the dank grass much longer, and she'd be too stiff to move. She'd let others split and roast the salmon tonight. She did most of the cooking yesterday. The sun squeezed itself down between two hills and disappeared.

Another thing about summer—the twilights. As the sun finally, after its long, long course across the day, settled down behind the hills, it dragged after it a lengthy train of color—blue and orange and pink and the softest purple. Stars fought pink clouds and lost. Light dawdled half of forever, running gray fingers across the hills.

Why did she not despise Anice anymore? Curious. Knowing Anice was now a widow and therefore, presumably, ready to find another man ought to make Treasa at least wary. Maybe learning that Anice fought at Culdrevny and then courageously defended Colm changed things.

She walked perhaps a quarter mile south down the track, loosening her tired muscles. She didn't mind fighting for hours and riding for miles and miles and struggling to survive, but, curse the idleness, didn't she hate standing around for days at a time!

She stopped, suddenly alert. On the open lea sloping up from the west of the track, other travelers had made camp. It was a large party, judging from the tents and fires. Sixty or seventy horses must be corralled within a makeshift paddock of stakes and rope. Armed monks stood watch on the four sides of camp.

Monastics on the move, especially a party that size, usually didn't worry much about safety on the track. Why would these be concerned?

Treasa hadn't done any genuine spying for years. Mostly for the practice, but also for the fun, she would check this group out at close quarters. She gathered her cloak into a wrap around her body, that it not snag on a stick and make noise. Bent low, she began working her way across the open lea, moving up a shallow draw from bush to boulder.

She reached a point where she must either quit her cover or quit the chase. She left the cover behind and began a silent skulk across the open pasture, keeping a cautious eye on the monk watching this quarter. The pasture, far from bare, was studded with random little rockpiles and outcrops. This was not some of Erin's better range. Darkness was getting deep enough now that, so long as she didn't silhouette herself against any horizons, she should be able to move fairly freely.

A familiar mountain-sized figure wrapped in a couple acres of cloak came strolling out to talk to the north watchman. Fascinating! Now why would Finnian of Moville bring such an elaborate contingent to a synod?

Finnian rumbled something Treasa could not discern. Finnian headed toward her, aimed more or less at a rocky outcrop across the hill to Treasa's left.

She moved to that outcrop, splayed like a lizard on a cool day, and perched cross-legged on a round, coarse boulder. "Good evening, Father Finnian."

He yelped like a dog whose tail a cow just stepped on.

"Treasa, of course." She smiled in the darkness. "I've always wondered, Father, why you want to be addressed as 'Father,' even by men who are fifty years old. That would imply considerable age in yourself, without necessarily the respect that comes to actual old age. A sort of flippant old age, do you ken?"

"What are you doing here?"

"Just practicing. I've a question for you. Answer truly, and I promise I won't practice on you again. You stole from Colm—stole time and a book—as surely as if you'd tiptoed into his scriptorium and tiptoed out with the goods. Why then did you speak up strongly in his behalf at Telltown?"

"That's none of your concern. Don't you ever come near me like this again." His cloak rustled.

"I promise I'll keep practicing on you until you tell me. You'll never be able to move abroad, day or night, without the thought

149

that perhaps I am lurking behind this tree or that boulder. 'Tis a fate I myself would avoid at any cost."

The cloak ceased moving. "Why are you doing this to me?"

"Because, fine Father, I want to know. I don't understand you, and I very much want to."

"Why?" He had her there.

From up by the camp, a man called, "Father? Is all well?"

"All's well." He said it grudgingly, she thought.

She considered his question a moment. "Until three days ago, you were Colm's enemy. The more I can understand about how enemies think and about how they may turn around, the more effective I'll be in my chosen trade." It sounded so right that its simplicity took her by surprise.

"I don't approve of your chosen trade."

"I know."

He hesitated in the darkness. "Guilt, I believe. Every time I serve the host in eucharist, I blaspheme."

"Because you know that the business about cow-book and calf-book was as much a cause of Culdrevny as the sanctuary violation."

"I should never have taken it to a secular court. To Diarmaid. I read Paul's letter to the Romans about a week later, a book that had just come in from Clonmacnois. He states unequivocally that the person in Christ is to suffer loss rather than drag another Christian into the courts, rather than air church problems in front of unbelievers. Defending Columcille at Telltown was an expiation."

"Why did you take his copy from him in the first place?"

Another hesitation. "I needed it for Dromin."

"Your other monastery. In Louth."

"We're desperate for material. Now will you leave me alone?"

"I will. Go in peace, Finnian."

The cloak rustled, headed around the outcrop and up toward the fires of camp.

Treasa twisted about to call after him. "One other thing. Why the heavy watch? Of whom are you afraid?"

He paused, partially blotting out two of the campfires. "Diarmaid wanted Columcille excommunicated, and if it hadn't been for Brendan of Birr and me, he would have been. What would *you* do?"

"Well spoken. Peace and blessings, Finnian." So Finnian didn't trust Diarmaid any more than Treasa did. She hopped off the rock well uphill and worked her way down to the track. She nearly missed it in the darkness and found her own camp more by luck than by skill.

The Dove of the Church himself sat asprawl beside the fire, turning the spit with three split salmon laced across it. For a man who had been challenged, excommunicated, and recommunicated, all within the last week, he seemed fairly well composed. Or maybe just incredibly weary.

Beside him Declan looked equally weary. Declan had come along uninvited by the synod, mostly as a lark. It's not every day a ri can attend a synod of this importance.

She picked up the lardpot and boar's-tail brush to baste the fish. "They're about done. Any bread?"

Declan answered. "Perhaps. Fergus took two of Colm's monks out begging at nearby raths."

"If 'tis Fergus you sent, you can expect the party back tomorrow, if at all. Fergus can get lost inside a ringwall."

She set the pot aside and hunkered down beside Colm. "You really are going into exile?"

"After a fashion. In a true exile, I would cut all ties with Erin and with my churches. I can't do that. They need me. But I'll set up a base church and monastery somewhere up within the Dal Riada, and that will be my world. Not this."

"Irish governance and the Picts conveniently close by."

"Precisely."

"To win three thousand Pictish souls to Christ."

"At least."

She watched his face a few moments. Was he teasing, serious, or something in between? "Why Picts? There's a multitude of unreached without stooping to Picts."

He watched the far distance beyond their salmon a few moments. "I don't know. The challenge, I suppose. They're strongly druid. So was my foster father, Cruithnechan, so I understand the mind-set. They're tough and respect strength—both brute strength

151

and spiritual strength. I have that. Mostly, I suppose, I need my clan. No man walks alone. The clan is everything. Up north, I'll still have the power of the clan behind me. On the continent I would not."

If they didn't eat soon, the salmon would start to dry out. She wagged her head. "I can't imagine you getting out of politics. You have too much the king's blood in you."

He smiled. "Maybe not clear out."

"See?" came a cheery young voice in the darkness. "I told you camp was this way."

Fergus's voice rumbled some sort of half-hearted acquiescence. He and two monks came hastening into the circle of firelight, pounds and pounds of loaves in their arms. Kenneth and Anice joined them.

"Time to eat. You sang Compline over an hour ago." Treasa hauled to her feet and retrieved the spit from over the fire. As Fergus broke the loaves in two, she laid slabs of broiled salmon out on the clean bread. *Aaaah.*

She faced a strange decision now—one she had not expected. She had planned to accompany Colm as far as Kells, then go home to the Monaghan with Fergus and Declan. Her own clan may have disavowed her, but she enjoyed strong support from her adopted patrimony. She was building a respectable estate there. She should continue developing her holdings as a client.

In a few more years her reflexes would slow up and her judgment falter. She saw it all the time in aging warriors. The thing to do was develop enough of an estate that she could give up defense and settle down as a client before the relentless deterioration of age brought her death on some battlefield.

It was a splendid plan designed to allow her a safe, happy old age.

So why did she suddenly yearn to sail north among the Picts?

16

Heroes' Good-bye

Year of our Lord 563

King of Heaven,
  King of life,
You make bright my drab places.
  You lift my heart.

Rich and dangerous, bold and bleak and subtle, the world between the tides . . .

Danger and aye. Rocky offshore reefs—skerries—studded the sea all around these islands, protruding at times, at other times lurking just below the glistening surface. The greatest of caution did not always prevent those below the surface from raking out the bottom of your boat.

Rich and aye. Festooned with seaweed and mussels, barnacles and slime, the rocks below high tide and above low tide seemed so barren. But seals hauled out upon them here. And over nearer shore, see the flock of oystercatchers, all brilliant black, white, and red, poking and prodding among them. A thousand small creatures lived in the goop and weeds. There was an urgency about life in the world between tides, a hastening to find food and respite before the sea returned to cover all.

Anice watched the skerries past which their curragh sloshed. Waves would break across the half-submerged islets, drenching their undulating seaweed. Sometimes you could not see the rocks —only the breaking water betrayed their position. With the wind against the outgoing tide, the sea chopped and dipped. She clung to the oak gunwales and tried to keep from being sick.

Treasa was complaining about how she despised boat travel, especially in rough weather. Even Colm up by the bow looked green. Only Gavin, the dark hawk, seemed immune to the pitching and yawing of this little craft. He leaned casually upon the gunwales at Colm's side, watching the distance ahead.

The smell of the mutton grease didn't help. Protective sheep fat dressed the hides covering the hull and the cordage securing the single sail. The hides themselves stank. The gray-stained, mildewed linen sail smelled musty. Come to think of it, the cordage smelled bad too. Anice hated all of it!

But then it was only a day, although a long, long day, asea from Drumceatt to the island Colm would soon call home. Gavin, the voyage leader, claimed that since the weather was fair they could safely sail to seaward of the islands on their right; Islay, he called one, and Colonsay, the next.

He pointed dead ahead. "The Isle of Mull. We're nearly there."

Good! Good! A large island it was, filling the horizon before them. It seemed somewhat barren, with scant trees and much bald rock, but few of the islands out here looked better. Even Erin to the south of them was taking on this open, windswept appearance.

One of Anice's uncles had lived for a time on Mull. He claimed it was the jewel of the Hebrides, its climate much more agreeable than that of the northern islands.

The little curragh angled to seaward. Its bobbing intensified. *Why aren't we landing?*

They rounded Mull to eastward and approached a tiny island off Mull's southwest point. The fitful wind and contrary currents drew them out to seaward somewhat, and the party had to take to the oars to bring them in.

"That's it." Gavin nodded toward that small bit of land in the roaring sea. "Iona."

The island rose in a dark, rocky mound off the surging water. A tangle of threatening skerries clustered along its coastline, daring the voyagers to venture closer as the sea slapped back and forth across a broad intertidal zone.

The island's whole south coast couldn't be but a mile wide at most. Gavin directed them to circumnavigate her; Anice realized belatedly that "circumnavigate" means "bob endlessly as you follow the island's perimeter."

They rounded a head and altered course toward the north. As they moved in closer to land than Anice cared to go, a white plume poofed up along the shore. Instantly, Colm and Gavin ordered the boat in closer to investigate. Treasa complained that she didn't care about strange plumes. She wanted the voyage to be over with. Besides, it would soon be dark.

The plume came from a cave sort of formation in the rocks of the shore. Now and then, the surf would strike just so and spout up in an impressive splash of spray. They bobbed onward.

Gavin pointed here and there. "On this bay is a machair with splendid pasturage. Good grass, level ground, rich loam. We can sow grain there and winter considerable livestock. There's an abandoned rath up on that head."

Waves crashed across partially submerged reefs all around them now. Gavin continued, "There are two or three raths on the landward side. They farm the machair, but mostly they fish—trade fish and shellfish to Mull and the mainland. The place used to be better populated; it's nearly deserted now that most of the trees are gone."

And then Colm, the lovely lad, was seized by a sudden, unexpected jolt of common sense. "Let's turn back. I saw a bay on the south coast. We'll put ashore there." The oarsmen turned them around.

Treasa moved in beside Gavin. Anice could tell that not only was her stomach threatening rebellion, she felt light-headed and her palms were sweaty. "Why not just land right here?" She waved toward shore; she didn't care where she was pointing to.

"No good place, with the tide going out." Gavin leaned casually on the rail, as if he were not the least discomfited by this hideous bounding. "Colm's got a good eye. That bay in the south end should serve us well. We can explore from there if we wish."

"How long is the island?"

"Three miles. Little less."

"Seems quite small to support a thriving monastery." She watched half a dozen intriguing black-and-white birds floating nearby like ducks. Their big heads sported the most amazing huge, brightly-colored beaks. They bobbed effortlessly, unbothered by the horrid swells. She pointed toward them. "I can't imagine a brotherhood the size of, for instance, Drumceatt or Moville on a barren place like this."

"Those are puffins." Gavin nodded toward those birds. "They nest in tunnels on the shore here. We might not become fully self-supporting, but we'll come close. And the whole world will have easy access to our gate."

"This is easy?"

He looked at her. "A day from Drumceatt. Half a day or less from the Pict mainland. A week or less from anywhere in Erin. We'll have scholars pouring in!"

Anice shuddered, and Treasa scornfully said, "Easy!" And this was a calm day.

Treasa was among the first to clamber over the side and struggle ashore. It was three hours past Compline before Anice could fall asleep. Three hours later, she was awakened by Matins.

They ate bread, broke camp, sang Primes, and took off to explore the island. Gavin sent four monks and the navigator north with the curragh to wait for them in the bay on the landward side, where the fishermen went forth.

Rocks. Mostly this island was rocks. Some were very pretty, a gentle white with greenish lines laced through them. But rocks are rocks, and beauty or no they don't grow much grain or leeks.

Colm pointed silently toward a ridgetop. Silhouetted against the overcast sky, a pack of dogs eyed them. The two parties watched each other a few moments. The dogs slunk off.

Colm grimaced. "Plague here also."

"Likely so." The mention of plague visibly sobered both of them.

Gavin led down a steep and rocky defile to the sea's edge. "I talked to a couple of the boaires here, and some fishwives. They say the population is perhaps half what it once was, but they didn't say why. I assumed clans had died out or moved to the mainland. No one mentioned plague."

They followed northward the slippery strip of land between the tides. This was not at all the sort of hospitable land Anice had envisioned. Moville lay in a fertile, productive vale. Drumceatt perched above a fertile, productive river valley. Clonard, Kells, Clonmacnois, Kildare—Anice had heard they were all surrounded by fertile, productive raths. They paused.

Anice looked around her at sullen sea and gloomy land. "I

can't imagine building anything substantial on this pile of rocks."

Gavin cackled. "You've never been to Skellig Michael."

She frowned. "No."

"A tiny, pointy island off the west coast of Erin. All bare rock and steep as a house wall. The monks there built themselves a substantial settlement. You have to climb hundreds of steps to reach it."

"Why?"

Gavin shrugged. "Close to God. Unfettered by the things of this world. Safe. No ri would care to conquer a little pile of rocks. The brothers of Skellig Michael are known the world over."

"For their foolhardiness, no doubt, as will Colm be if he establishes his fraternity here."

"It's not his choice. This is the island Conal gave him."

"Generous Conal."

Baithene the Tender-hearted, a rather pale and soft-looking young man, pointed to a squirt of water arching straight up out of the mud among the skerries here. He poked and pried with his walking stick. A clam popped to the surface. Baithene swished it in a little tidal pool, washing the mud off. In a matter of minutes, Baithene and two others dug cloakfuls of clams.

Anice had never cared for clams.

Continuing north, they entered a rolling meadowland studded with rocky little outcrops. Three ringwalled raths perched on rises. From only two of them did smoke drift. The milk bags on the spare, runty cattle promised little in the way of butter and cheese.

They walked on north, following a track leading to pasture land nestled among rises. Stumpfields and small groves of gnarled oaks gave way again to bleak grass patches and hawthorns.

Land ended. Angry seas shattered themselves against the rocks on this north coast.

Gavin pointed northeast. "The island glowering at us there is Mull. It wraps in something of a backward C-shape with us at the bottom of it. And off to the northwest there, there's our old friend Tiree. And Coll. Beyond them, as you know, there isn't much except a chain of outer islands. Iona here is fairly well protected compared to them."

Colm nodded as he stared off at the globs of gray on the horizon. "By that, I trust, you mean there are worse places to be."

"There are always worse places to be, Cousin."

"Ironic. My whole childhood, I grew up being able to see Islay, and sometimes Mull and Tiree, from the seashore north of home. Never dreamed that one day I'd be standing here."

Gavin smiled. "Irony? That's the half of it. You in the church and I outside, traveling our different ways, but the end is the same. Now you're an outcast like me. Going to a desolate place where there is nothing."

Colm's intense blue eyes seemed to be seeing far, far beyond the globs of gray. "Then we will make something."

He turned suddenly away from the brow of the ridge and the roaring sea and started back southward. "Earlier you said something about contacts on Mull."

"People who can provide supplies and timber until you become established."

"No timber on the island here?"

"None to speak of and hard to get to. It's easier to float it across from Mull."

Colm nodded. "We'll pace out the ringwall and decide how big to build the oratory this afternoon. When you take Anice to the mainland tonight you can arrange—"

"What?" Anice shrieked. She skipped forward six steps and turned to see his face better. "I'm here! To build, with you."

"We brought you along only to help you return to your clan at Drumderry. I thought we made that clear." And just like that he abandoned his attention toward her and shifted it back to Gavin. "Send word to Kieran, Kenneth, and Comgall asking them to join me here, at least for a while. They're splendid teachers, and we're going to need good teachers to get the school going."

Anice planted herself squarely in front of him and stopped. "You claimed at Telltown that you were coming here to bring Jesus to the Picts. You need someone who can speak the local dialects as well as Gaelic. That's me. You need me!"

He had to stop or run over her. "There are no Picts on Iona."

"The Dal Riada is both Picts and Irish. You—"

"Not here. On the mainland. I don't need you here, and this will be a male fraternity. No marriage, no adjacent sisterhood—at least, not in the beginning."

"Dove, old cousin, you never could figure out women. Go find your curragh." Gavin wiggled his fingers toward Colm, a dismissal. Then he stepped to Anice's elbow and turned her around. Firmly, he led her off southward down a cow path. "Colm's not always the best at explaining things to a woman. His tongue even gets tangled when he's yakking with Treasa sometimes."

"Yes, but—"

"Those oak trees down there—let's talk about this." He clambered over gloomy gray rocks, working his way down to a small grove of stunted oaks nestled in a draw.

Anice followed as best she could. Her legs weren't nearly as long as his. Here was a sprawling little oak, sheared and shaped by wind. Its lower limbs spread out across the rocky turf, nearly touching ground in spots. Gavin slipped in under it and sat down on one of those nearly-horizontal branches. Anice perched farther out the branch at an angle, the better to face toward him.

"I think," he said, "—and this is just an idea I have without a whole lot of reason behind it—that's Colm's afraid to trust himself around women."

"You're not."

"I'm different. I don't have to represent Jesus in everything I do or say. If I sin, I sin. If Colm sins, he gives his Lord a black eye. See the difference?"

She scowled. "No. Finnian always said that every Christian is a mirror of Jesus."

"Right. But Finnian doesn't notice that the outside world—the unbelievers—hold church people to a different standard than they measure common people. Or kings, for that matter. As a ri, I can marry, divorce, remarry, challenge and kill, steal cows. As a church brother I couldn't do any of that, at least so far as the outside world is concerned. See what I mean?"

"I see what you're saying, but it doesn't apply here. I'm not going to jump in Colm's lap or anything." She flapped a hand helplessly. "He's safe. I won't try to marry him."

"You tried to marry me."

She watched him a bit, calculating her answer. "The offer is still open."

"Anice, I'm already married."

Her jaw dropped, and for the longest moment she couldn't close her mouth. Shock and despair, anger and confusion swamped her the way the tide swamps the skerries.

Of course he would be married! All those years in exile, not among strangers but among a branch of his own clan—why wouldn't he marry? And listen to his words: "As a ri, I can . . ." He's a king among his clansmen, living a life far different from that of the footloose youth she knew. Why, he was probably grooming himself for the high kingship, should Diarmaid suddenly drop over with a spear through his heart or something.

Gavin stood up suddenly and drew her to her feet. His head loomed up among the leaves and branches of this oak arbor. "I've made two disastrous mistakes in my life. Letting Diarmaid chase me away was one. I should have challenged him right there, somehow. The other was walking away from you."

"Why did you walk away from me?"

"I didn't think I had any prospects to offer a wife. Up here, I didn't need prospects. In fact, a wife came with the kingship I have now, so to speak. As a favor to Conal, I married a widow with a different pedigree to bring together two ruling houses, ours and an Erse clan along the coast. I suppose you could consider that a third mistake." Gavin shrugged. "It seemed all right at the time."

She didn't know what to say.

He chuckled. "I remember the first time I saw you, climbing through our gate with that ax. Your first words were 'Help me!' And it never crossed my mind that maybe helping you wasn't the smartest thing to do. You could be a spy who would chop me in two or find and kill Finnian. You've haunted me ever since. You were a beautiful child. You're a beautiful woman."

"Yes, but—"

"But I'm committed to another." He led her by the hand out under the sheltering oak. "We should get going."

Unbidden, her mouth blurted, "I loved you."

"I loved you. And I always shall." He kissed her. Sweetly. Gently. Not with the kind of passion that leads to other things. It was, most of all, a good-bye kiss.

Good-bye to happiness.

17

Brude's Guests

Year of our Lord 565

*How beautiful upon the mountains
  are the feet of the one who brings good news.*

Thirty years ago, Gavin Mac Niall couldn't understand what Colm saw in Comgall. He still couldn't.

The gaunt old monk, now pushing fifty years of age, hadn't mellowed a minute in all those years. If anything, he had grown grumpier and less tolerant of any whiff of happiness or comfort. He stood at Gavin's elbow and complained that this ill-fated venture had not been planned nearly well enough. Where, for example, would they obtain fire? They certainly wouldn't be welcomed into any rath.

Kenneth was still Kenneth, copper-haired and youthful. And the silent, enigmatic Kieran hadn't changed all that much either. All in all, it was not a crew Gavin would choose for their daring adventure, but he wasn't doing the picking. This was Colm's expedition.

As Comgall and Gavin watched, Kenneth and Kieran climbed out of their curragh and picked their way up the rocky tidal flat, here where Loch Linnhe met the Firth of Lorne, toward clean grass.

The effusive greetings finally gotten out of the way, the four old friends settled onto the sward to wait. Kenneth described his new monastery down near Cashel with such enthusiasm that Gavin wouldn't have minded going there, and he hated monasteries. Comgall opined that the proper place for a contemplative society would be somewhere such as Loch Erne, where you could truly cleanse the soul. Then the two of them started talking about setting up churches out on Tiree beyond Iona.

Gavin listened to their gaggling with less than half an ear. Among the little fishing boats off the east head of the Island of Mull, he sighted a curragh under sail. Unless her master played the currents right, he was going to find himself sitting off Lismore Isle until the tide turned.

Brightly, Kenneth cried out, "Why, look!" and leaped to his feet.

Gavin looked. And gaped.

From the shore a quarter mile to the south, a woman with rich auburn hair approached. She came stumbling across the bog between the beach and the moor trying to balance herself with a crook, like a shepherdess without sheep. Kenneth ran down toward her with all the grace and dignity of a fifteen-year-old, calling greetings.

With a winsome smile, Anice returned his greeting.

Anice! What is she doing here? How did she learn of our journey? It was a sure bet Colm didn't invite her. Now what? None of them had seen Anice since she left Iona two years ago.

Gavin watched her greet Kenneth with an enthusiasm to match the copper-haired monk's. She too displayed the exuberance and artlessness of a fifteen-year-old. No crinkles in the corners of her eyes, no gray hairs, no wrinkles in her hands or feet betrayed the decades that had passed since the first time ever he saw her.

He found himself comparing her to his wife. *Foolish Gavin! There is no comparison, nor is comparison appropriate! For shame.*

Flush with happiness, or perhaps merely with the strain of crossing the bog, she climbed onto the sward and settled demurely beside Gavin, her legs tucked under her skirt. Perspiration trickled down the side of her face. It must have been the bog; one does not sweat with happiness.

She greeted Comgall and Kieran politely and Gavin very politely. He greeted her in kind, all false smiles, and turned his attention back to the sailing vessel.

Its master indeed knew the currents, for he hugged Lismore Isle until the last possible moment before cutting across the firth and gliding in onto the tidal flats. Gavin recognized the bright, bald head of Trena of the Mocuruntir even before they beached. Trena could take Colm's boat anywhere anytime in nearly any weather. He could make the trip from Iona to Erin and back in just under a full day, and that included lading supplies at Derry or the Inishowen.

Colm came climbing out of the boat looking a wee bit rocky. Behind him, a blonde woman with a long braid draped over her shoulder tumbled over the side and slogged wearily ashore. The moment she climbed above tide line, Treasa flopped onto her back and lay with her arms and legs splayed, her eyes closed. Half a dozen monks began unloading enough supplies to keep an army in luxury.

What is Treasa doing here? Gavin hopped to his feet and strode down to meet Colm.

Colm glared past him at Anice. He shifted his glare to Gavin. "I didn't imagine you'd be so stupid. You invited her, you can dis-invite her. I'll wait here while you dismiss her."

"Wait a minute! What do you mean me?"

"Enough!" Treasa bellowed. Without moving an eyelash of her sprawl across the grass, she snapped, "You two bickered like bantam roosters when you were kids and you're still bickering now that you're goats. Let her stay, Colm. You need her."

"Not that much."

"How well do you speak Pictish?"

"We can—"

"How well do you know Pictish protocols? You're walking into a king's lair on a political mission, right? Does the wife come with the guest bed, like she does in parts of Erin, and do you insult the king if you turn her down? It could go either way with these brutes, you know. You need an insider to plead your cause and lead you around some of the sharper stakes in that pit." She still didn't move a hairbreadth.

Gavin stepped past Colm and walked down to Treasa. He poked her in the shoulder with a toe. "Rough voyage?"

"I don't want to talk about it."

He sniggered loudly and deliberately. Taking up the call, a sea gull soared in a tight circle and alit on the shingle near the growing pile of supplies. It opened its hooked beak and laughed harshly.

Treasa snarled, "Go ahead and laugh, you stupid bird. If you weren't geis I'd skewer you."

"That's right; I'd forgotten. Sea gulls are taboo for you. Too bad you can't have the fellow for lunch. How'd you get the Monaghan to let you come?"

"Brought 'em with me. Recognize Fergus over there?"

Now that she mentioned him, Gavin remembered the fuzzy little ri tuatha who served under the ri ruirech Declan. The man looked older than he had two years ago at Culdrevny, which was patently ridiculous.

Treasa lowered her voice. "Things are quiet among the Monaghan for the moment, and they're all getting bored. Besides, Fergus's wife died a couple months ago and he's restless. He cared about her. And Colm wanted a female warrior along to show the Picts we're just one of the folks."

"You mean that, fundamentally, we're no different than they are."

"Brothers and sisters under the skin, that sort of thing. So he sent a monk down to invite me, and I invited Fergus." She lay still as a stone except for the rise and fall of her chest as she breathed slowly, deeply.

Gavin cast another glance toward the Monaghan. The little man was directing unloading operations a bit more imperiously, perhaps, than a guest ri ought. So recently bereft, would he crack or go crooked when things started going wrong? Gavin wished she hadn't brought him.

They were unloading a donkey now, or trying to. He squatted down near her and purred, "We're practicing eating the specialty dishes our Pictish hosts will be serving. When your tummy stops rolling and you feel less like throwing up, join us for lunch. Lots to eat besides sea gull, since it's taboo for you. Besides head cheese, of course—what else would you do with the brains?—there's haggis. That will be your mutton liver and lungs boiled in a sheep's stomach. And we have finnan haddie, which is your raw, smoked haddock. Then there's—"

She moved. And only Gavin's agile leap saved him from the wild swipe of her sword. *Glory be, she can draw a blade swiftly when provoked!* He strolled back up the slope to Colm as Treasa roared lurid aspersions on Gavin's ancestry and character.

Colm smirked. "Some things never change."

Gavin looked past him to Anice, still seated. "How did you know about this mission journey?"

"'Tis all over the district, how you'll be traveling to Inverness. There be only one way to go to Inverness, and this is it. No one, though, knew when. Then yesterday Comgall passed through Lochaline and asked my second cousin the whereabouts of Gavin Mac Niall's tuathe."

"You thereby learned when, and came up the rivershore, knowing we'd pass through here." Gavin had never doubted she was smart. He regretted that she was clever. He nodded toward the pile of duffle by the curragh. "We've become materialists."

Colm looked grim. "We accept hospitality when it's offered. I doubt it will be offered frequently. We'll take our own bread, bedding, and fire."

Dismal thought, that hospitality might be withheld. Gavin could not imagine a people who did not extend hospitality to any and every traveler who passed through. That was one of the fundamentals of life, one of the things that made a man a man. Until now he had avoided most contact with the uncultured Pictish warlords in his area. On purpose.

The Dal Riada, an enclave in itself, allowed him social congress with his own kind, with Irish wit and culture. A pleasant life. He didn't need this now, and he had no idea why he so eagerly jumped at the chance to come when the monk appeared at his gate with Colm's invitation. In promising Colm that he would come, he had promised himself a lot of sweat and work.

And that was another thing. What was this request of Colm's that he bring along no clients? As a ri, Gavin did no work and sweated very little. He had become quite comfortable with that. Here he sat with no retainers except for his valet. A ri without retainers was a ri undressed. He didn't like traveling naked through hostile territory.

But the adventure was commencing, with or without Gavin's full understanding and agreement. Quite a parade they made, traveling northeastward up the rivershore. Three monks and a donkey

165

served as burden bearers. Without an attendant, Treasa carried her own javelin and ax, her sword slung casually at her knee. Fergus rarely left her side, and then only to berate the donkey. Gavin gathered indirectly that Treasa had warned him against lording it over Colm's monks.

The weather sweetened, which Gavin took as an omen. They traveled a well-used track along riversides and lakeshores, an unbroken chain of valleys carrying them rapidly toward Inverness. A softly beautiful route it was, with mounded woodland hills to either side and the ribbons of glistening water.

The monks pitched a lot of tents, for no rath along the way offered them a night's repose. Anice did, however, enquire of fellow travelers regarding distances and directions and got what seemed to be fairly forthright answers. Days passed.

On a nicely sunlit day, they paused for rest and Tierce at the shore of a long, narrow lake hemmed closely by hills. Gavin took this opportunity to press Colm to explain the purpose of their trip.

"Didn't I tell you?"

"No, dear Cousin, you did not."

"Well, 'tis no secret. My chief purpose, of course, is to bring the gospel straight to the king of the Picts—Brude himself. But I also need to tie up some political loose ends. Even though it was within Conal's auspices to give me Iona, protocol dictates that I also gain formal permission from Brude. And I think it wise to ask for his pledge of safety for the brethren who will more and more be wandering his lands."

"What if he won't receive us or even gets hostile? A party with only four warriors certainly can't protect itself, let alone assert itself."

Colm smiled. "If God wants our mission to succeed, He will provide the way."

Gavin grunted. Then Fergus hinted broadly that a bit of bread would go well just now, and no one argued.

Kenneth brushed crumbs off his fingers and pointed toward the lake. "You're sensitive to spirits, Colm. Don't you feel the evil here?"

Colm frowned. "You're more sensitive than I. Evil people near?"

166

"A presence. Not people."

Colm twisted to look at Anice. "The name of this place?"

"Loch Ness."

"We'll have to cross it. Either cross the lake or cross the river beyond." Colm glanced at Kenneth. "Which?"

"The river."

Anice nodded agreement. "I already asked about a fisherman to ferry us. No one wants to cross the lake. No reason why."

The party took up their burdens then and continued on. The Loch narrowed and poured through a strait defile. You could nearly walk across this River Ness in places. In other places it widened out gracefully, reflecting the forested hills upon its bright and placid surface. Anice engaged a ferryman with a round oxhide boat. It took him three trips.

The sun had about spent itself for the day as they approached the cashel of the high king. And what a fortress! Certainly, Erse strongholds needed a palisade and gate against the blackguards and pilferers. But this stone wall was obviously designed to repel the gods—splendid rockwork, with every dressed stone fitting against its mates. They had catwalks up on the palisade inside, obviously. Gavin could see the heads of patrols pass back and forth up there.

And druids. Apparently, Brude's bards and druids were up there as well.

With Anice at his side to translate the sticky spots, Colm stepped forward. In his limited Pictish, he addressed the porters and requested audience with Brude, King of the Picts.

Brude, King of the Picts, Colm was informed, did not wish to entertain him. The gate, tall enough and strong enough to withstand a stampede of twenty-foot-high bulls, remained locked.

You can lead a horse to water, but you can't make him drink. You can present yourself at a king's door, but you can't make him accept you. A fine end this was to a grueling journey. Gavin's distaste for Picts was growing rapidly into plain old hatred. *How crass can a king be, to refuse guests?*

"Vespers," Kenneth announced quietly. He arranged the monks in a semicircle before the massive gate, gave them a pitch, and intoned the invocation. From up on the catwalk, an old man and two or three younger fellows, all of whom appeared to be druids, began a raucous singing chant.

Treasa stepped in by Gavin's elbow. "A magical incantation to cause your, uh, body to malfunction. They're weaving a spell and making sport of us."

Laughter from inside the gate blotted out part of the collect the monks were praying.

Gavin loosened his sword. "I didn't know you knew Pictish."

"I don't. But my father's a druid. I know the tone pattern and breaks."

"Well, the charm's not working."

"You sure? I've seen that charm reduce ri ruirechs to tears."

And then Colm began the anthem—the Patrick hymn. Gavin grinned. Even he knew that one.

"You the King of moon and sun, you the King of stars, beloved. . . ."

Treasa, loud and clear, picked up the melody. Anice smiled as she sang lustily. Gavin might stumble over a couple of the phrases, but he knew enough of the verses to keep up with the crowd. Even his valet added a rich baritone to it.

But Colm's voice! In rare form today, Colm's voice climbed out over the assembled singers. It rang against the stone wall, it rang against the clouds above. The druids' heckling chants ceased, powerless against it.

The anthem ended. In the penetrating silence that followed, Kenneth commenced the litany unopposed by druidic forces inside the wall. The office ended without further problems.

Gavin watched heads come and go on the catwalk. "We're being scrutinized, I'd opine."

Treasa snorted. "But not taken seriously."

"Seven monks and an occasional ri? Hardly. The donkey's probably getting as much respect as we are."

Then Colm stepped forward from his place in the office circle. Gavin looked at his face and felt for all the world like taking a rapid step backward. He'd seen that look on the Dove before— anger and fierceness. A determination that could rock the pillars of heaven.

Up on the catwalk, someone called to someone else.

Colm raised his hand and arm. He signed the cross but not extravagantly; if anything, the gesture was understated. That arm remained extended.

On the other side of the gate, someone dropped something heavy and metallic. On this side, an iron bolt or rivet, round-headed and flush against the gate's latchplate, backed out and dropped in the beaten dirt. It made the same kind of sound when it fell.

Others fell inside; another backed out and dropped on this side. Colm was doing it again—performing the kind of miracles old Cruithnechan used to pull off—and Gavin again was here to see it. His breastbone vibrated like a lyre string.

Men inside were shouting and running around. Were the gate's defenders trying frantically to stick fallen bolts back in? The notion tickled Gavin. If this kept up, the gates would soon simply come apart.

The bar fell away inside; you could hear it slide down the gate and slam in the dirt.

Treasa handed Gavin her javelin and pulled her ax, balancing it lightly in both hands. There was a vivid excitement in her face, a heady anticipation. Gavin felt it too.

The gates creaked and sagged. With an eerie moan, they separated.

Whether Brude, King of the Picts, liked it or not, he was about to receive guests from Erin. Guests from God.

18

Broichan's Slave

Bless the Lord O my soul!
  You, my Lord, are so very great!

Gavin might bad-mouth the Picts every chance he got, but even he would have to admit that when Brude really wanted to he could put on quite a feed. In fact, Treasa made Gavin do so.

This feast was sumptuous indeed, with roasted pigs and sheep, fish piled high on platters (firm yet delicate white meat, not the smoked haddie stuff Gavin talked about), warm, rich loaves of wheaten bread, and a vegetable called cabbage. Treasa would rather eat pasture grass than that stuff. But the rest was good.

The banqueting hall was a match for anything in Erin. It was just as warm, just as smokey, just as noisy as the best Erin had to offer. Come to think of it, this was probably the equivalent of Tara, for Brude, as overlord of the Pictish clans, claimed primacy over nearly as vast an assemblage of oddball families and political groups as did Diarmaid.

With her belt knife, Treasa shaved a splinter off the table edge to get the pork out of her teeth.

The Pict beside her, one of Brude's major warlords, Treasa gathered, pointed to her knife. "An excellent edge on your blade there."

Anice translated throughout, for Treasa's Pictish was nonexistent. She even had a hard time understanding Anice at times.

"A good edge is the equal of three dull weapons." She pulled her sword far enough to give him a better look at the sharpening job on it.

He ran a cautious finger across the edges. His finger paused on the intricate silver inlay down the blade, and he nodded admiringly. Good. Colm wanted to impress these crude country bumpkins. Her damascened sword, made to her specifications by the Monaghans' best smith, would impress a caesar.

"Ayaah! You slut!" The rumble of conversation ceased.

Treasa leaned forward to see who yelled. Brude's chief druid, soaked in amber beer, backhanded the little girl behind him.

She was crying out, "I'm sorry, Lord!" even as that powerful hand struck. And her speech was Irish.

A memory popped into Treasa's mind. She leaped to her feet and grabbed Gavin beside her, dragging him from half-standing back to sitting.

She kept a strong lock on his throat. "I share the thought. That slave girl the farmer speared, way back when as we were traveling to Gemman's. This is not the time. You ken?" He relaxed in her grasp, so she took that as a sign that he kenned, let go, and sat down again.

His face was tight with fury. She leaned forward and twisted to see Colm's.

The man's hard war-face was back, fearsome. That long-ago memory, obviously, still burned bright in his heart too. "Broichan," he said in measured tones, "hear me, for your life depends on it." Brude's frightened translator stumbled a bit with the recasting. The flabby old druid did not look very intimidated.

Colm kept his voice low. "I beg you to liberate your Irish slave girl. Her soul cries out to me."

Broichan's beady little eyes glittered. "I can't believe that, Wizard. She's Irish." His voice hissed, nearly a whisper. "She doesn't have a soul."

Treasa kept a strong grip on Gavin's sword arm. She whispered in his ear, "This is Colm's game."

Colm raised his voice enough to be heard throughout the hall. For him, that wasn't hard. "Know this, Broichan. If you refuse to allow her to go free as I've asked, you shall die suddenly— before I have left Brude's clan lands."

Broichan rasped, "Never."

Colm turned to Brude. "We came with three missions, Lord: One was to invite you into the company of the faithful; one was to ask permanent residency on Iona; the third was to gain your grant of safety for our hermits and wandering brethren who take haven in your northern isles. By your gracious mercy, all are accomplished. You've given your word regarding our monks' safety, Iona has been granted, and my invitation is made known.

"We are men of peace." Treasa almost guffawed aloud. Colm continued. "Because ill will has risen between me and your chief druid, and because ill will of that sort so frequently erupts into bloodshed, we beg your leave, while all is quiet." Colm raised his arm, that amazing right arm, and signed the cross in front of Brude's face—but just as closely in front of Broichan's. "God bless and keep you in His abiding love."

He rose, so Treasa rose. Gavin bolted to his feet and stood with legs braced, glaring at Broichan. Treasa whispered to him harshly not to forget her javelin. He scooped it up. He probably would have walked off without it.

In rapid Erse, Anice spoke to the cowering slave girl. "When Columcille begins a thing, he sees it through. Be patient."

Their three serving monks hurried out into the night. Colm paused to greet by name every ri ruirech and ri tuatha there; how he remembered them all, Treasa could not imagine. He blessed each of them in turn.

They were edging their way toward the door of that warm, stuffy, smokey hall, and suddenly they were stepping into dank and clammy darkness.

Gavin snarled, "I can't believe you walked away!"

"What was my purpose in coming into Pictland?"

"To save three thousand souls for Christ. And you sure as blazes aren't going to do it that way. Not with these people. The only thing they respect is a fist and a blade, and you can wield both with the best of them. You should never have run."

"God's purposes are better served this way. Watch." Colm headed for the gate. It had been repaired, but this time it stood open for them.

Treasa kept her hand on her sword hilt. "I can't help but expect Brude's retainers to fall upon us."

Suddenly cheerful, Colm pointed skyward. "Clear overhead, but for scattered clouds. No chance of falling retainers."

"Imagine, prince. A man of your education unable to discern between literal and figurative. I'll try to be clearer."

Gavin's eyes were flitting everywhere at once, and he held the javelin at ready. "Let's banter later, folks."

Treasa wagged her head. "I didn't expect Brude's druids to blow kisses our way when we left, but this isn't the way I expected to leave, either."

"Blow kisses?" Colm looked at her with one eyebrow cocked.

"Another figure of speech." *The joker.*

Their party, with Gavin as well as Comgall still complaining bitterly, was well outside the gate and down the track when the three monks and the donkey came stumbling and trip-trapping, trying to catch up. The donkey was half laden, the monks overladen. Colm stopped and helped them put things together right.

They made it down to the River Ness without incident. Still, Treasa couldn't shake a feeling of grim foreboding. The moon rose, skipping among black clouds. Its pallid light, waxing and waning, made the eerie surroundings eerier.

Colm stepped down to the river's edge and picked up a small white stone. "With this pebble, God will effect the cure of many diseases among these heathens." Treasa's father, good as he was, couldn't use a little stone that way.

Colm sat down at streamside, staring into the darkness. "We'll wait here a while. Broichan is being chastised at this very moment. God has sent an angel to strike him. He's gasping for breath and half dead. Two of the king's messengers have been sent after us."

Treasa snorted. "I watched Brude's face while you and Broichan were locking horns there. I'd call the old goat's expression 'bemused,' if anything. I can't see that he cares whether his druid lives or dies."

"He cares. Broichan is his foster father."

Anice frowned. "How do you know that? He addressed Broichan only once with the familiar term for father, and you were talking to someone else at the time. Besides, he spoke in Pictish."

From up the track came the sound of galloping hooves. Two horses, Treasa guessed. She yelled. If she hadn't, the horsemen would have thundered right on by.

A slight lad who looked as if he should be covered with pimples leaped off the horse and knelt at Colm's feet. "My lord Brude asks that you return quickly and help. His chief druid lies at death's door." His semi-soprano voice squeaked. Brude must have really laid a do-or-die command on him.

"I begged a favor of the chief druid. Will he grant it?"

"At my lord's insistence, he has consented to set one of his slave girls free."

Comgall barked, "Sure and you don't expect him to do it once he's well again, do you?"

But Colm was handing the tyro that white pebble. "Hear carefully. If Broichan really does set the Irish slave free, immerse this little stone in water at once. Let him drink from it, and he'll be cured instantly. But if he breaks his vow, he'll die instantly." The snap of his fingers echoed like a landslide through the silent night.

The lad and his companion stared a long moment at that small, ordinary, millions-more-just-like-it stone. Their faces fell virtually to mud level. "My lord . . ."

The other mumbled, "Our lord told us to—"

Colm repeated, "Instantly. I'll send two of my people with you to bring the freed girl to me. Comgall? Anice?"

Treasa wished he would have sent her. How she wanted to see this!

The retainers gave Comgall and Anice the horses and ran off alongside, carrying that river pebble.

Gavin growled, "I've always suspected that your load is tied on a little too loosely. This proves it."

"Patience, cousin." He nodded toward his monks. "Matins in less than four hours, but we'll sing Compline anyway, using the twofold hymn of praise, alternate tune."

Kenneth led. He seemed not the least perturbed by the thought that Colm might be wrong or that Brude might decide to take an eye for an eye and slit Comgall's throat if Broichan died. All sorts of possibilities loomed, and Treasa didn't like many of them.

Like a wolf in a cage, Gavin paced back and forth in the near darkness. Then a solid overcast blotted out the moon completely. When he bumped into the donkey, Gavin quit pacing and limited his fidgeting to sharpening the javelin blade. It was already as sharp as he'd ever make it, but the man needed something to do, so Treasa kept her mouth shut.

It couldn't be much more than an hour later that footsteps up the track told Treasa they were back. Not the heavy tread of warriors. Women's feet, and Comgall.

Colm put them to the track again, the donkey leading the way. Donkeys are much better at feeling out the track in the darkness than are people. The little Irish slave—make that ex-slave—said nothing. Her eyes wide with fear and misgiving, she kept glancing over her shoulder, and not even Treasa walking strong beside her seemed to allay her terror.

They stopped where the river began to widen. Despite that the eastern sky glowed pink and gold, Colm ordered the tents pitched.

"Not to be critical or anything," Treasa commented, "but if the idea is to put miles between us and Brude, is it wise to stop dead here? I use 'stop dead' figuratively, I hope."

Colm smiled. He seemed peculiarly at ease and lighthearted for a man who had just butted heads with the most powerful druid in Pictland. "We left without supplies. I'll send the monks around tomorrow to beg us some bread. Anice will try to secure a curragh with a sail for us. We can use the boat for nearly half our journey by sailing up the loch. It will be easier than walking, even if the winds aren't favorable."

"You plan to sail with a donkey?"

"Trade it for meat."

"Ah." But that put the donkey's burden on their shoulders. *Oh well. With half the journey behind them it wouldn't be totally terrible. Just half terrible.*

Treasa planned to sleep a day or two to make up for the lost night, but she lay in her tent wide-eyed. She couldn't stop thinking about Colm and Broichan matching magic. She grew up with Broichan's kind of wizardry and knew it well. Colm's magic—God's handiwork, he insisted—never ceased to amaze her. In this titanic struggle of wills, Colm seemed to be winning, but Treasa wasn't about to wager any cows on either of them yet.

If Colm's miraculous powers were so great, why did he suffer a sword wound the time Curnan Mac Colman was ripped from his protection? Why was he nearly excommunicated? That wouldn't have bothered Treasa particularly, but the mere threat of it devastated him. How come his God worked mightily one moment and with a divine yawn took the next moment off?

Anice found a fellow with a beat-up old boat. The man offered to help them repair it and even provided the mutton fat. He claimed it belonged to his foster brother up at the head of the lake, and he didn't have time to take it back.

The little Irish slave girl was a worker. Treasa could see why the druid would be loathe to lose her. The child stitched torn hides on the boat. She smeared mutton fat on the rigging, the hull, and herself. And then, just after Nones, she dropped the paddle she was whittling—the boat did not come with paddles—cried out, and fainted dead away.

Broichan the druid stood beside the alders near the boat. Behind him clustered three younger druids and a couple of burly retainers. Treasa loosened her sword and moved in close, where she could leap between the retainers and Colm if things came apart.

Either totally unafraid or totally stupid, Colm stepped up to Broichan with an effusive greeting.

Broichan waved a hand toward the alders beside them. "It's bad luck to pass alders on a journey."

"So I've heard. We camp beneath them."

Broichan nodded. "So tell me, Dove of the Church, when do you propose to sail?"

"As soon as the boat is ready, if God permits."

Broichan dropped his voice down to that hissing, menacing wheeze he had so beautifully perfected. "On the contrary. I'm going to make winds unfavorable to your voyage and cause great darkness to envelop you in its shade."

Colm switched into his preaching mode. Treasa had been expecting it long before this. "The almighty power of God rules all things, and in His name and under His guiding providence all our movements are directed."

He went on and on, but Treasa paid more attention to the retainers than to the sermon. They were obviously waiting for a word, and obviously the word didn't come.

The assistant druids bravely tried to keep up with Colm's arguments; that was clear. Within five minutes, their eyes glassed over.

Broichan removed himself then to a nearby hillock topped by a long-abandoned ringwall. In Erin, people already were claiming that these grassy mounds were fairy rings and attributing magical qualities to them. The thought that they were simply farms from the distant past never seemed to enter anyone's head, despite that ringwalled raths in various states of decay studded all of Erin. Just in the last twenty years, the plague alone had created scores of them.

The boat was ready the next morning, so Colm ordered everyone aboard. In lieu of the donkey they stowed a sack of dried peas, two of those miserable cabbages, and a bushel of stripped beef jerky. Whoever now owned the donkey got the better of that trade.

The wind kicked up from the southwest even as Treasa was stepping aboard and came down the loch a-whooshing. It churned the water into muddy froth along the shore here.

Absolutely terrified, the Irish ex-slave clambered into the boat and huddled in a tight knot up in the bow. No doubt it appeared she was doomed any way she saw it—drowned if she stayed with this mad monk, garroted if she returned to her former master.

Gavin shoved them off the bank into deeper water and crawled into the boat. The wind should have driven them right back up against the beach. They floated free, ten feet offshore.

"Raise the sail." Colm untied the reefs.

Gavin opened his mouth and closed it again. Nobody on this boat had to tell anyone else that the wind was blowing in the wrong direction.

By jerky, creaking increments, the sail climbed its greased mast.

Treasa watched the hillock beyond. A thick mist was rising off the river, climbing that gentle slope. Up on the grassy old ringwall—or fairy ring, if that's your preference—Broichan raised both arms. His exultant cackle carried clear to the boat here.

Colm began a song, quite likely one of the psalms from that contentious book he and Finnian had fought over. He sang of monsters sporting in the deep and of ships going down to the sea.

His voice gained power as the boat began to bob and move—upwind!

The Irish maid uncurled from her knot and stood up to look, as incredulous as everyone else. The contrary wind was pushing the sail back, yet they surged steadily forward on their way.

Against the wind, against all reason, they were heading home.

19

Gavin's Loss

Year of our Lord 564

Once I tasted joy with every meal
* when you loved me.*

Treasa sat cross-legged and draped her elbows across her knees. Beside her, Fergus stretched out in the warm grass. With a contented sigh, he closed his eyes.

Comgall and Kenneth had embarked for the Irish coast very early this morning, before first light. They were probably there by now, or nearly so. The slave girl with them was certain to find a good life at Drumceatt or Aghaboe, wherever they left her. With her industry and cute looks, she'd snare a man in no time at all.

Colm and his assistants were this moment bobbing their way toward Iona. Treasa could see his shining blond head in the boat, nearing the southern point of the Isle of Mull. Better them bobbing than she. Still, she was going to have to face the sea voyage sooner or later.

Anice had gone home. Where did she live? Some tiny rath alive with mud and fleas, no doubt.

And Gavin. He too had left the party early and angled off across the hills to home, but he could look forward to a king's life and a king's bed with his wife in it.

What a motley crew it had been. And what a splendid adventure! *Those bolts falling out . . . sailing against the wind . . .* Sure and Treasa would never see the like again! Her father had worked some amazing magic in his day, but nothing like that.

She jabbed Fergus's ribs and whipped around to her knees. "Horses."

He sat bolt upright. From beyond a little oak-hazel grove on the hillcrest came a ri's party—a king and half a dozen retainers. Treasa had her sword halfway out before she recognized them.

She dropped around to sitting again. "Gavin."

Fergus growled something unintelligible and flopped back onto the grass, prostrate—his natural habitat. The dark prince rode up beside them, slid off his horse, and handed the reins to an aide.

Treasa wiggled a finger. "New horse. I haven't seen him before. Nice color, sorrel."

"Thank you. It's a gift from my ri tuatha out on Skye. Pictish, taken in a recent raid of which I was not part." Gavin settled down beside her and pointed seaward. "That's Colm's boat, isn't it?"

"Just now rounding Mull there? Yes. He got a late start. After you left they decided the girl's fate. She's going with Kenneth, either to Aghaboe or Drumceatt. Comgall's not real pleased with following Colm around the world, so he's making noises about becoming a hermit." Treasa shrugged broadly. "In short, nothing's new."

"It'll never happen—Comgall becoming a hermit. He wouldn't have anyone to bellyache to. Greetings, Fergus."

"And the best of life to yourself, Prince." Fergus didn't twitch a finger.

Treasa smirked. "We wore him out that that last thirty miles."

"He didn't have to carry the full load." Gavin paused. "Though it's nice that he did. Colm's talking about building a circuit of missions around through the islands—Skye, Ardnamurchan, Kintyre, Lochaber, maybe clear over to Loch Ness. I think he kind of likes that area."

"And why not? Spectacular scenery, an air of mystery about it, the center of the heathen realm, and the site of a major victory over the region's biggest druid. He didn't say anything about such a plan to me, but I wouldn't really expect him too. You're his confidant."

"It wasn't a confidence as such. He was dreaming. You know how he does."

"Going to go with him?"

"Probably. At least part of the time." Gavin cooled noticeably. *Now what's going on?* "We brought lunch. Interested?"

"Always."

Fergus sat up. The quickest way to get that man's attention was to mention food.

Gavin twisted around and signaled his retainers. There were times Treasa rather wished she were a queen. Meal times, mostly. No preparations, no cleanup, no fuss.

As his retainers unloaded the leathern bags slung across their saddles, Gavin prated on. "I tried to tell Colm he's not the only fish swimming in this sea. Many are the Christian proselytizers working this general area, or did once. Ninian, of course, back in Patrick's time. Kentigern, south in Strathclyde. The church down in England made him a bishop and a war drove him to Wales, but that's over and he's back, I hear. Then there's Kessog. Hey! He might be a relative of Colm's on his mum's side."

"Cashel area?"

"The same. He died only a couple years ago. Worked out of a fraternity down on an island in Loch Lomond. South of here a-ways. I think the brotherhood is still there."

"But nobody up here in the Dal Riada."

"Going to be. Kenneth is all enthusiastic about building out on Tiree. In spitting distance of Iona."

"So is Comgall of all people." Treasa cast a glance toward meal preparations. ""The whole world is going to build on Tiree, it sounds like."

"Beyond me." Gavin rubbed his face. "Iona is as dreadful a slab of nothing as you're likely to find, but Tiree's worse. Worse weather, worse wind, worse land to raise cattle on. What gets into these people?"

Stiffly, like the old man he was fast becoming, Fergus stood and stretched. "Hiding in the farthest corner of the world can appeal mightily when life weighs heavy—especially if you've no ties of land or goods to keep ye home."

Gavin chilled again. Fergus, bless him, wandered off then, probably answering a call.

Treasa lowered her voice. "You went home yesterday. Why are you back here?"

"My wife greeted me with the news that she's decided she can do better without me. It might have been my home yesterday, but not today."

"Gavin—"

"Divorce is common. You know that. Her brehons are—"

"Not among people of God."

He snorted. "What makes you think I'm of God? Colm worked the miracles. Not my sword or yours kept us safe—it was his God. His relationship with God." Gavin flapped a mitt, a random gesture. "Anyway, her brehons are working it out, and I have no say whatever in the matter."

"No more kingship?" Treasa dipped her head toward the retainers.

"For a few weeks, until her people make the arrangements. I'm a prince by blood. I'll keep that. But since it's her brehons, I doubt I'll get much more than the horse I'm riding."

All manner of thoughts clamored in Treasa's head. *Don't just lie down and quit! Fight her! Bring in your own brehons! You're in with King Conal. Use the contacts your royal blood provides. Let Colm put a whammy on her or something.*

She held her peace. If Gavin hadn't entertained all those thoughts himself, he soon would. What Treasa saw beside her now was a man who had been soaring two days ago and now was utterly crushed. The sight pained her more than she would have believed possible. He didn't deserve this. But then, he probably deserved better than that wife to start with. He was a king's grandson. He should be ard ri himself, not a ri ruirech in a backwater of the Dal Riada.

Fergus returned in good time to partake of the boiled mutton, the barleycake, and the jug of ale. They ate in silence, taking their time, savoring the peace.

The mutton had been rubbed in garlic. Delicious. Treasa licked her fingers. "So where are you going? Iona?"

Gavin shook his head. "Too much daily offices. I don't want to know what time it is that badly. I thought maybe I'd go see a town. I've never seen a town."

"They're probably just big monasteries. I hear Glasgow is a town now."

"I don't mean Glasgow, or the little Angle and Jute towns. I mean a big one. One the Romans left behind. Londinium is big— what do they call it now? London town. Or Bath. Or someplace in

France." He grinned. "Think of it, Treasa! Hundreds of people in one place and not one of them a monk."

London town. A world away. Two or three worlds. She would never see the regal Hawk again. She ate his bread, and she ate his mutton, and down inside she mourned.

Gavin and his retainers saw Fergus and her down to the shore. The prince bartered their passage with a fisherman for the balance of the ale, bread, and mutton. It crushed her that his generous gesture was probably one of his final acts as a ri ruirech.

The fisherman took the food home to his children before he launched his curragh. They bobbed to Inishowen Head because that was the quickest Erse landfall. The fisherman didn't want to spend any more time with this fare than necessary, and Treasa didn't want to spend a moment longer in the boat than necessary. Everyone went home happy.

They stopped at Drumceatt to pick up their horses, but they didn't linger there. It didn't feel the same with Colm gone. Apparently the Irish ex-slave had continued on to Aghaboe, for she wasn't here.

Fergus and Treasa arrived home to learn that raiders had run off three thousand Monaghan cattle, a hundred of Treasa's among them. Surviving boaires suspected the Mountain Behr. The resulting planning and preparation and then the retaliatory raids kept her busy for the balance of the year.

20

Colm's Messenger

I am the rising sun,
* Singing my Lord into the morning.*
I am the setting sun,
* Crooning my Savior into the night.*
See the darkness flee before my song!

A brisk windchop lifted Colm's curragh high, then shot it nose-down into the next trough. The tough little boat bolted straight up and plummeted again. Colm's oarsmen were rowing for all they were worth, but most of their progress was horizontal and vertical; the shore of Iona and home remained tantalizingly distant.

The sea had been relatively munificent until they rounded Mull. *Grace be served,* Colm mused, *Treasa would not have these conditions on her return to Erin. A horseman she was, and superb. A sailor she was not.*

Colm braced against the stern gunwales, but he was only moderately successful in compensating for these unpredictable lunges and lurches. "Trena!" He waved an arm southward, sort of. "Put ashore down there. It's easier."

Trena scowled. "And carry the blooming curragh home, Father?"

"Beach it until the wind shifts. It can't blow in this perverse direction forever. Fetch the boat home tomorrow or whenever."

Grumbling something about a mile-long hike, Trena thrust his long oar off the stern and ruddered the little boat aport. Riding the tide at this southwesterly angle did wonders for their progress. They raised the rock-studded cobble beach within fifteen minutes.

First over the side, Colm dragged the boat into the shallow, as the sea lifted it and dropped it on the shingle with each wash of the waves. The oarsmen, and lastly Trena, tumbled over the gunwale. Together they pulled her above high tide line and left her

184

right side up to fill with rainwater if she wished. After weighting her down against the wind with boulders, the seamen-turned-hikers grudgingly began slogging upshore toward the monastery.

Colm paused. "I feel like walking up over the ridge in that direction. Tell them not to expect me till supper." He angled away from the disgruntled hikers and worked his way northwestward across the island, picking that particular route and direction for absolutely no reason at all.

Everywhere around him, short, dense bushes turned their rounded backs to the wind; the constant breeze off the open water seemed to trim them all to the same hunched slant. Wildflowers galore peeked out from creases in the rocks, from under the shelter of the bushes. None stood boldly against the wind. Flowers know better than to buck the irresistible. Tufts of grass grew long and rank anywhere they could gain a purchase. Sheep had not grazed this area in the recent past. This was the wild side of the island, the land not well used, and Colm loved it.

He strode amid smooth, domed rock and loose stones, reveling in the stability beneath his feet. He was of necessity becoming a fairly good seaman—so much of his ministry took him from island to island and occasionally to Erin—but he still preferred walking to bobbing any day of the week.

He exulted. He felt good! Like the cool wind at his back, he possessed great power and traveled far. Brude and his Picts—Inverness—the whole Loch Ness region—what a fertile field of endeavor! The Dal Riada required attention too. Every day Colm saw the need for churches and centers throughout Aberdeen, and at least one per island and coastland, to teach and preach and lead the people up out of depravity into a higher, holier walk with God.

So much to do!

He ought to sail out to Hinba one of these days and check into how well they were getting on. He could go over to Tiree, a short hop from the northwest shore, and try to develop a feel for the lay of that land, since Kenneth and Comgall were talking about building communities there.

By and by he stood on a rocky spine much farther north and west than he'd intended to walk. The machair stretched out before him in its vivid green. It rather surprised him that he'd come this far so fast. Beyond the flat and spacious patch of the machair, the sea stretched on forever until it met the sky.

He followed the ridge, the open meadows and barley fields to his left, the stony backbone of Iona to his right. He had to rock-hop, and he stumbled a lot. Such cross-country hiking was harder than one would think. He crossed the east-west track that carried the workaday farmers and the less adventurous between the machair here on the west coast and the monastery on the east shore.

He sat down on an inviting boulder to rest. The view from this spot was nothing short of spectacular, with the hill behind, the rocky ridges to either side, the machair before and the sea beyond. He felt comfortable here. It was a rather bright place, well exposed to the sun from before noon till nightfall.

He could build a clochan here as a retreat. A getaway. A haven apart for meditation and contemplation. This place lay only a couple hundred yards from one of the sheep trails coming off the main track. Easy to get to and yet remote. Yes. He'd do it.

The sun was headed inexorably toward its daily dousing in the western sea. The light ought to be turning warmer, yellower, softer, and so it did out across the leas and rockfields. In this immediate area at least, though, it seemed more a cold blue.

Colm leaped to his feet, wheeling. He flung his arms up in defense against an apparent attacker. The attacker sat quietly on a nearby rock, looking bemused. He was a man approximately Colm's size and build, as blond and fair complexioned as he. He wore a tunic but no cloak at all. The hems of his tunic didn't seem to flitter in the breeze the way Colm's hem and cloak did.

"I didn't hear you approach, and I've never seen you before. Who are you, and why are you here?"

Smooth, sonorous, and mellow, the fellow's voice suggested to Colm that perhaps God talked with just this sort of tone and inflections. His Erse was cultured yet casual. "To take your points in order: no, you'll not hear me approach; you've never seen me before, but you'll see me many times in the future; I am a messenger from God, and I'm here to deliver a message."

This had to be a dream. Colm often experienced strange and interesting dreams. Surely it was a trick of the mind brought on by exhaustion from the harrowing journey to Inverness.

Colm shook his head. "The voice of God has spoken to me on occasion in the past. I've recognized it. You're different."

"Very different." The fellow actually radiated a soft, bluish light now. "Not too many hundreds of years ago, Sadducees and Pharisees argued about whether we existed. Rather silly argument, when you think about it. Specious. Scripture treats angels matter-of-factly. Flatteringly, I'd like to think—at least to those of us who stayed true. You know the passages well. So why are you surprised?"

Colm weighed the wildly strange improbability of this whole ridiculous encounter. If the fellow meant him harm, he was doomed; no way could he win a contest against someone who glows with holy light. He forced himself to relax and sat down again on his boulder.

He thought a moment about the man's question. That moment also allowed his jangled nerves to quiet themselves a little. "No, actually, I don't think I'm surprised that an angel would exist. I am surprised that an angel would deign to sit down in conversation with me. And I'm wary. Satan disguises himself as an angel of light. I've many a battle with Satan. This may be one more manifestation of that war."

And then Colm's intense curiosity overcame his caution. "Angels are supposedly noncorporeal. Yet there you sit. I see you."

"And if you touch me you will find me solid." The angel smiled, and Colm would have to say it was an infectious smile, utterly candid and happy. "Remember when Jacob wrestled with an angel and almost won?"

"In Genesis. I've read Genesis several times."

"Jacob was pretty evenly matched. If you wrestle an angel, you'll be evenly matched. If instead of being one of the most powerful men in Erin you were five feet high and weighed less than an iron cauldron, you'd still be evenly matched. We assume form recognizable and comfortable to the people who receive our messages. We have enough barriers to overcome without adding a too-alien appearance to them."

"So if I were dark like an Ethiopian . . ."

The magnificent head nodded. "You've studied the Acts of the Apostles. You know Philip's story—how he ministered in the conversion of Candace's eunuch. An angel told him to go down the Gaza road. Philip was a puny little fellow. He looked as if you could push him over with a barley straw. I have no idea how he managed the strength and stamina to achieve all he did and travel so swiftly and steadily. Anyway, his messenger appeared to him in a puny form. Black hair, crackling black eyes. Much like Philip but not resembling him in the face."

Colm chuckled. "And here I always thought angels would be bigger than life, with fiery eyes. Imposing. Frightening."

"Oh, sure and we can do that when it's to our advantage. You should have seen how we came to the shepherds at our Lord's birth. We were all over the sky."

Colm was still suspicious, still felt that he had to be talking to an instrument of Satan. Disguised, the creature was. Surely so. And yet, there was a complete comfort about this situation. For once in his life, Colm felt at a total loss.

Wait! Not at a loss at all! "If you be of God and not of Satan, you will be able to praise God freely for me. Extol Jesus Christ as Lord of lords."

And the brightest, sweetest smile spread across the angel's face. Colm would have rather expected Greek or Latin. This being, though, sang in clear Erse. And what Erse! Colm heard the deepest, the most poetic, the most moving paean of praise he ever could have imagined. Beyond imagination! He tried to remember the words, at least some of the phrasing, but the moment the song entered his heart, it evaporated from his memory. The hymn ended.

Brusquely, Colm wiped the tears off his cheeks. "You are wholly of God. Speak to me."

The angel bobbed his head. "You like this place."

"I do."

"So do I. Build your clochan here, your haven of respite."

"You can tell what I've been thinking."

"No, I can't. That's the Father's prerogative. He tells me what you're thinking."

"You're in communion with Him now?"

"Constantly. No sin barrier. Continual state of prayer, you would probably call it. Usually, we deliver our message and be done with it. I've taken a while here, though, to establish myself because we will talk from time to time, you and I. I'll be able to offer guidance at times, and solace. A sympathetic ear."

Colm smiled grimly. "Sure and you've not forgotten that I'm on the other end of that particular ax handle. People bring me their problems."

"That hardly means you don't need the same ministry served to yourself. Your feelings toward Treasa, for example. You've no one to tell them to. Now you have me."

Colm's mouth sprang open to deny. It closed, the denial unspoken. Whether it be God's eyes or an angel's, this being saw into the deepest corners of Colm's heart, corners Colm himself dared not carry a lamp into. Yes, he admired Treasa—her gifts. Admired. Valued as a friend. Prurient thoughts? He did not allow them. Love? Not the man-woman kind. No. That temptation would be too much to bear. True, were he a king instead of an abbot he might even marry her. But . . .

The angel seemed to accept that absence of denial as a confession. He nodded slowly. "When you feel a strong urge to absent yourself and come away, do so."

Colm dumped the subject completely. "I'll begin the clochan tomorrow. That is the message?"

"No, this is: You have a rocky field to plow, Columcille. Keep in mind our Lord's words, that no one who puts his hand to the plow and then looks back is worthy. You must press forward with what you know is God's will despite the personal heartache it will cause you."

"I'm no stranger to heartache."

The angel smiled sadly. He seemed to glow a bit brighter now. "You haven't experienced what I'm talking about. You will turn everyone against yourself—your closest friends, your clan, even your cousin, the closest companion of your youth. Your friends will hate you. The church men will envy you and outlaw you and refuse to raise you to a bishopric despite your work. Press on."

189

"They outlawed me already. You must know why I'm on Iona in the first place."

"Your self-imposed exile is basically over one occasion. And you still travel freely in Erin. We're talking the long run here—the lifetime."

Colm sat back, locked his elbows, and braced his palms on his knees, digesting this. It would not digest. It whirled about inside him. "So I give up everything that's important to me to serve people who don't particularly want to be served in a land that has no real meaning for me."

"You've established churches in Donegal, your home. You've been given the Sight, and you receive power for miracles. Some would say you've gotten the better of the trade."

"What about my work?"

"Angels just deliver messages. We generally stay out of the prophecy business. We can't see the future any better than you can."

"But it can be revealed to you by God." Colm resisted a strong impulse to throw himself pleading at the angel's feet. But he didn't want it to seem a sign of worship. "Please! I need a reason to keep struggling."

The being dipped his head, a sort of *that's reasonable* gesture. He hesitated long moments, studying the ground, before speaking. "As regards your scholarship and copying. You and others of like mind will almost single-handedly save the Word of God for posterity. Remain diligent—the work is vital. Your work down in Donegal will stand through time. Many will evangelize the north here, as many already have, but the churches in Aberdeen will point to you as their father. Hinba will fall into eclipse. Lambay will die. Durrow and Drumceatt will be much altered. Lindesfarne will glow and suffer. The name of Kells will live in the work done there. Iona will stand as a beacon to the ages. Fifteen hundred years from now people will still be speaking your name as a hero of the faith in Erin and all these northlands."

The angel stood, and in his standing he became taller than life. "Try as you will, you are not a man of peace, Columcille. Too much of the hot blood of warlords rules your life. It will be your stumbling block and your grief—the grief of many—but not your undoing."

What do you say to a departing angel? Godspeed? Go in peace? Blessings on you? They all seemed so trivial in this situation. Colm stood up, but before he could collect his thoughts enough to say anything at all, this cosmic creature seemed to expand, to whisk upward and away, to disintegrate, all at the same time.

Stunned, Colm stared at the silent, empty, golden, twilight sky.

How often had he sung of his Lord Jesus, "You the King of moon and sun, you the King of stars . . . ," never thinking, never grasping that his Lord was indeed the King of the cosmos. This creature beyond ken belonged to the cosmos; he belonged to God. As messenger he tied Colm directly to God. The enormity of it all sucked his breath away.

Incredible, and yet engraved upon his memory indelibly. He remembered every word, except for that hymn of praise. Of that he remembered only the intense feeling of worship it resonated inside him. It must have been a dream of some sort . . . But no matter the vehicle. The message had been delivered.

Many, many thoughts scrambled for the chance to be pondered first. The thought that actually emerged for consideration first surprised and embarrassed him. He was going to have to dredge up his feelings about Treasa and do something about them. They hovered far closer to the light than he had suspected. She represented a much greater temptation than ever he had guessed. If he was going to give up so much (lose Gavin's support? God, no!) and gain so much, he must minimize every temptation he found lurking.

He looked about at this place, this holy spot. He would build immediately. His life was going to require a lot more separation for prayer and contemplation than he had anticipated.

21

Anice's Light

Light of the world,
Light of my life,
Light of my day,
Today,
O Three in One.

The wolves were howling tonight, and within a quarter mile of her door. Anice could hear them coming closer, closer. Wolves weren't known to fall upon people, and she owned no livestock. Still, she wished she had some dogs. Truth, she didn't even have a ringwall. Her hut sat amid pines and yews, unprotected. She settled in close to her little fire, such a tiny orange dot in a vast black world, and laid the last of her birch branches on it.

She would wait a while before going to sleep. Too often, disturbing dreams marred these long, long winter nights. The oxhide over her doorway rattled, and she jumped. *Wind.* A fitful wind was picking up out there. She could tell because a gust now and then would backdraft down her roof hole and swirl the pall of smoke below her rafters.

The last of the birch. At her right hand, a stack of oak branches. At her left, a stack of rowan. Anice almost didn't have the courage to do it.

She must break her ties with the past if she would bind herself to a bright future. She'd figured that much out. She forced herself to pick up a length of oak limb. She made herself lay it across the burning birch and the coals. Again, another. The oak was slow to catch, slow to burn, and very warm.

Oak, the sacred tree of this land's druids. It felt so strange to deny the druids' hold over her by burning their wood. She knew their magic and their deep, deep wisdom.

By the time the bulk of her oak pile had dissolved to ash,

Colm and Gavin were probably sound asleep somewhere, the Compline long since sung.

On her left, the rowan. Mountain ash is such a lovely tree. In fact, even these broken branches had a grace about them, with pretty bark and a slim line. The sacred tree of Erin's druids. Erin, her adopted home. She was sorry it had un-adopted her. It was not nearly so hard to lay the rowan branches on her fire, denying the power of Erin's druids over her. Would that she could so easily deny the power of Erin's brehons.

She heard rustling in the forest duff very close to her door-way. Quickly she laid two additional sticks on the fire. Long moments later, it crackled brighter.

Once, long ago, Gavin had told her that Colm's father, Phelim, wanted Colm to be named Phelan, Wolf. It would have been so much more apt than Dove. Colm enjoyed many traits in common with the fierce predators outside her door.

She dozed. She melted to half-lying. She startled. She sat up long enough to add the last of the oak and bank the back of her fire, then curled up beside it to sleep.

Anice awoke still nicely warm, her fire reduced to coals but not out. She cooked up the last of her stirabout and was eating when it dawned on her that she had not dreamt last night. No bad dreams, no ordinary dreams—no dreams at all.

She ought to take her iron pot. It was a very nice pot. But it was also very heavy. She must leave it. She ought to take the battle-ax her husband had given her, the one she carried the day he died. She tucked it in the rope at her waist. Should she encounter predators of either four or two legs, it might prove valuable. She ought to take her ladle and meathook and the bit of hide left over from when she'd made her shoes. No. Too heavy.

On second thought, she would need barter to get where she wanted to go. She scooped up the iron pot, the implements, and the hide. Burdened as little as possible, she stepped out into the cold, clammy gray of first light. She left the hut to whomever might happen upon it. *Let them listen to the wolves. Perhaps they would have dogs.*

By sunup she stood on the seashore, watching fairly quiet waters slosh listlessly against the cobble beach. On the last leg of their journey home from that fateful visit to Brude at Inverness, Colm and Gavin talked about a mission circuit of some sort. Colm spoke of traveling to areas in and near the Dal Riada, exhorting believers and making new converts. What areas? Her memory groped in dark corners, seeking names.

Skye for sure. Ardnamurchan. That was within walking distance. Kintyre? Lochaber? Which place? One of those or some other?

She had abandoned the druids of her fathers without really adopting any substitute. She felt empty, bereft of comfort or security. Finnian of Moville and Colm both claimed that all miracles come from God, who holds all power. Anice couldn't accept that. Druids held immense power. On occasion, Finnian attributed great power to Satan, the master of all evil.

Finnian, you can't have it both ways. Either God is all power or He isn't.

She didn't dare call upon a God she'd never really learned much about, but she had no alternative. She should not have burned her bridges, literally and figuratively.

She began to walk. She did not even consciously form a prayer along the lines of "Please guide me." She simply walked. By noon she was getting very hungry. Having no meat in it, nor even any flavoring, her stirabout did not last long. She walked on.

Sometime in midafternoon, she came upon a pair of beggars —cheery fellows. Some passing woman had thrown them a loaf of barley bread. For no particular reason that Anice could discern, they gave her a chunk of it when she greeted them. She thanked them profusely and walked on.

The sun was setting when she passed a rath on a hillside near the track. Its dogs warned her not to come near, but the goodwife chased them off to the bier and called to Anice to enter if she wished. She wished. That night she ate pork and slept on a pallet before the fire. She had not expected any of that luxury.

The goodwife's wooden ladle had fallen in the fire and burnt past use, so Anice gave the woman her iron ladle. It was a few pounds less to carry more than charity.

The next morning she walked on. If God was leading her to Skye, He was going to have to provide a ferry. If He was leading her to Ardnamurchan, He was still going to have to provide a ferry, or else she would have to walk all the way around Loch Sunart.

Another day's walk brought her to the loch. Now what? With no clear direction, she sat down on the shore. Perhaps she should walk west and find a boat to take her across to Mull. It was a very short distance. Then she would walk to the west coast of Mull and go to Iona. Rather than walk all over seeking Colm, she would simply wait in his lair until he returned home.

But she did not want to wait. Local gossip claimed that he was on the road. No one knew for how long.

The sun had nearly set when an aged woman came dottering in from the same track Anice had traveled. The woman's eyes watered, very bleary, and she didn't have a tooth in her head. She settled on the shore near Anice and wrapped herself tightly in her cloak.

She grinned, baring pink gums. "Y're going to hear duh great monk too, are ye?"

"The great monk?"

"Columcille. He'th coming down from Thkye today or tomorrow." Every *S* she pronounced sounded like a drop of water on a hot rock—whooshing, hissing, breathy, almost a *th*—but not quite. "He healed Muriel, ye know. Th-e had arthritith tho bad th-e couldn't pick up a thtick uhff ffirewood." Her *Fs* were just as mangled as her *Ss*. "He put hith hand on her and healed her." The ancient head bobbed. "I thaw it!"

"I heard he healed sick people on Iona."

"Health thick people anywhere he wantth to."

"He's coming from Skye? Where? To Ardnamurchan?"

The woman twisted to stare at her. "And where elth but Ardnamurchan? Why elth would we be thitting here but to go to Ardnamurchan?" She leaned forward, thrusting her face toward Anice's. "Thith I heard ffrom duh ri himthelff. Columcille and two ffriendth are croth-ing that rocky country below duh poin'—"

"Over there, you mean?" Anice pointed across the loch.

"Where elth, aye? And hith companionth are talking about two kingth. What doeth Colm thay but, 'Why do ye talk ffoolithly of duh kingth? Both had their headth cut off today. Thith berry day thum thailorth ffrom Erin will come and tell ye tho.' And it happened!"

"Sailors from Erin and everything, exactly as he said?"

195

"Egthakly. Muirbolc paradithi, it wath. Pordnamurloch in Lithmore. I know it'th true becauth I even know duh nameth uhff duh companionth. Laithran Mac Fferadach and Diormid."

Anice didn't know the location, couldn't understand its name, and doubted if the old woman had gotten it right. No matter. She was well aware of Colm's ability to see things that were happening elsewhere.

Three other people, two men and a boy, had arrived. They settled on the shore near enough to listen.

The crone leaned even closer. She wanted greatly for a bath. "Thure and y'rthelff hath heard a tale or two about duh bleth-ed abbot."

"Many a tale. For instance, he has a very good friend, Kenneth, who is the founding abbot of a monastery in Ossory. That's down near Clonmacnois. Aghaboe."

She wrinkled her bird's-beak nose. "Cow pathture?"

The three near them were joined by two more from the track.

"Right. That's the translation. Anyway, Columcille, you see, was caught in a storm while he was sailing, and he told the monks in the boat with him, 'Don't fear. This very moment Kenneth is running to pray for us with a single shoe.' And Kenneth at exactly that time got a powerful urge to pray for Colm and hurried to his oratory with one shoe on and the other in his hand."

The woman's watery eyes sparkled. She nodded, immensely pleased with a story that was obviously new to her.

The five were also nodding and murmuring. Four others approached from the south tract and joined the general group. In the distance, on the far shore, dozens of people were walking west.

Anice decided not to mention that she had heard the story a scant two years ago on that mission journey to Inverness, from the mouths of Colm and Kenneth themselves.

The woman said, rather accusingly, "Ye thpeak ffunny."

You think I speak funny? But Anice didn't say it aloud. "I lived for many years in Erin, the wife of a ri tuatha near Derry."

"That'th it. Duh ackthent. Y're not married now?"

"He died in battle. Then his children and brothers conspired against me to take the property." She shrugged. "I fought them as

196

best I could, but I was Pict and they were clan. I came away with nothing."

"No sthildren uhff y'r own to take y're cauth?"

"No children of my own to take my cause." What an empty life!

"Thad. Tho thad." *Yes, it was.*

Anice could see nearly a mile of the far shore and nary a boat. Why were they all sitting here? People kept arriving.

Then from out in the sound, a four-oar curragh appeared. Its two boatmen rowed right up to the party here. One of the oarsmen twisted and called, "A cow or the equivalent, and you all may cross."

A few of them grumbled about walking around the loch. Anice stood up. "An iron pot, a meathook, and half a hide."

A man stepped in beside her and held up a dirk. "This knife."

The boatman and his companion decided those goods would do and began ferrying people across, beginning with the barterers —Anice and the man. The old woman displayed an amazing agility, hopping into the boat unbidden. Three others boarded as well, bringing the water line to within six inches of the gunwales. But the loch was calm, the air still. They made it just fine, and the boat headed back for the next load.

Anice let the old woman and the man lead. They seemed to know where they were going as they left the shore and pressed up into the tangled hills. They fell in among dozens and dozens of others, all traveling in the determined manner of people who want to get somewhere. They ought be determined—night was coming on rapidly.

Anice heard the buzz of conversation somewhere in the distance ahead, hundreds of voices. And then they ceased as a most familiar and powerful voice rolled forth in song. *Columcille.*

"Glory to duh Ffodder! Hear duh boith uhff an anthel!"

Voice of an angel indeed. Colm communed with angels on occasion, he told his close friends. No wonder he would sound like one.

Anice let the crowd carry her over the lip of an open, rounded hill into a natural amphitheater. People sat all over the hillside, wrapped in cloaks against the November chill. More and more

197

people shoved in among them until the hillside was virtually packed.

Down in front, two bonfires and a row of torches lighted the choir of monks singing vespers. Colm had completed the solo anthem and stepped back among the brethren again. Although he sang as just another monk, Colm stood a head above the others, his white-blond hair gleaming in the flickering light.

What a splendid husband he would have made, if only . . . If only. What a splendid ard ri, as well.

The final "Thanks be to God" echoed away into the night air. Colm stepped forward. With words that covered the hillside, reaching every ear, he praised the wisdom and nobility of the druids. Anice's mouth dropped open. Never in a lifetime would she have expected this from Colm!

For a hundred generations, he claimed, the druids had been earnestly seeking the highest level of truth and knowledge. In that search they achieved amazing insight and power. They long recognized Mabon, the child who sacrificed himself for the world, the divine child who desires to live in every human being.

And then, in less than five minutes, Colm identified the promised divine one of the druids as the Christ, Jesus of Nazareth. From his Scriptures, from his beloved books, he showed that what the druids had so long been seeking had now come to pass.

He told a story then that he claimed was true: How wise magicians, the far-eastern equivalent of druids, saw a star that led them to the Christ. He told about the duplicity of the ri ruirech—Herod—and the Baby's flight to avoid death. A thousand heads bobbed knowingly. Yes, that's a king for you. The magicians were wise enough, he concluded, to go home by some other route and avoid the ri ruirech.

With an expansive gesture, hands raised, Colm invited everyone there to claim the Christ as the Savior their druids had so long been seeking. "Come," he called in that voice that tickled heaven. "Come, accept the Divine Son into your hearts as the druids and the Scriptures all foretold. He died for you. Live forever in Him."

He said other words of encouragement, but Anice didn't hear them. She sat entranced, remembering scattered bits of things Finnian had said in his many homilies. They had never come together before this moment. They made sense now. Finnian had been speaking to people he assumed already knew about Jesus and wanted further enlightenment. Never, that she could remember, did he speak as if his hearer did not know the least thing about the Son of God. She wondered how many others in that monastery, like herself, possessed no real grasp of the Christ.

Somewhere in his exhortation, Colm called all new believers to baptism. Many a baptism had Anice watched at Moville, as kings' children and the offspring of various royals and civil servants came to Finnian to be blessed. None but a fool would immerse herself in the frigid waters of November. The monks picked up the torches then and led the way eastward across the hill, singing. Hundreds of people followed them. Anice leaped to her feet and pushed in among the crowd, ready, even eager, to become a fool.

The vast assemblage, some of them converts and some of them merely curious, swarmed across the hill behind the monks to a small loch in a glen to the east. Other monks, attendants for the faithful, stood waiting on the shore. The first few people to be baptized, Anice guessed, were being re-baptized, for without prodding or instruction they knew just what to do. As an attendant held a broad linen sheet up protectively, they shed their warm woolen clothes. Wrapped in that flimsy sheet, they splashed down into the lake. Other monks led them out, signed the cross before them, and dipped them under the surface. Anice shivered just thinking about it.

Already the monks with the torches were igniting fires laid along the shore. Huge fires they were, bright and cheerful, dancing with joy. Finnian's words: "All the stars sing for joy." The same joy, no doubt.

As cold as it would be for her, imagine the misery of the poor monks who stood out in the lake receiving converts. Where would Colm station himself? It startled her to see him wade out into the lake when he could so easily stay warm ashore. But then, come to think of it, that was typical of him.

Hundreds pressed around her, in front of her, behind her. Anice could not hope to be baptized by Colm himself when scores of freezing monks out there awaited the new believers. She let the crush move her forward. And now there was no one before her save an attendant. He held up a soaking wet linen sheet to pre-serve her modesty. She shed her warm cloak and tunic with more reluctance than was holy, probably.

Without even looking toward her, he wrapped that cold linen around her. She gasped with the shock of it. Thoroughly chilled and not yet in the water, she stumbled down the shore. With the firelight behind her, she walked out into the unbelievably cold, unbelievably dark lake. Curiously, the water felt warmer than the sheet.

Strong arms seized her and dipped her under. She barely had time to grab her nose. The strong arms swept her up out of the water, out of death and the grave. And the voice who blessed her in the name of the Three was Colm's!

Her eyes and ears drenched, she could neither see nor hear worth anything. Then Colm's voice, alive with joy, cried, "Anice!" The distant firelight made his face glow, and he was laughing as she had never seen him laugh before. He hugged her, praising God over and over. He put her on her feet and sent her shoreward, calling, "Stay with our party! I want to talk to you!"

Her attendant met her with her tunic. She dropped it over her head and for the first time felt that possibly she would survive this. She wrapped in her cloak and headed for a fire.

Many were the ways Colm from time to time had described the Three in One. He used Patrick's figure of the shamrock—three distinct leaves, yet one leaf. He cited water as an example—snow, rain, and steam but water all the same. But none of the world's figures explained it. Finnian certainly never did. Even quiet, schol-arly Kenneth had not been able. The Trinity had always confused Anice to the point that she simply dismissed the whole puzzle.

To her utter amazement, as she huddled with the scores of shivering, babbling, singing converts around the fire, the puzzle faded. She would never be able to articulate it the way Colm and the others so carefully tried. No scholar, she. But she sort of understood.

From the time as a child when she burst through that monas-tery gate until this moment, Anice had been surrounded by men and women who hungered for the Word, for the Christ. Now, for the first time ever, so did she.

22

Comgall's Plight

The Year of our Lord 574

I arise this day
  through a mighty strength.

Gavin Mac Niall. A prince of Erin by blood and birth. A prince of Erin because he'd done everything else, and being prince was the only thing left to do. A prince of Erin because the rest of the world was pretty well tired of him.

He leaned on the oaken rail of this sailing curragh, let the rain splash his face, and watched gray haze dissolve into gray haze before them. Away to the northeast, a squall line of wind ripples ruffled the sea.

The master of the little vessel stepped in beside him and draped an arm casually over the forestay. "We'll not be going clear to Mull and Iona. See the wind changing? I'm going to put you ashore at Bangor. 'Tis quite as good a place as Iona. As many monks and always more of 'em arriving. Yourself wouldn't be planning on being a monk, would ye, I mean, since ye be going to Iona and all?"

"Wait a minute! I have to get . . ." Gavin looked at the weathered fisherman's face and didn't bother to argue. When an old bird that crusty makes up his mind, not even a prince is going to change it. "No. I'm not a monk. A prince of the Ui Neill, but not a monk."

Unimpressed, the master grunted. "As well, I aver. Y' seem too restless of nature to be a decent monk." And he wandered off.

Why thank you kindly, humble fisherman. Gavin allowed his mouth a little smirk. *I'm as natural a monk as Colm. We're cut of the same length, and he does just fine as a monk. Maybe starts a minor war now and then, but sure and nobody's perfect.*

201

Bangor full of monks? The last Gavin heard, and that was years ago, Bangor was a meadow beside Belfast Lough, full of cows. *Full of monks now, aye? Perhaps it was one of Colm's monasteries, and I won't have to sail clear to Iona after all.*

They landed on a sandy strand at the mouth of the loch. The master put Gavin and three sheep ashore and took on two leathern bundles of coarseweave. With none to claim them, the sheep wandered upslope to a grassy lea.

With none to claim him either, Gavin wandered upslope as well, picked up a well-worn track, and followed it to a community every bit as grandiose and populated as Finnian's Moville. Three ringwalls contained oratories, various roofed buildings, and clochans, the cold, damp little beehive huts that abbots are so fond of thinking enhance the piety of their cold, damp inhabitants. Scores of them.

Gavin saw none but women scurrying about one of the ringwalled fraternities and none but men in the other two. No children laughed in any of them. With Christians called to this separated monastic life, who would provide the next generation of the faithful?

The monasteries were wealthy enough—cattle and sheep by the hundreds dotted the slopes around. Mound fences, nothing more than long narrow piles of dead brush, kept animals out of grain fields and vegetable plots. Once the crops were harvested, the brush would provide the winter's fuel. Perhaps the thought of plenteous fuel triggered Gavin's memory—perhaps there was no reason at all—whatever, old Swaya leaped into his mind. She had to be dead twenty years now. She was older than dirt when he visited her that time.

The wind picked up sharply, driving the rain at an angle. He flagged a passing young fellow in a coarseweave dalmatic. "Greetings. Is this a monastery of Columcille?"

The lad studied him as if he had warts in his hair. "This is Bangor of Comgall, lord." *Any fool old enough to walk knows that.*

"Comgall! Well, I'll be. So he came here instead of Lough Erne, eh?"

"No, lord. He spent years at Lough Erne, till the bishop roared, 'Enough!'"

Gavin mulled this curious revelation. "Is he in residence at the moment?"

"Aye, lord. The mother is that group there." He pointed to the middle of the three ringwalls.

"Thank you, lad. Blessings on you." Gavin continued up the track to the center doon. He paused in the gateway. The two porters there, monks both, watched him silently. From inside the ringwall came occasional sounds of industry but no voices. Dozens of people. No voices. A facility this size ought to be rattling with conversation and laughter.

A rule of silence? Gavin tested it by walking past the porters. They did not challenge him. *What kind of guards are these, to let a stranger pass freely?* Were they guarding *his* doon, their heads would roll.

If this was the mother monastery, Comgall's seat, he would probably be in the oratory, the scriptorium, or his quarters. There didn't seem to be a separate structure for administrative functions. The oratory contained at least two dozen monks in prayer, none of whom was Comgall. Just to be sure, Gavin stopped by the kitchen. Not there. In fact, no one was there and the fire was banked.

The biggest roof in the place sheltered the scriptorium. Monks of all ages, sizes, and degrees of baldness worked on what had to be a hundred book projects. Some paid Gavin no attention whatever. Those who deigned to notice him spent almost no time at all doing it. Busy bees, these scribes.

Gavin stepped out into the daylight. The wind blew stronger, if anything. He walked over to the largest of the clochans and slapped on the oxhide covering its doorway.

A monk he had never seen before shoved the oxhide aside and looked at him. From inside, someone spoke without being spoken to—or rather, moaned without being moaned to.

Gavin frowned. "Infirmary?"

"Yes."

"Comgall's clochan, please. I'm seeking him."

"Near the west wall, marked with a cross."

"Thank you."

The monk nodded and stepped back, letting the oxhide fall loose.

If Gavin were, instead of an old friend, an old enemy eager to stick a dagger into Comgall's heart, the brothers in this monastery certainly weren't erecting any barriers to his intentions. But then, Gavin himself had always rather held that opinion of the surly monk.

Marked with a cross—two bare sticks lashed together with a bit of thong—sat the smallest, crudest, ugliest little clochan in the ringwall. In Erin. In the world. No oxhide on the door, no light ports in the wall. Wet and windy out here, dark and cold in there.

"Comgall? Gavin Mac Niall, returning in friendship after many years."

Rustling inside.

A gaunt stick figure appeared in the gloom—a tall stick figure who weighed at least three stone less than Gavin.

Gavin should speak, but the apparition robbed him of words.

The haggard monk squinted a moment. "Gavin. Yes." He stepped out into the doorway. "Indeed. Gavin. Welcome to Bangor. What brings you?"

"A fisherman reluctant to sail against the wind. I was headed for Iona. I didn't even know about this place."

"Then you've been gone a while, friend. We've been here several years, and we're growing rapidly. Come in."

"Thank you." Gavin had to duck to get under the oaken lintel. *It's dreadfully unlucky to use oak for roof rafters, Niall! Don't do it. Our Lord's cross was made of oak, you know.*

Casually, Gavin reached up and knocked on a roof beam. Also oak, like the lintel. Comgall settled cross-legged onto one end of his pallet, so Gavin sat down likewise at the other end. The pallet contained no padding whatever. For all practical purposes, Comgall was sleeping on cold, bare ground.

Gavin glanced roofward. "Just out of curiosity, of what was the Lord's cross made?"

"Some say oak, some say hawthorn. I tend to think 'twas alder, myself. The leaves turn black as His birth celebration draws nigh."

Gavin grunted and wrenched his attention to the conversation at hand. "You've been gravely ill, friend. I'm pleased to see you on the mend."

Comgall looked at him curiously. "No. Not recently."

"You look like death in a handbarrow, Comgall." The gaunt monk glared at him; there was a little life left in the carcass yet, apparently.

Gavin drew his knees up and draped his arms across them. "All right, old friend. What's been going on? Why have you been starving yourself, or whatever it is that brought you to this state?"

"Austerity purifies. Finnian taught it. I am fully convinced of it. Patrick himself engaged in purification through austerity."

"There is austerity, and there is suicide."

"God calls whom He calls." Comgall sat still a while, so Gavin waited, watching, as if expecting more.

The device worked. Comgall began to squirm a little, then continued. "A group of us of like mind established a fraternity on a little island in Lough Erne. Perfect place. Secluded. We were a contemplative group, devoted to prayer. Very little in the way of Scripture and almost no copying or writing. Just prayer and meditation."

"And austerities."

Comgall nodded. "The church is the bride of Christ. We were her purifier, you see. Through us the bride would come to the Bridegroom washed spiritually, as the bride the Groom deserves."

Gavin pondered this, weighing it against the grim, glum, let's-overdo-it Comgall he had so long known. "How many died?"

"Seven."

"At least you were smart enough to abandon the notion."

That glare returned. "Bishop Lugid meddled where he should not have."

"In other words, he made you ease up on the privations."

"Not privations. Minimalisms. We ate just like anyone else but not as often. We slept as others do but not as much. And so on. And of course, we cleanse wrongdoing whenever it turns up. For a loss of seed, wear cold iron thirty days. For a lie, a minimum of one week's fast and more, according to the severity. Strike another, forty days' fast. If one—"

"Colm adheres to the same monastic rules in his fraternities."

"But not as fervently."

Gavin let it go. "Wasn't Bishop Lugid your mentor? Like Cruithnechan was Colm's?"

"He still is, unfortunately." Comgall shifted uncomfortably. "Let us discuss other things. You. You've been traveling?"

"Amazing places, Comgall. But the call of home was too much. Other places are warmer and sunnier and bigger and brighter, but this is home. I'm done traveling. My goal for the balance of my life is to achieve a high kingship—either Tara or the Dal Riada. I should have pursued it from the beginning. I'm ready for it now. More than ready." *Let my sweet ex-wife who so summarily dumped me against my will find out she dumped a king.*

Comgall wagged his head slowly, that perpetual scowl firmly in place. "I'm not as savvy regarding politics as you or Colm, understand. But I see no immediate prospects for you here in Erin. The Dal Riada possibly. I hear Conal is aging and infirm."

"That's what I wanted to talk about with Colm. He's never lost his interest in things political, or his ties to the royal houses. He knows who's going to die and who's going to take over before the ris themselves."

"You've returned to your clan?"

"Not yet."

Comgall bit his lower lip. "They are in eclipse, if you will. 'Hard times,' one of my monks calls it. Raids, crop failures—all Erin is suffering, but they seem particularly hard-hit—and a paucity of heirs. And the plague. Virulent in that area. It continues to spring up here and there, no doubt a judgment of God for Erin's many sins."

Gavin felt the hairs bristling on the back of his neck. "Because my clan is particularly sinful, no doubt."

"I wouldn't know," Comgall drawled, absolutely lugubrious. "I do know that if you plan to further any intention whatever of a high seat, you're going to need material resources. The means to hire mercenaries, because your clan can no longer field an adequate fighting force."

"You don't know that for certain. You just said you're not all that current in political matters."

"What is the most dangerous enemy of a monastery?"

"Satan. Just a wild guess, understand."

Comgall's sour puss darkened further. "Satan need not bother himself. His desires are more than adequately served by man's depravity. You know from your youth at Finnian's that our greatest danger has always been raids by ris and interlopers. The theft and butchering of livestock, stealing a choice slave now and then. I keep tabs on the strength of local ris as a matter of basic defense. Bangor offers much in the way of wealth."

"I noticed."

"We've nothing to fear from your clan."

Gavin would have responded with something, but the conversation dropped cold as that sank in.

Does Colm know? Of course. He knew everything of that sort. But with no political aspirations, he would have no vested interest in a strong clan. To him, it wouldn't matter.

Gavin understood full well that the power of clans waxed and waned with the generations. He just never expected that his own would ever wane, and certainly not in his generation.

As his mind galloped like a terrified horse from thought to thought, Comgall was explaining why, because of this very depravity, it was so important for God's own to purify themselves, to counterbalance the evil of everyone else. Gavin interrupted the sermon. "Do you know where Colm is now?"

"On the high seas. He was here less than two months ago on his way around the coasts. He's established a splendid string of churches up through the Dal Riada and down the Erse coast. Now—"

"He did that years ago."

"Right. Now he's adding to the chain and visiting the old places. He came here from Lambay Island, and before that, the Jute coast and Lindesfarne—from up in the Orkneys. Stopped at Inverness, of course."

"Brude's still there."

Comgall nodded. His positive voice and gestures, like the nod, were every bit as lugubrious as his negative ones. "The last I heard, he was. The little slave girl Colm pulled from the druid's grasp those many years ago talked freely and long on our voyage home. She claimed that when Colm's voice penetrated Brude's fortress—"

"When he sang the anthem for vespers. I still remember that."

"Precisely. She says Brude was absolutely terrified. He thought Colm was somehow in the very room with him. Or his ghost was. It sounded so. Then the bolts fell out of the gate, and it swung open."

"I thought it fell open."

"She claims it swung, as if drawn by angels. When the slave was wrested away from his chief druid, that put the garlic on the roast. *But*. . . I don't think he actually converted to the faith. In awe, certainly. Magnifying the Lord along with the rest of us, perhaps. But not truly converted."

Gavin shifted on the uncomfortable pallet. "You're worried about Brude's soul?"

"Sure and he is one of the three thousand Picts Colm dedicated himself to convert."

"In other words, you think Colm failed his ultimate mission."

"I wouldn't use the term fail in its usual sense. Not a moral shortcoming as such."

"But failure all the same. And I assume that your austerities are also to cleanse failures like that one."

"Imperfections like that one."

Gavin found himself laughing aloud, but it wasn't merriment. Not in this place. "You are subjecting your monastics to every discomfort the bishop will allow, and subjecting yourself to even worse deprivation, to tidy up the work of Columcille, the Dove of the Church!"

"Now I wouldn't phrase it that way."

"I just did." Gavin stood up. His legs and backside were stiff. "Thank you, Comgall, for the conversation. It's been good to see you again after all this time."

Comgall was so creaky he nearly didn't make it to his feet. He embraced Gavin coldly, said the words people ought to say in parting, and sent Gavin on his way with God's speed.

Gavin stepped from the deep gloom into, by comparison, a bright and cheerful rain.

23

Gavin's Price

The old woman am I, the hag, with
  Aged skin stretched tight across the bone
where once kings pressed their lips.

His wearied and lathered little horse was half the size of theirs. It might be running its heart out, but they were gaining anyway. Gavin was a big man and therefore a heavy load, his pursuers small and fierce.

He glanced over his shoulder. Like a pack of wolves, the half-dozen warriors howled gleefully, knowing they were closing and the chase would soon end. They spread out across the lea knee to knee, with only the middle two riders on the track. Their cloaks flapped like banners behind them.

With a squeal, the outermost of the horses went down; what it tripped over or what hole it stepped in, Gavin neither knew nor cared. No one slowed or turned back to render assistance. Why pause to aid a comrade when you can fall upon prey?

He thundered past a threesome of gentle old birches growing along a rivulet's bank. The stream was too small to bother bridging even in freshet. Today the little horse barely broke stride jumping it. They raced on.

Gavin enjoyed one advantage and one alone. He was entering his clan territory. He grew up in these hills, and he knew the terrain. Leaving the track would pose a serious risk; his horse could easily go down too. He'd just have to take the chance, for he knew where he must go.

He reined the pony aside, up around the crest of a grassy hill. *Has the alder grove by the spring been cut? No. Praise God!* With open arms, the alders appeared around the hillside, beckoning. The grove's understory of elder, haw, and brambles had not been burnt off or cut in recent years. He plunged his little horse straightway into the grove.

Thorn bushes raked his knees. Leaving behind skin and ripped bits of cloak fabric, he turned the horse straight uphill past the spring, angled to the north, and galloped out the far side of the grove. Protected by trees and bushes from his pursuers' eyes, he forced the horse up over the hill into the seaward drainage. Down the hill they flew.

The horse dropped. Gavin pitched forward over the sweaty little ears and hit the grass rolling. *Of all times for the horse to trip . . .* !

It hadn't tripped. It wheezed a couple times, shuddered all over, and died.

Gavin scrambled to his feet and started running. He ducked in among a field of outcrops, ragged piles of rock emerging from the grassy slope. He turned aside and skidded to his knees behind one of the larger ones. Lord willing, he could hear his pursuers well enough to elude them by slinking around among these rocks.

He heard hooves a quarter mile downslope and raised his head cautiously. The five riders—one must have fallen—obviously reluctant to let the brambles rip them apart, had circled around downhill of the grove, crossed the creek well below the spring, and continued across the hill. It was the logical course a pursued man would take, if he did not know the countryside. They would have to look uphill behind them to see the dead horse.

Soon enough they would realize they were chasing nothing and stop to reconnoitre. They'd probably notice the horse then. Gavin wasn't about to wait and see how long it took them.

He continued north, as much as possible keeping the concealing outcrops between him and the downslope. That fallen rider. Did he remount and continue his pursuit? That would depend on whether his horse broke a leg. Following the map of his memories, Gavin jogged northeast now, down this dale and across that cut. There should be an oak glen in this area. He passed a glen studded with stumps. Erin was no longer the land of his childhood. So much had changed. He passed the abandoned rath of his second cousin Gaitth and jogged east.

Whenever he paused for breath he listened for voices or horses. Nothing came to him across the deserted moors.

The sixth rider had gone down just about exactly to the south of this little tor right here. Gavin circled around it and headed south, to come upon the fellow from behind.

He stopped. Below him, halfway down the hillside, the track lay deserted in both directions as far as the eye could see. Gavin loosened his sword and realized it was in his scabbard to stay. Somehow he had bent the tip over, probably when his horse crashed. He took the time to take off the scabbard and stomp the sword straight inside it. When he could again draw his sword comfortably, he put himself back together and started west, a quarter mile above the track.

There on the track ahead lay the downed horse in a pool of dark blood. Its rider had cut its throat, which told Gavin it had broken a leg. *Pity.* He needed that horse just now. Where had the rider gone? With care, Gavin moved down the open lea to the track.

Footprints aplenty told him the rider's story. The fellow had dispatched his horse, rested nearby on a roadside boulder, then continued west. The man was limping. A few hundred yards later, he rested again. And again.

The rivulet and its three birches would be about a quarter of a mile ahead, around this hillslope. Gavin left the track and moved uphill. If the fellow's leg or foot were really hurting, the stream and the protection of its birches would provide an inviting place to await his companions' return.

Crawling downslope on hands and knees, Gavin approached the birches, listening all the while for distant hooves. He crept in behind a clump of coppiced hazel.

The fellow sat against the trunk of the birch that leaned, his head rested against the bark, one leg stretched straight and the other cocked. He was dozing, at least, or perhaps asleep. Besides the sword at his side, he carried a bronze-tipped javelin. The spill had netted him a bloody nose—his tunic front was all streaked and blotched.

Ever since he had so artfully cut those step-holds in the palisade of Finnian's monastery wall, Gavin had taken a certain heady pride in his own stealth. That pride boiled up again as, undetected, he moved in behind the fallen horseman.

211

The pride abated somewhat when Gavin discerned that the man was sound asleep. The prince crept cautiously in behind the leaning birch and very, very softly lifted the javelin out of the fellow's lap. He stood up then, extended a leg out beyond the birch, and oh so quietly pressed his foot upon the man's sword blade.

The sudden downward pressure of hilt and scabbard at his side aroused the fellow. By the time he realized what that foot was doing, though, his sword blade was kinked inside the scabbard. He cried out and twisted toward Gavin.

Gavin shoved the fellow down brusquely. The warrior fell on his side in the streamside mud. Gavin dropped with a knee on the man's neck. He gripped a wrist. With the other arm pinned beneath him, the fellow had not much choice but to lie there.

Just to emphasize who was boss, spreading the butter thick, as it were, Gavin pulled his dirk—"lady knife," Colm always sneered—and pressed it to the luckless fellow's throat. "You've one chance and only one to survive this. Talk."

Big as hen's eggs, the man's eyes rolled. "What would I say to a prince, lord?"

"From the beginning. Why this pursuit? And quickly! I'm short on patience."

"We were seeking cattle, lord. The reward is in cattle. The price Diarmaid Mac Cerbaill placed on your head, lord, has doubled through the years. You've become a major irritation, I aver— an itch he cannot scratch."

"How did you know when my foot touched Irish soil? I've been gone for years."

"You were on Man for a time. A cousin of our ri saw you there. He bribed the fishing boat to bring you to Bangor—three cows to deliver you into our hands—and immediately thereafter sailed to Down to tell our ri. He sent us north to seize you."

Gavin twisted his knee a bit. "How did he know which boat?"

"Did not that particular fisherman give you an excellent price for the voyage, lord? A low fare you'd be foolish to turn down?"

He did indeed. Gavin seriously toyed with the notion of breaking this oaf's neck. The only reason he had been able to thwart their plan and slip out of their grasp was that he left Bangor much more quickly than they had anticipated. Had he waited but another scant hour before departing Comgall's monastery, he would have walked right into them.

Come to think of it, had Comgall served regular meals the way normal people do, Gavin would have stayed. Sure and his empty stomach, so often his worst enemy, had saved him this time.

He leaned down close to the man's face. "Hear me and tell your ri, lad. I will be prince in Erin. And when I am, I will reward my friends handsomely and slay my enemies. Your friends and your ri will want to know which side of the fence to be waiting on when I come. Am I understood?"

"Clearly! In your mercy, lord, spare me! I beg you."

"This one time only I'll demonstrate my mercy to you. I give you back your life. Lie still and take care not to stretch my mercy past the breaking point." Gavin stood up. Glory, how he loved this! It had been a long time since he exercised his royal blood in a land where people recognized it.

He stepped back, scooped up the javelin, and headed downstream. When he glanced toward the track, the fellow still had not moved.

He took refuge that night at the rath of a second cousin once removed, a circuitously related boaire Gavin's enemies probably wouldn't know about. The man gave him a horse, a most generous gesture, for the fellow lived in penury.

Weary as he was, he couldn't sleep. He thought about Diarmaid. With loyalty as fast as the ri in Down demonstrated, the man would be virtually impossible to unseat. Was it loyalty or greed? Gavin should have asked just how much the reward was now. Comgall seemed to think Gavin should work his luck in the Dal Riada. However, was not the Dal Riada a minor province of Erin, a sea away but populated by dispersed Irish under the ard ri? Still, it could be a stepping stone to Tara.

And those retainers on his heels. He praised God he'd been sufficiently alert to notice them coming, while he still had enough distance to make good his escape. He might not be that fortunate next time.

Mercenaries and the means to engage them. There was a slim chance. . . .

He left before first light next morning while the daughter, all sleepy-eyed, was headed for the cows with her milk pail. His father's rath, the family farm in dreadful ruin, lay less than ten miles away. He rode that way, then rode a great circle around it, watching for strangers. They could be waiting for him here if they knew where he had lived. On the other hand, why would anyone come back here?

Finally convinced of safety, he rode in the ringwall gate and tied his horse to a fallen timber. The memories of childhood assailed him all over again. He beat them back. Childhood is not all that gay and free a time anyway. He had chores a-plenty; kings' sons' character seems to be shaped mostly by drudgery. And he got into trouble then just as much as he did now. On the other hand, his childhood was not fraught with kings' retainers out to catch him.

The troll's nest of thatch that had once been his father's roof had rotted down to black slime. No one had dug in it, it would appear, since last Gavin had been here.

He walked down to the spring. The springhouse roof had caved in. Gavin retrieved one of its poles and returned to the house.

He began not with the house itself but with the souterain, the tunnel dug back into the earth-and-stone ringwall. Scavengers years before him had cleared it of storage jars and baskets. The granaries and woodpiles up against the back wall had also been stripped. No milk pail anymore. Even the stool was gone.

And now for the house itself. Others had dug into the rotted rushes along the wall approximately where Mum's pallet had been. He held scant hope of finding anything. Still, thieves digging at random weren't likely to hit on the precise spot where something of value might lie. Gavin, who knew things about his parents' habits others did not, just might.

Normally, one put one's pallet close to the wall. Mum, claiming the cold wall sucked the warmth out of her, slept a good three feet away from it. He dug accordingly.

He reached dirt floor in a quarter of an hour and began stirring and shifting the heavy compost. An hour passed.

This was a far more difficult project than he had first envisioned. He went out and laid his cloak across the saddle, and still he sweated as he worked. Besides digging, he had to keep an eye on his horse's ears and head, depending on the animal to tell him if someone was coming.

The end of the pole hung up on something momentarily. He needed a shorter digging stick, and it took him a good ten minutes to find one. He had reached his mum's pallet. Here were the sheepskins, now rotten, that she lay on, for how many years?

He dug for her pillow, the loosely rolled sheepskin that would be at the west end of the pallet. She liked to sleep with the cold wall at her right hand, for she was left-handed. Here it was, nothing more than a thick resistance to his probing stick. Rotted even worse than the thatch, the leather roll fell apart as he prodded it. The wool, somewhat more durable, gripped his stick in its matted mess.

His stick clunked on something. Viciously, he shoved more of the thatch away. Then he abandoned tools and dug with his fingers, ripping apart the stinking, slimy mass where once his mother's head lay.

A torque. Another.

So she did stash her treasures in her pillow roll. Later he would dig up Da's pallet too for whatever it would yield.

Eagerly he worked every strand, every slippery bit of the stinking sheepskin. His fingers popped a brooch out of the mass. He recognized it instantly. Its enameling had peeled, but the beautiful metalwork remained undamaged.

Mum had always treasured this brooch, a gift from her own grandmother, intended for her granddaughters someday.

He paused then for the first time to rest, seating himself precariously on the slippery thatch. He turned the brooch over and over in his hand. Ever so softly, he ran his fingers across the carefully worked flowers in the middle, along the wound wire border. The brooch was damp; with a fingernail, he dug the goo out of the indentations. He polished it on the hem of his tunic, cleaning away the muck. It shone.

Mum.

For the first time in his adulthood, he wept.

24

Gavin's Sorrow

I would host an ale-feast for the King of kings
  With the angels a-dining for eternity
And Jesus' hospitality in all things.

"And so, Mum, if he comes round again, I'll stab him. I want nothing at all to do with him, and ye ought tell him so." The girl's scowl, not to mention the blasphemies she uttered only moments ago, looked out of place on such a tender child. Treasa rather expected the scowl—the girl complained constantly. The blasphemies, though, were what interested her. *Where did the lass learn such choice words?*

Treasa pointed a finger directly at the girl's nose. "Now you listen, Lass. You'll not stab anyone so long as you're in my service. The lad may be a bit single-minded, perhaps even overly persistent, but he's useful to me. Damage him at your peril. Am I understood?"

"I want him kept away from me, Mum."

"I want him in one piece."

"Don't see what ye like about him," the girl pouted. "He ain't worth the grass ye wipe your shoes on." With a final, well-phrased aspersion on the boy's ancestry, she shuffled away.

Treasa sighed heavily.

She took her time walking back to the kitchen shed. She knew what the answers to her questions would be even before she got there. She would ask if the broken quern had been replaced yet, and the cook would reply, "Not yet." She would ask if the beans and greens were planted and the cook would reply, "I can't do it all, Mum." Her cook made a hedgehog look speedy as a deer.

Treasa stuck her head in the shed. No one there. The quern still lay in two pieces where it had fallen. *How can one manage to split a good, solid rock that big?* Treasa couldn't imagine anyone being that clumsy, but then Maive was a paragon of clumsiness, the like you'd never see.

The cookshed fire looked either out or nearly so. Maybe the cook was picking up chips and twigs to resurrect it. Treasa checked behind the woodpile. "Maive?"

Stretched out flat among the kindling, Maive yelped, caught in a catnap. Treasa sighed heavily. "Maive, dinner will be on time tonight or else. And you ought attend your fire fairly soon." She walked back out toward the gate. How she hated spring!

Three base clients in service were supposed to be cutting brush to fence the vegetable plots. The way her luck was going so far, she thoroughly expected to find them playing brandhub out behind the bier—probably wagering her best iron pruning blade on the outcome.

She stopped cold in the dooryard as her past rode in through the gate, ignoring her protesting porters. Gavin Mac Niall, the black White Hawk.

He needed a hair wash and trim and probably a bath. Dirt streaked his face and made the color of his tunic impossible to guess. The sorry, ragged little pony he rode would need to eat three meals to outweigh him.

The years had not dimmed the hawk eye. He spotted her instantly and the most wonderful smile lighted his face. Arms akimbo, she stood in the beaten dirt and let him come to her. She couldn't repress her own grin any better.

He slid off his pony to the ground—no big accomplishment, considering that the ground was less than two feet from the sole of his shoe. He just stood there, looking at her. "You've not aged a day since last I saw you."

"You've not changed a minute since last I saw you—still lying like a horse trader."

He wrapped her suddenly in a monstrous, engulfing bear hug. She hugged back just as powerfully. As far as she was concerned, he was right—she hadn't aged significantly. She could still lift him off his feet, so she did so. Briefly.

He stepped back, laughing.

217

She laughed too. "My world was coming apart by bitty pieces, and you've set it right again. What a pleasure to see you! My house is at your disposal."

She whistled to her porter, a piercing whistle most often used to call the dogs in from somewhere around Lough Erne. The gangly young man came running.

"Leod, a feast tomorrow night; relay the word. Music and wine and none of the fat trimmed. And take care of this man's horse, such as it is."

"Yes, Mum!" Leod scooped up the reins and turned away.

Three of the dogs came loping around the ringwall and through the gate. They circled Gavin warily.

"Hold!" Gavin laid a hand on the bridle, pulled a double saddlebag off the little runt's withers, and stepped back. He nodded and the horse disappeared out the gate. The other four dogs burst in the gateway.

"Not quite the mount you rode before. Where's the sorrel?" She rubbed Fat Hoo's head without thinking about it.

"In my ex-wife's stable. Where's that big bay I loaned you awhile back?"

Treasa made a messy noise. "Been dry bones for decades. Stupid horse! Almost as porridge-brained as you. Look at your legs! Riding through brambles isn't the smartest thing you can be doing, you know. You've got furrows in your knees you could plant onions in." She shoved the two bitches away and gave Onyx a cursory pat.

"Better brambles than swords. I'll tell you all about it. What about my horse?"

"Come." She turned toward her house. "I was charging a chariot, intent on taking out the near horse and dumping them. I kneed that brainless bay aside, but he kept going straight; ran right into the chariot pole. It spilled the chariot, all right, but it spilled me as well and killed him. Next time loan me a smarter horse."

Gavin wrapped a long, solid arm across her shoulders, and he was chuckling. "Some things never change."

She shooed her house wench off to start a bath warming. She measured the steward by eye and hand, but the man was hopelessly too small to loan Gavin a tunic, and he was the biggest person around. She sent him up the road to Leod's uncle's for a clean tunic and cloak.

She waved toward the sheepskin-draped back-prop by the fire. "Sit. Relax while your amenities are being prepared. Is it too soon to ask what brings you?"

"Best to get the business done quickly, in case some army comes after me." He settled by the fire, threw his cloak back off his shoulders, and dragged that double saddlebag around in front of him.

Treasa sat down cross-legged near his knee.

He groped around in his bag a moment, staring off into space while he let his hand do the thinking. He fished out a fistful and extended it.

She opened her hand. He dropped into it a heavy gold brooch. "Recognize it?"

She tilted it toward the fire. "Your mother's. The enamel's worn off, but it's your mother's, I think." Her brain belatedly put two and two together. Her eyes snapped up to his.

He smiled wanly. "Been in the family a long time. Now the family's about died out. I'd like you to have it."

"I can't." She held it out to him.

"Yes, you can." He leaned back against the flat, tilted back-prop and sighed.

"Your parents were raided. I bought your second cousin Gaitth, incidentally. One of Diarmaid Mac Cerbaill's princes took him in a raid. They passed by here seeking hospitality. When I found out Gaitth was related to you and Colm, I asked how much and paid the lout off."

"Appreciate it. Where's Gaitth now?"

"Went back west. Said something about settling north of Oran's territory. He talked about your parents, Gavin. He says your mum and father both put up a dandy fight, a resistance to be proud of. But the raiders hit them too heavy and too suddenly. Oran came along soon after and buried them. Oran told Gaitth and others that the place was pretty well cleaned out by looters." She hefted the brooch. She'd figure out how to give it back to him later. "Looks like they missed this."

The black look on his face frightened her, and she was not a person subject to fear. His voice rumbled, "The house and sheds were burnt out. Scavengers dug around the thatch a little but didn't find anything. I found all."

"All your mum's gold."

"And Da's, under his spare saddle where he usually kept it." He paused, apparently reining in either his voice or his fury or both. "And I found Mum."

Treasa's heart thumped. "In the house?"

"Burned to death or crushed by the falling roof. I doubt she had a chance to fight. No weapon in her hand. I found her when I was digging near the cauldron." He reached deep inside his tunic to the belt and pulled out a fine torque of twisted wire, a woman's collar. The gold caught the firelight and juggled it brilliantly. "It was still on her skeleton. Do you know that the whole jaw just sort of drops down on the chest as soon as it has the chance?"

"I'm sorry, Gavin. I'm so sorry."

His voice droned, flat. "Da wasn't there; at least I couldn't find him; and neither was his sword or shield. I found her ribs with the probe and dug her out. I tried to be careful. She was on her back. No cloak. I don't think her cloak would have rotted away completely, and there was no brooch to hold it."

"No cloak. No shoes?"

He shook his head listlessly, barely a gesture.

She pondered the mind's picture. "The raiders hit in the middle of the night. She was asleep. Your father may have heard something and gone out to investigate. Did you see any weapon wounds?"

"Couldn't tell. Just bones. Nothing left but bones."

"It's hard to kill somebody without marking up a couple bones. If she was in the middle of the house . . . Gavin, when your house burned, she was already dead. She wouldn't just stand there and wait for the fire to drop the roof on her."

He stared at her, but he probably didn't see her. "Could Da still be alive?"

"No. I met him only a couple times when he came to Moville, but I remember he was too much like you. You can't stay hidden; he wouldn't be able to either. If he were alive, you'd know it by now. Rumors. It sounds, though, like your sweet cousin Oran isn't being totally honest. Wanna go talk to him? I'll go along. Take along a hundred men or so, just so Oran listens nicely."

Gavin sighed to the soles of his feet, to the depths of his soul. "Da's cattle are long gone, of course, but I dug out enough gold to buy mercenaries for a year. I was going to use that to make a bid for one of the seats. Tara or Dal Riada. Not Cashel. Colm is linked to Cashel. I'm not. I still will secure a kingship—a big one—and use the power in that to wring the truth out of Oran." He looked at her.

"Sounds good to me. What mercenaries?"

"Monaghans."

"Ah. Of course." She thought about this whole thing a while. She was very good at making snap decisions in the heat of conflict. But to plan and determine and consider took her a longer time than it took most people.

Her house wench announced that the bath was ready. With a face full of relieved gratitude, Gavin heaved himself to his feet and followed her outside.

Treasa took the back rest, since Gavin had abandoned it. She sat down at its base, relaxed into its thick sheepskin, and stretched her legs out. She could safely assume that the lad's brain was muddled by the shocking discovery of his mother's remains. That meant any and all plans he made ought to be subject to review. So she reviewed them.

She also shamelessly went through his saddlebags. A year of spears? Either he tended to be unnecessarily generous with mercenaries or he could afford a year and a half of them. She would advise him not to be generous. Her first gift to him ought to be a hairbrush. He had none.

Maive had gotten the word, no doubt from Leod, about an important guest for dinner that night as well as the feast for tomorrow night. Considering that she probably had to borrow fire from the blacksmith, she did a pretty good job—halved piglets with field greens, the last of the winter's ham basted liberally with butter and rich with smoke, curds-and-honey, wild strawberries, and ale from the better of her two recent batches.

Treasa and Gavin ate together, just the two of them, and lingered long over the ale pot. They chatted of light things, happy things. She would advise him later, after she'd mulled his situation a while longer. This was not the hour for business.

They talked about how nice it was not to hear offices every three hours, day in and day out. The measured tread of time grew boring in an awful hurry. And yet Colm doted on it. They both noticed that. They decided it was because he could sing and they couldn't.

Gavin told her about Comgall's austerities. They agreed quickly and thoroughly that good food and soft sheepskins are gifts of God and certainly not to be snubbed. After all, how would you like it if someone you cared about refused your carefully considered gifts? And God must indeed have considered His gifts carefully to have come up with such delightful ones.

Gavin loosened up greatly. Sadness still dragged the lines of his face down, but he acted more relaxed. She sent him off to the guest clochans with fire, a bowl of strawberries, and the last of the ale.

Drowsy enough to trip over broomstraw, the steward came in to clear the table.

"Baeth, did you send out the invitations?"

"The O'Conor brothers on the two black ponies, within the hour of when you announced your intention, Mum."

"Any returns yet?"

"Fergus. The Gawley clan. Always ready for a party, the Gawley clan. So far, that's all."

She sniffed. "Fergus is always ready for a party too. In the morning, send an invitation to Fergus's steward. The man's a genius at trading up something like a gold torque into more slave girls than it's worth and more cattle than the girls are worth. I have a project for him."

"Aye, Mum. You asked about an enameler. I was thinking that Declan's smith is about as good as you'll find in the Monaghan. I've seen work by the Mountain Behr, also, that is nearly as good but not better."

"The Behr are too wild for my taste, and that's saying something. Invite Declan's smith tomorrow also."

"Aye, Mum. Will that be all?"

She smiled. "Go to bed before you fall into the other ale pot."

"Thank you, Mum."

She took her own advice and went to bed also. But her sleep was marred by dreams of blackened skeletons with their jaws dropping loose upon their chests.

25

Swaya's Bones

Sad cry, hawk, wind, wolf.
So distant, only my heart hears.

"Now how did this happen?" Gavin glanced across at Treasa, riding on his right.

Treasa had to admit she'd made a good match, picking that particular horse out for him. The horse's name around the stables was His Bulky-ness. Still, the hulking brute of a gelding appeared none too large when ridden by his burly-ness.

She had chosen the horse for size, not value, despite that it would be ridden by a prince. She hadn't chosen it for stamina either, or snappy action.

To say the gelding was entering its latter years would be an understatement. The old nag's teeth no longer hinted at its age, and its dun coat had grayed almost to white. *Ah well.* For some reason, white horses, pound for pound, looked larger than dark horses. A trick of the eye, surely. Gavin needed a horse that looked like one of Hannibal's elephants that he'd told Treasa about.

Gavin rolled on in almost a whining tone. "When I arrived at your rath, I fully intended to buy an army and sail north. Here I am on the track to Oran's, with a flock of fifty unruly, battle-happy Monaghans following along."

Treasa twisted in her seat to Fergus behind her. "Did you hear that? He's complimenting us highly."

"Highly indeed. Meself likes the 'unruly' best."

"'Battle-happy' isn't bad either."

"Aye! And so we are." Dumpy old Fergus grinned. "Nobody challenges Declan, and Declan challenges nobody. It was getting pretty rotten boring at home."

Gavin spat in the dirt. "It is not my province to entertain you."

She claimed he would do better to confront Oran and maybe threaten to dishonor him if he didn't adopt Gavin's cause. His ranks swelled considerably by Mac Nialls, Gavin could then make quite an impressive show up north. She claimed too that he needed to learn what happened to his parents if he was going to find peace of mind, and the truth wouldn't get any easier to uncover as time went on and those who knew the secrets passed away. He had admitted that she probably had a point. For him, that was an out-and-out admission of agreement.

Away at the back of their column, callow Leod kept falling behind and catching up. Fortunately, he rode a strong horse, for he was doing two miles to their one. He claimed that the bow and arrow was the wave of the future and was practicing his archery on the many hares they put up along the way. So far, he had no hares tied to his saddle.

Gavin grinned and jabbed Treasa's arm. He pointed beyond her. "The track north to Derry along the River Foyle. Remember when you rode my horse right into the banqueting hall to rescue me?"

"Could I ever forget? Nor does a certain ingratitude slip my mind."

He ignored that. "And the price on my head back then, engendering all that greed, is even higher now."

"So they say."

Within a quarter of a mile, they arrived at Oran's gate. There seemed to be fewer cattle in the leas round about, and the pigs were penned near the gate. That was highly unusual. Common practice allowed pigs to roam free and forage.

Treasa rode boldly to the gate and told the porter in no uncertain terms, "A delegation from the Dal Riada to meet with Oran Mac Niall."

The porter studied her a long moment. Common sense won out over training, and he took a fearful step backward. "Oran no longer holds the office of ri ruirech. Another has taken his place."

"News to me. Then we'll talk to the other."

"An aide is announcing you even now, Lady."

Treasa dragged her horse backward to Gavin's side. She muttered, "The lad is green enough to bend double without snapping if he thinks me a lady."

Gavin gaped at her wide-eyed. "You're not?"

She would have belted him were it not so pitifully unladylike.

A band of perhaps two dozen riders, well armed and well mounted, appeared over the hill to the north. They rode to within a quarter mile of the rath and drew in, watching the Monaghan. Another band arrived from the south. And here came two parties from the west.

Gavin grimaced. "He saw us coming, I suspect."

"Prompt response from his clients, even so." Treasa raised her voice. "Whatever happened to good old Irish hospitality? We have here a welcoming party with scowls on their faces, and a king who will not greet his guests. I tell you, Erin is going to the dogs."

At her horse's feet, Onyx barked happily. She should have remembered she'd trained Onyx to bark anytime he heard the word "dog."

She slid off her horse and snapped her fingers, drawing her dogs around her. "I shall greet this unsophisticated king." She loosened her sword and marched forward purposefully with no resistance from the porters. Of course, being accompanied by seven fairly large dogs didn't hurt her chances of walking in unopposed.

Across the dooryard, an armed guard, like one hastening to dinner late, scurried into the banqueting hall. He wouldn't be defending the cook. She continued directly to the two great doors and shoved one open.

At the upper tier of tables in the central seat of honor a man Treasa had never before seen sat with a bowl near his elbow. Four guards, naked but for torques and striped trousers, clustered close to him. *Fascinating, those striped trousers.* Treasa had heard tales of them from Kenneth and others, people who had traveled in France and eastward. It was quite an affectation, dressing local lads in them. That told her something about this man.

She dipped her head, but she did no obeisance due a ri ruirech. "A stranger in sovereignty, I see."

"I am." He had a rich, fluid voice—deep, as in a cavern. "You know of me."

"I never heard of you. How long were you on the Continent?"

He frowned. "Ten years. Who are you?"

"Treasa of the Black Battle, leading the Monaghan on behalf of the Niall. I fault your hospitality, Cautious Stranger. You dine and leave us sitting at the gate."

For long, long moments, he studied her, granite-faced. "I've no time to banter words, Woman. If your company came seeking a specific boon, ask it."

"Ah, good. Unlike your lad on the gate, you know a lady when you don't see one. I've always preferred 'woman.'" She walked forward another ten feet, until she could see the pupils of his eyes. "Where is Oran?"

"With a cousin or half brother. I'm not certain of the relationship. Blood relationship."

"That's not much help. The Niall count cousins like fleas on a dog."

Onyx barked happily.

The ri glanced uneasily at the clustered pooches around her knees. "Oran plans to study for several years, and then travel north, up into the Dal Riada, somewhere with that whole branch of the Ui Neill."

"Study where?"

"Wales. Under Cadoc."

"The name of the cousin."

"Columcille."

Treasa would never admit it out loud, but the man's answers sounded truthful. "How do you come to fill the seat of the Niall in place of Oran?"

"I am of the Ui Neill."

"But not of the Niall whose territory this is. No one of the Niall would ever dress his men in these unmanly clothes." She waved toward the retainers. The Ui Neill down at Cashel, she had heard, sometimes used them on court warriors to differentiate the court staff from all others, but what these people didn't know wouldn't hurt them.

One of the lads stiffened. *Delightful.*

"You've stepped too far beyond mere boldness, Woman."

227

"I step anywhere I please. I earned myself that privilege long ago with the edge of my sword. The last time I entered this hall, it was astride a great bay horse. The next—"

"So that was you! Of course. Your ride made you something of a legend here. Rescued a prince with a price on his head."

"The next time I enter the hall, it will be in the train of Mac Niall, restored to his rightful place." She dipped her head again, more so to the stripey-pants lads than to the ri. She owed them an apology more than she owed this usurper anything.

She strode out the double door unchallenged and left it standing open. *Now what?* Her hand on her hilt, just in case, she walked out back to the kitchen shed.

Three cook's helpers cranked away at lovely, unbroken querns. They eyed her curiously, but then grinding grain offers precious little challenge for the mind or eye. Their cook was a man in absolutely the greasiest tunic Treasa had ever seen, and many a time had she watched people render hogs. He was preparing for at least a hundred people. Either a party was in the offing—and the Monaghan not invited!—or they were keeping a lot of retainers in close.

The dogs found all sorts of intriguing scraps and bones here, and immediately fell to exploring. Fat Hoo challenged the cook to the lamb quarter in his hand. He snarled right back at the dog and Fat Hoo moved off, his tail between his legs. Treasa continued twenty feet and whistled them to her. They rejoined her most reluctantly.

She swung on around the back of the wall past the smithy. The armory had been effectively doubled by simply building another shed onto the existing one. Recently too—the new wood was still yellow and unweathered.

Cattle tracks all over, and fresh droppings. Despite the heavy build-up of warriors, they worried about the cows enough to bring them in at night. The milk pails and stools were stacked neatly inside the mouth of a souterain. An orderly household run by, obviously, a well-organized steward. Alert to any signs at all of trickery or attack—not that she didn't trust their boorish host, mind you—she continued around and out the gate to Gavin.

She turned suddenly on a porter. "Your lord's name."

Wide-eyed, he stammered, "Jesus Christ, Lady."

"I mean the lout inside there." She waved an arm toward the banqueting hall.

"Scanlon of Ossory, Lady."

Treasa glanced at Gavin and swung aboard her horse. As she kneed the mare away from the gate she whistled the dogs up. Fat Hoo paused to look wistfully off inside the gate, then fell in behind the mare. They rode perhaps a quarter of a mile as Treasa worked on her observations and the little details her eyes may have seen that her mind had not yet identified.

"Well?" Gavin was looking at her.

"The porter's a Christian. Let's assume he came with the ri, since the ri wouldn't trust a local to guard the gate. So he's from Ossory. The big monastery in Ossory is Clonmacnois; Kenneth's monastery is farther east."

"Diarmaid Mac Cerbaill's spiritual center."

"Right. As if he had one. This Scanlon is from Ossory. Southern Ui Neill. Clonmacnois is in Ossory."

Gavin rode in grim silence. Treasa didn't blame his grimness a bit. He said his family was in eclipse. That's the way he put it. It was beginning to look like Diarmaid was helping the eclipse along.

Behind her, Fergus asked, "What about the retainers?"

"Scanlon's running scared. I doubt he feels the least bit secure, what with all the people he's keeping on the premises."

"I didn't see many."

She twisted around to talk to him better. "Those retainers that responded weren't from surrounding raths. They probably live there, or at least stay there most of the time. They eat there."

"We challenge them? Fall upon them and restore Gavin here to his seat? Steal their dinner?"

"No, no, and no. They outnumber us at least two to one, and Scanlon likely has Diarmaid to back him up if he needs it; Tara's not far enough away. However, sure and we'll party a little. I wouldn't want your tummy to feel neglected. When we get closer to Gavin's old home, send Murphy and his cousins off to kill a pig. They can take the dogs."

229

Onyx barked happily.

"Aah!" Fergus smiled. The word he wanted to hear—"Party"—had been spoken.

Late that afternoon, Gavin began to point out things and places that had significance when he was a youngster. Oftener than not, his sentences started out, "There used to be a—."

Treasa was now so comfortably ensconced amid the Monaghan that she hadn't been home in many years. Were her childhood surroundings as altered as Gavin's apparently were? She almost didn't want to know.

They had to swing wide round a bog, picking their way along a hillside single file. Gavin swore that a togher somewhere down in the bog offered easy passage, but they couldn't find it. Treasa hated bogs.

Gavin drew the old gray gelding to a halt. "A crone named Swaya lived off that way. You're good at reading the scene. Do you suppose we could find out what happened to her?"

"Worth a try, if you like."

The hunters and dogs rode off in search of someone's feral or not-so-feral pig, preferably a sow, although a boar would do. The rest of them turned aside down a narrow and neglected tract, effectively widening it to a highway in their passing.

The grass grew rank, and the scant manure sign was aged—not many sheep or cattle grazed these parts lately. Gavin described in detail his last visit with the old woman and the nuts and firewood he brought her. Some time later, he pointed out a tiny, disintegrating rath ahead as Swaya's. He slid off almost reverently by the gate and gave his reins to Fergus.

Treasa dismounted beside him and also handed her reins off to Fergus. On impulse, she ordered, "Scatter out and find the grave or ash pot. A barrow, probably. This area is too rocky; the bedrock's too close to the surface to dig far. Probably a barrow."

"We'll see what we can find. You stay, Leod." He put the horses in charge of Leod and rode off. Left behind, denied the heady excitement of seeking a pile of stones, the incipient archer pouted. There still were no hares on his saddle.

In a sudden, uncharacteristic fit of charity, Treasa took the reins. "Go shoot some hares for dinner."

230

No need to tell the lad twice. With a brilliant grin he leaped aboard his little horse and galloped away to the northeast. Treasa let the reins fall. Her mare wouldn't go far with all this grass around and the old gelding was so tuckered he wouldn't go far if a fire were built beneath his belly.

Three feet or less separated the ringwall gate from the house door. Treasa had never seen such a small, squalid rath. She stepped in under the lintel.

Gavin rapped on it. "Ash lintel." Whatever that had to do with anything.

The place smelled musty, like stale urine. It must have stood vacant here ten years at least. Mice had riddled the rolled sheep-skin pallet. *Stink! What stink!* Treasa unrolled it, bringing to light all manner of fluff-ball mouse nests and tiny black droppings. Well worn at hip, head, and shoulder points, it had been none too plush to start with.

The rest of the house, bare and empty, appeared to have been scavenged by neighbors or perhaps even passing strangers. Few were the travelers who stopped here after the crone was gone, though; there was very little footprint activity around the fire pit.

Gavin squatted beside a round stone. "This is the stone I brought her to crack hazelnuts with."

"Still some nutshells lying about. The only sign of food." Treasa picked one up. "Raw. She didn't bother to roast them. She was hungry a lot, I'd guess."

"She was blind. Depended on the largess of others."

"What others?"

"Oran."

"Indeed." She stood up and walked outside, mostly to breathe some real air. Scanlon of Ossory's usurpation had occurred quite recently if his nervousness and the armory shed be any indication. Scanlon wouldn't even know about old Swaya, but then her fate was sealed long before he appeared on the scene.

Gavin ducked out from under the lintel and stood beside her. She rapped a knuckle on the door post, pointing out a weathered nick near the top.

Gavin scowled at it. "Made with a spear?"

"My guess. Who would raid this place? It's too small to be a calf shed." She silently pondered the whole matter a few minutes. "If her grave were anywhere near, Fergus probably would have turned it up by now. I speak figuratively. There are no trees around, so the wood to cremate a body would have to be transported in, or the body transported out for cremation. A lot of trouble for an old hag. So it's not likely there's an ash pot to find. Where would someone hide a body if all he wanted to do was get rid of it?"

"You make it sound like murder."

"She didn't die in her sleep. The pallet was rolled."

Gavin chilled. He was usually very sharp at deducing things. She attributed his present numbness to the emotional whacks he'd received recently upside his head.

She softened that hard thought with an easier one. "It wouldn't have to be murder. If she died sitting by the fire, during the day presumably, whoever found her would still have the problem of what to do with the body."

They sat down by the gate, leaned against the ancient ring-wall, and talked about the old woman's youth, Treasa asking the questions and Gavin expounding. The horses hadn't wandered fifty feet. They grazed with determined industry, ripping at the short, tender, fresh growth beneath the long, tough stuff.

The Fergus folk started drifting back in. No barrow, no marker. Two of his people reported spending some time probing the bog beyond the hills, thinking a body could have been left there. Nothing turned up, so to speak. Five of them brought in firewood, so they all must have ridden afar.

"Mum!" Leod's voice rang cross the hillside. "Mum!" In a rumble of hoofbeats he came racing in. "A skeleton, Mum, stuffed back under an outcrop!"

"The caves! Of course!" Gavin bolted to his feet and ran for his gelding. He swung aboard and took off with his heels in the old nag's ribs. Treasa was hard pressed to catch up, and she had a fine distance horse. Gavin didn't seem to need Leod to lead him anywhere. He rode out round the side of a slope and across a shallow drainage onto another. Half a mile from Swaya's ringwall, he drew his lathered horse to a walk and started reading trail sign.

The hillside consisted of an almost solid mass of rocky out-crops and overhangs. As Treasa topped the crest she could see in the far, far distance the level line where sea met sky.

Leod's horse had flattened the grass enough in passing to make the tracking easy. Treasa kept an eye to the trail and an eye to Gavin. He was backtracking Leod, but he seemed to know where Leod had been. As he slid off his gray, the horse's head immediately dropped to graze. Treasa rode in beside and swung off.

Gavin pointed in half a dozen directions. "Overhangs. We called them caves when we were lads and made lairs out of them. You can't dig back under them very far, though; it's solid rock back there."

"Scanlon of Ossory wouldn't know about these. A local lad, yourself or Colm, would."

"Or Oran." He leaned forward toward a large one.

"That's the one!" Leod dragged his horse to a stop. He hesi-tated. "I think that's the one. They look a lot alike."

"It's the deepest." Gavin folded himself up like a linen hand-kerchief and still his back scraped the overhang. "I don't fit quite like I used to."

Leod was rattling away excitedly. "I wounded a hare, and it bounded up the hill into this cave, with the arrow still in it. When I tried to crawl in and retrieve it, I saw—" He took a breath. "That."

Gavin backed out. "I can't see much. Dark."

"Give me your cloak." Treasa dropped down to her knees.

He unpinned his brooch. "Why?"

"To put the skeleton on. I want to bring her out and look at her. If it's a her."

"Why not *your* cloak?" With a grandiose swirl, he whipped it off his shoulders and handed it to her.

"I certainly don't want mine to stink." She dragged his cloak in under the overhang. It smelled cool and dry, it felt cool and dry. Immediately, when you pressed in under the rock, it became very quiet despite the nervous tread of horses and men outside.

The body had been jammed back as far as the rocks would permit. A few stones had been shoved in front of it, perhaps to keep dogs at bay, but the ploy hadn't worked. The skull had been disarticulated; the head lay a foot away. The bones separated one from the other easily in Treasa's hands. The spinal column came away in three chunks.

She spread out the cloak and on it arranged the bones as closely as she could to the position they had held for so many years. She backed out, pulling carefully, keeping the whole thing as undisturbed as possible.

She dragged the cloak with its skeleton out into the light of day, the first light these bones had ever known. She would start at the head end.

"It's Swaya." Gavin stood by Treasa's shoulder. "The hair. Those few shreds of hair stuck to her skull there yet; it's hers. And the teeth."

"There aren't any teeth."

"Right." Gavin sat down rather suddenly. Ashen-faced he stared beyond the skeleton.

Treasa studied the skull and jawbone carefully. "The gums are all shrunken. She didn't have teeth for a long time before she died. Must have swallowed nutmeats whole."

And then she sucked in a deep breath. She was toying with the idea of just keeping this to herself, but Gavin caught the gasp and demanded, "What!"

She sighed. "You said she was blind." *How do you deliver this news gently? You can't. Why try?* She scooted in closer to Gavin and tilted the skull so that the waning sun shone onto the backs of the eye sockets. Fergus moved in behind, blocked the light, realized he was doing it, and shifted position.

"Here." She laid Swaya's skull in her lap a moment and held her arm toward Gavin. "Remember when I broke my arm, right after I arrived at Moville? Feel along here."

When he pressed a finger to her arm she guided it across the place. "A rough spot right here, feel it? Damaged bones don't heal smoothly. The injury leaves a bump or rough spot."

"Like the knob on my rib."

"Exactly." She picked up the skull and pulled a stalk of grass to use as a pointer. "These little holes here are supposed to be there, but this surface at the back of the eye should be smooth. See where I mean? Now, can you see the tiny mark here? A bone scar. That's how bone heals itself when it's been nicked or chipped. And here in the other side? One off to the side, the other in the middle of the space."

Gavin's voice, normally so rich, croaked. "If they were natural, they'd be in about the same place—symmetrical—the way the holes are." It dropped to a harsh whisper. "A blade tip. A knife or javelin or something. She didn't just go blind because she was old. They put her eyes out."

The enormity of it slammed Treasa's thoughts to a muddled standstill. *Oran. Who else?* Oran had joined Colm or soon would.

Gavin would head north, she knew, because his quests now all lay in one direction only. North, with Columcille.

26

Gavin's Chance

The moon rides high
* to show the alien sky*
What beauty lies
* Beneath the angels' sighs.*

As miserable a sailor as Treasa was, why did she even try? There were surely dominions enough to conquer in Erin without taking to the high seas. There she went, headed for the stern gunwale again. Fergus at the other stern rail wasn't doing any better.

The fourth member of the party, the gangling and callow Leod, moved from rail to rail, not the least big discomfited, enthusiastically absorbing his first ocean voyage. The young archer enthusiastically absorbed everything life offered. Gavin envied that. He was losing it.

Gavin sat down amidships, between the fore and aft oarsmen, and leaned back. He was big enough that he could splay his elbows out along the elm gunwales. He wondered why the builder of this curragh used elm instead of oak for the framing and decided it was laziness. Wych elm bends much more easily than does oak. *Doesn't last half as long though.*

Treasa had a point, claiming that God had quenched hell and substituted the strait between Erin and Iona. The seas ran particularly high this evening. Their doughty little curragh clambered up one wave and slid gracelessly down the back. Up the next and down. Up the next and down. The wind worked at such cross purposes to their desired direction that the sail had been furled completely.

Trena of Mocuruntir seemed immune to the ups and downs of this existence, but then he made the trip from Iona to Erin and back four or five times a month. Maybe oftener in the summer.

Trena assured Gavin that Colm was on Iona. Who better would know than Colm's own ship's master?

Trena called to Treasa, "Iona dead ahead."

She replied mournfully, "Promises, idle promises."

Many the time had Gavin depended on Colm, and just as often Colm depended on Gavin. Neither had ever let the other down. Gavin could depend on Colm now.

Colm was an intimate in Conal's court. Despite his activity in the church, his first love was ever and always politics. He dabbled in it; he kept up on it. He would know who was where; he would know about Scanlon from Oran. But did he know about Oran?

Gavin couldn't shake the memory of Swaya in her last days, cold and hungry, and of her bones. Treasa showed him from the bones where the old woman had been stabbed in the chest—unhealed marks on her ribs—and her head severed—an unhealed clip off two of the neck bones.

"It took a lot to kill the tough old gal," mused Treasa.

Gavin didn't want to think about how Treasa had acquired all that esoteric knowledge of how bones heal—or don't have time to heal. He assumed it involved exhuming people. Ghoulish. And she took such great delight in it, flippantly handling the remains, running her fingers across them—that bothered him most of all.

Gavin hiked himself up a little and twisted around to look at Iona's south coast. Off to the west lay that bay where Colm first landed on Iona. Why did he not choose that landing for his monastery? Instead he had built halfway up the east coast of the island, amid some fishermen's cotts and a few raths. No protection along this flat coast—when the wind came howling straight down out of the north, landing became difficult and sometimes impossible. "I'm here to serve the Erse of the Dal Riada. Might as well build right among them" was Colm's rationale.

"Pick a sheltered harbor" was Gavin's.

Colm the poet, Colm the singer with the voice that could call in vessels at sea, was able to praise God in three languages. Gavin, having never mastered Greek, could do so only in one, for his Latin consisted primarily of "Have you lodging in this monastery for the night?" The crazy languages of the Franks and Angles he never did attempt.

But at least he could praise God now with a clear conscience, for a tiny monastery near the baths away down south had shown him the way to eternal life. With a smile, the quiet little prior, Brother Pax as he called himself, claimed, "Salvation does not come automatically with attendance at a monastery. Not even Finnian's at Moville, splendid as it is. It does not come through blood relation or social status or a pilgrimage to Rome. It comes from Jesus, and to Him you must declare your allegiance. Heart as well as head."

Now that Gavin could look back with new eyes, as it were, he saw that Colm had tried to explain the same thing, though not in those words. Finnian had never tried.

No matter now. When the time was right, Gavin would casually declare his new faith to his beloved old cousin Colm. Ah, how the man's blue eyes would light up! Gavin relished the thought almost as much as he would the eventual reality.

The swells abated to a coarse wind chop as they entered the protected channel between Iona and Mull. That ought to ease Treasa and Fergus's discomfort, but it didn't seem to. Perhaps motion is motion, for all that.

Two young monks Gavin had never seen before awaited them at a rickety wooden pier. Trena tossed a line to one and motioned to Gavin to heave the stern line to the other. As the rowers shipped their oars, the curragh clunked in against the pier. Treasa and Fergus shouldered each other roughly in their eagerness to clamber ashore. Treasa flopped flat on her back on the stony shore and closed her eyes, her arms splayed wide.

"He's gone," is all one monk said.

Trena nodded gravely. "Not unexpected."

"Who's gone?" Gavin looked from face to face.

"Ard ri of the Dal Riada, Conal."

Treasa sat up, suddenly alive again.

Gavin practically shouted, "Where's Colm? Columcille?"

The monk glanced nervously toward Trena. *Who sent this madman?* "Our father has gone to take part in arranging for a successor."

Gavin climbed back into the boat. "Take me there, Trena. Immediately."

"Oh no," moaned Treasa.

"Oh, hush," snapped Gavin. "You'll live. This is exactly why we came!"

Trena motioned her into the curragh. "'Tis only across to Mull."

Very reluctantly, the Seasick Twins crawled back over the elmwood gunwale.

"Stay in the middle," Gavin suggested, not for the first time. "The least amount of movement, in the middle."

They made it across. But this final leg of the voyage was less than ten minutes long.

Strange it is, how when you wish to hasten, so many barriers slow your way, and when there is no need to rush the trip goes smoothly. Gavin encountered obstacles galore on his way to, so to speak, the Tara of the north, the seat of the Dal Riada.

Along the way, Gavin learned details of Conal's passing. He learned that Colm and just about everyone else favored Iogenan as Conal's successor. Iogenan might not be tanaiste, exactly, but he was certainly well favored. Many were the praises heaped upon him by those who seemed to know. Gavin took it all in. When he made his own bid as ard ri of the Dal Riada, he wanted to be able to claim superiority in as many areas as possible. Sure and that wouldn't be too hard to do.

On the other hand, if Colm favored Iogenan, the man must be good. Colm had no way of knowing Gavin was done traveling. Still, wouldn't he send word somehow for Gavin to come running?

Silly goose. How would he ever do that?

As at last they entered the gate of the king's seat, whoever the king might be, a zipping hum vibrated his breast. He had tasted the life of a monk, the life of a ri ruirech, the life of a wanderer without status. He'd explored all the possible corners of a man's experience. This, assuming it came to pass, would be the ultimate experience—high king.

He and Colm were born to this. Colm abdicated.

Half a dozen men, brehons and monks, were just coming out of a common hall. Head and neck above them, Colm still shone as blond-bright as he had at fifteen. Gavin anticipated the effusive grin Colm always broke out in when he saw Gavin.

He saw Gavin, all right—and stopped cold in his tracks, dumbfounded. He looked perplexed and then puzzled, and then, finally, a thing untimely born, the grin appeared. He surged forward, scattering brehons, and greeted Gavin with the mutual exchange of bear hugs that was their habit.

Gavin waved an arm toward the rest of the party. "You remember Fergus Gray Beard. The tad there is Leod of the Bow, one of the Monaghan. And What's-her-name."

What's-her-name participated in a hug just as wild as Gavin's.

Colm studied his cousin who expected a kingship for a few moments, holding him, literally, at arm's length. "You're aware that the high seat is empty, of course."

"Of course. That's why I'm here."

"I thought so." Colm draped an arm over Gavin's shoulder and started off toward the gate. Fergus was about to follow, but Treasa stiff-armed him to an instant standstill, hissing something in his ear. Colm and Gavin left the gate without an escort.

Gavin noticed then that Colm too had a companion. A young lad, dark-colored like Gavin, tagged at Colm's heels, but he stopped in the gateway.

They strolled out across drab and barren pasturage, more rock than grass, more gray than green. Colm pondered the ground before them a while. "Sometimes, Fierce Hawk, the Lord's will appears before me as clear as spring water. Other times, I've no idea of His leading and have to follow my instincts. But this time—this time is different."

"I've been getting the impression from people I've talked to along the way here that you have a firm say in who will next rule the Dal Riada."

The Gentle Dove wagged his head, smiling. "Rumors of my power are grossly overstated. The group of us who have the final say—representing most of the region, one way or another—have all agreed on a candidate named Iogenan."

"So I keep hearing. I understand he walks on water."

Colm chuckled. "No, but he does pretty well in loose sand. And his military skills are second to none. We need someone who can stand up to the ard ri at Tara. To maintain our independence. We're not the tail on the hound of Tara; we're our own hound."

"As well I know, having lived here all those years. It would help, if you want to assert your independence, to have a little military muscle to back you up." He watched Colm's face for cues. "I have almost five hundred spears waiting near Drumceatt. Combined force, the Niall, the Monaghan, some others. Treasa thinks we can have them ferried in within two months, maybe. I think six weeks at the most."

Colm looked even darker than he had a moment before. No, not darker. Sadder. Perplexed. "I was certain Iogenan was the one. We all were. His war muscle is pretty impressive too. Then out of the blue, God presents you as a strong possibility. A fighting strength makes your nomination even wiser." He looked at Gavin quickly. "I don't mean as a threat; you'd never turn that force against us. Against me. I mean as a thing we could use."

"Not 'could use.' A thing you absolutely need. You're not going to convince Tara without a spear in your hand." Gavin pressed on. "Besides, his fighting clans are scattered all over a nest of islands and mine are centered within two days of Tara. And none of them wasting any love on Diarmaid."

"True." Colm turned around and started back up the lea at that leisurely stroll. "Now I don't know what to do. But I do know what you must do. Go around to every ri ruirech in the area. You know most of them already. Introduce yourself to the two who took their seat since you left. Present yourself to them."

"Plead my case, so to speak."

Colm nodded. "I'm going back to Iona to pray."

"What? God doesn't hear you anywhere else?"

"If He could hear me at Moville, He can hear me anywhere."

Gavin chuckled. He could amen that.

"That's home, Hawk. I don't feel restless there. When I come in to that pier, I'm where I ought to be." He shrugged those still-mighty shoulders. "I don't know how to explain it." Colm's voice drifted, wistful. "I built my clochan on a ridge above the monastery, not to elevate myself but to enjoy the view—a smoothly functioning community of the faithful, and I started it."

"You started many."

"This one's special."

241

Gavin snorted. "That's what you said about Hinba. Remember?"

"All right, so Hinba's special too. Particularly since Brendan came to visit. Did you know Brendan of Clonfert stopped by Hinba for a while?"

"I've been out of the area."

"He claims he sailed to Tir Na n'Og."

Gavin stared. "To paradise? And returned to tell about it?"

"The Land of the Blessed. Ah, Gavin, you should hear his tales. Not something you can make up. These are so fantastic they have to be true."

They had arrived back at the gate. His friends were outside the gate, off under an oak. Fergus had fallen asleep, and Treasa was sitting with her back against the trunk, showing Leod how she sharpened her javelin.

Colm dropped his voice to nearly a whisper. "There's a place on the far side of the island, on the slope of the hills facing out on the machair, where I built a little hut. Just a camp. I go there for solitude. Meditation. Angels have come to me there, Gavin."

"A dream. A vision."

"Perhaps. One angel in particular—a faintly glowing being who speaks perfect, fluent Gaelic in pure poesy. My poetry or Gemman's—nobody's poetry can come close to matching it. And he upbraids me when I need upbraiding."

Gavin watched Colm's face a moment, wondering if one showed external signs when one has flipped one's internal apple basket. "How many people have you discussed this with?"

"Few. Very few."

"Good. The fewer the better. I shall do as you recommend. Godspeed home, Fierce Dove."

"Blessings on you, Gentle Hawk." The world's tallest dove beamed at Gavin. "It's good to see you, Old Cuz." He strode inside and disappeared beyond the oratory.

That evening, Treasa and Leod went boar hunting, she with her javelin and he with his bow and arrows. Fergus accompanied them out of boredom, Gavin would guess. He guessed too that this was a rivalry of sorts, Treasa and Leod, over who used the superior boar-hunting weaponry.

The sky cleared with nightfall, washing the world moon-gray. Colm took off immediately after Complines. The third-quarter moon would give him light the night through; why lie a-bed when you can be returning to Iona?

Treasa and party got back around midnight with a boar slung on a pole between the horses—a boar with a javelin through its ribs.

Gavin set out on his quest early next morning with Leod and Fergus, leaving Treasa to assay military forces in the area and sort out the various clan connections and loyalties. It took him over a month to reach the ri ruirechs of these tangled islands, to be feasted at each rath, to talk far into the night about the needs and problems of the area.

He heard a lot about Iogenan. He finally got to meet the man about three weeks into his grand tour. Iogenan and his brother Aidan hosted a fine feast, particularly considering that they were feeding and feting a rival. Aidan graciously gave Gavin his own seat next to Iogenan and sat instead with the brehons. Everyone, Gavin included, seemed immensely relieved when he rode out the gate.

Gavin discerned that having been married into a kingship and divorced out of it didn't help his cause a bit. Apparently he should have murdered his wife before she could dump him and thereby hold onto the seat as a stranger in sovereignty. Frankly, it had occurred to him.

And deep, deep down inside, a bitterness gnawed, a jealousy for his cousin's gift. For Gavin talked to kings, but Colm talked to angels.

27

Gavin's Betrayal

If I speak with the tongues
of men and angels
but have no love
the noise is meaningless.

"The Sweet Isle of Hy," poets called Iona once. Obviously, they were poets who had never actually visited Iona, hearing about her only from others' songs and lies. There wasn't a blasted thing sweet about this chunk of rock and fish smell. Denuded of trees, the island provided nothing, not even a stone wall or thorn hedge, to stop the cold wind coming off the sea from the northwest. And if Iona felt the cruel bite of autumn, what must Tiree, lying to windward of Iona, feel?

Yet Kenneth, Comgall, Colm, and a dozen other people were starting monastic colonies on Tiree. Colm talked about building a sister monastery to Iona there. Gavin couldn't understand it. In fact, he couldn't understand building one on Iona.

Kings and abbots by the score were pouring onto Iona, though, as if a balmy climate and rich delicacies awaited them. Gavin had seen the monastery's stores. He could only hope Trena would get back from Erin soon with some decent food. They were down to barley and seal meat. Period.

No building in the monastery was big enough to put a roof over this whole august assembly, so Colm had built a temporary banqueting hall on a fairly sheltered flat south of the landing. Coppiced hazel wands and sturdy reeds were woven among oaken uprights. Colm insisted on oak roof beams so that he could space the houseposts farther apart. Gavin tried in vain to talk him out of oak and into alder or pine instead.

Iogenan and Aidan arrived with the kind of panoply you'd expect of an ard ri. "A bit presumptuous of him," mused Treasa.

244

She stood at Gavin's side on the cobble shore as they watched Iogenan's party disembark from the first of seven boats bringing his retinue. "He has fifty spears with him and another hundred over on Mull. Maybe two hundred on call besides, but it'd take them a while to get here. Allied clans, another six hundred."

"Aidan have any of his own?"

"Not that I could hear of. He just sort of cruises along with his mouth shut. Weird little man."

Gavin had received the same impression. In fact, he'd call her assessment charitable. "The quiet ones are the dangerous ones. When the tide turns against Iogenan, we want to make sure Aidan isn't coming up behind us."

Treasa nodded. "Incidentally, I have Fergus and Leod and a handful of trusties from the monastery looking for Oran. We figure he'll be coming in on one of the boats. Being a ri in the same clan you are, he won't want to miss the fun here. I didn't tell them why I'm anxious to find him."

"His monk-mates are covering for him. Protecting him."

"Don't think so. I'm certain they aren't lying. They say he hasn't been on the island for several months, but they expect him back any time."

"Anyone indicate in any way that they suspect he's a murderer?"

"Nary a hint. Oh, good!" Treasa pointed to Iogenan's third curragh. "Their cook brought some dressed hogs. One way or another, I'm going to eat pork tonight. If I have to face another slab of seal, I'll lose my guts clear down to my feet."

"Better reconsider, Tree. I've heard that seal fat retards the aging process. Prevents wrinkles."

Her reflexes were slowing down. It took her a large enough fraction of a second to realize what he said that he could bolt and run successfully.

All over this side of the island, from a quarter mile below the landing to a quarter mile above it, energetic crews of retainers were jockeying for the most favorable campsites, erecting elaborate tents and marquees, building fire pits, picketing horses that were still soaking wet from the swim across from Mull.

It was going to be quite a party.

The ri tuatha of this island greeted each of his guests as they landed. Gavin would expect Colm to be right in there, glad-handing with the ri. So where was the blond giant? Out of curiosity, Gavin wandered up through the monastery gate and checked the oratory. No one there.

Here came that dark-complexioned young man who assumed the role of Colm's shadow on Iona whether the sun was out or not. Colm had presented him to Gavin as a cherished assistant. *What was his name? Lugbe?*

Gavin flagged him down. "Where is the Father?"

"I don't know, lord, and neither does Diormit. I was seeking him myself. He didn't attend Tierce or Noonsong. That's not like him."

"He mentioned once about a clochan he built as a retreat, somewhere over against the Machair."

The lad waved an arm vaguely toward the west. "Over the rise and take the causeway across the lake. Follow any of the tracks over the hill and seek out a lone hawthorn on a grassy slope. Near there. Diormit and I aren't permitted to go there, but he said nothing about you not going."

Gavin climbed the hill. If Lugbe couldn't find Colm around the monastery, Colm wasn't there. His getaway clochan was the best bet. He crested the rocky little ridge and walked downslope toward the lake.

Like strands of rope come together to the twist, so a dozen little tracks converged upon a causeway across the south end of the lake. This togher was quite a feat of engineering, shored up along the way with posts and piers, its jumbled rock core here and there held in place by wicker basketweave walls. The grass tufts that so bravely grew in this alien rubble were trimmed close by sheep and cattle. Hoofprints and droppings confirmed their passing.

Could you drive a chariot across this togher? Probably, but you'd have to have an awfully good charioteer to avoid getting tipped into the drink when a wheel went off one side or the other. The passage wasn't much wider than a chariot's wheelbase.

Which posed another problem. Here came half a dozen beef steers, no doubt the guests of honor for the feasts Iona's ri tuatha would be providing his distinguished visitors. *Upon their departure,* Gavin thought. *Please let the beef age a couple weeks at least!*

He stopped and stood solid in the very middle of the causeway. The cattle balked; the boaire behind them yelled and swatted rumps. Lowing and shying, the cows pushed past him, jostling him, threatening to flatten his toes, smelling like cows.

Gavin continued across the togher to solid land on the far lakeshore. He followed a clear, well-worn track west through and over the island's spine. Easy going. Just past the crest, the track looped out across flat rock for a few yards. Ahead of him, blazing brilliant green, the broad, level machair opened out at the base of the west-facing slope. Gavin knew good grass when he saw it, even from this distance. Within it, a few small truck gardens were fenced off with brush and rocks, protected from ranging livestock.

Glistening sea rippled in the far distance. It stretched away forever, hiding mysteries beyond ken, unbroken except for a tip end of Tiree huddled in the misty middle distance to the northwest. So Brendan of Clonfert sailed across that sea. Brendan, Colm claimed, took the last journey, as all must do, and came back, as none had ever done before.

Gavin stopped cold, slammed breathless by a hideous thought. *Is Colm losing his sanity?* Colm believed Brendan's tales. But then why not accept the word of an eminent church father? Did not others claim to glimpse the glowing land from afar? Finnian told of a respected church leader—was it Enda out on Aran?—who claimed to see Manannan mac Lir come riding a white horse across the waves and mount into the sky right beside him, returning from Tir Na n'Og.

Colm talked to angels. Nothing too strange about that. Many were the people, Christian or not, who claimed congress with the wee folk, with the dark people of the netherworld set abroad at Sammhain, with human souls trapped inside wolves, seals, or swans. No one, Gavin least of all, suggested that reality was limited to the everyday. Still, if it were such an expected occurrence, Colm would spread the word abroad more, wouldn't he? Why tell very few people if this were a noble thing?

The sun was waning, slipping out from over the dull roof of overcast on the way to its nightly plunge into the western sea. Its orange glare hit Gavin in the face at just the right angle to blind him to the track ahead. *How am I going to get back across that togher in the darkness?* The worn track splintered into a score of much fainter tracks fanning out in all directions down the slope. He pressed forward more or less at random, seeking a tiny clochan built of rocks and sitting somewhere amid a ragged array of all sizes and shapes of rocks. Rocks in rocks.

Colm's peculiarities could be neatly explained away. And Gavin didn't believe any of it. A foreboding, almost a fear, gripped him. He felt so vividly that he was in the presence of something dangerous that he glanced behind him a couple times. Surely this tree-raped island harbored no more wolves, if ever it had any in the first place. What else, other than human beings, could be dangerous? He had sharp enough eyes and ears to know when lurkers hid. Gavin White Hawk Mac Niall was safe enough. Why the discomfort?

Just short of its final plunge, the sun splashed orange light liberally against the slope. The garden pens threw long shadows across the machair. The world glowed warm, except for a notch in the slope well to the north of the track. There the glow looked cold, bluish.

Not even as bright or as definite as the phosphorescence that occasionally flashes light across breaking waves, or an aurora early or late in the season, that soft blue glow fascinated him. And terrified him. Maybe his eyes were playing tricks on him and it was merely a reflection off the sea. Maybe not. It hovered near something like a pile of stones.

In his youth, Gavin would have hastened forward to investigate this thing. Now he couldn't bear to approach it. Suddenly, violently fear-struck, he turned on his heel and ran back up over the hill. He need not have worried about negotiating the togher after dark. He was safely across it before last light.

* * *

Treasa, true to her word, didn't have to eat greasy, fishy seal again, and neither did Gavin. They drifted among the campsites from feast to feast over the next week, usually together but sometimes not, sipping wine and dining on imported meat.

Kenneth, Comgall, and Kieran arrived late in the week amid rejoicing (where was Colm?). Their monasteries on Tiree gave them a vested interest in the appointments and declarations to be made here, they claimed. Gavin suspected that plain old fellowship had as much to do with it as anything.

Kenneth showed with pride a beautifully carved walking stick one of his monks had made for him. The whole top end was an intricately interlaced tangle of ribbons and cords. It was the only time, in all the years Gavin knew Kenneth, that the quiet little monk displayed interest or pleasure in anything material. That tickled Gavin. *The copper-haired monk is human after all!*

Although Gavin lived within the monastery, a guest of Colm, he really ought to host a feast of his own, so he sent Fergus and Leod to Erin for mutton and venison and anything else they thought might be festive. Kenneth went with them; he knew some sources, he claimed. They brought back wine from Moville, wheaten bread, venison, and freshly caught salmon.

Treasa took the role as cook, and that made Gavin shudder. She could ride a horse better than anyone, man or woman, Gavin had ever known; she could sharpen a blade that could split a whisper; but cook?

"Bread, no," she claimed. "At wild game, I'm the best." She roasted the venison with ample garlic over carefully tended coals. The salmon she slow-broiled before alder fires. On the flat sward below the landing, Gavin borrowed monastic labor to set up temporary slab tables beneath the stars. He sent invitations via Lugbe but he needn't have; the aroma of the venison drew the guests, and the flavor of the bread and salmon kept them there until dawn.

Sometime during those last few days, Colm returned as furtively as he had left. His path and Gavin's failed to cross.

Gavin began to fear that Oran had fled for good. When this was over, his first order of business would be to find the ri wherever he may be hiding, in a monk's cloak or not.

The great convocation assembled on the first of the three days of full moon. They began early in the morning with introductions and speeches, even though everyone by now knew everyone else. Thanks to a cold, persistent rain, most of the participants arrived well after the festivities, if one could call them that, commenced. Treasa settled in beside Fergus near the bards' corner. As princes of the Ui Neill, Gavin and Iogenan sat side by side in honor seats. The candidates, Gavin noted, had all arrived on time.

Colm ranked high enough to sit beside the princes. In fact, here in the Dal Riada he could justifiably sit above them. Instead, he took the host's place next to the ri tuatha of Hy. So Colm was adopting his church persona rather than his royal identity. That probably meant something, but Gavin couldn't figure out what.

Next came the Great Pretense. Brehons pretended they were impartial and valued all candidates equally, as they extolled the qualifications of each of the top ten people whose genealogy and status qualified them for the kingship. All pretense. As the brehons spoke, the candidates themselves feigned indifference, pretending to be paying no attention to the recital of their sterling virtues. Another mockery. The assembly applauded each candidate with a hearty "Well done! Worthy to be king!" whether the fellow possessed the slightest trace of merit or not. Still more pretense, and in that one everyone took part.

Everyone but Treasa. Gavin noticed that she kept herself aloof from the responses.

The introductions at length complete, Colm took over, and Gavin could see why. The blond abbot's stentorian voice vibrated the crickets right out of the matted roof overhead. And when the assembly grew noisy and inattentive, Colm shouted a single word, "Peace," curing both problems instantly. The six brehons and ris whom Gavin had seen with Colm when first he returned to the Dal Riada now moved forward through the assembly to take their places beside Colm. They carefully arranged themselves by rank around him.

He scanned from side to side across the room. "Discomfort and a restive spirit have plagued me as this convocation gathered."

A general murmur of agreement rose. Did that mean that everyone else was restive too? You wouldn't guess so from the degree and extent of partying over this last week.

The elder of the six took a step forward beside Colm. "Interesting that our esteemed host should open with that. I have been plagued by an ill-defined urgency. I can neither describe it nor justify it. I hope for enlightenment."

The younger brehon on the end said about the same thing. So did the elder ri. All this talk of vague irritation was contagious; Gavin also was beginning to feel a vague irritation. Through his mind flashed his own feeling of panic when he saw the cold blue light. He chased the thought away.

Colm laced his hands behind his back and studied the brand new roof a few moments. "I have labored these years among you to bring each of you here today into a saving knowledge of Jesus Christ and to save as many Picts as will enter the kingdom. Some of you deny Jesus or simply ignore Him. But most of us confess the Christ. Also, the Dal Riada is rich in churches and monasteries, whose interests must be served. Therefore, God's guidelines should prevail when we choose a successor to Conal—rest his spirit—for the high seat."

Gavin saw movement in the corner of his eye and turned to look. Treasa was standing in closer, her sword loosened in its scabbard. She looked so relaxed, her thumbs hooked casually in her scabbard-belt. Through long association with her Gavin knew better. She was looking for trouble, ready to leap instantly into action.

Colm went on. "You all know that since Conal's death I have leaned heavily to Iogenan as his successor. But God will not permit me to support Iogenan. As strongly as I believe he is the perfect successor, God has other plans."

Gavin forced his face to remain relaxed and noncommunicative. Here it came. Treasa obviously was expecting an eruption of some sort among Iogenan's faction. Her mouth tightened down to a thin line. She kept her eyes on Gavin.

Colm looked to his six. "Is there comment so far?"

The elder mumbled, "Continue."

Colm continued. "My cousin, Mac Niall, has been making himself known to you as a possible successor. No need for him to make himself known to me. I grew up with him. We got into trouble together and saved each other's lives and hides. We worked together in a dedicated effort to give Finnian of Moville fits."

Treasa laughed aloud and Gavin couldn't help but cackle. He nodded, "Extraordinarily successful too."

Colm grinned. "Extraordinarily. I know his strength of character and his skill with sword and tongue. His faith is not where I would want a king's to be, but he is open and charitable toward the church. In fact, supportive."

My faith is where you want it to be, Cousin! Quit consorting with angels and hang around the monastery long enough to let me tell you about it.

Colm went on. "I can without reservation identify Gavin Mac Niall as a worthy successor to Conal, a candidate just as well qualified as Iogenan. Perhaps better. But God won't let me."

Gavin's ears and eyes and heart froze. *What?*

"I can't force the final decision, which rests first with the committee and then with the assembly. But I can and will insist that I have been shown that it's God's will, in no uncertain terms, that we give the high seat to Aidan." He stepped back a foot to lay a hand on Aidan's shoulder.

Treasa, a score of Monaghan whom Gavin didn't even know were here, and Fergus slipped instantly between Colm's six and the rest of the assembly, a bristling, formidable, protective wall. Iogenan's people lined the outer perimeter, their hands on their swords. You could have heard a mouse sneeze.

The elder brehon stood. "Columcille's pronunciation of that name has lifted the unrest from my heart. I still can't explain it. I refuse as unstable the doctrine of a trinity, so I'll not call it holy or a holy spirit's pressure on me, as Columcille claims. I can only say the pressure has evaporated."

The elder ri rose. "Phrasing it another way, I'm comfortable with the choice, and I don't have the slightest idea why. Up until a moment ago, I would have said Iogenan or Gavin."

Statements and claims swirled around him. Gavin sat in stunned silence. The chance of a lifetime had just been ripped out of his hands. He was there! He was in. And now he was not.

Thanks to his betrayer, Columcille.

28

Oran's Confession

Though all men turn against me
  And the heavens fling their wrath,
Your protective hand hovers near,
  O God.

She leaned against the back wall of his little clochan, her wool cloak scant protection as the stones sucked the warmth out of her. She folded her arms and waited.

Just outside the doorway, he crooned a good night to his valet, Diormit, and shoved aside the oxhide door covering. Fortunately, the burly Columcille built his beehive hut here extra tall to accommodate his height. Even so he filled the little hut simply by entering it. He paused, kneeling on one knee, to stir his banked fire and stuff a handful of sticks into it.

It flamed up, sending orange light to flicker and dance across the stones. And then he saw her. His head snapped up, his mouth dropped open. "Treasa!" He recovered almost instantly, studied her a moment, and sat back cross-legged on his rush-covered floor. He fed his fire a few more branches.

She didn't move. "That's a relief. I wasn't certain you'd recognize me. We've only known each other most of a lifetime, and you don't seem to regard old friends too well."

"Gavin didn't come near me to let me explain. I tried to find him. How's he doing?"

"Since you're the weapon of his destruction, I doubt you care, but I'll tell you anyway. You know his silences. When he gets bored, he's silent. When he's brooding about something, he's silent. And when he's too furious for words, he gets silent. That was the one. I followed him down to the curraghs; stuck with him. Took a pair of oars and helped him row to Mull. He was going to cross alone, and I said, 'Oh, no you're not.'"

Treasa kept her eyes, unblinking, on his. "I finally got him to explode. After the screaming and cursing and throwing things, he ended up weeping in my arms like a lost child. That's how he's doing, since you ask."

"Where is he now?"

"Out looking for Oran."

"Oran's here."

"No, he's not."

Colm frowned. "He might be with Baithene. Why does Gavin want him?"

"For the murder of Swaya in cold blood and possibly Gavin's parents in a midnight raid."

"Swaya! The old woman down by . . . that's ridiculous, Treasa. He's acting on misinformation. And his parents? No. Some of Diarmaid's outer clan might have been responsible, if my aunt and uncle actually did die in a raid, but not Diarmaid himself and not Oran. No."

Treasa shrugged without unfolding her arms. "So Gavin gets the wrong man. Won't be the first time injustice prevailed." She paused for effect. "As well you know."

"It wasn't my choice. I made that clear."

"It was within your power. I hated like nettles having to step forward and defend you when you made the nomination. I would have preferred the assembly stand up as one and tear you apart."

"I explained before we walked into the hall what I had to do."

"And I explained what you would do to your cousin if you did it. Well, you did. I doubt you'll ever get him back."

Colm sighed as deeply as a sigh can penetrate. "I didn't want to, Treasa."

I didn't want to. This physically powerful, politically powerful man, this charmer who could sway kings and talk the husk right off a hazelnut, didn't want to. But he did. That was the end of it. Treasa did not believe in theory. She did not believe people's words. She believed in what happened. And yet his tone of voice, his utter sorrow and defeat, suggested that he really did not want to—that forces beyond her ken were at work in the political structure of the Dal Riada.

It was all beyond her, and she thought she knew power politics. "So what are you going to do about it?"

"Where's he looking? Do you know?"

"I have no idea. Wherever he hears a rumor."

Colm tossed another couple sticks on his fire. "Be here at first light. We'll build a search party and leave right after Prime."

"Whoa! Search party? He's not lost."

"Perhaps not physically."

She couldn't fault that thought. She left him, pushing out through the oxhide-sheltered doorway into briskly chill night. The sudden shift from warm to cold gave her the shivers.

A moon the size of a rendering cauldron coasted at leisure high overhead. She walked down the gentle slope and out the monastery gate, awash in silver brilliance.

She paused short of entering the Monaghan camp. They were heartily celebrating their part in preventing bloodshed this afternoon. What else but the Monaghans' show of military strength would cause Iogenan's minions to abstain from a display of force to place Iogenan on the seat? The fact that Aidan was Iogenan's brother, to whom Iogenan's forces were equally committed, didn't seem to dampen their pride or their spirits any.

Treasa didn't feel like partying. She turned aside and walked the half mile up beyond the monastery to the rocky little draw where Kenneth, Comgall, and retinues had camped. In contrast to the happy shenanigans going on with the Monaghan, these people were engaged in a sober prayer meeting. Actually, Treasa didn't feel any more like praying than partying.

She turned away and was starting down toward the shore when Kenneth called, "Treasa! Join us!"

Why not? She turned around and paused. Here came that sparkly-eyed aide of Colm's, Lugbe.

He hustled right into the midst of Kenneth's encampment, effectively ending the somber prayer. "Father Kenneth, my Father asks your company tomorrow. We are going to Gavin Mac Niall."

Treasa moved into the circle of firelight. "So Colm does know where he is."

Lugbe shook his head. "My Father thinks Brother Oran may

have gone over to Tiree, as do I. He proposes to find Oran, then simply wait until Gavin finds him also."

Treasa nodded. Good plan.

"Terrible plan!" Comgall snarled. "Why think he'd seek Oran's company?"

"They're cousins, aren't they?" Kenneth asked.

Treasa looked at Lugbe. "And Gavin really, *really* wants to find him. You know, as I know, once Gavin decides on a thing, he does it. Why Tiree?"

Lugbe lost some of his eager sparkle. "Oran and Baithene are friends."

Kenneth explained, probably for Comgall's sake, "There were some problems at Maigh Lunge. We needed a prior who could address them and Baithene is very good at administration. Plus, he knows copying. So Colm sent him to us. A permanent loan, so to speak. Maigh Lunge is the monastery in the Plain of Lunge on Tiree. One of the better ones, once its problems get straightened out."

Clear as porridge. But then Treasa wasn't interested much in monastic problems.

Lugbe was nodding. "A very good copyist. I recall last year, Baithene wanted someone to proof a copy he'd just made. The Father said, 'Why? The only error is a missing i.' He was right."

Treasa asked not Lugbe but Kenneth, "How many spears will you want? I'll line up some Monaghan."

"None. This is not a military sortee."

"You don't have to be a military sortee to benefit from a little muscle, Kenneth."

"We can ask Colm tomorrow if you think it best, but I'm sure we won't need them." Kenneth rubbed his hands together. "My cook is just preparing a bit of supper before we retire. Please join us."

"Sure." Treasa tried never to turn down food. Against her principles. Kenneth's menu, though, delivered her principles a crushing blow. *Seal meat!*

They embarked upon one of Treasa's least favorite activities horribly early the next morning—sea travel. Colm brought his Lugbe but left his valet, Diormit, at home. Treasa brought Leod, who loved voyages, and left a grateful Fergus behind. Kenneth, Kieran, and Comgall all brought their own aides, and Colm identified a mousy little brother with a stained dalmatic as a cook. The brother never said a word the whole time.

Their curragh bounced on the windchop up the passage between Mull and Iona, swung around Iona's north coast, and plowed out across wild, wind-torn waves. Spindrift blew across their bow, soaking everyone and everything. Treasa dreamt of a warm, dry land where nothing was out on an island. No matter where you wanted to go, a horse or chariot would get you there. There was no such place, of course, but one can dream. She lost breakfast and, she suspected, some of the seal meat an hour before they beached on Tiree.

Tiree was just as unimpressive as Iona, but there was six times as much of it. Listen to the wind whistle across the tops of its rocky rises! Such a dismal moan. If ever it had trees, they were long gone now. Treasa didn't even see stumps. They would have to import just about everything—grain, firewood, carpentry timber, metals, and cordage.

Maybe a score of fishermen's cottages dotted this protected east side, scattered like forlorn sheep across the green-and-gray landscape, none closer to another than a quarter mile. The cattle looked runty and hollow-flanked, the sheep ragged. Treasa saw no hogs at all, nor could she think where they would sequester themselves for shelter.

Comgall hiked off to his own establishment somewhere back in the hills. Colm and Kenneth led the way to Maigh Lunge. As promised, the monastery sat out on a relatively level place. The only fresh water Treasa could see was a small brook tracing out across the north end of the plain. Surrounded by close-cropped pasturage, the ringwall and everything else were all built of rock. *Of course. What else is there with which to build on this God-forsaken lump?*

God-forsaken? Treasa snorted at her own gaffe. If God had forsaken this place, a whole lot of monks were fresh out of luck.

In fact, they seemed to be swarming all over Tiree. A group of them were walking a track single file back into the hills to the west. Perhaps half a dozen tended the livestock or jabbed with

257

sticks at vegetables behind brush enclosures. Three sat on the rocks above high-tide line mending nets. Another two were sewing a ripped hide on a little curragh turned upside down on the shingled beach.

Treasa stopped to search the sea to the southeast. Yes, there in the distance lay Iona, looking much smaller and more vulnerable than did Tiree from Iona's shores. She pointed south. "Is that Erin? I can barely see something in the haze at waterline."

Colm stepped in beside her. "It is indeed. And Mull, of course." He swung a long arm up toward the east. "And beyond it the mainland of the Picts. See the ridge?"

"And on the west side looking out, nothing. Right?"

"Right."

"Across which Brendan sailed."

Colm nodded. "An interesting number of monks have voyaged out there, some at the mercy of the sea. They'll cast themselves adrift without sail or oars and go wherever God takes them."

"To the bottom, it sounds like."

"Sometimes. Brendan says he met Gaelic-speaking colonizers on most of the islands between here and the Land of the Blessed."

Treasa smirked. "So the Land of the Blessed is Gaelic. Let's not tell the Picts, if you want to evangelize them."

Colm chuckled. He turned and headed up toward the monastery.

Treasa fell in beside him. The rest of the party must have gone inside. No doubt, so would Colm; it was nearing Vespers.

She stopped, staring at the beehive granary out beyond the biers.

"What?" Colm stared at, obviously, nothing.

"The wind kicked a tag end of a cloak out from behind that granary—the one on legs beyond the bier. I think someone's hiding behind it."

"Why would anyone—"

A hint of a head appeared. The fellow saw that he was being watched, turned, and ran directly away from them, up a track toward a small knoll in the distance.

Treasa was after him at a dead run even before she realized

what she was doing. She slid her scabbard a bit aside to give her leg free movement.

Colm was faster than she, and why not? Longer legs. Still, the lad sat around most of the day copying letters from one book to another. You'd think he would not be in such good shape.

Oh, for a horse! Treasa saw none nearby that she could borrow or steal, and the cattle were absolutely emaciated. She was reduced to running pell-mell through countryside she had never before seen to grab a person she did not know for no reason she could discern.

The track the fellow was following looped up and around the knoll. Treasa glimpsed it winding up through a draw beyond, to the north. She left Colm to keep to the track and run the man down through brute speed. She angled aside, straight for the knoll. Colm might be faster, but she was agile at cross-country. She would cut the corner.

She scrambled up the knoll, leaping at times from boulder to boulder, crested, and came down the other side within a hundred yards of the monk they pursued. The man had left the track and was heading for a craggy outcrop, the only good hiding place around. Colm galumphed into view another hundred yards back the track.

Their quarry was running out of energy, wind, and time. He had been trying to hold his hood on. He let it fall away. His strides were shorter now as he put less energy into each step.

Colm's voice boomed out, "Oran!" Treasa suspected so all along.

The monk had slowed almost to a staggering walk as Treasa came in behind him. She lashed out with a foot against the back of his knee and broke it forward. He skidded on his nose to an ignominious stop in the mud.

All right. So maybe the run took a little more out of her than she would admit. She flopped to sitting on a boulder nearby and sucked in air as if her life depended on it. She was sweating freely.

Colm wasn't in any better shape. Puffing like a winning racehorse, he jammed a toe into Oran's side and flipped the subdued monk onto his back. Oran's nose was bloody.

Everyone just sort of looked at each other and gasped for air a while. Treasa got her speaking voice back first. She wiggled a finger at Oran's balding head. "Last time I saw you, you had hair."

"I . . . don't know . . . you."

"Sure you do. I rode an incredibly huge, incredibly stupid bay horse down the middle of your banqueting hall."

He closed his eyes. "Gavin . . . Mac Niall's . . . paramour."

"Whoa! That's a new one." Treasa had to chuckle. "Paramour and confidante don't necessarily equate. The confidante part is what you'd better be worried about. He told me all about you. More than I wanted to know at the time, actually. That knowledge, though, is coming in handy now."

Colm glanced at her. "Does Gavin have a basis for his accusations against Oran here?"

"Ample basis." Treasa looked down at Oran. "He's out to destroy you because you destroyed his parents in a middle-of-the-night raid. When you and your raiders struck, his father heard you and made some sort of defense. His mum rolled out of bed but never made it to the door. Her remains were still inside when the burning roof collapsed on her."

"You don't know that."

"Obviously, I do. Every detail. Now let's talk about old Swaya." Oran, despite the sweaty flush from running, turned white.

Treasa pressed on, assuming that Colm hadn't heard any of this yet. "Old Swaya was the only surviving witness. She probably happened by, or was visiting or something. Gavin says she sometimes visited his parents' place. He also says that Swaya kept up on all the latest political gossip, that she kept track better than Gavin's da did. So she might know who did the deed even if she didn't see it done. For some reason, you didn't kill her. I'm assuming your geis protects old women, right?"

Oran opened his mouth and closed it again. He was finally getting some breath back.

Treasa nodded. "Geis it is. A taboo against killing an old woman. So you put both her eyes out. Why? So that she couldn't support herself anymore as a baker and wood gatherer? I'm guessing you fixed it so that she had to depend entirely upon the people you sent to sustain her. You made sure she had enough bread to

260

survive and a few sticks to burn. That was about it. If she wanted to live she had to keep her mouth shut."

Colm was watching Treasa. "That *is* his geis. Also, Swaya was his elder aunt."

"Bad luck to kill her." It fell together now, everything Treasa had heard in bits and pieces. "Some time later, Gavin came home. You didn't expect that. He looked up Swaya. You certainly didn't expect that. Why, of all the people in his father's tuath, would it be old Swaya whom Gavin visited? You couldn't afford to let her live any longer, so you or your minions came to her rath and started tossing spears. Actually, javelins. One stabbed her in the chest. She didn't die right away, though, so you cut her head off. You stuffed her body back in an overhang half a mile away because digging a grave is too much work just to get rid of an old woman, and she was puny enough to fit clear back in that hole, particularly with her head separated. Now do you see why Gavin wants to reach you?"

"You're a witch!"

"A lot of people say that, but they're usually referring to my sweet personality."

"There's no way you could know that!"

"There's more. When you held a feast, Colm's parents sent their brehon but refused to come themselves. They were wary of you, either suspecting or knowing you were responsible for the murders at Gavin's father's rath. Gavin showed up at your feast, so you sent killers out back to the guest clochan where he was freshening up. No geis against harming a prince, I take it. They came away empty-handed because Gavin, not trusting you, had abandoned that clochan immediately. He's really proud of that little move, especially since it saved his life."

"No!" Oran wagged that bald, sweaty head. "I didn't send anyone out back after him. Those were Mountain Behr. They heard about Diarmaid's bounty on Gavin's head." He looked at her with terror pooled deep, deep in his eyes. "Believe me! I would never kill a guest at my feast!"

"How noble of you."

Colm grabbed the front of the man's dalmatic in one big, burly paw and dragged Oran to his feet as if he were a sack of barley. A small sack. "Swaya!"

Either the fellow's knees collapsed or he figured kneeling was a better posture to take against this enraged giant. He flopped around in front of Colm like a salmon on a gaff. His voice croaked. "Lord, hear me! Hear me! I am innocent!"

That voice that frightens children a mile away boomed. "You are guilty! You saw Treasa and me coming up the strand and panicked out of guilt. You recognized her as Gavin's friend from the past. Of course you did. A woman with a long braid and a sword. There aren't that many of those. I am looking at your face now. Your face tells me."

Treasa added, "Did the new ri ruirech of the Niall, Scanlon the stranger in sovereignty, let you know we were looking for you?"

Oran stared at her. He glanced guiltily at Colm. "Lord—" It piqued Treasa's curiosity that this man who was a close cousin to Colm, and by some forms of blood reckoning considered a brother, called the man "lord."

Then Oran gave up. You knew it instantly from the way he melted into a lax lump. "Yes, I killed Swaya. I justified it to myself by thinking she was miserable and I was ending her misery. I wasn't harming her, I was helping her."

"Who was with you?" Colm's voice cut, brittle as ice.

"No one. I acted alone. That's why I'm certain this woman is a witch, and you'd better beware of her." Those terrified eyes turned up to Colm. "She wanted to die. She taunted me as soon as she heard my voice. She said she was going to tell all she knew. She wouldn't have taunted me like that if she didn't want me to end her misery. She would have been obeisant."

Treasa wasn't going to let him off with that. "Misery you yourself created."

"Swaya wasn't obeisant toward a single soul her whole life, and you know it," Colm snarled. "Aunt Glenna and Uncle Niall."

"A raid. My people. Yes." The lax lump sagged further. "I saw Tara within my grasp, but I didn't act quickly enough." The miserable little bald murderer.

262

"How did Glenna die, exactly, that she never left the house? She was a fighter, like my mother."

"I don't know. I wasn't there."

"But you reaped the profit of it."

"A profitable raid politically and as regards cattle and horses. I knew he didn't keep many retainers on hand." Oran's voice cracked.

Treasa glared at him with what she hoped was a see-all's witchy stare. "You were there on the raid. Otherwise you wouldn't have known that Swaya posed a danger. If someone else had seen her as a witness, they would have skewered her on the spot. I doubt that killing an old woman violated anyone else's taboo. You were on the scene."

Colm gave the man a shove with his foot, a nudge toward truth, so to speak.

Oran's voice barely rose above a whisper. "I was there. When I put Swaya out of her misery, though, that's when my life began to fall apart. I violated my geis, and, of course, ruin would result. I lost my wife, my clients, my holdings. Everything. Already, my power base had disintegrated so badly that when Scanlon appeared, he didn't even have to fight. He took over and allowed me my life if I gave him the seat. So I adopted a life in the church. It was the only way to eat regularly. I had nothing left anyway." He spread his hands helplessly. "I have nothing now."

Colm stared down at him, those crackling blue eyes unreadable. "Many's the time I begged fresh wheaten bread from Swaya. And my aunt and uncle . . . I'm too close to this to be able to be realistic about your penance. Your only chance is to do exactly as I say. Hasten down to the shore and take the first curragh you come to. Row north beyond Ardnamurchan. There are monasteries on Rhum and Eigg with good saints. Wise men. Confess everything and let them give you a fitting penance. Perform that penance completely to excess."

"Yes, lord!"

Not one to have to receive an order twice, the sweating baldy lurched to his feet, nearly dumped himself because he was standing on the hem of his dalmatic, got himself freed up, and ran away down the trail toward the plain. All in all, his performance was not one you'd expect from an erstwhile ri ruirech.

Treasa watched the fellow disappear around the knoll. "Why did you let him go? Gavin—" She quit. Colm knew Gavin as well as she did, probably better.

Colm began walking out toward the track, so Treasa walked beside him. "Couple of reasons. For one, Gavin's father had a bad problem with indecision. He'd let a situation go and hope it resolved itself. Gavin usually isn't like that except when he's being pushed hard, as he is just now. When things are weighing heavily on him. You ever meet his wife?"

"Don't like her, but I never met her."

Colm smirked. "She's pushy. Aggressive. She knew Gavin wouldn't fight her. She played her game assuming that he'd let the situation go too long. Which is exactly what he did, and he lost everything."

"So?"

"Gavin is certain to hear the connection of Oran and Baithene and come here soon. Oran must be gone."

"Yes, but—"

"Think, Trees. Sure and Gavin will try to kill Oran if he finds him. But in his present state, his indecision might give Oran the opportunity to kill him first."

"I can't picture Gavin losing to that dumpy fellow."

"Oran may be ruined and guilt-ridden, but by blood and training he's a king. Never underestimate him."

Treasa nodded. She should have thought of all that herself. Possibly she would have, eventually. The fact that Colm came up with a complete analysis of the situation instantly impressed her. It really impressed her.

No, she would not underestimate Oran. And she would not again underestimate Columcille.

29

Kings' Penance

As you course the heavens, moon,
  Chasing and calling the high tide,
Your face shines for us.

"Looks like your informant this morning was right. Here he comes." Treasa pointed offshore to a bobbing curragh in the distance headed this way. Already you could discern in it a tall, big fellow with dark hair. Beside her, the callow Lugbe beamed.

Colm slapped Lugbe on the back and nearly capsized the little monk. "Well done, Son. Go tell them he's here." Lugbe ran off, up the shingled beach toward Maigh Lunge.

Kenneth and Comgall stood beyond Colm in silence. Probably praying. Treasa wouldn't guess what was going on inside the sour Comgall. But she could win any bet that Kenneth was hard at prayer.

She watched the bobbing curragh and praised God it was not she out there. She sat down on a broad, flat rock, cocked her knees up, and draped her elbows over them.

In a surprisingly accusatory tone of voice, Comgall rumbled, "He's going to ask you where Oran is, Colm. How are you going to avoid lying? 'I don't know' is a lie."

Colm sat down beside Treasa, his legs sprawling out over the bulge of the rock. "Not exactly. I sent him to Rhum or Eigg, but that's no guarantee he'll go there. Still, I won't imply a lie either." Colm bit his lip a moment and poked Treasa. "How did you know so much about Swaya?"

"I already told you how Gavin found his mum. Strictly by chance, we found Swaya—"

"I don't mean finding her. I mean ascertaining how she died. Oran says no one else was there, yet his whole demeanor revealed that you described it right."

"Marks on the skeleton."

"There's more to it than that."

"Infinitely more." Treasa watched the curragh a moment. It didn't seem to be making much headway. "In a skirmish some years ago, I got hit in the side of the face by a hoof when I was unhorsed. Broke off a molar back here." She pressed a finger to her cheek. "A couple years later, I happened upon a skull at a place where some people had been attacked. The previous owner had a tooth broken off exactly like mine. I got to thinking what my skeleton would look like after I'm gone, and what it would tell about me. That got me started, interested. I started looking closely at bones we'd find here and there."

Comgall droned, "Grisly."

"But helpful. A rath of the Monaghan were wiped out. Mountain Behr claimed that when they happened to pass by everyone was already dead, so they buried the remains and rode on. Declan didn't believe that for a minute, but he didn't know what really happened. Here was a chance to put my interest to the test. We went out and dug up the victims. Everyone of the rath whose grave we could find."

Comgall growled, aghast, "That's absolutely ghoulish! Not to mention disturbing their souls!"

Treasa ignored him. She was talking to Colm anyway. "One of the fellows we identified right away, because a couple years before—his ri tuatha knew—he'd lost three fingers in a harvesting machine. But his skeleton didn't just have three fingers missing. The bones of the three stubs were lumpy; shaped oddly where they healed. So I started looking for other healed bones—lumps and rough ridges. A broken arm. A broken hip on an old lady. Her bones healed in pieces; they didn't knit together. She probably lay around for six months before she died."

Colm was frowning, puzzled. "And you could tell flesh wounds from the bones? I don't understand. What purpose—?"

"Not flesh wounds. But think how many wounds occur in battle, and almost always a bone is damaged. We looked for cuts on the bones that would be a gash to the bone, speaking literally. And we found them. The closer, the more carefully we looked, the more we found. That and cracked skulls. That whole rath had been engaged in a life-or-death fight, and they lost."

Comgall interrupted. "See? No point to it. So the Mountain Behr were lying. Your Declan knew that anyway."

Treasa sat up straight, telling a favorite story now, and immensely proud of it. "No, they weren't! We found some blades with the skeletons. Lance points, a javelin tip, and one sword tip that broke off inside the body. The Mountain Behr smelt their own iron. Good quality stuff. These were poor quality bronze."

Colm was watching her intently. "Only ones using that kind of metal now are the Coast Behr, and not many of them anymore."

"Exactly! Exactly! Mountain Behr and Coast Behr might be two lines of the same stock, but they hate each other. They don't cooperate in raids or anything. So when we found the bronze blades, it implied that the Mountain Behr weren't the killers, you see? Declan gathered up a thousand-man force, including a couple clans of Mountain Behr, and we hit the Coast Behr. Found a lot of loot and jewelry, especially the torques, from his tuath. If we hadn't dug those skeletons up and studied them, Declan would have retaliated against the wrong clans and *really* started a war."

The curragh was nearing shore now at last. How could Gavin ride in a thing like that so comfortably?

The silence grew heavy. Treasa wasn't expecting a response. She'd asked or said nothing requiring one, but she didn't like the silence either. "Besides," she added, "I've been thinking about the afterlife. Remember how Finnian used to say the dead in Christ will rise first, and then the living go up with Him? I've been hoping that studying skeletons will give me some kind of understanding about life after death. Do we just whisk away to the Land of the Blessed? Or heaven? Or sleep? What? And how much of our body goes to heaven? If none of the body goes to heaven, how do we know where we are if we don't have a body to be someplace with? I have all these questions."

Comgall said something in a derogatory tone of voice, but the questions would have to wait, for Gavin's curragh was riding in on the tidal wash. It grounded out on the shingle and flopped listlessly aside to port.

He jumped the gunwale, nimble as a yearling, and sloshed ashore. Behind him, half a dozen well-armed retainers hopped out, some of them with grateful expressions on their faces. Treasa recognized none of those faces. They weren't Monaghan. She adjusted the scabbard at her side.

Grimly, even say angrily, Gavin strode up the shingle to Treasa and Colm. "A welcoming committee. I suppose a feast follows?"

"As a matter of fact." Colm nodded without otherwise moving.

"I don't eat with enemies."

"I'm included too, huh?" Treasa was watching the face of a dangerous man on the verge of exploding. His neck muscles were so tight they built grooves near his throat.

"Yes, you. You talked me into leaving my military strength back in Erin when here is where I needed it. Was this all planned out between you and Colm? Am I victim of a conspiracy, or are you each working individually to destroy me?"

The nerve of this spoilt brat! Treasa kept her arms flaccid, kept the fury and tension out of her voice as best she could. "It would have taken you five or six weeks and a whole lot of wealth, which you happen to lack, just to ferry them out to the islands. And then you would have been too late anyway. The assembly would have appointed a successor while you were still lining up your fleet. And you know it."

He ignored her, which, when you think about it, is about all you can do when faced with a truth that doesn't fit your fond misconceptions. "I've come for Oran. Then I'm leaving."

"He's not here." Colm hadn't moved either.

The retainers gathered in closer and spread out, forming a semi-circle around Treasa and the august monks. They were good. They knew what to do without needing every step explained to them. Did they know they were surrounding three of the biggest abbots in Christendom?

"My sources say he is."

Colm nodded. "Thank you for not calling me a liar directly. At least you've kept your tact if not your temper. Oran confessed to the deaths of your parents in a raid he instigated and attended, and the death of Swaya by his own hand. He's abroad now doing penance meet for his crimes."

Gavin's neck tightened further. Treasa wouldn't have thought it possible. "Death is meet for his crimes."

"His death would avail nothing for God. Give God the pleasure of receiving the man's penance. God is much better at vengeance than you or I could hope to be. Let Him handle it."

"Was He handling it when Oran fell upon my mum and da in the dead of night?"

That one would have tangled Treasa's reins past answering. She waited for Comgall to answer it with ridicule, in which case she would lash out and kick the old curmudgeon.

Colm came right back with, "Penance is to atone for sins done against God, not sins done by God, if such there could be."

Gavin was in the midst of retorting—at least he'd gotten as far as the open-the-mouth part—when Colm's penetrating voice silenced him.

"Hawk, of all God's people, I know about penance. I'm here on Tiree, on Iona, at the court at Inverness, up on Ardnamurchan —all because of penance. My home is Erin. Penance has driven me here. Three thousand souls, and not even a thousand of them secured so far. Penance can never replace what's lost, and you've lost all. But Oran's penance will serve God far better than would his death. I'm trying to soften the ruins of Culdrevny. Oran's trying to soften the ruins of the people you loved." His voice fell. "Never forget that I ate Swaya's bread too."

And then Colm raised his hand, his arm outstretched toward Gavin. He signed the cross, just a small, contained sign. "Find peace, Cousin. God's peace. Retribution won't give it to you. Only forgiveness will. You have enormous injustices done against you. Call on Him for help, and forgive, for your own sake."

Treasa didn't think it was going to work. She tightened up her right arm, ready for a quick grab of her sword. The retainers watched Gavin for their cues. After a long, long moment in which Treasa failed to breathe, Gavin turned on his heel and strode back down the shingle to the boat.

Like a pack of boar dogs, the retainers followed him. He spoke to them in undertone. They scattered out across the shore. Now what? While Gavin stood with his back toward Treasa and Colm, his retainers talked briefly to everyone they found. They were, no doubt, asking where Oran would have gone, and everyone wagged their head. No, no one knew anything about an escaping monk. No, no one could help the Hawk or offer suggestions where to look.

They shoved the curragh off, the retainers sloshed out and one by one clambered aboard, and Gavin gave it a final shove. He rolled in over the gunwale. A tidal surge lifted the little boat as the retainers set their oars. Gavin was leaving.

Kenneth sighed heavily. "My heart aches for him."

Colm nodded agreement. "Thanks for your prayer support. That's the only thing that saved the situation from exploding."

"Six to four," Comgall whined, "and only one of us armed. It would have been a massacre."

Treasa lurched to her feet. "Don't wager too much on that. I've seen Colm and Gavin best armed veterans bare-handed. Remember at Gemman's, Colm?"

"I remember the horses we stole."

"Yeah. That big bay, the absolute stupidest horse in the Gaelic-speaking world, and you picked him. The only smart thing you did was palm him off onto Gavin the first chance you got." Treasa braced one foot against the rock and offered Colm a hand to his feet.

Colm accepted her hand. "He looked good."

She hauled back, yanking the blond abbot to his feet. "Lots of things look good."

Kenneth grimaced. "Amen to that. Colm, I'm going to head back down to Erin. The priories there require attention, I'm certain. I've been gone too long as it is."

Colm braced two fingers against his front teeth—Treasa tried for years to master that and couldn't—and whistled down the shore. In the distance, his boatman, Trena of Mocuruntir, waved and headed out toward their big curragh lolling in the shallows.

Comgall allowed as how his work here was done also, and he was expected as a visitor down in Coleraine. For Comgall, it wasn't too clumsy an exit. He usually messed up good-byes pretty badly.

The friends of a lifetime bade their adieus, as the Franks would put it, and pledged mutual visits. Colm invited them all to a major political conclave at Drumceatt next year. They all agreed it would be a good thing to attend.

Treasa remained ashore as the three monks waded out into the restless surf. They talked a while. She saw gestures, but she could discern no words above the harsh and throaty whispers of the surf, above the alternately raucous and mournful calls of sea gulls.

The curragh reached them shortly. Four monks at the oars move a boat that size quickly. She watched Colm assist his two old friends aboard. He gave the curragh a final push. With much waving and signing of the cross, the friends parted.

He stood there a long while watching them, the surf swirling against his legs and tugging at his dalmatic, in all his cold alone.

Trena raised sail, enlarging the dot that was the boat. Winds were swirly here along the shore, but the old seaman obviously picked up a favorable breeze out beyond the point. Leaning slightly, the little vessel shrank until it faded into mist.

Colm waded ashore, his bedraggled dalmatic slapping and clinging against his legs. Treasa watched his sorrowing face a moment and sighed. Gavin had wept on her arm. Colm looked ready to. She wished she could just be a warrior and avoid all this emotional stuff.

He studied the ground intently. Absently, his thoughts suddenly dispersed on the fickle wind, and he strode up the beach toward the monastery.

Treasa stood alone on the shore, with none but complaining sea gulls around her.

30

Love's Quest

Hart and hind
*   bull cow kine*
boar sow swine
*   me and mine*
love entwined.

Dismal. So incredibly dismal, this abandoned place. And to think that once it had been Anice's home. Gavin felt his spirit sag, and he didn't live here. He was only standing here. Dark pines and melancholy yews blotted out the sunshine that Gavin knew was up there somewhere. And this hut! Gavin knew of cattle biers bigger than this. The mud-and-clay wall siding had all but melted away, leaving the woven wattle to weather in the gloom. The thatch was intact, but something had been digging around in it—dormice, perhaps, or a stoat seeking dormice, or both. The place smelled very musty inside. The only fresh tracks in the powdery dirt floor were his own.

The neighbors claimed that Anice had been gone for years. Gavin believed them. Still, for some reason, he felt driven to come here and see for himself. Now, in a way, he was sorry he'd done so. On top of the gloom he could feel his anger building rapidly.

He led his horse out of the pine grove onto a hillside of waist-high brambles and hazel. Soft spring sun warmed his face. He swung aboard and pulled his knees up high on the horse's neck to avoid being raked by the stickers. He rode almost a quarter mile before the brambles gave way to open lea and he could lower his legs.

He followed a faint track to a heavy track and reined his horse aside onto it, headed uphill. Presently he heard the baying and yowling of dogs off to the north. Hoping a huntsman was with them, he turned the horse aside toward the noise.

In a swale a quarter mile from the track, dogs had brought a boar to bay. When Gavin arrived, the huntsman was just pulling a javelin out of the boar as his lads drove the dogs aside. Easy to see which man was the ri—a king and his wife, glorified in a rather garish tartan, sat their horses off to the side.

Gavin was not wearing colors today. They'd just have to take his word regarding his pedigree. Paying the hunt no mind, he rode directly up to the ri. "Gavin Mac Niall, Prince of Erin."

Denied their boar, the dogs gathered yapping around Gavin's horse. Gavin ignored them. "The boaire at the rath where I stayed last night says that a woman, Anice of Drumderry, belongs to a clan in these hills, the Laine. I'm looking for her ri."

This was not a man whom you'd care to engage in a friendly game of brendubh. He glowered at the world from beneath thick, wide brows. His salt-and-pepper beard was carefully trimmed and carefully dressed. Dour men who attend to their appearance that carefully usually haven't a cheerful bone in their bodies. "Anice of Drumderry. She was of the Laine, yes."

Gavin's heart thumped. "'Was.' She died?"

"Might as well have. Gone."

"Sources I've found all say she was kidnapped, sold to a princess, and taken to Erin. She returned many years later and left again. I'm trying to find her."

The ri's lady spoke for the first time. "Don't trouble yourself. She was one of the South Burn Laine. Not worth the effort. Certainly not for a prince, if prince you be."

The anger, simmering a moment ago, boiled over in his heart. "I just came from the hut where she lived after she returned. To call it 'squalid' is being charitable. You're her king. She was your responsibility." He glared at the man and was delighted to see that his old gift for frightening a person with a strong look had not waned. The king actually backed his horse up a step.

"I deal with what's brought to my attention. None in her clan brought her to my attention."

The woman seemed not the least cowed by Gavin's anger. She rode in closer to his side. "This interests me. What does a prince want with the likes of her?"

"More to the point, why do you despise her?"

"And why should I not? Look at her clan! Kidnapped? Hardly! Given to Forba of Drumderry in return for royal favors. Not foster-age, mind you. It's one thing to sell war captives or debtors into slavery. But not your own kin."

"What favors?"

"Land and recognition at court. Of course, soon after, Forba picked up and removed to Erin, so there went the recognition up in smoke."

"Chasing after Finnian." Gavin nodded.

The woman's eyes lit up like a Beltaine fire. "You know about that! Whatever came of it?"

"Of Forba, I have no idea. Finnian is still waddling around his monasteries. He has several." Here might be an ally. The woman seemed open to gossip, and it was gossip that Gavin sought. "And he's not one of those abbots who marries or permits marriage. Ever see Finnian?"

"No. You know him?" She was all ears.

"Very well, in peace and in war. He's immensely fat. Rotund. Scholarly. He tries to be fair, at least when his personal interests aren't inconvenienced too badly. He's the friend of Diarmaid, ard ri at Tara, particularly since the king's favorite monk at Clonmacnois died some years ago."

"Fat. As in repulsively fat?"

Gavin shrugged. "Repulses me. He's this tall"—he held out a hand, palm toward the ground—"lying down."

The woman cackled as if she'd just received a hundred cows. "They say the woman was mad about him."

"She spent several years that I know of camped at his gate. Anice took refuge in his monastery, and Finnian ended up having to pay for her. Something about a wrecked chariot also. Anice didn't find out she was redeemed until years later when she married well and sought out the princess to buy her freedom."

"Amazing. Forba came back, you know—eventually. Married a regional king and, I suppose, gave up pretensions to any thrones of her own. Pretty woman, but an absolute witch."

Gavin nodded. "That's the impression I received of her."

The hunt was resuming, with or without the gossipers. The king's lady invited Gavin along, and he accepted. The woman's blood lust matched her hunger for tales. She rode with an eager disregard for anything save the chase, and once in a while actually used her horse to shoulder her husband's aside.

They finished the day with two boars and a stag and a dead hound gored by the cornered deer. Gavin accepted their hospitality and that night feasted on boar that had been dressed out several weeks ago and aged properly. He slept in a cozy nest of two-year sheepskins—the wool-on hides of sheep that had been allowed to go two years without shearing before being butchered. These little royal touches were a nice change from the errant, even say impoverished, life he'd been living lately.

That was one of the troubles with monks. They tended to consider hardship a virtue.

Once he heard that several in this Pict's clan had married Erse, he admitted that he was for some years a ri ruirech of the Dal Riada.

"Ah," purred the goodwife, "so that's why you mutilate the language so."

That startled him. He thought he was doing pretty well with Pictish.

Friday when the king sat at court, luck struck. By invitation, Gavin sat beside him. And by chance, the first case to be heard was a minor ri of the Drumderry Laine. Anice's clan.

The ri was interested in getting his petition made. Gavin was more interested in Anice's bloodline and present whereabouts.

The ri's brehon knew the bloodline and recited it twice, since Gavin didn't handle pronunciation of names well. Anice possessed quite a nice pedigree. Nothing royal, though a couple clansmen were civil servants. But nice. Did she even know that?

Her whereabouts? She disappeared. No one knew anything.

"Just disappeared?"

The ri fidgeted. "Her uncle mentioned about her disappearance, and I sent a party out to check on her. They found nothing. There are wolves in the area."

"What did they find in her hut? Belongings?"

"If she were gone some time, they could have been pilfered by beggars or madmen passing through."

That fury flared again. It happened often lately, this barely containable anger. Gavin glared and the fellow shrank back, but no more information was forthcoming.

The next morning he left the area, and not a moment too soon.

Disappeared ... wolves ...

Gavin was not ready to buy the wolf theory, however obliquely it was suggested. Wolves for all their reputation usually limit their diet to livestock. He returned to her hut and spent a full day examining the area. He found absolutely nothing.

He sat at her wretched little doorway that evening beneath the melancholy yews and pines, while his horse pawed the duff, hungry for grass that didn't grow within a half mile of this miserable place. She owned no livestock, obviously. This hut was nowhere near open arable land where grain might be raised. So far as he knew, she possessed none of the arcane skills of an artisan —no metalworking, specialty weaving, or such.

How would she make her way, living in this hole? She couldn't. No wonder she left. Where would she go?

Her clan here, and even her king, certainly didn't care about her. Her connections were primarily in Erin therefore. Her Erse clan in marriage had kicked her out, so if she sought her fortune in Erin or the Dal Riada she would probably use a church connection. Drumceatt. Moville, perhaps. Not Iona; Colm didn't allow women in that monastery.

Tiny golden speckles of the setting sun pierced the gloom of this woodland, dappling the black trees overhead. Drumceatt was also one of Colm's. So was Durrow. Gavin would use them as a last resort.

She might be dead. As thoroughly as she seemed to have disappeared, she probably was dead. Gavin would not accept that. He could not. From the first moment he espied her coming through the broken gate until the last moment he watched her auburn hair catch the sun just so, he had never forgotten her, never eased her from his mind.

Oran and Anice. He would give Oran time to do his penance, whatever that was. Then he would seek him out and kill him. That task was for another day. Anice was today's.

276

He needed her now. No more would he fret about not having a kingly life to give her. No more would he worry about ruling a domain. They would persevere somehow and build a good life. He wanted her. No one else. Her.

He would find her. He would.

31

Treasa's Betrayal

Year of our Lord 575

This I know of love,
  'Tis lost as soon as found.

Treasa *hated* being wealthy! She absolutely hated it. Sure and it was fun in the beginning. She'd receive a hundred cows as a bonus for good work; she'd garner another hundred in a raid. She distributed cattle generously as gifts to the men under her and that largess almost always came back to her in good will and improved heart. Heart more than anything else makes the warrior. The people under her had heart and to spare.

But those cattle she kept, leasing them out judiciously to boaires she knew well, just went on multiplying. Her flock increased fivefold, her hogs went—well, hog wild.

The not-so-fun part that made the whole pursuit so odious was the management of her growing holdings. Declan had given her the wasted rath of a family decimated by the plague. He made the gift sound so generous. She knew better. The rath stayed in the clan whether she or someone else lived here. It would not be hers even if she had heirs—which was certainly not likely. She was building up a rich property for someone else's benefit and in the process going fruity trying to keep it running.

As she watched her latest ex-manager amble out the gate, better off by a good bit than when he ambled in six months ago, she wanted to just dump all this and ride away. She couldn't. It was too much to give up. Her pride wouldn't let her.

She clapped her hands once and slapped her right palm down on her left knuckles. Her aide, a callow lad on the new end of puberty, leaped to his feet and ran out the gate to fetch her horse. Nabb, his name was. Nabb of Clogher. His mother, Treasa heard, was a Tyrone, which wasn't bad. Minutes later he returned with the little charcoal mare. Though making no comment she noted that he had made a good choice. The mare hadn't been exercised recently and needed the work. Treasa scooped up the reins, dismissed Nabb, and swung aboard.

Phenomenal luck she had, finding good people in a military capacity, like the aide there. Fine lad, Nabb. Quick. Why couldn't she get a decent seneschal? She urged her mare to a lope as she headed for the gate.

The path through her gate was a sea of mud again. The manager should have strewed straw and stones there days ago. Details. That was it. She despised details. The mare skidded a little on one stride, recovered, and continued.

Now that Treasa was a-horse, her natural condition, where should she go? She reined the mare roughly to a halt. Then came the dawn. *Of course!* She wrenched her mount's head around and sent her back in the gate. The mare slipped in the goo and very nearly went to her knees.

"Nabb!" She pivoted the mare in the dooryard, looking about.

The lad came running around the side of the house, furiously brushing bread crumbs off his tunic. *Less than two minutes, and already he's in the kitchen.* She kept forgetting how much food a lad that age consumes.

"Nabb, you're in charge of the rath. You can commence your duties by correcting that mud problem in the gate before some king gets sucked down into it and disappears."

"The manager, lady—"

"You are the manager. You've proven yourself by handling my arms and my stable faultlessly. Take over here."

Her announcement effectively reduced her new manager to a blathering mess. His mouth bobbed open and shut a few times, achieving nothing of importance.

She twisted on her mare toward the gate. Hoofbeats, a horse at a canter, were approaching. Hers was not a gate to be approaching at that speed. She knew what was very likely to happen; she just didn't know yet to whom.

The rider angled in from the north track as the porters stepped forward. He drew his horse in at the last moment—deliberately, no doubt. The great, bulky dapple tossed its head high and sat back. Nabb gasped.

A big man on a big, dancing horse cuts quite a figure. A big man on a horse that keeps right on sitting is not so impressive. A big man on a horse that slams back on its rump, its legs flying, and flops onto its side appears singularly unimpressive. A big man who is unceremoniously thrown off his fallen horse into mud pasty enough to calk a boat looks downright ridiculous.

Casually, straight-faced, Treasa rode over to a fallen prince of Erin. "Welcome, Gavin Mac Niall. When you've rooted about there sufficiently to serve your fancy, do join me for a light meal. 'Tis about that time of day."

She expected him to erupt in fury. She expected him to laugh it off. She did not expect the utter dejection and loss on his face, or the way his shoulders sagged when he dragged himself to standing.

Nabb leaped forward unbidden and had his hands on the horse's bridle even before it struggled to its feet. "I'll have his horse cleaned up and see to this immediately, lady!" He jogged away, carefully, the big dappled horse in tow.

Treasa slid off her horse and let the porter take care of it. She watched Gavin slog his way to firmer ground inside the gate yard. "Cold rinse or warm bath?"

"Warm bath."

She flagged the porter. "Leave the horse and see to the guest's bath."

The porter dropped the mare's reins and strode off behind the house. He wasn't in any better mood than the ex-manager.

"This"—Gavin spread his arms, a look-at-me gesture—"is my life in a nutshell. Right here."

"I daresay you look defeated. I just dismissed a manager and hired anew, or my service would be far speedier. As soon as he returns, I'll have him tap the ale. You look as though you could use some."

"Name anything in the world. I can use some."

"Not a horse. Nice dapple you have there."

"Clumsy."

He could blame her mudhole for the spill or he could blame his horse. This was a time to keep her mouth shut.

He pulled the pin on his brooch and dragged the muddied cloak off his shoulders. It was plainweave, without colors. For the moment, he was not advertising his princehood. "Anice. Ever hear anything about her?"

"No, but then I haven't been asking. Doesn't she live up in the Dal Riada? Somewhere near the Lochaline inlet, I thought."

"I've been to her home there. She disappeared."

"Mm." *Why would he want her?* Treasa would no doubt learn in time. "Outside chance, but Colm might know."

Silence. All right, she'd allow silence. She opened her door and with a wave of the hand invited him in. Gavin. She was afraid she'd never see him again, and now here he was. She would rejoice in life's little mysteries and not pry.

Her housemaid, somewhat surprised, built up the fire and scurried off to the kitchen.

Gavin lay back against the leaning board and watched the fire slither around on the birch branches for a while. The lad looked incredibly wearied.

Treasa dug into the head roll at her pallet. It took her fingers a few moments of groping to find what she was looking for—she hadn't had it out since it was repaired. She took it over to Gavin and settled beside him. "Hold out your hand."

He did so with a puzzled scowl on his dark face.

She dropped his mother's brooch into it. "Enameled again, just like new."

He stared at it the longest time. Did his eyes glisten? She was hoping so, but she didn't really see it. He closed his hand over it and grimaced. "Thank you, Treasa. Now I feel particularly like an oaf. This is . . ." Whatever it was, he let it ride with a silence instead of a statement. "I suppose before I ask a favor I ought to apologize. So I do. That's not what I came for though."

She snorted. "Obviously, apology comes very hard for a prince. Whatever it's for, it's accepted. What did you come for?"

"I've just been to Finnian's. Moville."

"How's the old blob doing?"

"He's getting pretty rickety. I doubt we'll have him much longer. Healthy enough but getting awfully slow. I was hoping Anice came down to Erin. If she did, she might make contact with a monastery. Apparently she didn't go to Moville. She never was at Gemman's. Glasnevin's gone."

"Glasnevin started up again. Still, she'd have no connection with it—with the new one. Kildare, maybe, if she heard about it. Excellent reputation, Kildare. If she came to one of Colm's, he'll know."

"That's what I was thinking. I'd like you to go ask Colm for me."

She mulled that all of two seconds. "Gavin . . ." And it made her mad. "Gavin, you're acting like a twelve-year-old! You know, the kid who won't talk to his foster brother, so he gets the sister to be the go-between? 'Tell so-and-so I said—' and so-and-so is standing right there. But the go-between has to repeat it. Ask him yourself!" She paused. "Besides, I am not about to float in a boat on that hell of a sea just so you don't have to talk to your cousin. Especially since you float in boats very comfortably, without losing any meals."

Gavin waved his hands. "No. You don't have to float anywhere. Colm and his new king are coming over to Drumceatt to a political assembly of some sort. Seventy, eighty miles overland, and you're there. Easy ride." He watched her a moment. "I'll loan you the dapple."

She wrinkled her nose. "Too clumsy. It's an easy ride for you too."

"That price on my head has never been lifted. Until there's a change in the high seat, I can't appear at any political assembly. Please, Treasa."

Curiosity got the best of her. "Why do you want Anice?"

"To marry her."

That was short and sweet. Why did it stun her so? She heard her lips say, "Oh, all right," but her heart wasn't in this house. It wasn't even inside her ringwall. It lay buried deep in the shards of shattered dreams she had never even known existed.

They headed north three days later, with a score of retainers and Leod at their heels and Nabb back home in charge of the rath.

Fergus claimed he'd like to come along, but he was afraid Colm would be out on Iona after all and he wasn't about to go there.

With his hood pulled forward and his dark face in shadow, Gavin was harder to identify. Not much harder. There was no hiding that big, brawny build. They waited until late evening before riding out onto the Derry plain. They camped on the periphery of a vast, amazing array of tents and marquees clustered amid a thousand fires—a thousand thousand.

Treasa thought again of those myriad warriors preparing to go forth to, as it turned out, Culdrevny. *Ah, what a time that was, and never the like of it since!*

Gavin was condemned to sitting by the fire hunched over, trying to look smaller. Leod and the retainers set up camp and took the horses out to water and graze down on a common by the river. Treasa walked up to Drumceatt to see what was going on.

Even before she entered the gate, she heard Colm's clear, ringing voice speaking. Was this the opening office? It was, after all, his facility and he the host. He could be greeting them. And yet the camps she passed coming up here appeared well established, as if these people had already been around a while.

Inside the ringwall, the oratory and scriptorium had been linked together with a breezeway roof of pole-and-thatch, providing dry seating for the entire assembly at once. And what an assembly. Tartans all over. Every ri ruirech, of course, an awful lot of ri tuathe, a whole flock of brehons, numerous bards, many, many monks, and a scattering of druids made conspicuous by their scarcity. It was the social event of the year, apparently.

She stretched on tiptoe to see faces. With just about everyone seated on rushes on the ground and she, taller than most, standing, she could see well. Aidan the usurper of Gavin's place was seated at Colm's right. Declan had come. There he sat, not far from the bishop of Armagh. Finnian? There he sat, taking up three or four spaces to the bishop's left.

She had about determined that she was entering the middle of a session when the words Colm was speaking sank in.

". . . no place on the battlefield. A woman is a nurturer. She can bestow mercy like no other can. She is grace. I quote the saying we have all heard since childhood, 'There is a mother's heart in the heart of God,' referring to His nurturing aspect. Only the triune God, who is all things, can be both warrior and nurturer. We faulty people of the earth cannot. We are fitted by God to be either/or, not both.

"I therefore propose that this assembly adopt the following: That henceforth women be excluded from the battlefield. That this rule will be binding upon all the churches and accepted by all the kings of Erin."

Treasa stared, open-mouthed. He couldn't be sane! He couldn't say that and—

Speak up, Declan! Tell this assembly that your best warrior's a woman! Tell them the wealth she's brought your clan.

Declan saw her standing in the entryway and averted his eyes. Debate commenced, and he did not offer a defense. When Colm betrayed Gavin, Treasa felt sorry. Now Colm had betrayed her, and sorrow was the least of it. Fury burned wild in her.

She pushed forward, striding amid seated delegates, until she stood virtually alone. Was Declan embarrassed? He looked so. *Good! Couldn't be better!*

Treasa quoted the only scriptural thesis she had ever learned during her years at Moville. Fortunately it fit the occasion. "In the letter to Corinth, Paul says that—"

The presiding brehon thundered, "Opinion is permitted of the privileged ranks only."

But Treasa rode her voice roughshod right up over his. "—the body is composed of many parts. Whoever is suited to a task, that is his task. His or hers. He never said that the arm must be female and the leg male, or that the—"

They were dragging her backward toward the entryway, one bear attached to each arm. She pulled forward against them, struggling.

"—head be a different gender from the breast. The job a person is drawn to, that is the job God made that person for. That is the job the person should do."

She was nearly in the entryway now, and she knew the dragging wasn't going to stop there. Instead of resisting, she stepped back and sat suddenly, dropping her full weight downward. The bears attached to her arms weren't expecting that. They lost balance, staggered.

She hauled her arms forward as hard as she could, crossing them in front of her. The bears collided.

Treasa leaped back a step to full standing, pulling her sword. "As I said, when person is created by God for a task, that's the task that person should do. I assume I have made my point." She put a bit of extra oomph on the word *point,* sheathed her sword, and stepped quickly out the entryway.

She heard Colm shout, not at her but, apparently, at the bears. No one followed her out into the clammy night.

Imagine that miserable cur! How could he?

She left the ringwall gate and walked in a huff to the biers, so irate she could not see. If this assembly voted to bar women, she was out of the Monaghan. Declan ran with the herd. Whatever they said, he would go along with.

She continued past the biers to the royal stabling. A voice in the darkness called, "Who goes?"

"Just me. Treasa. Columcille knows me." *But that didn't stop him from proposing to destroy me.*

The guard loomed, nodded, and stepped back. There is value in being a well-known figure, the only woman around with a braid and sword. She chose a stout length of rope that happened to be coiled and hung on a paddock post.

With it, she continued around to the back of the ringwall. She built a loop and tossed it up over the stockade post. A few tugs—it held firm. It didn't take much trouble at all to scale the wall, haul the rope up and toss it to the inside, and roll over into the compound.

Colm ran quite an extensive school here for kings' and nobles' sons. Had the eager and pious young students thought to carve handholds up the inside of the stockade yet? Not along the back here, at least. She might have to give some lessons of her own to these lads; they appeared to be pretty slow.

She worked her way among the jumble of clochans until she could see the refectory and most of the backyard. She would wait.

From the scriptorium/oratory/marquee came a chorus of yeas.

Shortly there followed a much fainter chorus of nays. Did Declan deliver one of the nays? Probably not.

The Compline sounded like it was being sung by a rehearsed group, not just your average bunch of monks.

The assembly was breaking up in a roar of conversation. The voices were slow to filter out the gate. They must be standing around talking. These privileged ranks sure knew how to throw a party. A boring, disastrous party.

It must have been an hour later that Colm finally appeared, taller than the rest, that blond head floating in the flickering half-light of the torches. He stopped here, he stopped there, talking, talking, talking. He moved from the dim circle of orange light this way, toward the clochans.

Treasa unpinned her cloak and drew it up over her head like a hood, putting her face in shadow. She threaded among the bee-hive huts, keeping an eye on that shining head, until she could gauge which hut he was headed for. She slipped in beside it and stood stock still, as near it as she dared, holding her breath.

He had no idea she lurked so close by. She heard a sigh, but she couldn't see his face in the darkness. At his doorway, he shoved his trimmed oxhide aside. She moved forward and slipped in behind him. Did he hear or note the oxhide's gentle delay as it fell back in place? He seemed to hesitate.

She stood in the blackness and waited patiently as he stirred his fire. A sudden problem reared its head. How would she an-nounce her presence without scaring the willies out of him? She pictured him bolting in startled surprise, perhaps punching a hole right out the back of this tiny clochan.

Which presented another problem. This place was so close, if he swung around quickly to confront the unknown—a gut-level reaction to having one's willies forcibly removed—he'd cork her in the chops. She minimized both prospects by hunkering down close to the dirt floor and very quietly snickering.

He jerked up stiff and straight, sucking in air—then heaved a sigh of disgust the like she'd never heard. He sat down cross-legged at his fire, his back still toward her. "Treasa, why do you always do this to me?"

"Not always. Only twice."

"Have you ever considered approaching and addressing me like normal people do?"

"And miss the opportunity to demonstrate that when it comes to stealth I have no equal? Open battle or covert operation, I'm the best there is. You ruined me. What Finnian and Cruithnechan tried to do and failed, you achieved. Why?"

"Do you remember the first time ever we saw Anice?"

"I remember I hated her, and I didn't even know her. She loathed battle, and I hungered for it. She got to be in the thick of it, and Finnian kept me out of it. She despised the opportunity I wanted most."

He sat silent a moment. "That's it exactly. She didn't want to be there. That gash on her leg went to the bone, you know. An interesting skeleton for you to examine someday, perhaps. How did a weapon mark end up on the back of a lower leg bone? That first sight of her haunted me for years. She had lost her zest for life. Living and dying meant the same to her. She didn't care anymore."

She found it disconcerting to talk to his back. She circled around the fire to see his face. "So to protect the likes of Anice the child, you deny a whole gender the ability to choose. As an adult she entered the battle voluntarily, you know. She fought for you at Culdrevny. So did I, and capably. I stood between you and trouble when you announced your decision for Aidan. We profit you. I profit Declan. Doesn't that mean anything to you?"

"Not as much as ending the forced service does." He nurtured his little fire (as if men had any ability to nurture) without looking at her. "You're furious. I guess I don't really blame you. But you're also resourceful. The good of the many defenseless girls and women outweighs your needs. You're resourceful. You'll make your way, whether there is fighting or not. You—"

"What about *dreams? Desires?*"

"Dreams are the first casualty in any battle." He looked at her for the first time. "You just arrived today, right? I didn't see you before."

"Hours ago."

"Then you don't know about the resolutions we passed before you got here. They were going to abolish the rank of bard. No more poets, no more oral historians. I managed to block the motion and save the position."

"Of course you would. You've always been a poet."

He continued as if he hadn't heard her. "Also, Aidan and I managed to get the Dal Riada declared fully independent of Erin. The Erse may live there, but we're our own entity."

"You were anyway."

He shook the glowing blond head. His fire crackled bright enough now that he practically radiated. "Not politically. Not in the ways that count." He watched her face a moment. "It's an important victory for the Dal Riada, Treasa."

"Forgive me if I'm unimpressed. We came to find Anice. She's not with her clan anymore. We're hoping you might know where she is."

"Who is 'we'?"

"Gavin and I."

"He's here?"

"I'm mediating because he doesn't want to look at your face, and neither do I anymore." She watched the pain spread from his pallid eyebrows down to his eyes, and brimming over. She almost regretted saying that, so she added, "Besides, he's still wanted. After all these years, he's still wanted."

"Not in the Dal Riada. Not anymore. See the value of complete independence? We still follow brehon law and church rule but with none of the rubbish that Tara would inflict on us."

"Anice. Do you know where she is?"

"Here at Drumceatt. She's in charge of our orphans and old people." He smiled for the first time in—well, in years, that Treasa could remember. "She's a part of the family of God now."

"Orphans and old people. Where's that?"

"Ask the porter."

She nodded. "That's what I came for. Good-bye, Colm."

She heard his good-bye behind her as she walked out into the clammy night. The gateyard was plunged into deep darkness, for the torches had all been snuffed.

So had she.

288

32

Anice's Glow

My love came a-seeking me,
  Derry down derry,
To bring me an apple tree,
  Derry down derry,
And pledge his true love to me,
  Derry down Dee.

Gavin stood a while on this rainy, windy lea, his back to the Drumceatt gate, and gazed out across the Derry vale. The setting sun burnished with orange the hills beyond. The valley itself lay in blue-gray gloom. Scattered across the river plain, a few small, poor, ringwalled raths awaited destruction from the next major flood. The prosperous raths, their houses and walls built of fitted field stone, crowned the gentle rises and distant hills beyond the vale. Cattle and sheep in their hundreds and thousands mixed with occasional swine to dot the hills here and everywhere in Erin forever. Beside him, the crabapple tree moped in the rain, its leaves growing hard and tough along with the dying springtime.

Just about every visiting dignitary to the big folderol at Drumceatt had packed up and gone home. *Good riddance.* The show was over, the party done. Without the noisy, stinking clutter of tents and livestock, the valley looked so peaceful in the dying day.

Old people without clan support were extremely few in Erin, though the plague had created more than you'd expect. Orphans? Even fewer. Children were the future of the clan and jealously hoarded. Gavin tried to piece together what had happened here.

Obviously, without her clan to take her in, Anice decided to return to Erin. Equally obviously, she had come directly to Colm, but that would be expected. Where else would she turn? And so Colm, with few options, would find something for her to do that would conveniently take care of her and yet keep her out of his

289

hair. Giving her old people and orphans to care for would be a perfect solution.

One of those ringwalled raths on the river bottom was the monastery's old people and orphans' home. Treasa said that the porter, with his wave of the arm, seemed unclear as to just which one. No matter. Gavin would find it.

Keeping his shoulders hunched and his hood pulled forward, he hurried down the slope, following a faint cow path. On an outcrop just above the river bottom, he paused to consider. This side of the river or the other? To the right or to the left?

Into the gate of the rath just across the River Foyle, a rather dumpy milkmaid was driving two cows. The robust laughter of young men floated up from the rath downstream on this side. Neither of those places was likely to be the one. He turned aside and rock-hopped down off the outcrop toward the other rath on this shore.

Two half-grown boys were driving five cows in from the hill. They hesitated when they saw Gavin, but the cows continued toward the gate, so they did as well. He fell in behind, just far enough off to the side to keep the cows to the straight and narrow. Many a cow did he drive in his own youth.

As the cows lumbered in through the muddy gateway, one of the lads raced around behind the house as the other kept a wary eye on Gavin. Three children ran across from the kitchen to the woodpile, spent a few moments studying Gavin carefully, then scooped up branches and hastened away.

Gavin dropped his hood and smiled at the wary-eyed lad. "I'm not about to steal your cows."

"That's good." The lad's hard gaze didn't soften in the least.

Gavin's memories skipped back to his own youth—he was about that size, in fact—when he killed the man who tried to steal a calf from Finnian. The night that happened, saying nothing to anyone, Gavin drove the cattle in as usual. When the body was discovered, he kept his mouth shut. No one suspected a twelve-year-old, of course, and as far as Gavin knew, someone somewhere still wondered by whose hand the man died. Gavin never, ever regarded twelve-year-old boys lightly.

And there she was.

Her hands nervously wadding a soiled towel, Anice stood between the house and the wall, between the other lad and Gavin, between heaven and hell. The first things ever he noticed about her when she entered his life were those huge, glorious, luminescent eyes. He noticed them now. Her hair glowed auburn, and despite all the blows the club of years had rained down upon her, she had not lost the sweetness in her face, or the youth.

She was trembling. "The moment the Leary said 'a tall man,' I knew it was you." Her voice seemed huskier than he remembered.

"Come walk with me."

"I can't. There's the supper to prepare."

"Sure and you must have a cook."

"We do, but she's three score and seven years old and stiff. Arthritic. She's as likely to fall into the fire as stir the pot."

"Let the Leary supervise her then. Come."

Behind her, the lad asked suspiciously, "You know him, Mum?"

"Since I was your age, aye."

The Leary's eyes went wide. "But y're so old, Mum!"

Anice stared at Gavin a moment, startled, then burst into a messy spate of giggles. "Aye, Gavin, I shall walk with you." She handed the towel off to the Leary. "Yourself is in charge of supper, Lad." And she marched boldly up to Gavin.

What was different about her? He would explore the question later. He swirled his own ample cloak out and over her shoulders, covering her threadbare shawl, drawing her in closer.

They walked out the gate through the mud. He watched it squish up between her bare toes and belatedly realized he had better watch the dirt at their feet less and look out for danger more. The kings and princes, brehons and abbots might be gone, but his head was never safe in Erin.

They wandered down to the river shore because that's where the cow paths led them. Amid a field of birch stumps at water's edge, a dozen alder trees had taken hold. This grove of little alders crowding close beside the river was hardly more than saplings. So few mature trees remained in Erin anymore. It wouldn't be long, Gavin mused darkly, before Erin would be as barren and treeless as the islands of the Dal Riada. He rued the day.

Anice slipped out from under his cloak and perched on a birch stump. "Does Colm know you're back?"

Gavin nodded.

She seemed so poised, so confident in herself. He, uncharacteristically, felt like a twit in a labyrinth, unable to think and clueless as to which way to go next.

"Treasa was here for the conclave. She defended the right of women to enter battle. If anyone can, she can." The luminescent eyes glanced up at his. "Did you know she was around?"

He nodded.

Anice looked at the river, at the mud, at the sky, at infinity—anywhere but at Gavin. "And Comgall. Comgall very nearly precipitated a fight, arguing about a monastery he's establishing near Coleraine. And Kenneth. Dear Kenneth. We were all here. All the old crowd. But so much has changed. Remember how Cruithnechan and Finnian were credited with miracles? Now Colm is too."

"Finnian was here too, you know."

"I know." Her voice hardened, not the least bit wistful, not floating gently the way it usually floated. "I spoke to him; introduced myself, for old times' sake. It was terribly obvious that he didn't remember me. So I explained that I was the slave girl he redeemed from Forba. And then he really got mad, so I walked away."

"Why does your clan not accept you?"

She shrugged. "My mother was clan, but her mother was from outside. My father was a murderer, and exiled. When my father left, my mother remarried—"

"Happens all the time."

"She married a fellow who killed the ri tuatha and tried to take the throne. That was the year after he sold me to Forba. I financed his campaign against the ri, in small part." She smiled at Gavin. "I suspect they rejected my stepfather not because he killed the ri and tried to take over but because he failed in his attempt. You know how it goes."

"Your parents come from good families, both of them."

"The families look good, perhaps. In truth, they're a conniving, stingy, bunch of cattle thieves, is all."

"Everyone's a cattle thief, or potentially so."

"Sad, isn't it?"

"So Colm put you in charge of old people and orphans." He tried to give his tone of voice a flavor of contempt—a very mild flavor, to be sure—to open the door to his proposal.

"The plague turned Erin upside down, Gavin. There was a time, my grandmum said, when everyone was safe within the clan. You took care of whomever you should, and someone would take care of you. Someone somewhere was closely enough related to you that they had to take you in. No orphans left without a roof. No old people cast out."

"It's still that way."

"Where is your clan, Gavin?"

She knew as well as he that it was devastated. It didn't seem quite fair to win an argument by pointing out a truth. He countered with, "Yes, but I'm a strong adult. If I were a child or—"

"Wars take their toll. They always have. But the plague, Gavin." Her voice caught. "So many small clans have been wiped out, or virtually so. Even not-so-small clans. A few members left, and they not strong enough to take over a full clan's duties. We don't have many here in our rath. But the few we do serve have no one else to turn to."

He shook his head. He was going to say "I can't believe you're as important here as you think you are" and managed to cut that off in time. *Tact, White Hawk! Tact.* Instead he said, "But what about the rest of the tuath? Shouldn't the king pick up where the clans beneath him fall short? It's his responsibility."

"These people have no one."

Now what? His delightful cousin Columcille, the sweet Dove of the Church, had just yanked Gavin off still another horse. Obviously, Anice considered herself useful here. He was going to have to lure her away. Gavin resisted the impulse to tell her to turn it all over to the Leary and then just scoop her up and carry her off. *Should I simply make my plea and then tear apart her arguments, or should I—?*

But she was still talking rapidly. "I'm a Christian, Gavin! I worship God through Jesus."

"Whom did you worship before? Jupiter?"

293

Her face fell. It brightened again. "I didn't really care much whether I lived or died. I had nothing to live for. Then I realized how Jesus died for me. Don't you see? If my soul weren't valuable, He wouldn't have done that!"

"He died for a few other people too, you know. Me, for instance."

She completely missed the reference to his own conversion and plowed on down the field. "For the first time, life means something! Colm brought me into his monastic ministry in a position where I make a difference—this one—and suddenly I have an important purpose. I never had a purpose before, not even when I was married to a ri. I was a convenience to him. Here I'm a necessity. Don't you see? I have a whole new life!"

Gavin had made a commitment to Jesus. Why didn't it change anything in his life? Because every time an avenue opened to him, Colm blocked it shut.

"Anice, you're not a sister. A nun."

"No. Many people work for the church without being monastics."

"So you're free to marry."

"If I choose." Her voice beyond words was telling him, *I do not choose.* "Before I came to this work here . . ." She frowned and started over. "Brendan of Birr died a couple years ago, you know."

"No, I didn't." *So what? And who was Brendan of Birr?*

She answered his unspoken question whether he wanted an answer or not. "Colm always admired him. Brendan of Birr was one of the few people who supported him at Telltown, who worked to prevent his excommunication. Anyway, he initiated a festival on Iona to commemorate Brendan. But he had to go to Durrow, and then he had to settle some problems on Hinba, so he gave me the task of preparing the liturgy honoring Brendan. You see? Another job with purpose."

"That's insane! You never studied. . . . You're not even lettered!"

She darkened instantly. "He wanted an expression of pure faith because Brendan of Birr was a man of simple, pure faith. Not scholarly preaching. Honest doing. He accepted my work almost without change."

This was the difference in her, the new Anice contrasted to the old. She glowed. She shimmered with life. Gone was the defeat, the blasé attitude. And there was only one explanation for it. "You're in love, aren't you? In love with Colm."

Her mouth dropped open. Fury ignited her eyes.

He grabbed both her hands. "If I'm wrong, prove it by going away with me. Colm has thousands of monks and nuns in his monasteries. He can assign any of them the task of minding these people. You're not the only one who can handle the task. Marry me!"

"Stop! You don't—"

He pressed forward. "Anice, you know I've always loved you. I haven't been able to get you out of my mind over all these years. When I had nothing, I thought—"

"Please stop!"

"—I would wait until I gained a position of some sort—a kingship. And I'd have to get out from under that reward for my head somehow. I doubt any of that will ever happen. I've given up the dream, but I haven't given you up. We'll make our way somehow, you and I. Mercenary in Pictland, with your own clan, if you like. Something."

Her luminescent eyes were filling up with tears, sparkling like stars. She wagged her head.

Time for action. He gathered her in close, and reveled in her closeness. Leaving no room for reluctance on her part, he cupped his hand behind her head. It tangled instantly in that luxuriant hair, and he dwelt happily upon the softness of it. When he kissed her, her lips resisted for only the barest moment before they softened and opened.

Never. Never had a kiss ever warmed him like this.

He whispered, "Please come."

She pulled her head back, surprisingly strong against his cupped hand. "Gavin, I'm a Christian now." She wrenched away.

He frowned. "So am I. That doesn't mean—"

"It means everything! Under brehon law, there wouldn't be a problem, but Christians answer to a higher law. We have to do things the way God originally intended."

"Well, uh, certainly." He should have said this first. "We'll get married, of course. I didn't mean—you know. Here!" He dug into the purse at his waist for the bit of sheepskin. Carefully he unwrapped it. His mother's enameled brooch gleamed in the palm of his hand. "I'd like you to have this, as a pledge. It was my mum's."

The luminescent eyes swam in crystalline tears. Her warm, delicate hands wrapped around his open hand and closed the fingers over the brooch. "I want to so much, Gavin! You can't imagine what a temptation you've set before me! I want—"

"Then let's go!"

"We can't, Gavin. Don't you see? Christians take but one wife. You may have been estranged for many years, but somewhere your wife still lives. I can't marry you. You're still married."

33

Finnian's Miracle

Year of our Lord 579

You will hear about wars
*   and rumors of wars.*

Treasa hated herself. Of all the people in this wide world whom she hated, she hated herself the most.

What she wanted to do she never got around to. What she desired most was ripped out of her hands, and she did nothing to recover it. What she hated doing, what she didn't want to do—that's what she did most all the time.

Today she was acting all too true to form. She rode with determination, but she was not determined in the least. She had a purpose in riding down these melancholy hills, but it was not a purpose she relished, and yet it meant her future. If God indeed be in heaven He knew how much she hated this!

Her horse moved at a steady jog across the open, sloping pasturage where in her childhood a forest stood. No sign of it now. Sleepy cattle grazed casually across the meadows or stood in brainless silence watching her pass. The slippery fog parted before her and closed behind her. With its steady *plik plik plik plik,* her gelding carried her to a place she absolutely did not want to be—Moville.

She reined her gelding in sharply. *What's going on here?* Directly before her rolled a broad river, right across the track. She expected a minor rivulet that, by the time it reached Moville, would have become the creek that once flowed past the bull pasture. This was her native territory, but she had just gotten lost. Well, perhaps not lost. Turned around. She was miles from where she thought she was. And yet—

I must have become disoriented in the fog.

She waded her gelding across the ford and up the slope on the other side. A moment ago she thought she was only about half a mile from Moville, but now the presence of the river made it more than two miles.

Half a mile later, she rode in through the familiar, time-worn gate, totally confused. But then other thoughts and feelings caught her attention. She detected a powerful tension in the air. Old Finnian had always been pretty lax about defense, but he must have abandoned defense entirely, for no porters greeted her. No monks challenged her. She slid off her sweaty horse near the oratory and found no stable boy or kitchen help to hand the gelding off to. *What's going on here?*

Finnian had torn down his old oratory and built a new one, no small feat considering that the old was one of the first stone oratories in the region, and certainly one of the sturdiest. She stepped inside the doorway, from foggy pearl-light into intense gloom. What Finnian had against windows she couldn't guess, but the man avoided light sources in his buildings at every opportunity. Here and there beneath Treasa's feet, cold, slimy-damp spots spread. This roof, unlike the first, leaked frequently and well.

As her eyes adjusted, details shaped themselves. Three or four women knelt in prayer, not near the altar at the far end but along the side walls. Finnian was not here. Six monks, two of them not old enough to shave, filed in and began the office of the hour. Thousands of monastics filled this place, and they could spare only six for offices? Either Finnian's enthusiasm for singing offices, which once burned bright as the summer sun, was at last waning, or Treasa had just ridden in on some problem.

Military problem? She stepped out into the filtered light and waited for her eyes to adjust again. Now Treasa realized why those women pressed away off to the side in their prayer. Had they knelt in the middle, the light-blind monks would have walked right over the top of them.

She stopped cold in the middle of the gateyard. Twenty feet in front of her, Anice of Drumderry stopped cold in the middle of the gateyard.

Treasa found a smile somewhere, and hung it out where Anice could see it. "I'm surprised to see you. Greetings."

"They sent for you too?"

"Who's 'they,' and why would they?" Treasa closed the distance between them.

"Finnian died."

"That explains much." *May his obese soul rest in peace.* "You're Colm's worker. Why are you here?"

"Colm will be here. He's coming in from Hinba. We'll lay Finnian to rest when he and Comgall and the prior from Dromin arrive."

"What about Gavin? He was Finnian's pupil also."

"I don't know." Anice crooked the corners of her mouth up, sort of, but sure and you couldn't call it a smile. "I have to go now. I'm making the arrangements."

Treasa wanted desperately to know *why you?* but she loathed having to ask Anice. That was crazy. There was that frustration again—Treasa working at serious cross purposes with herself.

Anice hastened off past the oratory. Treasa wandered back to the kitchen. A rather morose-looking monk was directing two callow youths in the butchering of a hog. Slight and skinny, he appeared to weigh less than the hog. Treasa hoped he wasn't one of the cooks. It wasn't the moroseness. Aileen, the grumpiest of cooks, turned out good food. She just didn't trust the culinary skills of thin people. They didn't love food enough.

"Is Aileen about?" she asked.

"Aileen died years ago." The morose fellow sounded just as lugubrious as he looked.

Surprising how heavily Treasa's heart received the news. "She was a friend of mine. How did she die?"

"Sickness."

"Plague?"

"No. Sickness." He didn't seem much interested in talking about Aileen and, in fact, turned his attention to the hog.

Rather offended that he preferred the dead hog's company to hers and was interested in Aileen not at all, Treasa walked away. She felt all at sixes and sevens. She would put up her own horse, it would seem. She found it over by the refectory, scooped up its reins, and headed out the abandoned gate.

What's this? Off to the north of the stables and paddocks stood a brand-new mill. Perhaps not brand-new, but fairly new. Some of the peeled poles supporting its roof had started to weather. And hard beside it, in place of the old, bubbling, teasing creek, flowed a flat, wide, muddy river.

The river was not supposed to be here beside Moville. Somehow it had been physically moved into a different drainage, into this idle little creekbed. Treasa plopped down in the damp grass and stared at that impossible river. Everything was impossible— Anice's presence and her participation, the loss of the old Moville, its old buildings, its old inhabitants. The loss of Treasa's livelihood as a warrior. And this.

Several separate parties appeared from beyond the crest of the hill to the north. They stopped on the slope behind the river and mill, large retinues indicating the arrival of kings and bishops and brehons and all that ilk. Among those camps, eventually, Colm's people would set up. Much as Treasa needed a place to be, she would not go there.

Think how fragile friendships are when they are hurled against the stone wall of time.

She sat there until late in the day, thinking and yet unable to think, her life and her thoughts and her heart all a-jumble. And then across the north ridge came a figure she remembered well. Comgall, with only a half dozen monks or so, was traveling to Moville to pay his last respects to the mentor of his youth. Treasa took her time mounting, riding down the hill, finding a ford. By the time she rode up the far slope, Comgall had staked out his camping spot above the river.

She rode into his camp and slid off. More on impulse than out of respect, she offered him the obeisance due an abbot. Instantly, one of his monks took her horse. Apparently, she was a welcomed guest. You wouldn't think so looking at Comgall's glum expression. If anything, he was thinner than ever, with a gaunt appearance that was more than simple lack of weight.

Treasa settled beside his pile of kindling. His attendants had not yet made it into a fire. "You look like a badger after the hounds have done with it. Not enough meat on you to feed the dogs."

"Infuriating." He sat cross-legged across from her. "I don't question others' acts of piety, yet mine are a constant matter of comment and conversation."

"Turning yourself into a specter to scare the children with on Sammhain is an act of piety?"

"Self-control is. But I won't argue the matter with an unbeliever."

"Wait a minute! Who are you call—"

He skewered her with his perpetual glare. "Are you committed to Jesus Christ?"

"That's been drummed into me ever since I left home. Even before I left home."

"That beggars the question. Your answer is your answer, and my statement stands." He wiggled a finger toward one of his aides, no doubt a signal of some sort. Treasa didn't see anything change because of the gesture. Everyone kept doing whatever he was doing.

She dipped her head downhill. "Did you happen to notice our new river out there?"

"You didn't know it was there?"

"And I grew up here. You sound like you know the story."

Comgall's visage darkened further, a thing Treasa would not have thought possible. "Finnian got his miracle. You'll recall he was capable of miracles in his early years, and he was somewhat jealous of old Cruithnechan's ability to perform them late in life. Well, there was a mill quite some way from Moville, and people had to travel from the monastery to there. Consumed much, much time doing so—time Finnian would rather they spent in prayer and pious acts. Travel lends itself to impiety, you know."

"Licentiousness, if that's the way you want to travel."

Comgall nodded grimly. "So Finnian prayed that the river change course, and when it did he built this mill here."

Treasa felt herself staring and closed her mouth. "He diverted a river miraculously?" *Amazing. Or maybe not so amazing when you stop to think how easy it would be to alter the stream at its headwaters. A small diversion dam . . .*

301

Comgall rattled on. "They're attributing miracles to others. Miracles attributed to Colm, for instance, that I doubt he could possibly be responsible for." He changed the subject abruptly. "Do you happen to know where Gavin Mac Niall is now?"

"Somewhere up in the Dal Riada. I don't know just where. He attached himself as a mercenary to a regional king, the last I heard."

"I'd like him as a mercenary. If you see him, tell him."

She tried not to let her eyebrows rise in surprise and interest. "To what end?"

"To win an argument. Why else?"

"Arguing with whom?"

"Columcille. You've heard about the business at Coleraine, of course."

"Of course." No, she hadn't heard. However, she didn't want to hear. Keeping track of politics is fun if you're listening to someone who knows what's happening. Comgall didn't qualify.

"That won't be tolerated. The Dal n-Araive and Ultonians agree with me. We need some spears to back us up."

Treasa pondered a moment. "Colm thinks women can't fight. What do you think?"

Comgall studied her intently. "I question Colm's judgment frequently."

Treasa, with some misgiving, bared her purpose in coming here. "Finnian carried more weight in the church than even the bishop of Armagh. I speak both literally and figuratively. If anyone could get that resolution rescinded, Finnian could. I came to convince him to throw his weight around—I speak figuratively—and help me out."

"Pity he died untimely."

"Whose death is ever timely?"

Comgall grimaced as if it were a smile. "I know your value in battle. Join my cause."

"Your cause doesn't interest me. The chance to fight does. Give me that chance, and I'll acquit myself well for you."

"I don't doubt it." Comgall nodded. "Stay nearby."

Treasa took that as a definitive yes, made as little small talk as she could politely get away with, and left, elated.

A chance to take to the field again! Now if Comgall didn't back out of the commitment he had not really made just now, she'd have that chance!

She stayed in Comgall's camp that night as much to avoid crossing that miserable river as for any reason of friendship. It was nearly dark, and whatever ford she had picked out in the kind light of day would now be lurking hidden in the dark waters. This river, of Finnian's miracle or no, was an irritating nuisance.

34

Forba's Fate

Kings once came to me—
  Meat and wine and loving promises.
Ah, sad glory!
  Nothing left now but to die.

Anice felt a foreboding, a sensation distinctly apart from her (frankly) mild sadness over Finnian's death. Something was wrong here, or at least upsetting if not wrong. She had not asked for a gift like Colm's, an ability to see parts of the future or to sense coming events. She didn't want it.

She stood by the altar in the oratory. Before her, Finnian's remains were laid out on a modest wooden catafalque, his wrists discreetly bound together so as to maintain the prayer position of his hands on his chest. A lamp burned at his head, another at his feet. They shed scant light on the mountain between them.

Finnian's monasteries boasted many monks and nuns. *Why did they send to Drumceatt for me?* No matter—she had come instantly, and she had arranged well. Colm claimed she possessed a gift, if you could call it that, for putting together an elaborate affair of state or a whole new ministry. Perhaps there dwelt some justice in his claim, for she had done so here, having assembled the necessary people and victuals within a day of her arrival.

Tomorrow, warlords and overlords, brehons and bards and monks by the thousands would stream through the oratory door to pray over the mortal remains. They would eat well at the tables laid continuously throughout the day and night. They would attend his final rites and follow him in a solemn procession to the particularly wide, particularly deep grave in the cemetery beyond the ringwall. They would greet each other and make many hollow promises. Some of them would end up fighting.

At the far end, a woman entered the doorway. Anice could tell nothing about her. She would not even have guessed "woman" had the person not been wearing a female's longer tunic beneath the hooded cloak—a cloak done in Pictish tartan. And well Anice remembered that tartan.

The woman approached slowly, her eyes watching Finnian as if he would perhaps sit up. She stood less than two paces away from his head, staring at him. She didn't cross herself.

Anice recognized the face belatedly. How time had ravaged it! The long hair Anice had spent hours brushing was nearly gone; wrinkled wisps of gray-blonde remained. Obviously the woman did not recognize Anice.

Should she speak or keep silent? Anice could not help herself. She spoke. "Forba. Princess."

The woman's head snapped up toward her. That withered face hardened. "So. Anice. Of course."

"I'm flattered that you recognize me. I was a child." Anice stepped forward into better light.

The woman looked at her with a poisonous glare. "You were with him to the very end, I see."

"You always suspected something unholy between Finnian and me, Princess. Jealousy, I presume. Never has there been. There. It's said once more, and it's true. I'll not say it again."

Forba the princess of Pictland looked not the least regal, even in her tartan. She looked weary, defeated. Anice watched her a moment, weighing what she saw against the Forba she remembered. "Life has treated you ill, mistress. God's blessing upon you."

"You bless a rival."

"Never a rival. I thought we'd settled that."

Forba for the first time, it would appear, might be grasping the truth. Her eyes drifted from Anice to Finnian's remains. She stared at him a long, long moment—minutes—before she spoke again. "Ill treated indeed. The dark forces in control of destinies do love to play their little tricks. Still, much of my fate, I suppose, was my own fickle fault. Five husbands, and not one of them was even half the man Finnian was. Lovers now and then. I had my own seat for a while, a regional kingship through my mother's side, until I married unwisely and lost it in the divorce."

"No royal seat now, I take it."

"No." Forba smiled then, and in that smile defiance glowed even yet, a shaking of the fist at fate.

Anice moved in closer beside Finnian's head. "Jesus Christ came to seek out and save lost Picts just as much as anyone else, mistress. Save them from the power of those dark forces you fear and abhor. Eternal life! Believe me, it's far better to have one's destiny shaped by a powerful God who loves you."

"I've seen the destinies God picks out for women. Nuns in plainweave, chewing prayer as a cow mouths cud. Staring at books? Toiling at the kind of work a royal would never dream of touching?" Forba smirked. "I think not!"

"You'd rather die in hell, in other words, than change the lifestyle that's giving you so much misery."

"Misery!" The woman cackled. "Ah, but never dull. A consort of kings. Courtly intrigue. Many the tale my life can tell."

Anice decided to skip off to other things and return later to the subject of eternal life. "I doubt courtly intrigues are a thing one can give up easily. I know Columcille still indulges in them, though he's never claimed a life in politics."

Forba nodded. She turned to study Anice closely. "Columcille. The Dove. Beware that one. I hear there's trouble brewing twixt him and Comgall, with the whole north lands choosing sides between them."

"Comgall has been his friend since childhood."

"I hear a different word." Forba's voice dropped to a conspiratorial hiss. "Comgall has watched the likes of the Old Little Pict, who has since died—what was his name?"

"Cruithnechan?"

"Him. And your Columcille and the gentle Kenneth and lastly Finnian himself, all of them a-working miracles in the name of God. And Comgall? As yet, not a one. It galls him, for he fancies himself purer and more pious than the rest. He's picking a fight over a monastery at Coleraine, but the miracles—they're what's at the bottom of it."

"If you so despise the church, why would you keep an ear to church politics?"

Forba grinned. Three teeth were missing in the top row. How she loved this gossip! "I may be reduced to penury, but I still live in the royal clan. The church is well established in my territory now, as it is in most of the Picts' lands. The abbots, the bishop, they all come calling by and by. The ri feasts them, of course. And there I hear all the foibles of the church as well as those of the court. Hear me and hear me again: sure and the leaders of the church be no less stained and tarnished than all the rest."

Anice wagged her head. "If your intelligence be accurate, a sad state it is. Jealousy."

Forba turned again toward the mortal remains of the abbot of Moville. "Jealousy. If anyone knows the power of it, I do. I let it eat me for years—hot jealousy toward any man or woman who took a fair place in Finnian's life, a place I wanted, marriage or no." Her voice dropped to a whisper, harsh in the dank, dark air. "Always, always have I loved the man. Nor shall my love end at his grave. Who knows what my life would have been had he not married the blasted church."

35

Colm's Culrathan

The king is the life of the clan,
  His integrity the clan's protection,
His honor the clan's name,
  His fortune his people's.

Who knows what his life might have been had he not married the church? Columcille. Had Colm not chosen the church in the very beginning, in the days of his youth, sure and he would be ruling Erin now with a benign hand, spreading the cause of Christ and preventing wars instead of being accused of fomenting them. Phelan, the Wolf. He would have excelled at playing politics. He did that well enough already. His kingship would certainly have operated on a higher plane than did this ard ri's.

The man knew what was right and what was wrong. He knew Colm's position was right. As the first among kings, he should have acted swiftly and wisely upon what he knew. But the high king was neither swift nor wise. A king sidestepping an opportunity to gain glory in combat is a king to be arduously avoided. Because the king in his dotage declined to rule vigorously, Colm must pick up the pieces—tie a knot in the rope to take up the slack.

Colm rode a white horse this morning, an animal he'd never seen before. He did not much care for white horses, but Diormit had assured him this beast was the best to be had. Perhaps Diormit was confusing "best" with "largest."

"He fits you well, Father" had been Diormit's comment. Not exactly a paean for a superior warhorse. Diormit, brilliant as an aide, left everything to be desired as a warrior. How would he know what a fighting man requires? Colm should have sent Anice out in quest of horses.

At his right hand rode his brother Eoghan—"The Dove's hairy brother." Eoghan loved to call himself that. Now he stroked his thick, silken beard. At Colm's left was Declan of the Monaghan. The man was graying at the temples, but he still cut a splendid figure on horseback. At Declan's left, Fergus Gray Beard scratched vigorously under his arm, then twisted on his pony to check the men behind. Colm couldn't exactly picture the slow and rickety Fergus as being good for much anymore. In fact, he couldn't exactly picture this slow and rickety horse beneath him as being good for much either.

Colm's gift of second sight proved a blessing at times, a curiosity at times, and much too often a source of sorrow. Today he would have welcomed it in any of its forms. He wanted to know what lay ahead, but God had for some reason veiled that from him. No dream, no angel, no quiet word. Colm was operating in his own strength now, and he didn't like that. He was accustomed to his Lord's leading.

They would reach Comgall's monastery before too long. Ideally, Comgall would size up the number of Colm's spears, instantly and prudently sit down, and then they would negotiate. This show of force was for purposes of bringing Comgall back to his senses. The half-starved monk seemed to think that his ridiculous extremes rendered him exempt from the counsel and opinions of others. Colm was proud of his own monastic rule—a rigid, disciplined observance of piety in strength. His system of penances and atonements was stricter than ever Finnian's had been, or Finian of Clonard's either, for all that. Keeping yourself weak from hunger, discomfort, and cold did nothing for piety and reduced your ability to minister to others. Even old Cruithnechan, rest his soul, had known to keep his strength up.

They flowed up over a gentle rise, the host of them, the thousand horses' hooves churning the wet ground, greeting grass before, leaving chopped mud behind. The sky shone pearl white —not quite an overcast, certainly not clear.

Colm raised his arm high as he pulled his horse to a halt. He gaped. *Why did God veil this from me?*

Arrayed on the far slope a hundred strong, a solid line of warriors stood waiting with shields and spears. Declan shouted and waved to the left, to the right, spreading their people out along the crest of this hill. He watched the shifts of position a moment and rumbled to Colm, "So where's their cavalry? Their chariots? Nobody fields just infantry."

"Where's their leader? No one stands to the fore."

Declan snorted. "We all know who that is, sure enough. But why would Comgall bring these people out here to preempt us?"

Colm needed scant moments to figure that one out. "The shape of the land here, that grove of birches—near perfect military situation. You can have any number waiting beyond view. You can hide a lot of chariots just over the hill and a lot of horsemen beyond those trees."

At his side, Eoghan blew a derisive whirlwind through his bushy whiskers. "And that, no doubt, is what's happening. Funny, though. I didn't think Comgall had that much military acumen that he'd pick good ground."

"He doesn't." And Colm's heart thudded into a pained lump as he realized whose military acumen was actually directing this situation. Even from this distance, he recognized the warrior at the center of the opponents' line. *Not only does she flout the proscription to which everyone agreed, so does Comgall for engaging her. Another black mark against him.* He pointed.

Declan swore beneath his breath. "You didn't tell me Treasa would be in on this. My people aren't going to fight her, and, probably, neither will the Tyrone. She's one of us as much as she's anybody's."

"Sure and she doesn't act like it." Colm waved an arm off toward a flurry of black-and-gray birds mounting into the sky to the southeast. "See how those crows are coming toward us? If these battle lines worried them, they'd be flying in the other direction. Something startled them into breaking this way."

"Troops or chariots coming in from behind." Eoghan grunted. "So she's setting up a trap. How many do you think they can array against us?"

"Too many. His clan, all the clans around Bangor, the Dal n-Araive, the Ultoni." Colm looked at Declan. "Might any Monaghan switch sides out of loyalty to her, do you think?"

"Against their own ri? They better not!" Declan wheeled his horse to face his warriors. "Hear me! Treasa has abandoned our aegis! She directs the line ranged against us. She fights with them.

Very well, she made her choice. We treat her as we would any other foe. I spear any man who shirks our cause on her behalf." He paused a moment and swung his horse around into the line again.

"Doubt that'll do any good," Fergus muttered, "the moment the swords are unsheathed. I cannot imagine raising m'hand against her."

Declan grimaced and rumbled in undertone, "Neither can I."

How did this mess happen? Colm depended on the leading of God. He welcomed it. He had come to expect it. Now here he sat, alone and forsaken, in an impossible dilemma.

No leader, religious or otherwise, who hoped to remain a leader would deliberately humble himself in the eyes of the warlords of the region he hoped to lead. Not in Erin—not in Pictland either, for that matter. To back away from a fight would destroy whatever respect Colm had built over the years. His reputation for bad judgment, if not actual cowardice, would haunt him both down here in Erin and north in the Dal Riada. He didn't dare back down.

And how he ached to do so!

Just as large loomed the problem of Treasa. She was dangerous. He knew that. It was no secret that in the past, when she controlled a military situation, the Monaghan won. There was one solution, and he could not bear to think about it—destroy her himself. Ride out onto the front line and take her out before her military prowess overcame them or the men behind him lost heart when faced with the prospect of fighting her. Killing Treasa himself would save many lives on both sides.

Unthinkable.

The warriors on the far hill parted. The emaciated Comgall came riding forward, through his line and on down the slope. Her lances laid across her shoulder at a jaunty angle, Treasa fell in behind him.

Colm dug his heels in and was surprised by how quickly his sorry old white horse responded. He tried a few subtle turns by kneeing the horse to left, to right. Obviously well trained, the horse obeyed instantly. Colm felt slightly better about having this particular animal under him. Slightly. Declan, the ranking warlord, rode down the hill beside him.

They all four met in the swale between. Treasa, her shield slung casually on her arm, watched Colm quietly, even say smugly. Her snide confidence had a strange tendency to infuriate him. This was no time to let himself be blinded by a personality problem. Declan, Colm noticed, was glaring at her.

She paid no attention to the Monaghan. She purred to Colm, "No song about the King of the stars this time? No war shout?"

"We weren't expecting to encounter you here. We're ready for you; we just weren't expecting it."

"This is no way for friends to meet," Comgall seemed irritated by his faux warlord. "Particularly not friends in Christ."

"I agree." Colm nodded, keeping his attention on the gaunt face before him instead of the contemptuous face beyond. "We've shared many an open sky together through the years. Now is the time to sit down and work this out."

"Turn around, Colm. Go back to Drumceatt. Tend to your affairs, as I shall tend to mine."

"The welfare of Ulster and the clans in it are my affair."

"You don't find me coming from Tiree to attempt control of Iona. I urge you to be as wise. There's nothing to work out."

Quite out of line, Treasa inserted, "Comgall's been explaining it to me for two days now, and, frankly, I still don't understand what the fuss is about. Why a territorial dispute over a church, for pity's sake?" She held one lance and slid the shaft of the other under her leg, holding it tight against her horse's ribs with her thigh.

Declan glared blacker. Colm didn't blame him. When the champions of the sides are conversing, the seconds in command stay out of it. She knew that. She was presuming too much upon their former friendship, casually making this war negotiation into a three-way chat among old chums.

A wild spate of yelling burst out on the hillside behind Colm. He kept his eyes on Treasa and Comgall, leaving it to Declan to find out what was going on. Bedlam erupted behind him.

Declan yanked his sword. "They're falling upon us from the rear!" He wheeled his horse around to strike at Treasa.

Colm shouted, "No!" in spite of himself and grabbed for Declan's horse's bridle. This was the answer to his impossible dilemma—Declan cuts down Treasa—and Colm couldn't stand to see it happen.

But Treasa was already lunging her horse at Declan, her lance clamped tightly between her elbow and her side and braced low. *What was she—?*

Declan's horse, speared perfectly at the point where throat meets brisket, squealed, spewed frothy red blood, and collapsed. Unhorsed, Colm's protector dropped out of sight.

Instantly Treasa, the seasoned warrior, in one swift motion pulled her second lance free and tucked it firmly under her arm, even as she kneed her horse at Colm.

She drew up short, her spear point inches from his heart. "You two fight it out. I have a battle to win." She wheeled her horse away, raised a shout that could shatter clouds, and galloped up the slope toward the fray. Howling, Comgall's mob behind her came racing down the hill, spears at ready. Half the warriors ran naked, save for their sword belts and the glittering torques on their necks.

And Colm on his ugly white horse sat right in the path of the screaming wave. Comgall turned his back to Colm and shouted something, but his puny cry was hardly going to deter a band of frenzied maniacs who love to kill.

Someone seized Colm's left arm and yanked him straight down off that white horse. He plopped ignominiously onto the swampy meadow grass. Declan it was who unhorsed him. And now the ri had grabbed the white horse's head. He hooked a heel behind the horse's foreleg. With a startled squeal, the white horse came down on top of Colm, falling flat on its side, pinning him beneath eight hundred pounds of writhing dead weight.

Declan's bad breath panted hot on Colm's ear. "Cover your head, you fool!" he roared.

Facing an army weaponless, there wasn't much else Colm could do. He lay squeezed between Declan's dead horse and his own kicking, struggling one, as the wave of warriors swept by, still howling.

Pressed against Colm, Declan moved, raising to see; he dropped again. "Stay down!"

The wet meadow rumbled. It vibrated. Somewhere out there Comgall's futile, pitiful shout melted into the thunder of a hundred iron wheels, four hundred hooves striking lightning from the ground. Treasa's corps of chariots was hurtling downslope toward them.

Colm couldn't stand it. He had to see. He lifted his head, peeking from beneath his protecting arms. In a ragged line, hub to hub they had swept up over the hillcrest. They were coming right at him. With no room for any to turn aside, they presented a virtually solid wall. Comgall danced his horse helplessly in circles, as trapped as Colm and Declan.

The charioteer bearing down on the two fallen horses apparently recognized Comgall barely in time. He hauled back, slowing his eager horses, dragging them aside. They fell in behind the chariot to his left, the one that swept close—very, very close—by Colm's fallen horse. The parting of the wave left just enough gap to spare both Comgall and the white horse.

The charioteer to his right, too slow to haul back and aside completely, came straight as a lance at Colm. The panicky horses shied away to avoid Declan's dead horse. At the last possible moment, the near horse dropped its head and leaped frantically to clear the barrier; its teammate slammed into the chariot beside it.

Colm was certain the great iron chariot wheel would flatten his head to the thickness of an oxhide. But somehow the wheel missed him, thumping into the dead horse, bucking high in the air. With unholy roars and crashes and screeches, the colliding chariots dragged each other down.

Colm's white horse was flinging itself to its feet. His legs freed, Colm scrambled up and swung aboard the horse even before it had fully gained a purchase on the soggy ground.

Weapons! The warriors in the star-crossed chariots were slung willy-nilly out across the grass, their spears available for the taking. Colm gripped tight with knees and heels, dipped low and snatched a spear up off the ground as his horse leaped forward.

What a splendid warhorse, this animal! With an enthusiasm to match Colm's own, it galloped up the slope toward the action, nose high and ears forward. Colm dropped the reins and gripped his spear two-handed. The weapon was too long for easy use from horseback, but he wasn't going to quibble.

He overtook the chariots, speared a warrior from behind and grabbed a smaller lance. The chariot line faltered and broke up as it reached the pitched battle. Colm kneed his horse in zigzags between chariots, taking out another warrior in the passing, and headed for a knot of fighters surrounding Fergus Gray Beard.

The grizzled old warrior was holding the enemy at bay almost long enough for Colm to save him. But he suddenly relaxed and slid off his rearing horse just as Colm arrived.

Fergus! Enraged, Colm lashed out wildly, letting his rusty skills from long ago hone themselves avenging the bushy-bearded old warrior beneath his horse's feet.

The line was breaking, and at first Colm couldn't tell in which direction. When he kneed his horse sharply aside, though, it slipped and went down. By the time they were up and into it again, Comgall's forces were abandoning the field up in the north end of the action even as Declan's men were falling back at the south.

Bronze horns hooted orders, but how could one tell whose was whose? The thrill of fighting subsided into confusion. Who was enemy, and who was ally? By now, mud-and-blood spattered, everyone still standing had vanquished his first foe or two and had no idea whether the warrior before him ought to be the next. The Tyrone had stripped for the fray, so you couldn't even tell by the degree of dress. When somebody's horn blasted Fall back, both sides obeyed.

Hostile, distrustful, angry, the sides regrouped and glared at each other. But the fight was over. You could tell it had ended in the heart, and that's where the end counts.

Where's Treasa? Colm pivoted his horse, searching. If she were still alive she'd be on her horse. She'd be here! A couple hundred horsemen churned about, but she was not among them on either side.

Treasa! Fergus!

And the truth forced itself upon Colm. God's silence should have been sufficient to dissuade him from this tragic, useless foray. This was Colm's doing, all Colm's, and no number of Picts' souls, however vast, would ever be penance enough.

36

Gavin's Games

In the leaping salmon He speaks
And in the whispering breeze.
In the galloping horse He speaks
And in the silence of trees.

Back at the rath, they had told Treasa that she could find Gavin somewhere down this way. Probably in a meadow beyond a strip of willows, they suggested. Spotting a line of willows just barely peeping above this slope to the north, she kneed her horse aside across the hillside. So what was the Man Who Should Have Been King doing in a meadow on a little backwater rath in Pictland? *Gavin White Hawk Mac Niall picking daisies? Why not?*

As she approached the creek with its bank full of willows, she spied a giant of a man beyond the trees. Gavin, on a nice roan gelding, was flapping his arms at a flock of mounted boys. The lads ranged in age, probably, from ten to maybe fifteen at most. They were dressed in striped trousers only. Most of them wore torques. Kings' sons. Half of them had tied strawberry-pink kerchiefs on the left arm; the other half wore blue kerchiefs on the right.

Treasa was coming up on war games, with Gavin the instructor. She laid forward low across her mare's neck and worked the pony at a cautious walk along the creek. She forded in bubbling riffles so that the noise would hide her mare's footfalls. She stopped the mare ten yards farther, still well screened from view by the trees.

She was close enough now to hear Gavin's voice, not so close as to grab the boys' attention away from their instructor. Gavin was explaining the strategy the Reds ought take in sneaking up on the Blues, and the strategy the Blues would need to meet the surprise attack. She listened a few moments and smiled. Gavin had just given her a perfect opening.

She ducked low and dug her heels in. Her mare came popping out of the trees like the bung from a jug of fermenting cider. The warriors-in-training cried out, terrified; Gavin's sword leaped into his hand. And then he froze, his gaping face expressing all the intelligence of a fish that's been lying on the shore for an hour.

Treasa rode in among them. "On the other hand, my doughty Red lads, you're likely to lose that way. What you really want to do is hold back a couple cavalrymen out of sight. Their drummer beats off ten minutes and then they ride forward and plow into the lines. If there's only six of you to a side, though, you might want to make that one minute."

Gavin's mouth moved, but he said about as much as the beached fish would. His sword tip slid in a lazy arc downward and pointed to the grass.

Treasa shrugged. "It worked for me at Culdrevny and Culrathan, and it worked for Columcille at Culfedha."

Gavin found his tongue at last. "Culfedha?"

"Down by Clonard. I'll tell you all about it later. You lead the Blues, and I'll lead the Reds. Here we go, lads! We're about to attack those lackluster Blues and beat the stripes right out of their trousers."

Gavin grinned suddenly, looking more like his old self and less like a flounder. "This is Treasa of the Monaghan. Go with her, Reds. You're about to learn from the best there is. Blues, here we go."

The war games commenced, played and replayed through the afternoon in half a dozen different ways. Treasa reveled in this. Use your brains, occasionally your brawn, outwit, outfight, outguess, and no lives lost. No blood drawn. All the fun and none of the horror. She should have taken up teaching war to kings' sons years ago.

Twilight had nearly melted into night blackness when the armies retired from the field exultant. The ponies were so utterly wearied that Gavin forbade the boys to ride at any gait faster than a walk, so they abandoned their horses and ran ahead to the rath. The dispirited mounts slogged riderless along the track behind Treasa and Gavin, noses low, equine hearts no doubt yearning for the barley and oats of home.

Treasa watched the laughing, joking, exuberant lads disappear around a bend. "Youth is wasted on the young."

"Oh, I don't know. We didn't waste ours. What's Culfedha?"

"A few weeks after Colm tangled with Comgall at Culrathan, he let himself get drawn into yet another battle. This one political, down by Clonard. His brother Eoghan was the warlord in theory; in practice, Colm told him what to do. I don't know how it happened—how Colm would manage to get himself tied into another one so soon after Culrathan. He was really smarting after Culrathan. Distraught. Maybe he just wasn't thinking. I assume you heard about Colm and Comgall."

Gavin nodded. "A monk from Bangor came through a week ago. Says Comgall's might prevailed under your inestimable leadership, and he won handily. Of course, we'd already heard from Iona that Colm won."

"It was a mangled draw. Everybody lost. Fergus died."

Gavin looked at her. "I'm sorry."

She nodded. The whole welter of anguish and remorse boiled up unexpectedly inside her again. She thought she'd taken care of all that, and now it was back.

Gavin's arm whipped out and grabbed her mare's rein. He dragged the little horse aside, turned a circle and came up behind the boys' ponies. With a yell and a wave of the arm he chased them on down the track. They lifted their noses enough to jog a dozen paces and settled back to a walk, headed for the paddock.

He kept his hand on her horse's bridle, and she let him. He led her mare up the hill, and she let him. They pulled to a halt beside a night-black oak grove. Like a bar to a gateway, a massive old oak had fallen right here in front of the grove. Its few remaining limbs, dry and crackly, attested that it had lain in state for years.

Gavin slid off his roan and tied it to a limb. He wiggled a finger toward the fallen tree trunk. Treasa slipped to the ground and sat down beside him on the rough oak bole. The seat was just the right height for comfort.

"I come here a lot." He waved an arm casually. "Great view when there's light to see it—hills, meadows. And I like the trees behind us here. They give a sort of comforting feeling."

"Nice spot." Treasa was having trouble keeping her emotions under her heel.

"I talk to God here." He paused, but she didn't know what he was waiting for. "Now you talk to me."

"That's what I came for, actually. To say hello, see how you're doing. Talk. But now I don't think I can do it." She shook her head. She had long since given up trying to figure out other people, such as the inscrutable Columcille. Now she'd be content just to understand herself, but that wasn't happening either.

"We're going to sit here until you do. I might mention that it gets pretty blasted cold out here at night."

She chuckled in spite of herself.

Somewhere in the woods behind them a small animal started rooting in the leaves. Hedgehog, likely. You could barely hear it. A star here, a star there pushed through the light overcast. The air smelled damp and oak-ish and hung very still.

There was a protectiveness to the thick and crowding darkness. He couldn't see her. She liked that. "I hid, Gavin. For the first time in my life I turned coward and hid. At Culrathan. There was a birch grove well situated; in fact, I stationed cavalry there for a delayed charge. I had a chance to spear Colm, and I couldn't. I rode up against the Monaghan and the Tyrone, and I couldn't. I angled off into the birches and hid."

He hated her now—she could tell because he waited long moments before speaking. "That's not cowardice. You're not capable of cowardice. That's love and loyalty."

"Nice words. It's cowardice. I'm a mercenary. That means when someone employs me I do my best for him. It doesn't matter who's right or wrong. You fight for your employer. Comgall depended on me, and I abandoned him. If I'd stayed on the field he would have won. Quite possibly Fergus would still be here."

Silence. "What did you tell Comgall?"

"I said I got knocked off my horse and offered to give him his cows back. He took them. I went down to the Monaghan, told Declan I was going, and left. I think one of Fergus's sons has my rath now." She snorted. "Listen to me. 'My' rath. It never was mine. It was in Monaghan territory, so it would always be Monaghan. I don't have status as a ri, so I couldn't take it over as a stranger in sovereignty. The only way I could legally keep it would be to marry into the clan. No thanks."

"There are worse things than marriage."

"Yeah. Managing a rath."

He laughed heartily, the old Gavin Mac Niall laugh that she hadn't heard for years. She twisted to look at him in the dark and saw virtually nothing. "You're doing well up here. What's been going on in your life?"

"Everything. I've made peace. Now I want to help you find peace."

"Fat chance. Tell me about yours." *Tell me anything to keep you from prying around any more in my life.*

His voice in the darkness sounded content. Gavin the Dark One, of all people, content. And she felt herself filling up with envy.

"Years ago, down among the Angles, I committed my life to Christ. At least I thought so. Nothing changed. You know all that's happened to me since; you've been part of it through the years."

"You never did marry Anice, did you?"

"She turned me down. Best thing that ever happened to me."

Her heart tickled, though she couldn't imagine why. "She's a good woman."

"And totally happy with what she's doing. It's the first happiness she's ever had in her life, and I almost spoiled it."

"There are worse things than marriage, I'm told."

There was that loose and happy laugh again. "Her reason for refusing me was that I was already married."

"So? By brehon law—"

"Not God's law. Had she accepted me, she would have felt guilty, and I'd be breaking the law just as much, whether I admitted it or not. She was right, in other words. So I came up here to lick my wounds, got this position teaching royals' sons martial arts, and spent lots of time on this very log thinking. And studying. Colm and his constant delving into books finally rubbed off on me a little."

"They say Colm spends hours every day copying books. Are you into that too?"

"No, but I'll ride up to Ardnamurchan or sail over to Eigg to read new material. I'll never be a copyist. Finnian was right about that. But I'm learning about God." He sniggered. "Believe me, it isn't quick or easy. I'm not a scholar."

She made a sort of grunting sound to fill up the silent space. "I'd heard you were a mercenary."

His voice took on a bemused twinkle. "I did get one job offer as a mercenary."

She waited. Obviously, this was near and dear to him.

"From my wife. Ex-wife. She was planning to divorce her current husband, and she was afraid he'd kill her if she tried. She wanted me to return."

"As a bodyguard or as a husband?"

"Either or both. I turned her down."

"Good. You always have been one smart dollop of lard."

He sobered. "She took refuge with the ri of Ardnamurchan, but her husband managed to kill her anyway before she could make the split. He's ri ruirech over three of the mightiest clans in the Dal Riada now. Real power base."

She drew her cloak closer around. He was right about it getting cold up here at night. "So now that you're free, whom did you end up marrying?"

"No one yet. I've read just about all the Greek letters now. Paul's writing. He urges you, whatever state you're in to be content. I'm not a king. Be content in that. I'm not married. Be content in that."

She made a derisive noise, her only necessary comment on an idea so stupid.

"And forgiveness. I talked to Finnian the week before he died. I went up to Bangor then, intending to come home, when Comgall got word of his death, so I returned to Moville. I figured Colm would show up, and I wanted most of all to talk to him."

Treasa's head snapped around. "I didn't see you there!"

"Nobody did. I'm getting pretty good at moving around in Erin without losing my head. I was even able to sneak up on Colm. You don't get to do that very often."

"I do it all the time."

He ignored it. "I forgave him too."

She had no idea how to respond to all this. "How'd he take it?"

Gavin's voice hardened. "He didn't believe me." It brightened. "It doesn't matter. Anyway, here I am, happy for the first time in my life."

Treasa wagged her head. "Born to be king, happy with nothing. Interesting."

"Amazing. Now I understand what Kenneth talks about when he says there's great peace in simply resting in Jesus."

Yes, it was amazing, and well worth some contemplation. Later. More to the immediate point though, she was freezing. Her backside was telling her exactly what it thought about being subjected to unmitigated oak bark. And come to think of it, she hadn't eaten since early this morning.

Apparently she wasn't the only one getting stiff as an ax handle. He stood up abruptly. She took it as her cue and leaped at the opportunity, literally and figuratively. She stood erect and arched, stretching her back.

She expected him to cross to his horse. Instead, he wrapped both arms around her waist and laced his fingers together behind her back.

Actually, that wasn't a bad idea. The overcast had won out over the stars, and the sky offered no light at all. In this dense gloom, the only way to know for certain where each other was would be to maintain physical contact.

"You can't imagine how stunned I was when you came popping out of the willows this afternoon."

"Sure I can. I saw your face, you know. Your jaw was dropped enough to drive a chariot into. Little delights like that make life worth living."

He chuckled. "So what are you going to do now that you've left the Monaghan?"

She laid a forearm on each of those big, broad shoulders because there wasn't a whole lot else to do with her hands. Were the sun suddenly to rise, they'd look like lovers standing there. Looks so often deceive. "I don't know. I thought maybe find a ri up here in the Dal Riada who needs a good military strategist, at least until Colm manages to mess me up in this kingdom too. I was hoping you or one of your friends might know some opportunities."

"I know one good one. He's not a ri, but he admires you immensely."

"Fairly secure? I don't have clan support worth mentioning. I'm going to have to start thinking about situating myself for old age somewhere. It was probably pound foolish to quit the Monaghan rath, but after opposing Declan in battle I didn't really have much choice."

"Very secure. Guaranteed lifetime support."

"Doing what?" She sensed a tenseness in him she hadn't noticed before.

The ham-sized shoulders shrugged. "Teaching princes war games. Running a sortee now and then if you want. Being married to me."

"That sounds li—*what?!*"

He drew her closer. "For years I fantasized about obtaining a kingship so I could marry Anice. Then she got married. Then I got married. Then she was free. Then I was free—sort of. And all the time I was chasing my tail in circles, there you were. I guess you've been too good a friend all these years—dependable, ready to help when I needed you, even when I was off hungering after another woman. I didn't think of you in any higher capacity."

"Nothing's higher than friendship."

"So true. Now I have no kingship, no prospects for one, and nothing really great to offer you. Except myself. So I do."

Her mouth stammered a bit. "What about love?"

"Man-woman love. Infatuation. I've had a taste of those. This is more. Sure and I love you, but it goes deeper than that. It always has. Nothing's higher than friendship, they say. I do have a little something to offer you." He released her to dig around in the purse at his belt. It took him a while. His hands found hers and opened her palm. He pressed a bit of metal into it. It took her both hands, fingers stroking, to work out what it was. "Your mother's brooch."

"Carried it with me all these years because I have no real place to call home."

She realized her breathing rate had doubled. She tried to slow it down, tried to think. Then she decided there comes a time when you quit thinking and let your heart just take over and do what ought to be done. You plan the strategy, but in the heat of battle you turn your fate over to instinct and reflex. This was a battle she'd never fought before, and sure and she was in the heat of it.

"You realize I have nothing to offer you in return. Nothing to bring. I left my cattle and sheep behind. They didn't mean any-thing to me a month ago." She snorted. "Now that I need them . . ." She let it trail off.

"I don't care to marry livestock."

"Then I suppose you're stuck with marrying me."

37

Colm's Task

I rise today
  In the strength of Heaven—
Light of sun,
  Radiance of moon.

A hundred years ago Patrick sang of splendor, speed, and lightning. Colm felt not the least bit swift or splendid or brilliant. He sat on the little stone bench at the door of his clochan, leaned back against its rockwork, and gazed out across the western sea.

The sun swam on the edge of the world, shimmered in its orange mystery, then dropped rapidly below the sea, leaving behind the colors of night streaked all across the sky. The moon was past first quarter. Colm would give it another hour, than walk back to the monastery by its waxing light.

Patrick the Singer, a man of men, indefatigable, wise in the faith. Already at Armagh they were raising Patrick to cult status. Colm wasn't certain he approved of that. He just hoped they didn't do that to himself or to the truly humble men of faith who would consider it an insult. Finian of Clonard. Brendan of Birr. Brendan of Clonfert, the Navigator. He didn't last long after he returned from Tir Na n'Og—a few years. But what a Christian! Colm cherished every visit the old man of the sea made to Iona and Hinba.

Those men didn't start wars. They didn't slip and fall as Colm did so constantly. They were saints. Colm was not worthy to breathe the air above their graves. He felt utterly crushed by sin. Not even when he exiled himself to these northern shores did his heart weigh this heavily.

He sat forward, listening. A horse was coming down the track in the distance. No, it was angling this way along the sheep trail. Standing orders at the monastery forbade the monks from coming out here. Who had the gall to break orders? Diormit, perhaps. He sat back again. There wasn't much he could do until the inter-loper got here.

The horse stopped just off the corner of the clochan. Scowling, Colm pushed to his feet. *Rules are rules.* "Who do you think—?"

The white horse stood there, its long, bland face more or less gazing right through Colm. No bridle, no saddle. "You toad." Colm stood there a few moments, arms akimbo. "Why did I ship you over here with me, anyway? I should have left you at Drum-ceatt. Go back. Go on home!"

When he waved his arms, the horse tossed its head high and flicked its ears, but it didn't move. It sneezed then, grotesquely as only horses can sneeze, blowing flecks of mucus all over his tunic. "Useless old nag!" Colm walked back to his bench and flopped down.

Useless indeed. A war horse for a man who would study war no more. The horse tipped forward apparently on purpose, ex-tended a leg to catch itself, and dropped its head to graze. It nib-bled a tuft here, a few blades there, step by slow step amid the rocks. The green machair with its lush pasturage stretched out below. It must appear inviting to a grazer, but the horse seemed content right here despite the sparse pickings.

Colm watched the old cob a few minutes. "We're going to have to find something useful for you to do. You have too much time on your hands. I speak figuratively." And that last phrase vigorously flung Treasa again into his mind.

He thought about that lance point stopping short of his ribs. Had a man come that close to spearing him, he would have reacted blindly and instantly, unhorsing the fellow and returning the favor if at all possible. But it was Treasa, so he sat there. He thought about his joy and relief when she appeared as if from nowhere after the debacle at Culrathan. *What am I going to do about Treasa?*

What was it in Peter's letter? Throw all your concerns over to God because He cares about you. Treasa, or rather Colm's feel-ings for Treasa, was a concern.

Very well, God. I commit to the truth that she will always and ever be a friend, and no more. I surrender her to You. Bless her. Give her happiness if You would. She is never mine, ever Yours.

His sins, so heavy, so numerous, so blatant. His sin of impulsivity and blindness, his failure to allow God to lead, his criminal disregard for life. Those weren't just concerns. Those were tragedies inflicted upon others, and many of those others servants of God even as he purported to be.

In his mind's eye, Colm rehearsed all the fallen he could think of, Fergus first among them. He begged God's forgiveness for each. Next he rehearsed his unconfessed sins chronologically, because that was his best hope of recalling most of them without forgetting many. He closed his eyes. His ears listened to the occasional noise of a hoof on rock, of the flaccid nostrils snuffling, the teeth ripping grass. His mind listened to the litany of wrongs, and he wept. He asked forgiveness for each remembrance in turn.

When he half-opened his heavy eyes, the moon coasted high behind him, flooding its half-hearted light across the machair and the glistening white rock. It made the old white horse fairly glow.

Not all the light was moonglow. That familiar, soft-blue haze, almost light but not quite, was brightening Colm's dooryard. He looked over at the rock pile.

Whether dream or reality, and only heaven knew which, the angel smiled.

"I was hoping you'd come. I need you."

The horse grazed on, oblivious.

The messenger nodded, still smiling. "Too much."

"I sinned grievously, stepping out beyond God's guidance."

The angel shrugged. "That's news to me. Your Father tells me you're sinless—for the moment, at least."

"But . . ."

Finnian preached it constantly; Finian of Clonard made it the linchpin of holiness; Colm himself preached it: Once sin is confessed and forgiven, it is washed away. Gone. The enormity of that basic tenet of the faith slapped Colm across the heart as if he'd never heard it before. *Of course! Sin dissolved in blood, and not my blood either. How easy to forget that! How easy to carry concerns and grief instead of casting them off where they belong!*

The angel grinned. "There, you see? I could have counseled you. But you worked it out on your own without me. You know the

Faith precept on precept. It's putting it into personal practice that's the hard part, but you did it, and you did it just fine."

The horse glowed brighter blue as it moved closer to the angel's rocks. It showed absolutely no sign of being aware of the cosmic creature.

Colm considered all this a moment. "If you didn't come to counsel, you came to bring a message."

His angel nodded. "Diarmaid Mac Cerbaill will die in a few months. You're to find Gavin, gather up the Niall, the Phelim, and the other Ui Neill, the Monaghan and the Tyrone, and seat Gavin at Tara. You love king-making. Here's the big one."

Colm grinned, and he couldn't stop, not that he wanted to. *Gavin's dream at last! Given by God!* The grin faded into perplexity. "Tell me if you can—Why did God not seat Gavin to start with? Why all the years of Diarmaid and his pagan practice?"

"Gavin wasn't ready."

Fair enough answer. Another perplexity: "What was the change, that he's ready now?"

"He coveted the seat then; he doesn't now. That makes him a better ruler. He was agnostic then; he's a Christian now, trusting in Jesus completely. He's grown immensely. Note, Columcille, how often you use the phrase 'in the fullness of time.' It applies to all God's work, including this one."

It constantly amazed Colm how often he knew something thoroughly only to find it had never penetrated to his heart. "Tanaiste?"

"Diarmaid's appointed a successor but to no avail." The angel seemed to be dimming. "Diarmaid was given ample opportunity to turn to God. Three consecutive abbots of Clonmacnois, Finnian of Moville—any number of godly men brought him the Word. He disregarded their pleas. He is the last pagan ard ri to rule in Erin. From now on Erin serves Christ alone."

"That's wonderful! That's splendid! Praise God!"

"I do. Glad to see you do."

Colm laughed out loud. Of course this creature praised God. It was his job. It was Colm's job just as much.

The angel absented himself with that incredible, swooping

zoom from solidity on the ground to nothing in the sky. The white horse flicked not a whisker.

Colm pondered all this a while. Not long though. He had no idea how to reach Gavin, and time was short. He walked over and ran his hand up the horse's neck, grabbed a chunk of mane near the withers, and swung aboard. He kneed the horse around and headed up the sheep trail to the track.

The breeze picked up a bit, ruffling the lake, kicking up ripples that tossed a million flecks of moonlight about. The horse splacked out across the long narrow togher without hesitation. Out on the causeway, Colm was surrounded by dancing moon sparkles. They seemed a bit bluish. Angel color.

His heart sang.

He was much too elated to sleep. Immediately he reached the monastery, he rousted Diormit out. "Work to do, lad! Right after Matins we're sending word to Erin. We're assembling a full force at Drumceatt."

Diormit stared. It sank in, apparently, because he wagged his sleep-heavy head. "Oh, no, Father! Not again. Please."

"Save your anguish, lad! This time it's of God!"

This time it's of God. How the flavor of that welcomed statement pleased his tongue.

It took him nearly three precious days to assemble and send the appropriate letters and messengers. There is a high degree of tact involved in getting a dozen ri ruirechs together to oust the tanaiste of a king who has not yet died.

He put out "Where is Gavin?" feelers through the Dal Riada. With Trena sailing to Erin, Colm placed young Colca in charge of the Iona-to-Mull ferry, taking the white horse across on one of the last trips.

On the Mullside Colm received no good word on Gavin. To his surprise, though, rumors of a Gaelic warrior maiden with a long braid reached him. She might be out somewhere near the Murchan, perhaps teaching tactics and strategies to princes. No, she's traveling up the valley Ness to sign on as a mercenary at Inverness. No, a friend of a friend swears she is building her own force to storm Tara.

Away in his clochan on the west side, the solution to his "Treasa problem" seemed so neat and simple, so easy to maintain. Suddenly it was not.

He traveled light on purpose, for light is fast. Diormit he left behind to handle affairs on Iona. As a valet and assistant he brought Lugbe. Young Lugbe, callow and full of wonder, was shaping up into a fine monk, but he needed a little more exposure to the real world. Sisan Colm brought to handle messages and correspondence. These and a hostler sufficed.

Every ri he met insisted on feasting him. He was going to get nowhere fast this way. And yet he dare not brush off their hospitality. That, the height of rudeness, would erode his work here in the north country faster than anything else he could do.

Nearly a week passed since his visitation before it dawned on him that God's time is God's time. He must put aside his anxiety, his desire to rush about, and get into the flow.

"Gavin Mac Niall? Aye and aye again, I know him." The ri ruirech of Ardnamurchan paused as the ale pot passed. He sipped generously as befits a king and passed the pot to Colm. "Up at Glenelg. You want your son to win on the battlefield? Send him up to Glenelg and place him in Gavin Mac Niall's hands for a month. The lad'll return telling you just what you're doing wrong as you conduct your campaigns." He hacked another hunk from his pork joint and offered it to Colm. "And the lad'll be right."

Colm accepted. Good, juicy pork, hand-fed out the kitchen door. There was no comparison between forest hogs that rooted acorns and kitchen hogs. This man lived well.

Next morning he sang Primes for the ri's household because no one was up for Matins. He left Sisan and the hostler behind. With only Lugbe in tow on the lad's favorite old roan gelding, he turned his white horse north.

He asked regarding Gavin at Glenelg and was feasted instead. "Plenty of time for fetching the White Hawk in," the ri assured him. *No, my friend, hardly any time at all!*

Colm did not wait to have Gavin fetched in like some field slave. He left Lugbe at Dun Glenelg and rode out along the coast according to the porter's vague directions.

To his left hand, the sea sparkled. Almost within touching distance, the Isle of Skye hovered close across the sound. Colm loved Skye, with its dense forests, its quiet people, and relaxed pace.

He would not visit Skye this trip. Another time.

A flock of plump, shaggy sheep scattered off the track as he rode by. He asked their shepherd, a half-grown girl, "Gavin Mac Niall?"

She pointed to a stone ringwall on a distant hilltop and giggled.

A herd of half a hundred sleepy red cattle lay across the lea at rest and watched him pass, their legs tucked beneath them, their jaws casually rotating. He asked the cowherd, a strapping lad, "Gavin Mac Niall?"

The lad pointed up the track and tittered.

This small stone-walled rath appeared deserted. The mud in the gateway had been churned up since the last rain, but no horses nickered at his from the paddocks. Someone here kept chickens. The rooster flapped clumsily up to the thatched house roof and announced Colm's arrival.

"Gavin? Hawk? Are you here?" He rode through the gateway into the yard, watching, listening. "Gavin!"

The rooster answered.

Colm was within moments of giving it up and looking elsewhere when he saw a shadow move inside the house doorway.

Wearing only striped trousers and a gleaming gold torque, Gavin stepped out into the doorway and leaned against the doorpost. He crossed his arms. "Welcome." Nothing about the man or the situation suggested Colm was welcome.

Colm slid off. "I have wonderful news, Cousin."

"Been talking to angels again?"

"As a matter of fact."

Gavin studied Colm a long moment. "Tell me something. Is there a sort of a hazy blue light associated with angels?"

"There can be. Often, yes."

He nodded. "Just before you threw me over for Aidan, I took that togher across the lake, out to a clochan your house man told me about, looking for you. I didn't know exactly where the clochan was. I saw a blue glow off to the north, down a sheep trail. Faint. Very faint. Almost unnoticeable. Big brave me, though, instead of hustling right to it to investigate, I ran back over the hill and across the togher and didn't stop until I was inside the monastery wall. That was when you were talking to your angel, wasn't it?"

Colm frowned and shook his head, suddenly confused. "I went over to Hinba. I was on Hinba when the angel came to me."

Gavin grunted. "Then maybe I didn't cheat myself as badly as I thought. I've always rather wanted to see an angel. I've long envied you for that. I've been kicking myself ever since, thinking I'd lost my only chance to do it by running away." Those snapping dark eyes held steady on Colm.

Colm had forgotten how intimidating Gavin's dark stare could be, even for him, who knew his cousin so well. He had a hard time keeping himself from backing up a step.

Instead, he forced himself forward a step. "A messenger came. You are God's choice for the next ard ri at Tara."

Gavin never twitched a muscle. "Why wasn't I the former one?"

"I asked. Apparently you had to grow first."

He stood there thoughtfully, digesting the news, surprisingly un-elated by it. He nodded slightly. "I'll accept that. Is he dead yet?"

"Going to be. I have forces assembling to back you up. You'll have to get past Diarmaid's tanaiste." Never before in his life had Colm felt discomfited or out of place—sure and never with Gavin! Just now, he did. He wasn't quite certain what to say or how to say it. He tried to keep the nervousness, the uncertainty out of his voice. "You probably ought to marry. The getting of children is an important part of the kingship."

Gavin burst out laughing, and so did a woman inside the house. Treasa, clad only in a linen tunic, moved in beside Gavin in the doorway, still laughing. "Spoken like a true celibate!" Unbraided, her hair was long enough to sit on. She had thrown it forward over her left shoulder. It tumbled down in wavy kinks.

Gavin's voice kept its dark edge. "So I ride up to Tara with my army behind me. Know this, Fierce Dove. My wife will ride beside me, as fully a part of the army as myself. I need her too much to give her up on your whim. If I tackle Diarmaid's forces, I intend to win."

Colm took a moment to gather himself back together. The news left him crushed, incredibly relieved, happy, sad. His Treasa problem was solved, but not the way he ever would have guessed. What could he say? "God's will prevail."

Gavin bobbed his head. "We agree on that, Cousin. We agree on that."

38

Erin's Ri

There is no authority except from God.
  He positions the powers that be.

Until two months ago, the victory at Culdrevny had been the high point of Treasa's life. But perhaps because time had dimmed it just a tiny bit, her wedding to the Hawk became the high point. What a splendid man!

Both those acmes were about to be superseded, she could tell.

To her left rode Gavin, straight and tall, regal in his magnificence. To Gavin's left, Colm on his goofy-looking white horse. To her right, Declan; to Declan's right, Eoghan; to Colm's left, Aidan. The Dal Riada might be independent, but they were also Ui Neill. Most of the ris out of Dunkeld seemed just plain eager to field an army to bring one of their own to the throne. The prospect of getting into a little top-of-the-pile action wasn't a bad incentive either.

Behind them nearly four thousand fighting men spread across the hills, a solid ribbon of marchers several hundred yards wide and two miles long. Cavalry, chariots, foot soldiers, Leod of Monaghan's crack corps of archers, a support column of wagons and smiths, some of the best lancers Treasa had ever seen in action— what a band they were!

And she rode in the van, their strategist, in charge even of Declan.

Colm raised an arm. Treasa and everyone else drew in, bringing the serpentine army to a halt. He announced, "Alither. He's abbot at Clonmacnois." A monk and party were riding down the distant hill, headed their way.

Declan nodded. "You know him, don't you?"

"Very well. That trip to Durrow, I went on over to visit him, since I was so close. Closely tied to Diarmaid, so I suspect he's bringing us news from Tara."

Treasa's breastbone gave a happy little thump. News from Tara. To Colm. To Gavin. She sat up straighter suddenly. *What is that?* She pushed her mare forward out of the line and reversed her, facing the host behind them. She drew her knees in and lifted herself off her horse's back, gaining a foot of elevation in order to see better.

Gavin twisted to look. "What is it?"

"I thought I heard horns. I'll let you know." She dropped down, kneed her mare aside and dug in. The little horse bolted forward, out around the column and back along its side. She was probably making a fool of herself. It was nothing. Still, she ordered "Alert! Alert" as she rode.

Half a mile from the front she pulled to a halt between divisions, for a unit commander was waving his arms and yelling, "Horns! They're signaling attack back there!"

Diarmaid's tanaiste wasn't waiting for negotiations at Tara.

She had no time to plan a strategy. *Do what must be done.* "You and you. Take your units and everyone in that direction and build a perimeter around the king and his abbot. You are his protection. Go!"

She kneed the mare and set her back to the troop line toward the rear. Bad strategy, to split your forces—unless the enemy is attacking your rear in order to draw you back away from the king. *Leaving the king with a token force is leaving him vulnerable, and it's the head the enemy wants to cut off, not the tail.* With that thought, she stopped long enough to send still another division forward as protection for Gavin.

She was left with half a fighting force now. Maybe less than half. No matter. She paused again at the supply wagons and pointed to the ri ruirech of the Murchan. "Protect our weapons at all cost. We don't want our superior edges turned against us!" Grenne of the Murchan nodded and began barking orders. The Murchan were worth diddly in open combat, but as a defensive force they were as good as any. It was not by chance that she had placed the Murchan next to the wagons when they set out.

335

Ahead, the trumpets, the shouts and screams. Even before she came within view of the action she estimated the engagement at four thousand men.

She reined aside and rode to the crest of a hill short of the action. A good two thousand warriors had engaged the rear of her column—and cleverly—cutting them at their most vulnerable point. She worked at a severe disadvantage—this was these people's home ground, and Treasa did not know the lay of the land.

She could see what was happening well enough, though, and what must happen if she would win. She kicked her mare forward, down the hill, her cloak flying. She hit the enemy line at what appeared the softest spot and cut herself a path through it to her beleaguered archers. They had taken refuge in a small grove of second-growth oak and coppiced hazel. She slid off her mare beside Leod.

"Break and run, Leod, up that hill. Tell your folks to look panicked. Cowardly. A small contingent will follow you, and they'll be pretty merry. Let them get in close but not too close—good target range for your arrows. Turn and hold your ground, and shoot them down."

Leod grinned. He'd never lost that boyish quality of being amazed at everything in the world, not even after all these years. "Perfect! Perfect!" And he turned away to set it up.

She continued on, sending the Mountain Behr around for a flanking movement, sending the naked Tyrone against what looked to be the worst of the ruffians on the other line.

Her mare fell once, tripped by a body. She lost her lance when she ran it into a ri and he dropped away from her, pulling it out of her grip. She snatched another out of the hands of one of her own warriors.

An infantryman speared her mare. She had to fight on foot until she managed to cut a bay gelding free of a loose chariot and swing aboard it. The stupid horse plow-reined—you had to drag his whole head around in the direction you wanted him to turn—and it knew nothing about cues, but it kept her up where she could see and fight.

Ten minutes ago, the battle could have gone either way. Finally came that sweeping feeling, that mysterious point she had

336

come to know so well—we will prevail. Men still struggled and died, horses still squealed, the fight went on, but you could feel the victory coming your way. She was never able to explain it, and she never really cared to. It was there.

She pulled a cavalry unit out of the action and sent them around to preempt a tribe she sensed was going to bolt and run north. Moments later, the horsemen charged the fleeing clan.

They were on the run. They were all in retreat!

"To Tara!" She shouted. "We don't chase them; we protect the king! To Tara!"

As the trumpets blasted, word spread through the ranks. Not everyone liked the idea, but they all obeyed, quitting the chase, hastening at double-step southward down the track. She brought the Leod down off the hill and sent them south. They had to pause to retrieve arrows from the fallen.

She fully expected to hear the tumult of battle as she galloped her horse south toward the rest of their warriors, leaving the forces behind her to catch up as they could. Any half-baked strategist would use that action at the rear to divert troops from the main battle at the front. What she came upon was a valley filled with men just standing there.

Standing there. The Dal Riada, the Monaghan, all Gavin's people formed a giant circle facing outward. The enemy formed a giant outer circle facing inward. And in the center of these unimaginable rings of people, all just standing there, Gavin sat on his horse. Twenty feet away from him, a horseman Treasa had never seen faced him.

A good riding horse will pay attention to where it's going in battle, lest it stumble. Chariot horses are trained to plow straight ahead, regardless what lies before. Fortuitous that Treasa now rode a chariot horse. She aimed it and dug in her heels; the little gelding shoved forward, muscling men and horses aside. Treasa pushed through the lines, both lines, in a matter of minutes.

Both men in the center of the circle had cast cloak and tunic aside. The foe looked every bit as husky and strong as Gavin. He also looked twenty years younger. Each wore his sword. Each carried a battle-ax. The ax was Colm's weapon; the lad was born to it.

It was not Gavin's best choice by any means. He should have a lance now if he were to enjoy any advantage whatever.

So they were reverting to the time-honored tradition of eld, letting heroes fight. It would be a battle not of armies but of champions, a single hero from each side to determine the outcome of the war, to determine the future of Erin. The winning hero would lead his people into Tara. The loser's forces would retire from the field without a blow being struck.

But why Gavin? Why put the ri-elect in such danger? He didn't have to die to lose his chance at kingship. Brehon law forbade a man to rule if he were deformed or mutilated in any obvious way. All this power-hungry foe had to do was maim Gavin to ruin him forever.

Colm claimed God's will in all this. Treasa could not bear to trust something so nebulous with so much at stake. If axes were the weapons here, why didn't Colm strip and meet the tanaiste's champion? He was the logical choice for a dozen different reasons.

And then Colm's clear, resonant voice began to sing. The incongruity of it startled Treasa. But it thrilled her too.

"You the King of moon and sun, you the King of stars, beloved . . ."

Others immediately picked up the tune, singing along. A thousand voices. Two thousand. This glorious song of praise to the Lord of the Cosmos swelled and rolled out across the valley. It reverberated off the naked hills around; its echoes returned in harmony with the singers. And above it all, above the thousands, rang the powerful voice of Columcille.

The rest of Gavin's army, their weapons-and-supply wagons rattling, were swarming down from the north now to spread out around the ring. The tanaiste's forces were being sandwiched between two lines of Gavin's people—not a good military position to find oneself in.

As the first verse of the hymn ended and the second began, the tanaiste's hero pivoted his horse a full circle. Treasa saw his eyes as big and wide as shields. The man was terrified. But a hero does not back down. A hero gives his life if necessary, but he does not shirk the fight.

He charged forward with a war cry that was buried completely by the song. Gavin's ax clanged against the boss of the fellow's shield. But the foe hooked his own ax down and around, chopping not at Gavin but at Gavin's horse.

The horse whinnied and collapsed. Gavin dragged his leg free of his fallen mount and, barely in time, reached his knees with his shield held high. The foe's ax split it in two.

Gavin ducked forward and darted under the belly of his enemy's horse, coming up on the other side. The fellow pivoted his horse for another swing of that murderous ax. Gavin broke and ran.

There came Colm's white horse across the circle! Riderless, the animal trotted right toward Gavin. Quick as a stoat, Gavin grabbed its reins and leaped aboard. He tossed aside his near-useless half-a-shield and drew his sword. His sword in his right hand, his ax in the other, he kneed the white horse around to meet his enemy.

The fellow started a charge and almost immediately aborted it, pulling up short. His mount danced in place. Gavin let his reins fall loose on his horse's neck. The big white warhorse stood rock solid, ears forward and nose high, awaiting the next subtle command to action.

Here that fellow came, shield raised, ax high. *He's going to try to cut this horse out from under you also, Gavin!* Treasa didn't bother to yell her warning. She couldn't have been heard above the final verse of the wondrous song.

At the last moment the white horse dipped aside and slammed a shoulder into the enemy's mount; both horses staggered and separated. The riders went down in a tangle, locked together as each tried to deflect the other's weapon.

What's happening? The song died on Treasa's lips; she couldn't sing, though all the rest of the world sang. Now both men were on their feet, parrying, struggling. Gavin's right arm was bloodied, as was the whole front of his opponent, but Treasa had no idea whose blood was whose; you never knew in hand-to-hand until it was all over.

The axes clanged. Blue-white sunlight reflections flashed off Gavin's sword, the torques. He tossed his ax aside and brought his sword up two-handed the way a sword must be used to be effective. With it he parried another ax blow and took a thick yellow chip out of the ax handle.

As the last words, "God of life," vibrated the valley and Colm's voice ceased, the tanaiste's champion, screaming, made a wild swing with his ax—a foolish act of fear, frustration, desperation. His final act. Gavin deflected the ax-blow with the sword haft and with the raw strength of his powerful upper body kept the sword moving. It arced in behind the foe's wooden shield. The shield fell aside; Gavin's sword had reached the neck.

The fellow's knees folded, and he dropped heavily at Gavin's feet. Utter silence rushed in to replace the music of the spheres, the hymn of praise.

Colm filled the silence with Patrick's great paean to the Trinity. Who actually won the epic bout? Gavin or Colm? Treasa couldn't say, and the difference wasn't worth thinking about anyway.

". . . Belief in the three-ness, declaration of the one-ness . . ."

Gavin Mac Niall, Ard Ri at Tara, ordained of God, stepped back away from his vanquished foe, raised his arms high, and slowly turned a full circle to greet his people Erin.

39

Colm's Repose

Year of our Lord 597

My heart unwearied sings Your praise.
My hands unwearied Your work raise.
My life lifts high Your name above
That others may come into Your love
To extol Your glorious ways.

Colm paused in his copying to run his fingers down the page at his left. The Psalms. Much as he ought to love the Psalms, they always gave him a sad feeling. It was this very book over which he and Finnian argued all those many years ago. If not for the Psalms, he would not have sailed to Iona. If not for the Psalms, he would not have taken the salvation of the Picts as his life's work.

He, Ninian, the monks from Eigg and Tiree—many were the workers who brought Pictland and the north under the hand of God.

He dipped his pen. *They that love the Lord shall lack no good thing.* He laid the pen aside.

He was tired. Seventy-six years old now, he probably had reason to be. *Still . . .* He thought of old Cruithnechan. No one ever knew how old Cruithnechan was; the saint seemed to spring from the cradle wizened just as he went to his grave wizened. But he had to be eighty or ninety when he died.

Colm picked up the pen again only long enough to write, *Here I must stop. Let Baithin do the rest.* He capped his inkpot and walked over to the scriptorium door.

He walked slowly across the slope toward the refectory because slowly was the only way he could walk these days. Shortness of breath dogged him now. Constant weariness dragged him down. Once upon a time he envisioned himself dying in the heat of battle. Now he tried to envision himself lasting until supper.

341

He sat down on the old ogham stone between the bier gate and the kitchen to catch his breath. They ought to move this stone. Either feature it in the courtyard or dump it out back. Here, it was merely in the way.

A milkmaid shouted angrily from out behind the biers. Through the gate came the white horse, that silly-looking old warhorse, with the milkskins slung across its bony back. Sloshing milk in all directions, it trotted through the gate, nose high. Colm chuckled. About the time the milkmaids decided the horse was getting old enough to settle down and behave, it'd take off like this. The creature must be thirty years old at least. You'd think the milkmaids would figure out by now that good behavior was probably beyond the old nag.

The horse jogged just fast enough to stay ahead of the milkmaid. Here it came, right toward Colm. Colm extended his arm. He had no treat to offer save a rub on the nose, a pat on the neck. That seemed sufficient. The horse stopped beside him.

The warm, velvety old nose pushed forward, muzzling deep in Colm's lap. Colm scratched behind its ears, under its throatlatch, beneath its chin—all the places horses love to have scratched.

The milkmaid tossed her rope belt over the horse's neck to lead it away. "Sorry, Father."

"Let him stay, please."

She looked at him oddly, as if he were as irascible as the horse. "Aye, Father. I'll fetch up another pony to take the milk to the kitchen."

"No need. We're going that way anyway."

The milkmaid sniffed, expressing the disdain due a couple old goats, and headed back toward the biers.

He wagged his head at the old nag. "We find you a job. One simple job, carrying the milk from the bier to the kitchen, and you mess it up." He stood up. "Come with me to the refectory. Perhaps we can find you a treat of roots or greens."

He leaned heavily on the horse's neck and welcomed the support. He could feel death drawing near, and he wasn't at all sure he was ready. Baithin, Colm's cousin, would probably do all right as his successor. Diormit, dear Diormit, was competent enough at the everyday administration. Probably, every founder prays his foundation will survive him well, even as doubts assail.

Colm stopped and spoke as if the horse could understand Gaelic. "Wait. Take me there first. I want to check on the lamps." He wiggled a hand toward the oratory. The old horse altered direction, and for some reason that didn't even surprise Colm. It stopped beside the oratory doorway.

Colm doddered through the door and down to the front. Everything was in place. Why did he doubt? He settled down beside the altar. He would sit here a while and rest. He rather wished he had the strength to go out to his clochan on the west side. He hadn't been there in years. He would like to see his angelic visitor one more time.

"Easily done. Turn around and look." That familiar, rich, flowing voice came from behind him. The vague blue glow lighted the altar.

Colm twisted around, scooting. He smiled broadly. "Ah. My messenger friend. I'm delighted you came." He hesitated. *This is a silly time to think of it, but . . .* "I have a question that's long been bothering me, ever since I gave Gavin his good news up at Glenelg. You came to me at Hinba, yet he says he saw you on Iona. Or at least, he saw a bluish glow."

The angel nodded as he hunkered down to sitting on the rush-strewn floor. "You understand that we have within us a bit of the nature of God, just as you do."

"I suppose." Colm had never really studied the spiritual composition of angels.

"And you're aware that God created this world to take pleasure in it."

"Yes . . ."

The angel shrugged amiably. "Well, so do I. It's a beautiful spot. I go there now and then."

Colm chuckled. "I keep underestimating you. Making you one-dimensional. My error."

"You've done well, Columcille. You've grown mightily. You're letting go well too. I wasn't certain you'd be able to do that. You tend to control tightly."

343

"I know you're not in the business of prophecy, but can you tell me if my work will go on as it is now?"

"Not exactly as it is now. Your monastic rule is going to be eased up considerably. Replaced by an order called the Benedictines. You're a little too harsh. Not as bad as Comgall, but harsh. Basically, though, you've built for the ages."

Colm nodded. "So long as God is glorified. Have you come to bring me a message?"

"No." The angel stood up. He smiled and extended his hand. "I've come for you."